A pickup
and stopped behind ⌐
the windshield, making it impossible to see the driver.
She shielded her eyes with one hand and gripped her
keys with the other.

A tall male hopped out of the driver's side. "Do
you northerners make it a habit of running out of gas?"

Grace loosened her grip on the keys, but she
looked around for a way to escape. Maybe a tornado
would appear and suck her up in its funnel. She'd
hoped Blaise would never find out about her stupidity.

"Did Beau make you come?" Her voice wobbled.

Blaise swaggered up to her. "Nah. After he was
done yelling about women and cars, I offered. Figured
I'd save Pete the drive and Beau the call to bark at
him."

"Beau was yelling?"

"Whole neighborhood could hear him. Where were
you coming back from anyway?"

She turned and looked toward the woods. That
might be a good place to run and hide. "I'm sorry I
inconvenienced you. I'm not the kind of person who
runs out of gas."

"Lighten up, Grace. Ain't no big deal." He pumped
up his southern accent. "Pop open your gas tank. You
know where that button is?" He laughed. "You weren't
trying to get out of dinner, were you?"

He poured the gas into the car, and she held her
nose. "It would've been easier to call and cancel, don't
you think?" she said.

"Depends."

A Second Chance House

by

Stacey Wilk

Heritage River Series, Book One

A Second Chance House

Cover Art by *RJ Morris*

The Wild Rose Press, Inc.
PO Box 708
Adams Basin, NY 14410-0708
Visit us at www.thewildrosepress.com

Publishing History
First Mainstream Women's Fiction Edition, 2018
Print ISBN 978-1-5092-1925-4
Digital ISBN 978-1-5092-1926-1

Heritage River Series, Book One
Published in the United States of America

Dedication

To Chuck, Joshua, and Samantha.
You are my home.

Kita —

How lucky am I
that you walked up to
my table at Old York?!
It was so great to see you!
I'm glad you enjoyed
Grace to Stay.

Stacey
Wolf

Chapter One

Grace Starr turned her Subaru Impreza into the driveway of her two-story gray colonial with black shutters and matching black double doors. She loved this house with its oversized deck she sat on at night catching the breeze and drinking tea, the big kitchen with plenty of cabinets, and the gas fireplace that burned clean. Twenty-Five Tudor Drive was the place she started a family with her husband and raised her daughter, Chloe.

She hated the For Sale sign in the front yard.

She had an hour before she had to be back at the library. She should get some lunch, take a walk, clean a bathroom. The bathroom would win, and if she had time, she'd throw in a load of laundry, wipe down the counters, sort the mail into piles. Her favorite pile being the one that went into the garbage.

The extra car was parked in the driveway too. What was Chloe doing home from school in the middle of the afternoon? Had there been a half day Grace had forgotten about? Some kind of teacher in-service thing? Possibly. Lately, she kept returning to the bathroom to touch her toothbrush just to see if it was wet. Her mind couldn't hold a thought if it were a vault. Problem was, she didn't know if the absentmindedness was her age or the stress of the divorce. Better to blame it on the divorce. She wasn't that old…yet. Maybe Chloe felt the effects of senior year ending and was ditching.

The garage door yawned open, and Chloe came out in bare feet, her blue-streaked hair bouncing off her shoulders. Her nose piercing sparkled in the sun, mocking Grace from its coveted place on Chloe's face. Her shorts barely covered the necessary parts, and her shirt showed too much skin.

Grace cringed at the uncontrolled appearance of her almost-eighteen-year-old. She tried to arrange her face in a way that said she was used to seeing Chloe this way. Larry had let her get the piercing. He had bought her the blue dye. Grace was always the bad guy. The boring parent.

Chloe waved something in her hand. "Mom, you've got to see this."

Please don't let it be a letter from the guidance counselor.

"What are you doing home?" Chloe said, slightly out of breath, through the open car window. "I thought you were volunteering at the library today."

"I am, later. I was wondering what you were doing home on a Wednesday. Did you get in trouble for wearing that outfit to school?" What was the point in fighting? But she couldn't keep her mouth shut.

Chloe rolled her eyes with the skill of a seasoned pro. "No one dress codes in June. School's boring. We're not doing anything. They won't even notice I'm gone."

The same arguments about doing the right thing bubbled inside Grace and died on her tongue. Did it really matter? And look what doing the right thing did for her. She had followed the rules and planned for all possible outcomes. She was the dutiful wife, and she had still been evicted from her life. "Don't make skipping a habit. I don't care that there's only two weeks of school left."

Ignoring her last remark, Chloe shoved the white paper at Grace. "This came in the mail today. I didn't open it, but it looks interesting. Did Dad get new lawyers or something? Did he move out of state and not tell us? It would be just like him, the jerk."

"Chloe, don't call your father names." Even if Larry was a big fat jerk. Grace inspected the envelope addressed to her. A postmark she didn't recognize. A law firm's name and address in the top corner. Pretty official. What had Larry gone and done? She shoved her way out of the Impreza, gripping the envelope. She took a closer look. Tennessee? "This must be a mistake." She handed the envelope back.

"Are you kidding? You've got to open this." Chloe shoved the envelope at her. "Maybe we won something."

"Wishful thinking. I've never even been to Tennessee. Take it inside, please."

"No, Mom. Open it." Chloe gripped Grace's hand and shoved the envelope in her grasp.

Why was this so important? "Oh, all right." She ripped the envelope open and scanned its contents.

A letter on the firm's letterhead. Her hand began to shake. She had to read it twice to make sure she was seeing things correctly.

"Well, what is it?" Chloe's blue eyes had grown to the size of sunflowers. Her face sagged when she stared at Grace. "Dad did something bad, didn't he? He's keeping all his money or not letting me go to college, right?"

Grace shook her head and searched for her voice. "Surprisingly, Dad has nothing to do with this, but it must be a mistake. There's no way this is real." She looked back at the letter. "It says someone has left me a house. Who would do such a crazy thing?" A laugh bubbled up into her throat.

"That's great. Now we have a place to live. You can tell Dad you don't need him anymore."

Grace thrust the letter back in the envelope. Chloe's loyalty was sweet, but it might not last. These days they got along one minute, and the next Grace had said or done something wrong. Having a teenage daughter could be wonderful and exhausting at the same time. "The house is in Tennessee. You don't want to live there. I don't want to live in Tennessee. I like it here, in this town. Like I said, I'm sure it's a mistake. You want to get some lunch?"

"Wait. Who does it say gave you the house?"

Grace folded the envelope. "I don't know. They don't want to be identified."

"And you don't think that's mysterious and want to find out more?" Chloe raised her eyebrows.

She envied Chloe's ability to still believe amazing things happened at random moments. That was a blessing of youth. "Even if it's legitimate, which I highly doubt it is, nothing good can come from an unidentified person giving you a house. It's unheard of and ridiculous. People don't do things like that." Well, not practical people anyway.

****

The darkness covered Grace like a cocoon. The only light spilling into the kitchen was the dim one over the sink. She liked this time of night when Chloe either

4

was out or barricaded in her room and she sat in the protection of the dark.

She sipped the white tea with citrus and stared at her computer. The law firm on the envelope had an impressive website. They certainly looked legit. But it still didn't make any sense. Who would leave her a house, especially one in Tennessee? No one she knew, and no one she knew had recently died. She had no relatives except Chloe. Her father had walked out of her life when she was too young to remember him, and her mother passed away when Grace was in her twenties. Both of her parents had no siblings.

What would it hurt to call? And what if someone had left her a house? The idea began to buzz around inside her head. She could sell it and buy something nicer up here. She had been planning to rent, but with extra money she could maybe buy sooner. Renting left a lot of unknowns, but buying at least would allow her to settle in and make the place her own.

She shook her head. What was she thinking? Stick to the plan. She and Chloe would move in with Grace's long-time friend, Jenn, until she found a place. She would have to find a job at some point too. The alimony was enough, but it wasn't her money. Never was.

She gripped the letter, ready to tear it in half. Her cell vibrated and interrupted her thoughts. Who would call at that hour? She checked the screen, and her heart sank.

"Hello, Larry."

"Sorry to call so late." His voice was low and raspy, as if he might have been speaking for a long time or didn't want anyone to hear him. "I haven't had another chance all day, and I wanted to reach you as soon as I could."

He had stood in their kitchen on a night not much different from this one and leaning against the gas range, confessed feelings for someone else. He had used words like *controlling*, *obsessive*, *cold*, and *buttoned up*.

She was controlling, but she wasn't buttoned up. She thought they were in a rut. Didn't all marriages have those after nineteen years? How excited could you get when you knew all of the other person's moves? It wasn't as if Larry was creative. While she was busy running their home, raising their child, and volunteering at the library, he was busy being creative with someone else, though. Someone younger than she was. Grace was the quintessential cliché. He had packed up and moved in with his young hottie whose skin still stayed in all the right places and who hadn't pushed a baby out of her hooha.

"I've got some news," he said.

"You're joining AARP?" She picked at the corner of her letter. She didn't want this man back, did she? No, not the man. She wanted a marriage and a large family. He never really wanted to share a marriage with her, and his cheating had proved it. He ended the large family dream back when her eggs still dropped on a regular basis. She thought she didn't care about the latter—how wrong she was—and was too blind to realize she was the only player on the marriage team.

"Stop being so bitter. I have something to tell you. This is going to come as a shock, because no one was more surprised than me. I can't believe I'm about to say this out loud—"

"Could you get to the point?" Why was he calling

her with his news? Did he really care what she thought any longer? What was he going to announce? Early retirement?

"Annie and I are getting married," he blurted in one swift breath.

The phone slipped from her hands. She grabbed at it like a hot potato. "What?"

"I want to buy your half of the house. Before you say a word, just listen. I'll pay more than the market value for it. You know as well as I do we'll never get full price for it if we sell, but if you'll sell your half to me, you'll get more than you expected."

She gripped the phone tighter.

"What do you say, Grace? It's a good deal. Better than you'll get any other way."

"Why do you want the house so badly?" She gripped the kitchen chair, trying to steady herself. She couldn't bare the idea of that woman living in her house. The house she had decorated with careful planning, from the colors on the walls to the pillows on the couch. The cabinets she kept cleaned and organized. The lamppost she had installed by the front walk because it was too dark for guests at night. All belonging to that woman? Over her dead body.

"I want to do this for you. I buy the house, you make the most money on your share, and you're rid of me. It's what you want. To be rid of me."

She wanted him out of her life—no point in denying that little truth. "We have a child together. I don't think we'll ever be completely rid of each other, as you say." She flopped down in the chair, creating a wind that sent the mysterious letter floating to the floor.

"Will you accept my offer?"

"I need time to think about it." The money would be nice. They hadn't had any bites on the house, and Larry couldn't afford the mortgage here and his rent forever.

"We could have the sale completed in thirty days."

"Thirty days? I don't have another place yet. I can't find a place that quickly." She had barely begun looking. Research needed to be done first. She wanted to create a neighborhood prospectus. The new house would most likely be where she'd finish out her later years. She couldn't buy a house that had the perfect number of rooms on a pretty yard without careful consideration.

He heaved a sigh. "Listen, Grace, I know this is coming as a shock. I'm a little shocked too, but we want the house."

"Larry, I can't make a split-second decision like that."

"Yeah, I know."

She wanted to reach through the phone and strangle him. "Don't make me out to be the bad guy in this one. It's not fair. I need some time."

Chloe shuffled into the kitchen in her slippers, yanked open the freezer door, and pulled out the cookies-and-cream ice cream. "Is that Dad?"

Grace covered the phone. *How can you tell?* she mouthed. It couldn't be the rise and tightening of her voice. Oh no. Not that.

"Did he tell you Annie is pregnant?"

"Your girlfriend is pregnant?" she yelled into the phone.

"What? How did you—"

"Shut up, Larry. Just shut up. Chloe told me. That's

why you want this house so badly, you jerk."

She stifled a groan and dropped her head between her knees to keep the room from tipping on its side. Larry, with his thinning hairline and paunchy belly, was getting married again and having a baby, having another child she'd wanted so badly her insides had ached for years. He had never wanted more children.

"I have my child," he had said, flipping through the newspaper as if they had been discussing the weather. "I don't want anymore."

"I knew you might be upset. I don't blame you."

"Don't tell me you know how I feel."

"You're right. I don't. Annie loves the house. It has everything we're looking for, including good schools. She wants to be settled in before the baby comes."

Annie loved the house? When had she seen it? They wanted their new child to go to the schools Chloe had attended. Grace thought she might be sick. "And if I say no?"

"You'd be spiting no one but yourself. This is the only way to guarantee more than a fair sale price. If you want to sell it to strangers, then we will. I'm going to get married either way."

Grace went to the faucet and filled the glass with cold water. She gulped it down, hoping to stop the sweats. She stepped on the letter, and the paper creased under her foot. Her damp fingers stuck to the paper as she swiped it from the floor.

Larry was getting on with his life. Had been even while they were still married. In a few short months, Chloe would be off at college getting on with hers. Where would that leave Grace?

She stared at the phone number at the bottom of the

letterhead. "You've got a deal." She ended the call and threw the phone down on the table.

She could go to Tennessee and check out this house. She could call the law firm in the morning for more details. If she liked what she heard, she would make a plan to go. What harm would it do to just see the house? She didn't have other options anyway. She hated when Larry was right. She stood to make the most money with his offer. She'd be an idiot not to take him up on it, and he was banking on that.

The idea of that woman living in her house still made her skin itch. "It's just a house, Grace. Stop being ridiculous." But it was her house. The house where she raised Chloe. The house she wanted grandchildren to visit. Was the house she shared with Larry ever really a home? Well, maybe, for about five minutes.

She could use a few days away. If this house in Tennessee really was hers, she could sell it and have extra money to buy something nicer than she originally thought. Maybe something with a porch she could sit on in the mornings with a cup of tea.

Buying a new house in town would be a fresh start. Didn't she deserve one too? A way to show Larry she didn't need him.

But did she really want to run into them at the grocery store? Or the library? Or any number of places the new Mrs. Starr would show up with her rounded belly and then later with her child in tow. It would be bad enough to deal with them at Chloe's college graduation in four years or when she married and had children of her own. She shook her head at the thought of Larry's new child possibly being close in age to a child of Chloe's. The man was pathetic.

She didn't want to move away. She loved Silverside with its tree-lined streets and parks. She could smell the ocean from her front lawn. Her life was there. How could she live somewhere else? No town would speak to her the way Silverside did.

She'd sell her half to Larry and hope for the best. In the meantime, she'd go to Tennessee and learn more about this mysterious house. She needed to start living again. Even though her insides shook with the idea of jumping on a plane to some area unknown without the safety net of a plan, she knew she had to. For once, Grace Starr would take a risk. Hopefully, taking a chance didn't backfire.

Chapter Two

Blaise Savage stared at his bandaged hand as if it belonged to someone else. The brace had turned gray from dirt and sweat, and it was starting to smell like old socks, although he'd only been wearing it for a week. He yanked on the garden hose with his good hand. He was convinced the stupid thing had tied itself in knots when no one was looking.

The hose barely moved. He kicked and cursed, hoping it would make him feel better. It didn't. How was he supposed to plant a garden without a working hose? Isn't that what regular guys did? They planted tomatoes and zucchinis and handed them over the fence to neighbors.

He glanced at the neighbor's house. Well, no one had been on that side of the fence in years. Surprisingly, the house hadn't been condemned. And he was going to have to look at that piece of shit for the next three months. Maybe less time. He wasn't going to wait for the okay from the doc. He was going back on the road as soon as the dates were ready. Colton was rearranging the schedule after Blaise's accident.

He didn't want to be back in Heritage River with a bum hand, but he didn't have anywhere else to go. A musician wanted to be on the road, playing in cities across the country. Behind his drum kit was the only place that ever made sense to him. He understood time signatures and rhythms. He didn't always understand people. Even people he thought he knew well. They were the ones who surprised him most. You thought you could trust someone, and then you were wrong.

He gave up on the hose. The idea of planting tomatoes made him feel like his grandfather, but the doc told him to do something to get his mind off his hand and his troubles. Planting wasn't getting his mind off his hand. All it was doing was getting dirt in his brace.

His phone vibrated against his hip. When he saw the number, he debated answering. The last thing he needed was Melissa's shrill voice in his ear, complaining about not having enough money. If he didn't have to pay her so much alimony, he might not be in this much trouble and he wouldn't need the tour as much as he did.

He would answer the call and put up with her sharp voice because of his son. He hit the button and tried not to sigh into the phone. "What's up, Melis?"

"Must you call me that?"

He sighed anyway. "What can I do for you?"

"I know this might not be the best time for you because of your hand—I read about it on Facebook—but I need your help."

"Then you know I can't give you any extra money right now. The tour has been suspended."

"This has nothing to do with money. It's Cash. He's in trouble again, and I'm out of ideas. He needs his father."

Blaise ran a hand back and forth through his hair. Cash in trouble again. When was it going to end? He had been wild as a kid, but not like Cash. Was it because he and Melissa were divorced? Was Cash constantly reacting to having a broken home? Or was he just mad at Blaise for not being around? Not coaching baseball games or sitting in at school conferences? Once he and Melissa split, she moved back to California and took Cash with her. What was he supposed to do?

"What did he do now?" The afternoon sun beat on the back of his neck. Sweat rolled between his shoulder blades.

"It sounds worse than it is, but—"

"You always try to put a good face on the things he does. Did you ever think that was part of the problem? Maybe if you punished him when he did something he wasn't supposed to, then he wouldn't be in another mess."

"Me? You're going to blame this on me?" She made muffled sounds with her phone. Maybe she switched ears. "Of course you're going to blame me. That's what you always do, but this has nothing to do with me. I've tried with him over and over. He doesn't listen. He doesn't care. There are no consequences strong enough to make him sit up and listen. Until now."

"So just do it, then. If you found the right button to push, do it." Why was she calling him about this? He couldn't do anything from this part of the country. "Do you want me to talk to him or something? I could do that video camera thing with him later and give him a lecture." It might not work, because Cash didn't listen to him either, but he was willing to try.

"You can do better. You're going to take him for the summer. When I saw the tour was suspended, I knew it was the best idea."

Blaise tripped over the hose. "Wait a second. I can't take him. As soon as Colton reschedules everything, I'm going back on the road. I might be back out there in a couple of weeks."

"Tell Colton to push the dates back to September. You'll probably sell more tickets that way anyhow. Your son needs you, Blaise. You're never around, and that's why he acts out so much. He's dying for you to pay attention to him."

"The whole summer?" He might be a great drummer, but he was a lousy father. He knew it. You can't be any good at it when you're constantly saying goodnight on the telephone. His father had given up his whole life to raise him and his siblings. Blaise hadn't been that unselfish.

"Yes, the entire summer. It will be good for both of you. Cash needs to see his father loves him and cares about what happens to him."

"I do love him. He knows that."

"No, he doesn't. Honestly, when was the last time you spent quality time with him? Christmas for a few days? You don't know how he's doing in school. You don't know that he has only one friend. Only one. You're not checking his computer history and reading his texts."

Melissa let out a long breath. "I love him, but I don't know what to do with him anymore. He's gone too far this time, and I need you to take him for a while. I need a break."

"For Christ's sake, Melissa, what did he do?" She was scaring him a little.

"You have to keep him at your house in Heritage

River, not in Nashville. And don't you dare take him on the road. You hear me? He needs stability."

He had sold the Nashville house, but she didn't know that. It's what he used to pay her alimony for the past six months. "You know he's practically an adult."

"Just because he's almost eighteen doesn't mean he's an adult. He's a child looking for approval from his father. I have him booked on a flight for tomorrow."

"Tomorrow? And you waited until now to call me?"

"I wasn't going to give you a chance to say no. He's already packed, and believe me, he doesn't like this setup. Only, I didn't tell him I hadn't spoken to you yet. He thinks you want him to come. I lied for you to try and help your relationship with your son. So don't say I never do anything for you. You need this time with him."

"For the last time, tell me what he did." His mind raced through possibilities. Did he rob someone? Hurt a girl? Cheat on a test?

"He burned a house down."

Chapter Three

Cash burned a house down. Blaise yanked on the garden hose enough to allow the water to run. He splashed his face and neck. The brace on his hand dripped. He shook his head and let the water run down his shirt.

Okay, it wasn't a full house with people inside. He breathed a sigh of relief on that one. It was just the frame of a new house. What the fuck Cash was thinking, Blaise would never know. Cash's acting out was his fault. If he had been a better father, paid more attention, this would never have happened. Would it?

The good news, if there was any—Cash was still seventeen. He wouldn't turn eighteen until September. Melissa bailed him out, hired an attorney, and got him off with community service. The judge liked the idea of Cash getting out of town for the summer. Now Blaise would have to find him the community service he would have to do.

The pounding in his head matched the pounding in his hand. He stepped inside the air-conditioned kitchen, leaving a trail of dirt and water on the tiles, and rummaged in the whitewashed cabinet for some Advil. The sun lit up the small space, accenting the dirty dishes in the sink. He'd have to do some housecleaning before tomorrow. Was there someone in town he could hire? He hadn't been back to Heritage River in six

17

months. But every time he walked into his childhood house, he felt at home. Probably because this was where their father had taught them about music and where they had played together as a family. Except for Savannah. She didn't play. Savannah, the youngest of the Savage kids, had baked cookies and hung a sheet up in the living room, pretending it was a stage, and ordered them around as if she were their manager.

Colton was going to blow a gasket when he found out the tour had to wait until after the summer ended. He was storming mad when he found out Blaise couldn't play and fifty dates had to be changed. Colton even threatened to leave without him. But it was just Colton blowing steam. His older brother would never do that to him.

He didn't want to think about the appearance of his bank account until the fall, when they hit the road again. And what if they didn't sell more tickets by making their already-dwindling number of fans wait even longer to see them? Summer was the best time to tour.

He yanked open the stainless-steel fridge when his phone vibrated in his pocket.

He frowned at the screen. Another call better sent to voice mail. "What's up?" His salutation sounded calmer than he felt. He popped two Advil and swigged some lemonade.

"I'm checking on how my kid brother is surviving in that matchbox-size house. That's what's up."

Colton never understood why Blaise kept their childhood home. He wanted to sell and split the money between the three Savage kids, but Blaise couldn't let it go. He bought out his siblings and kept the house for himself. "What's really up?"

"Can't I ask how you're doing? Christ, man, you've been in a lousy mood since you busted up your hand."

Blaise let out a sigh, wiped his face with his bad hand, and bit back a groan. "You're right. Sorry. My hand is getting better." If he ignored the pain.

"Listen, Joe Kelly called. He can line us up dates to finish out the tour. You know, the ones we had to reschedule."

There was the truth. Colton tried to hide it, but Blaise knew Colton blamed him for postponing the tour, even if he never said it. It didn't matter that accidents happen. "Sounds great. When exactly?"

Colton took so long to answer Blaise thought he'd hung up. "In four weeks."

He stared at the ceiling. Four weeks. Of course. That was just his luck. He was hoping to postpone this conversation at least until Cash had arrived, but that wasn't in the cards. "I can't be ready in four weeks." He braced himself for the explosion.

"What do you mean you can't be ready in four weeks?"

Blaise held the phone away from his ear.

"As far as your hand is concerned, you'll be fine." Colton surprised him by lowering his voice. "Look at the guy from Def Leppard. He plays the drums with one arm. What are you whining about? Your drumming can't get any worse. Trust me." He laughed at his own joke.

Blaise wanted to deck him. He gritted his teeth. "It's not my hand. Cash is coming to stay with me for the summer."

"Why?" The question wasn't as hateful as it sounded. Any other time Cash wouldn't be staying with him. Colton loved Cash. They were buddies. Maybe that was part of Cash's problem.

He told Colton the whole story.

"Wow, man, I didn't know your kid had it in him. He makes what we did as kids look like amateurs."

"I know."

Colton laughed again. "Okay. Whatever. Doesn't matter anyway, does it? Melissa got him off, and your punishment is to spend the summer trying to make your kid feel guilty about what he did."

"It's not punishment spending time with my kid." Was Melissa trying to punish him too? Was there any chance she exaggerated the offense? Probably. She resented how he picked music over her. Except when she bought whatever she wanted with the money he made. Then she didn't seem to mind his career choice. And would she have ever looked twice at him before they ruled the airwaves? After all the years of fans chanting his name, he still couldn't believe the guy staring at him in the mirror was a famous musician. He was and always would be some awkward kid from a small town in the South.

"Take Cash with you on tour," Colton said, bringing Blaise's thoughts back to the present.

"I can't. He has to do community service, stay put, and learn some responsibility."

"He can work as a roadie."

Blaise walked to the back door. The neighbor's house mocked him with its slanted roof and broken shutters. "Working as a roadie doesn't count as community service."

"It does in my book."

He stepped outside and stood at the fence. Maybe the town would let Cash fix up that house. "I've been writing music. I want us to record it," he said, not sure now was the time for this conversation.

"I've said all I've got to say, Blaise. You know that."

Colton hadn't written a thing since he dried up and got clean and didn't want anyone else in the band to write either. "You don't have to write anything. Just record it. My stuff's good, and we need new music. We can't keep playing the same old shit. Nobody cares."

"Not happening, little brother. I'm the songwriter in the group."

"I can write music too, you asshole."

"Yeah, but you suck at it." Colton laughed.

"Listen, I've got to run." What was the point discussing new music? The band's name might be his, but Savage was and always would be Colton's.

"Remember we take off in four weeks."

"You saying you'd leave without me?" His blood heated up to the temperature outside. "After what I just told you about my son?"

"I'm saying we've got our fans to think about, not to mention our careers. We don't get back on the road soon, there won't be any more fans, and don't go bringing up songwriting again because that store is closed. Besides, the only place you're ever happy is on the road. Do you really know how to be a father who hangs around the house doing something stupid like planting that garden of yours?"

Blaise continued to stare at the neglected and forgotten house. The gaping windows stared back.

"Fuck you." And he ended the call.

Real mature, Blaise. He shoved the phone back in his pocket. Then with another thought, he yanked it back out and hit a button.

He was about to disconnect when an out-of-breath voice answered. "Hey, sis." He smiled into the phone.

"Oh, Blaise, can I call you back? I'm about to run the kids to the pool for the afternoon, and I'm supposed to pick up their friends, and I have to stop at the library to grab some stuff for the fundraiser, and of course, I'm running late. Hey, why don't you come over for dinner?"

He laughed at his sister's ability to say all that in one breath. She definitely had inherited their mother's aptitude to accomplish ten tasks at once and never lose her cool. She made being a mother, a wife, and the head librarian, not to mention all her volunteer work, look easy. He couldn't help but be proud of his little sister, who wasn't bitten by the music bug and never felt any less important because her brothers could be heard on radios around the world. Well, they were heard a lot more years ago, but he didn't want to think about that.

"Thanks for the invite, but I can't make it." He had too much to do before Cash arrived tomorrow. "I just wanted some advice, but it's not important. I'll talk to you later."

"Hang on. A Savage man calls looking for advice, and you say it isn't important? Spill. The kids can wait." He heard a chair scraping the floor behind her.

"No, really, Savannah, it can wait. Can I take a rain check on the dinner and bring a guest?"

"You're seeing someone." Her voice squealed. "You want advice about a woman."

"No, no. Your mind always goes to a woman. I'm not interested in getting involved with anyone. There isn't a woman out there who understands what my life is like, and inevitably she will hate me for always being on the road."

"You just haven't met the right woman yet." Savannah never gave up. She was so much like their mother. Blaise missed her.

"My guest is Cash. He's coming for the summer. I'm picking him up tomorrow at the airport."

"And you want a buffer of my crazy family his first night in town?"

Heat filled his cheeks. "I thought—"

She laughed. "I know what you thought. Tomorrow at six. We'll throw steaks on the grill. And then you can tell me what happened that brought Cash here, because I know he didn't call begging to spend the summer in town."

"Yeah, okay."

"Blaise, I'm glad he's coming. It's exactly what you and he need, and don't let Colton bully you into going on tour before September."

"How did you know about that?"

"I know my brothers."

Chapter Four

Grace hated lawyers. It was an irrational hate, but lawyers represented the end of her marriage and the division of her assets. Lawyers signified the moment in her adult life when nothing would be the same. All her careful planning for a life without turmoil had been for nothing. A lawyer had seen to that. Okay, Larry had seen to that, but why split hairs?

She fidgeted on the blue silk sofa in the lobby of Hoke Carter, Attorney-at-Law. The office smelled like a bottle of gladiola perfume exploded. The smell made her head hurt. The southern summer heat had followed her in and clung to her skin despite the air-conditioning humming in the distance. A glass of untouched iced tea dripped condensation on the coffee table in front of her. The receptionist had added sugar. *Who takes sugar in their tea?*

A picture of a horse and his jockey winning first place hung askew on the wall. Was Mr. Carter one of the people surrounding the horse in the picture? He must be a successful lawyer if he owned a racehorse.

Jenn came barreling through the glass doors. "I'm so sorry about that." She dropped down on the sofa, brushing her damp hair off her face. "It is so hot in this town. Anyway, you won't believe what's happening back at my shop. I won't bore you with the details now because I know you have a lot on your mind, and rightfully so, but when I get home, some heads are going to roll. I'm telling you that." She fanned herself with a *Forbes* magazine.

"Ms. Starr," a sweet, southern voice said. "Mr. Carter will see you now."

Grace and Jenn followed the petite blonde woman wearing a black pencil skirt and white blouse through a maze of hallways. Grace wasn't sure if she'd remember how to get back.

Her hands began to sweat. How was she going to sell a house in Tennessee when she lived in New Jersey? She couldn't possibly live in this heat box of a state. Not with her daughter up north. And then what if it didn't sell? She needed a better plan. She had let Larry's news get the best of her, and now she was sweating buckets as the reality of her decision to fly south hit her. "Maybe this is a bad idea," she whispered to Jenn.

Jenn placed a hand on her arm. "You're the brainchild of this one."

The sweet blonde gestured them into the corner office. Mr. Carter came around his executive desk. He was a short man with a shock of white hair and a smile that crinkled up his eyes. His hearty handshake had Grace's elbow feeling overworked.

"This is my friend Jenn Caldini. I brought her along. Hope you don't mind."

"Welcome." He pumped Jenn's arm too. "Please have a seat."

Grace perched on the end of the antique-style chair and gripped her hands in her lap.

Mr. Carter pulled his chair in and moved folders to the corner of his spotless desk. "Would you like some coffee?"

"Yes," Jenn said.

"No. Thank you, Mr. Carter. I'd like to get right to the point, if we could."

Jenn's forehead wrinkled, and her hands shot out, palms up. Grace shook her head. Jenn slumped in her chair.

"Please call me Hoke. Even at my age, when I hear 'Mr. Carter' I look over my shoulder for my daddy, and he's been gone some years." He pressed the button on the phone. "Ginny, please bring in that strong coffee I like so much. Thank you." He turned back to Grace and Jenn and offered a smile that warmed up his blue eyes. "My wife only lets me have one cup. I have to sneak the other one here." He clapped his hands together. "Let's get right down to it, then. The donor of the house wishes to remain anonymous. I have papers for you to sign that state you won't go looking for their identity and if you happen to stumble upon it in some fashion, the gift is void and the house is no longer yours."

"I still don't understand how or why this person chose me. I've never even been to Heritage River."

"I assure you the donor knew exactly what they were doing. The house is yours."

Ginny entered carrying a tray with a carafe of coffee and three mugs.

"Ah, finally, my second cup." He stood and offered a mug to Jenn, who gladly whisked it out of his hands. "Are you certain you don't want any, Grace? I can call you Grace, can't I? I feel like we've met somewhere before."

Heat filled her cheeks. "Of course you can call me Grace. But I know we've never met, unless you've been to Jersey."

"Can't say I have." He tipped the mug as an offering and savored his first sip. "Now where were we?"

"You were saying Grace can't find out who gave her the house." Jenn cradled her coffee. "Isn't this kind of thing unusual? She can't even know why she was chosen? There has to be a catch somewhere."

Hoke eased into his chair. "Oh, there's a catch."

"I knew it." Jenn slapped Grace's arm.

Grace jumped in her seat. "Ouch. What's this so-called catch?" Did she really want to hear this?

"The house needs some fixing. You have to live in it during the renovations. You can sell or stay after, but if you don't live in it during, there's no deal."

"We might as well go home now." Jenn stood.

"Sit. I haven't decided to go home yet." But going home was exactly what she wanted to do. She was just thinking she couldn't live down here, and now she would have to? That was insane. She had a life in Jersey. She couldn't take a sabbatical from it. How could she agree to such a thing? "Can I see the house first before I decide?"

"Of course. The donor is providing money for the renovations. No need to worry about that."

"Is there a time frame for fixing the house up?"

"You aren't seriously considering this offer, are you?" Jenn returned her coffee to the tray. "This could be a scam. I know I agreed to come down here with you, but now that I'm hearing you have to live in the house while you fix it up, something sounds wrong. We should go, Grace."

Hoke stood and pulled up his trousers. "Ms.

Caldini, these circumstances aren't ordinary, I grant you, but there is no scam involved. My law practice has been around for decades. My granddaddy started it up when that road out there was nothing more than dirt. I wouldn't scam anyone anymore than I'd steal their seat at church on Sunday."

He turned to Grace. "If you decide to take on the house, you'll sign the papers that say you won't try and find your gift giver. The other papers you'll sign put the house in your name. The house is yours. If you decide you don't want to fix it, you sign the house back to me. You can't sell it as is. The donor doesn't want that either."

"Let me make sure I understand you. I live in the house and fix it up. When that's done, I can sell it?" She wiped her sweaty hands on her legs. She might be able to pull this off. Chloe could stay with Larry. Grace tried not to picture Larry padding around in his boxers with the hottie sitting in her kitchen. "If I change my mind at any time, I sign the house back to you and I walk away? No questions asked." An escape hatch. She could swallow that.

"That's right." Hoke's smile warmed his eyes again.

"This is crazy. You can't possibly be considering this," Jenn said.

"Let's go see the house. How bad could it be?"

****

The house on Dogwood Drive tipped on its side. Or maybe that was the panic making her head spin. Grace took four long slow breaths. Of course the house was a piece of crap. What did she expect to see? A mansion? Well, at least something that had seen the wet bristles of a paintbrush in the past ten years.

That wasn't the worst of it. The broken front wooden steps led to a sagging porch. The shutters—maybe in their prime the color green, but now the color of overcooked broccoli—hung on their sides. Yellowed curtains hung like limp pasta in the dirt-covered windows. The grass was nothing more than sand worn over by years of footsteps and quite possibly a car. Grace took another four slow breaths.

"We're not going in there. We've seen enough. Tell Mr. Carter he can keep the house. Grace doesn't want it," Jenn said to Dixie Bordeux, the realtor who was squeezed into her white linen suit and whose ankles puddled around the tops of her white pumps. She dangled the house keys off her perfectly manicured pink nails. The polish matched the pink stain on her lips.

"Hang on a second." Grace gripped Jenn's arm for support. "Let's just take a look. We're here, aren't we?"

"Why are you so bent on seeing more of this house? Look at it." Jenn stabbed a finger toward the leaning structure. "You can't live here." Her eyes grew to the size of boiled eggs. "Maybe Larry is the giver. He's trying to get you out of the way while he slides into your house with his floozy. He forces you down here for eternity, thinking you're getting something great out of the deal, and he never has to run into you again."

She dropped Jenn's arm. "Stop it. Larry doesn't have anything to do with this. This is about me. I'm going inside that house, and I'm going to take a look around. You can wait out here if you want." She headed for the porch but stopped and turned around. "If I

Stacey Wilk

decide to keep this house, it's because I need something new in my life. Everyone around me is moving on. What will I have after that?"

She didn't want this house. She didn't need this house. But she didn't want anyone telling her what to do either.

Sweat trickled down the back of Grace's neck into the collar of her cotton buttoned-down shirt. The southern sun was hotter than she was used to. All this sweating would ruin her clothes. The mold-filled air inside that house would probably do it faster. "I still can't believe this house was meant for me. Why would someone choose me? I'm nobody special."

Dixie offered a thin smile. Grace wanted to like her. Dixie's pale blue eyes smiled back at Grace, but the house and the situation made it impossible to warm to her. Her soft voice held a hint of southern charm. "Everyone's special, darlin'. You can rest assured this house is a gift from the almighty." She pointed to the sky. "I've known Hoke Carter for years. His daddy and mine used to go fishing together. Why, he practically grew up in my backyard. He's the salt of the earth, that one. He wouldn't let anyone pull a fast one on you. This house was meant for you. I know she doesn't have on her prettiest face, but give her half a chance. She'll be a debutant before you're done with her."

"See," Grace said. "Dixie knows."

"You're a lucky woman, is all." Dixie wrestled the key in the lock and swung the door open. "My momma always told me to count my blessings. I'd say that's what you should do with this house."

"This house is not a blessing," Jenn said.

"Hey, Debbie Downer. Keep it to yourself." False

30

bravado, the desire to prove to herself she could move on, and the desire to prove Jenn wrong pushed Grace's legs forward and through the doorway.

She ran a finger along the wall and brought it back covered in grime. She tried not to gag.

"This is the living room." Dixie swept the room with her elegant hand. "You see how much natural light you get in here. With a little elbow grease, you can have those windows sparkling."

Pounding began behind Grace's eyes, and she pinched the bridge of her nose. She wanted to go home. And that was the problem, wasn't it? There would be no home. Larry and his chick were there now, measuring windows. So the idea of turning around and flying back north to the shattered remains of her warm and safe life made her skin itch almost as badly as this house did.

"Jenn, look." Grace glided across the room on her make-believe positive attitude. "This mantel is mahogany. I could sand and restain it. It would be pretty."

"Since when do you know anything about mahogany?"

"I watch home-makeover shows." She stuck out her tongue and took off for another room. "Look in here."

Dixie and Jenn followed.

"The kitchen is cozy. Sure, the appliances have to go, but a little paint on the cabinets and they'd be good as new. I really could fix this up and sell it." Grace leaned back against the cabinets as if she'd discovered some gem, while hoping she wasn't ruining her clothes. She ignored the cabinet door that fell off its hinge.

"The kitchen receives a lot of morning light," Dixie said.

"From that tiny window?" Jenn said.

"Just use your imagination, Jenn." Grace wasn't sure she had an imagination of her own. She'd start with a list. Lists always made her itchy skin settle down. Lists meant order, and order meant peace. Larry hated her lists, but she didn't know that until recently. She didn't know her ex-husband at all, it seemed.

Dixie handed her the keys. "Will you be hiring someone to do the work, or will you be doing it yourself?"

"I, um, didn't realize how much work there would be." Grace peeked around the corner to the pink bathroom that screamed 1953. Well, that would have to go too. She didn't know the first thing about renovating a house. Sure, she could decorate. She'd pulled every detail together in her house back in Silverside, but she didn't know how to restain hardwood floors or break up tile, and what if they needed to rip out walls and fix electrical? She took another long breath. "Do you know anyone?"

"The local contractor is Beau Carroll. Everyone hires Beau. I'll send him by later today to have a look-see, and he'll tell you what you're up against." Dixie waved her hand in the air, and the dust particles danced around her fingers.

Grace suppressed the urge to sneeze and wash her hands.

"But honestly, sugar, nothing a little bleach won't fix." Dixie pushed her smile higher, forcing her cheeks to close her eyes.

"This place needs more than a little bleach." Jenn

crossed her arms over her chest.

She ignored Jenn's comment. "I might like to get multiple estimates." How could she make an informed decision by speaking to only one person?

Dixie laughed. "Beau is the best. You won't need anyone else. You know, I'm surprised he never bought this house for himself. He could've fixed it up real nice and flipped it." Dixie shrugged. "No matter. You're here now, and we're right glad to have you. Welcome to Heritage River."

"What are the neighbors like?" Jenn peered out the dirty window.

"Most folks keep to themselves. You've got the Bucknells across the street. Sady and Mo been there forty years. Raised four boys. They're good people. On your left is Miles. He lives alone since his wife died in 2005. He knows when you can rake your leaves and place them at the curb and when you have to bag them. He keeps track of the sprinkler rules too, but you don't have any here, so he won't be reminding you to turn them off."

"He sounds like a peach." Jenn turned back toward them.

"The house on your other side is only occupied once a year or so. That family has owned the house for a long time. First the parents and then the middle boy. He won't bother you. He sleeps all day and works at night. And like I said, he isn't there much."

"What's he a bartender or something?" Grace said.

Dixie laughed again. "Far from that. He's our resident celebrity. You must've heard of the band Savage?"

Jenn took a step toward Dixie. "Savage was my

favorite band growing up."

"Well, lucky day. Blaise owns the house now. Bought it from his siblings some years back."

"I remember that band. Whatever happened to them?" Grace said.

"They're playing amusement parks and small theaters now. It's a shame. They used to sell out arenas," Jenn said.

"Is he married?" Grace had read about the rock bands of the past and how they tore apart hotels and had women in every city. Not to mention the drugs they did. What kind of a neighbor would this Blaise Savage be?

"I heard he got divorced because his wife couldn't stand his cheating. I read it in one of those trash mags," Jenn said. "Supposedly he'd have hot women ride the tour bus with them while his wife stayed home raising their son."

Dixie's eyebrows squished together. "I don't know the details. He never brought his wife here. I heard she didn't like our small town. Wanted the bright lights of the big city. When they got divorced, she took their son and moved back west."

If the mother took her son and ran, there must be more to the story, but Grace didn't bother to say anything. She wouldn't be making friends with her neighbors. That wasn't the plan.

"Is he there now?" Jenn wiped the dirt from the window and peered out.

"Jenn," Grace warned.

"What? I'm curious."

"Back a few weeks now. Hurt himself. Taking some time off to heal. I'm sure you'll see him over the fence. Not sure how long he's staying, though.

Probably be out of here like lightning. Well, I must be running along. If you need anything, don't hesitate to call me." Dixie waved and marched out into the hot sun.

Grace closed the door and leaned her back against it. The heat forced itself against her. She was hot, and the house was miserable. And now she'd be living next to a rock star. He probably had parties all night long and played loud music. Women probably paraded in and out of that house. Just thinking about the number of women he must've slept with made her skin itch.

"This isn't going to be a quick flip like you were hoping." Jenn held the curtains between the tips of her fingers before she let the material drop back against the wall.

"I need a new adventure." Grace pushed the curtains aside to let in the view of the street and wiped her hands on her pants. No sign of the neighbor.

"You'll probably have to stay the whole summer. Maybe longer. And what about Chloe? Do you really think she'd want to spend her last summer before college down here in Tennessee?"

"Chloe can stay with Larry in her home, in her room. She isn't going to miss me, that's for sure, and I can fly home right before she leaves for school. If she needs me to buy anything for her, I can do it online and ship it. But she'll want to do that herself. She always has." Every time she thought about Chloe leaving, her breath stuck, but the truth her daughter had one foot out the door by the time she was twelve. As much as Grace wanted to be right there with Chloe, staying in Heritage River would be good practice for when Chloe left. Grace would just have to remember not to cry.

35

"I still say you're nuts. This place isn't you. It's a mess and you hate messes. You don't know what's lurking behind these walls."

"Why are you so against this? I need something new in my life. I need to find myself again, and this house might be the answer."

Jenn smirked. "This house isn't going to help you find yourself. It's going to give you one giant pain in the butt." She grabbed Grace's hands. "If you want to find yourself, let's go on a spa trip or find a yoga retreat in Arizona or something. Taking a risk like this isn't you."

"Maybe it's time for a new me." She pulled a notepad from her purse. Playing it safe and being predictable had gotten her nowhere.

"What are you doing?"

"I'm making a list of things we need to get through the night without wanting to throw up. Flip the switch and see if we have electricity."

"This is crazy." But Jenn flipped the switch.

"Let's say a prayer the water comes on." Was she actually going to make this work? She'd start with cleaning the bathroom and the kitchen. Just enough to make a cup of tea. They'd have to eat somewhere else. She wasn't going to put a single thing in that fridge. As for sleeping arrangements, they'd have to figure something out. One step at a time. There was no point in getting ahead of herself. She'd just go running scared.

She looked around the house again. Maybe things wouldn't be so bad, after all.

Chapter Five

"That must be Blaise Savage," Jenn said over her shoulder.

They were staring out the kitchen window into the neighbor's backyard. A tall, sinewy man with salt-and-pepper hair hanging in his face and wearing a ripped T-shirt fought the garden hose with one hand as he dragged it against the house. The other hand was wrapped in some kind of a bandage.

"He's dirty, whoever he is."

"He's not dirty. He's dreamy." Jenn turned in circles with a cat-eating-the-canary grin on her face. "I used to have posters of that band on my wall. I went to their first concert when I was a kid."

"Well, your childhood crush, if that's even him, needs a bath."

"I'd give him one."

"Of course you would." Grace stepped away from the window. "We need to get some cleaning supplies. I don't care that we're here for just one night. I've got to get my hands on those bathrooms."

"Do you think we could find a hotel to stay at? I wasn't planning on this house being in such bad shape. Did you see the mold around the tub?" Jenn made a face.

Truth be told, Grace wanted to disinfect the house for meningitis. "We'll get a couple of air mattresses, and I'll clean the bathroom so your butt has a nice place to sit."

"What did you do with my friend? Two days ago, you wouldn't have come within a hundred feet of this place, and now you're ready to throw everything away and move in?"

"Yeah, well, two days ago Larry called with his big announcement. I want to try this. I need to try this. Please understand."

"This is scary, Grace. You don't know who gave you this house. What if they show up here in the middle of the night and attack you? Take you hostage or something."

"You've been watching too many serial-killer shows."

"This place could be a money pit. It might have to be condemned."

Grace laughed. "It's not that bad. I think Dixie is right. With a little bleach and some fresh paint, it will be fine. Okay, the porch looks a little rough, but there aren't any cracks in the walls. The foundation is probably fine. I'm doing this, Jenn. I want to remember who I was before I married Larry and had a child I've spent the past eighteen years revolving my life around. I can't stay in Silverside no matter what. I can't run into Larry and Annie with her big belly in the grocery store."

"But it's your grocery store. It's your town. Don't give them the satisfaction of running away."

"Larry doesn't care about me or what I do. I'm not sure he ever did. I'm going to fix this house up. I don't care what papers I signed, because I'm going to try and figure out who gave me this house. I have no idea where to begin on either count, but I'll worry about that later. And after all that, after I've had a chance to get to know myself again, I'll sell this house and move home, having been a better person for it."

What kind of an example would she be setting for Chloe if she sat around and let the world run over her? Never mind that she felt exactly as if the world had crushed her. Being dumped by your husband for a younger woman was embarrassing. The tears threatened to come, and she bit down on her bottom lip.

"I still think you're making a mistake. You don't have anything to prove, and you can find yourself in Jersey, where you belong."

"I don't know where I belong anymore." Grace swung her arm in the air, taking the room in. "This old, decrepit, smelly, disaster of a house is my second chance."

Jenn laughed. "Well, it looks like you're going to take that chance no matter what I say. I never would've believed it possible if I wasn't standing here watching you lose your mind."

Grace's back stiffened. "I'm not losing my mind. I'm going to know what I want for the first time in a long time. I wish you could be more supportive. Of all the people, I thought you'd understand."

Jenn ran to her and grabbed her hands. "I do understand. Larry is an ass for what he's done to you. You are the sweetest person I know, but to throw caution to the wind like this just isn't you. You're a planner. You don't make a move without assessing the situation first. And now you want to nose-dive into an empty pool. You don't have to do this to spite Larry."

That wasn't what she was doing, was it? "How is

taking this house spiting Larry? If I'm spiting anyone, it's myself. I'm the one with something to lose if this doesn't work out." She swung her purse over her shoulder and pulled open the front door. She'd had enough of this discussion. She needed to do something, and she'd start by buying the items on her list.

The smell of fresh air and cut grass swooped in and settled around her, drawing her outside. Children laughed somewhere down the road. A large poplar tree decorated the front yard. She hadn't noticed it before. The tree offered the porch some shade from the blistering heat. Maybe she could put a swing there some day.

"Grace, I'm sorry." Jenn yanked the door closed behind her.

Grace waved her apology away. "This is a cute neighborhood if you look out from the porch." A much better view than standing at the street and looking at this eyesore.

"How could someone let this house get so bad?" Jenn said as the stepped off the porch and into the rays of summer sun.

Sweat ran down Grace's spine. The back of her blouse would be completely wrinkled. She was glad she usually wore her hair pinned up. She forgot to check if the house had air- conditioning. She'd grab a fan just in case, and if it didn't, that would have to be on the list of things to change.

"I will admit whoever gave this house to you has me curious," Jenn said. "You sure you don't have a long lost aunt or something?"

"I wish." She pressed on the key fob, and the rental car chirped to life. "Why me? Why do something so nice for me?" Not knowing had had her running the vacuum over and over. She really didn't have any relatives. Her mother was an only child, and she had passed away years before, when Grace was twenty-two. Grace hadn't spoken to her father since she was five. She didn't know any relatives on his side, if there even were any.

"I've wondered the same thing. But is strapping you with a house that's been neglected for years really doing something nice? It seems whoever gave you this house wants to see you sweat." Jenn wiped the back of her neck. "This heat alone is enough torture. You should give the house back to Mr. Carter."

"Enough." Grace raised her voice. "I brought you with me because I needed my friend's support. Instead, all I'm getting is this negativity." She shook her hands, trying to find the right words. "You don't have to understand why I'm doing this, and if it's the biggest mistake of my life, then it's my mistake to make. All you have to do is stand there and nod your head. If you can't do that, then get yourself on the next plane home."

"She told you," a male voice said.

Grace's head snapped around. The dirty neighbor stood yards away. He brushed his hair out of his eyes. He had high cheekbones and a defined chin. His shirt stretched across his muscular chest, but he didn't look as though he'd be rock hard to the touch. When had he walked up? His pickup door was open, and he was halfway back to his house. Maybe he had forgotten something.

"Excuse me?" she said.

The neighbor's full lips spread into a crooked smile, revealing straight white teeth. "Pardon me, ladies, but here in the South we don't air our dirty laundry on the front lawn. I'm not used to such a scuttle out in public." He tipped an imaginary hat. He was mocking them.

"I don't believe we asked for your opinion," she said.

"You asked by yelling in my earshot with your Yankee accents." He laughed.

Yankee accents? She'd show him. "In the North, we mind our own business, Mister…"

"You can call my Blaise."

"I knew it," Jenn shouted. Her face and neck bloomed red. She stood up on her toes with her hands clasped together and a teenage twinkle in her eye. "I'm a huge fan. I have all your albums, and I've seen you in concert at least ten times. Can I take a picture with you?"

Grace thought Jenn would begin fanning herself any second or, worse, faint. "Jenn, shush."

"What's the big deal? I can put it on my Facebook," she hissed back. "What do you say, Blaise? One picture?"

Grace hung her head. It was like being in high school all over again. Jenn wanted to be the center of attention, acting like a groupie, and Grace wanted to hide in the shadow of her embarrassment.

"Sure. I'll take that picture."

Of course he would. He probably never told a woman no.

Jenn glided across the lawn, placed her cheek against Blaise's, and with smiles the size of Tennessee, hit the button on her phone. How many pictures had he taken just like that? Pressing his cheek against some stranger's? Probably grabbing her butt too. Why would any self-respecting woman want to flaunt herself in front of a man like that? He wasn't about to take her seriously when around every corner another Botoxed bleached-blonde bombshell was waiting.

"Can we go now?" Grace repinned her hair and adjusted her blouse.

He returned to his truck. "That house belonged to a nice family once. With a little help, it could belong to a nice family again. You planning on buying it?"

"I think she should knock it down," Jenn said.

"That isn't very nice." Blaise wagged a finger at her. "How would you like to be knocked down before your prime?"

Grace ignored his sarcasm. "I haven't made any decisions yet." Why was looking at him getting harder? Her gaze kept returning to the cheek he pressed against Jenn's. She was being ridiculous. This man was of no interest to her.

The weight of the situation, the summer heat, Jenn's obvious disdain of the house and infatuation with the neighbor wore Grace out. She wanted to get inside air-conditioning with her thoughts and make more plans.

"Sorry to bother you. Thanks for the picture." He jumped into his truck and pulled away.

"I've already got twenty likes." Jenn held her phone up as she slid into the passenger's seat. "I've always wondered what it was like to sleep with a rock star."

Grace slid in after her. "How could you fawn all over him like a schoolgirl? He looks like he hasn't bathed. He must put on a show for every woman in a five-mile radius. He can't possibly take a relationship seriously. I bet he's been married like five times."

"Someone has a crush."

She ignored Jenn's jeer. "That someone would be you. He probably thinks his twinkling gray eyes make every woman gush over him. Well, not me, no thanks." She swung her head to the side to find Jenn looking straight ahead and a large smile plastered to her face. "Stop laughing. It isn't funny." But she found the corners of her mouth twitching up. No one made her laugh like Jenn.

"He does have twinkly eyes. And did you see his butt?" Jenn said.

Grace couldn't help but laugh.

They found the local grocery store and stocked up on cleaning supplies and a few basic nonperishable food items to hold them over. They would eat meals out during their time in Heritage River. They were scheduled to go back to Jersey the next day, but it looked as if Grace would be back to the little southern town as soon as she could pack. There wasn't any time to waste. The sooner she could fix the house, the sooner she could return home a new person ready for a new life. She hoped this idea of hers was going to work.

When they returned to the house on Dogwood Drive, they passed a Cherry Street, a Spruce Street, and a Meadow Lane too. A red pickup waited in the driveway. The truck was faded from years in the sun, with a worn-out sign on the side reading Construction. She couldn't make out the rest.

"Looks like Dixie sent her man." Jenn opened the car door and peeled herself out.

Grace followed.

An older man shoved his way out of the truck. Even in the heat he wore jeans and work boots. He was tall and thin, but his shoulders stood military straight. What was left of his hair was white and stuck up in different directions, and the lines on his face drew a picture of years of hard work outside.

"You must be the contractor Dixie mentioned." Grace plunged forward with her hand out and her best library-volunteer smile plastered on.

The man didn't budge. He shoved his hands in his back pockets, and Grace came up short. "Oh," she said.

"I'm Beau Carroll." His voice rubbed the air like sandpaper. His gaze turned to his boots, then back up at her. "You bought this place?"

"Well, it's a long story. But it's mine, and I need to fix it up. Dixie said you could help with that?"

He glanced back down at the ground, then over at Jenn. "You moving in too?"

"Me? Uh, no. I'm just the friend hoping to talk some sense into her. This house isn't worth fixing, is it?"

"Nothing wrong with that house." He hitched a thumb toward it. "She's still got her bones just fine." He turned to Grace. "When do you want to get started?"

"Don't you want to take a look around?"

"Don't need to."

"Have you seen inside the house before?"

"Worked in this town a long time. Seen every house at least once." He walked up to the porch and pressed on the step with his heel.

Where was he going? Grace hurried after him, but his cold stare stopped her on the sidewalk. "Could you at least provide me with a detailed estimate of the work

45

included and the cost? I might not want to complete every job, or I might want to do some myself. I'm not entirely sure what my budget is yet."

He kicked the step. "You figure that part out and let me know. I'll stay in your budget. You'll need to do some of the work anyway. I don't have my crew no more."

How could he possibly do it all alone? What happened to his crew? There must be other contractors around she could hire with a full staff. She'd check into it. "Mr. Carroll, I think I need to get additional estimates. If you could just leave yours with Dixie, I'll pick it up when I return to town, and then I'll let you know either way what I decide."

"You either want to hire me or you don't. I don't have time for you to go shopping around for another contractor."

"If that's the case, then thank you for your time, but I think I'd like to go in a different direction." Who did this man think he was coming in and ordering her to hire him? They might handle business that way in Heritage River, but it's not how she handled things.

The growl of a truck engine grew louder as it approached and then quieted down in the driveway next door. "Afternoon, Beau." Blaise's voice floated in from behind her. He grabbed a brown paper bag from the bed of the truck.

Beau Carroll nodded his head. "Blaise."

"These ladies giving you a bad time, sir?" He edged his way along his front walk.

Grace stamped her foot. "Excuse me?"

Beau gave her a wide circle on the way back to his truck. He yanked at the truck door. "Ms. Starr and her friend are deciding on another contractor."

"You're not going to hire Beau? You're nuts. Because he's the best around. You won't find better. You could try, but old Walt Ramsey is a drunk and never shows up on the job. It will take you a year to fix this place up with him. You could try a big company out of town, but a little job like this won't be a priority. Besides, we like to stick to our own here." Blaise shifted the bag in his good arm, keeping it away from the brace.

She wouldn't be steamrolled by these men. "I haven't made any final decisions. I'm still in the stage of collecting estimates, that's all. Mr. Carroll, if you're certain you can't provide an estimate, then I'm sorry, but our business is finished."

Blaise placed the bag on his porch and crossed the yard in a fast-paced stride. "Listen, Miss I Don't Trust Anyone Because I'm From the North, you won't find a better man than Beau to do your work. He fixed my place up for me and practically every house in town. Go ask the ones who didn't use him how sorry they were."

"It's about the money, that's all."

"It's not about the money. It's about integrity and honor and decency. That's everything Beau is. He won't waste your money." Blaise moved into Grace's personal space, causing her to back up, but there was a softness in his gray eyes and a smile on his face.

It appeared he genuinely cared about this man.

Beau fidgeted with his keys. "I best be going. You let me know what you decide, Ms. Starr. I'm ready to start when you are."

Those were the most words the man had said the whole time.

"I like him," Jenn whispered in her ear.

"Beau?"

"And Blaise."

Chapter Six

Her muscles ached. What was she thinking, tearing out a carpet at her age? Grace sat on the front step of her disaster house. That was the new name she was going to give it. Disaster House. Kind of went with her life at the moment. The irony wasn't lost on her.

The cool night air blew on her damp skin. The shorts and T-shirt weren't enough. She should have brought out something to wrap herself in. The hot Earl Grey tea would have to do for now. She cuddled the paper cup for warmth.

Fireflies chased each other under the poplar tree, and the smell of honeysuckles coated the air. A peaceful quiet settled around her. Most of the lights were out in the other houses. The street was tucked in for the night. Even Jenn was nestled deep in her sleeping bag, with a movie playing on her tablet. They'd be going home tomorrow, and then Grace would return to Heritage River alone.

The house didn't fit her. Oh, she wanted it to now that she decided to plunge headfirst into this scheme. But the house pressed against her skin like a sweater shrunk in the dryer. Sure, they had cleaned until their fingers were raw and her arms screamed for her to stop, but she couldn't stay inside just yet. Maybe she would feel differently in the morning or when she got back. Or after she moved her things out of her home and Larry's

49

hoochie momma with the new-baby belly moved in. Because the Disaster House would be her new home until she could fix it, sell it, and find a real place in Jersey. Just not in Silverside.

She tallied potential projects in her head. How long was all this going to take? She was actually considering hiring Beau Carroll. She kept thinking about Blaise's set face while he spoke those words about Beau. He meant them. She could tell. It was just a feeling, and maybe she was a bad judge of character considering she didn't even know her husband, ex-husband, but she believed Blaise trusted Beau.

And did she really have the time or desire to find someone else? She wanted the house fixed up as soon as possible. Beau Carroll could do his work—of course, his working-alone part had her concerned—but the house had to be sellable. It didn't have to be perfect. Once it was good enough to satisfy Hoke, she'd call Dixie. Maybe she could even start showing it before it was completely finished. There weren't any rules about that.

Her phone buzzed next to her. She yanked it up. "Are you all right?"

"Mom, jeez, I'm fine."

Grace let out a breath and held a hand to her chest, as if she could steady her racing heart. "You're calling so late."

"I know. Sorry. When are you coming home?"

"Tomorrow. What's up?" Because Chloe didn't call just to say hi.

"I want to know when we're going house hunting because I can't live here with *them*. They make me sick. Dad fussing all over her—"

"Chloe, stop." She held her palm up, as if her daughter could see. "I don't want to hear the details."

"Sorry. I just want to know when we're going house hunting."

"We aren't. I'm going to spend the summer down here fixing up the house, and then I'll sell it. You'll have to stay with your dad. You can hide in your room when you're at home." She told Chloe about the stipulations.

"You're actually going to take this stupid idea on?"

"I thought you wanted me to check this whole thing out."

"I did and you did, and now that you know you have to live there during the renovations, I think it's a stupid idea."

Of course Chloe didn't like the idea, because she didn't want to live with Larry. Why wasn't Grace shocked? "I need to try something new."

"If you want to try something new, how about sushi? Picking up and moving to another state isn't like you, Mom."

It wasn't anything like her. At least not the Grace in her adult years. Adult Grace planned and weighed the risks. She kept the house clean and organized everyone's life. Adult Grace would never take on something like the Disaster House.

"I'm sorry this isn't what we planned, but I want to do this, Chloe. I need a new chapter in my life. In a few months, you'll be off to college, doing amazing things and meeting new people. This is my time. Living with your dad won't be so bad. You're hardly home anyway."

"What about me? Who's going to get me ready for

college? I have a ton of stuff to buy, and Dad isn't going to shop with me. And living with him like he is now will suck."

"Don't be ridiculous. You lived with him your entire life. Why is now any different? And buy what you need online. You know what you want. I'll be back before it's time to move you in. I wouldn't miss that for anything."

The lights went on in the house next door. Blaise glided past the windows. Grace tried not to notice.

"You know, I'm affected by what's happening too. Do you think I like the fact my father is hooking up with a woman not much older than I am and they're about to have a baby? I don't want to be an older sister. It's creepy."

"I'm sorry your father's choices have upset you, but you'll have to discuss that with him. As for me, I'm fixing this house up and then I'll be home. You're an adult now, at least that's what you've been trying to tell me for the last four years. You will have to learn to live with disappointment. If all you need me for is to shop for you, you can do it yourself. I thought maybe you were calling to say you'd like to come down and see the house."

Classical music drifted over to her from Blaise's open window. She didn't take him for the classical music type. His curtains billowed in the night breeze. Her tea had grown cold, and her skin crawled with goose bumps. She should have grabbed a sweater.

"Come to Tennessee? No, thanks. What could possibly be worth seeing there?"

"It's a nice town." Heritage River wasn't Silverside, and if you blinked, you'd miss it, but the streets were tree lined and children played in the front yards. And neighbors didn't mind their own business, but they did play nice music.

"I still think you should come home. You don't know what you're doing renovating a house. You run the PTA. You organize cabinets. You plan dinner parties. You shelve books. Do you really want to be alone all summer?"

Right at that moment she did. She pinched the bridge of her nose. "Chloe, somehow I managed to survive into my forties. I'll figure out what I need to do." She took a deep breath. She didn't want to fight. She just wanted someone to understand. "Besides, I won't be alone. I've already met people. And you could come and visit. It won't kill you." Probably not the best thing to say.

"It might. Goodnight, Mom. I've gotta run." Chloe ended the call.

Grace pushed the phone away and let out a large breath. Parenting was never easy. She kept waiting for the moment her sweet daughter, who once had chubby cheeks and pudgy hands wound tightly around Grace's, would come back to her. The library ladies with grown children said the girls return. She found it hard to believe. Every conversation had the potential to explode. Talking to her teenager required navigating a daily trip across a land mine. It didn't matter Chloe had turned eighteen on May thirty-first. It didn't matter she had graduated from high school the week before and was about to go off to college in Virginia. She fought with Grace every chance she could, just because she could. And Grace was exhausted.

Blaise stepped onto his front porch, his good hand

shoved in his pocket and the other holding a guitar. A man that good looking who plays in a famous band must be nothing but trouble. She could feel it in her belly.

The classical music was gone. He must've turned it off before he came out. She liked the music. It soothed the muscles in her shoulders.

He pulled up a rocking chair and rested the guitar on his knee. He strummed with his good hand and stopped from time to time to rub the injured one. She couldn't hear what he played, but she heard the cursing that went along with the breaks in his playing.

"Are you ever coming in?"

Grace jumped at Jenn's voice. She stood in the doorway, wearing pink shorts and a black tank. Her brown hair was sticking up in the back.

"I can't fall asleep. This house makes too many noises. Not to mention I'm afraid it will collapse around me." Before she could answer, Jenn went on. "Oh, now I see why you're out here. Let's stay outside and enjoy the music. Blaise, woo hoo," Jenn yelled and waved her arm.

Grace jumped to her feet trying to grab Jenn. "Stop that. He might hear you."

"That's the idea. Hey, Blaise." She pushed Grace out of the way. "The only redeeming thing about this house is him."

Grace glanced over her shoulder. He turned in the direction of Jenn's ruckus and smiled. He waved back. When he put the guitar down and headed across the lawn, Grace thought she'd die of embarrassment. If she didn't kill Jenn first.

Chapter Seven

Why the hell was he walking across the lawn?

Because Blaise couldn't stop himself. And because the friend—what was her name? Jenn, that was it—was giving him an excuse. He had to see his pretty neighbor up close again. The hour of the evening was in question, but hell, that never stopped him before.

"Hello." Not his most original opener. "Enjoying the evening?"

She tucked a strand of blonde hair behind her ear and looked down at her bare legs. Her legs were long and toned. Her toes polished in red. She cleared her throat and brought his gaze back up.

"We were just going inside." His neighbor tried to steer Jenn toward the door. Why hadn't he asked for her name earlier?

Jenn pushed past her friend and flew down the steps. She tucked an arm through his good one. "Not at all. It's such a beautiful night. Grace and I thought we'd have a glass of wine on the porch. Would you like some?"

Her name was Grace, and she was giving him the cold shoulder. "You got something besides wine?"

Grace's eyebrows furrowed. Was she hoping he'd say no thank you and walk away?

"How about an iced tea, then? Doesn't everyone in the South drink iced tea?"

"Around these parts they do." He boosted his accent for fun.

Jenn was persistent. He'd give her that. He was used to women invading his personal space, so he laced an arm around her shoulder to see what Grace would do.

Her eyes grew to the size of cymbals, and she backed up toward the door. Okay, the arm-around-the-shoulder thing might have been a mistake. He stepped back. The face Grace made, as if he were singing out of key, gave her feelings away, and he didn't want to run her off completely before he got a chance to get to know her a little.

"I'm heading inside. Good night." She pulled her clothes into place and smoothed down her hair.

"Did you decide to hire Beau?" He couldn't let her go just yet.

If he had a type, which he did not, Grace was not it. After Melissa left him, he didn't want to be tied down or involved with another woman not even for a night, which most men would not believe. He'd run into his share of problems with a one-night stand. Anyone so uptight would never understand him or how music was in his blood and he had to be playing no matter what. No matter when. No matter where. Her blue eyes and the way she tucked her lip under her teeth made him want another look. What would one more look hurt?

She stood with her hand on the door, ready to make that quick exit. "I think I will be hiring Beau."

"You will?" Jenn said.

"I hadn't decided until tonight, but I don't want to waste time searching for another contractor. The sooner we get started, the sooner I can sell."

"You're not planning to live here?" She was a house flipper. It was all business to her. He should've known. Someone like Grace wouldn't want to stay in Heritage River. Only a special person would see the beauty of this small town. She was probably a city girl and liked the noise and the action. She probably wanted a Starbucks on every corner.

"I'll be here through the renovations, but that's it. I'd like to be finished before my daughter goes off to college."

"Good luck with that," Jenn said. "This place needs way too much work. You might be here through Christmas."

Here through Christmas? She'd never stand it. Not that he'd be around until then either. As soon as Cash went off to school, he'd close up the house and hit the road. "Why did you choose this house to flip? There must've been ones that required less work." She didn't look like someone who got dirty doing the fixing. She stood there in crisp shorts, showing off her legs, and a sleeveless shirt that exposed her toned shoulders, but earlier she was all buttoned up in a top his third-grade teacher would've worn and pants that belonged in a cubicle.

"It was a gift." Jenn picked at her nails.

"Jenn." Grace looked as if she wanted to choke her.

He tried not to laugh. The lady didn't like her dirty laundry hung on the line. She'd fit right in, after all.

Jenn looked at her and smirked. "It's true. What's the big deal?"

"Someone gave this house to you?" Blaise said. "That's a mighty nice gift." Maybe house flipper wasn't her business. Then she had no idea what she'd gotten herself into.

"I'd rather not discuss it. Now if you'll both excuse me… We have an early flight tomorrow."

"I'm headed to the airport tomorrow morning too. Do you need a ride?" Why was he behaving like a teenager who never spoke to a girl before? He could clearly see the rental car parked in the driveway.

"Yes," Jenn said. Of course *she* did.

"No, thank you." Grace turned her back and marched inside. The door shut behind her.

"She's not a lot of fun, is she?" He shoved his good hand into his pocket.

"She was once. Anyway, how about that iced tea?" Was she batting her eyes at him? This one was trouble. He should send her to Colton. Colton could handle trouble way better than he could.

He stared at the door. "No, thanks. I think I'm going to call it a night."

****

He hated early mornings, which was probably why Melissa booked Cash on a flight that would force Blaise out of the house before noon. The airport buzzed around him. Haggard people dragging luggage behind them as they navigated their way. TSA agents patting down families without shoes on who just wanted to go on the vacation they had saved five years for. He wondered if Grace had arrived yet. And then decided it was better if he didn't know. She'd be back in town, and he'd see her every day. Was that really going to be a good thing?

Blaise pulled down on his baseball cap, trying to hide his eyes, and made his way to passenger pickup downstairs.

"Hey, excuse me." A man with thinning hair and a portly belly ran up alongside him. Blaise didn't flinch but kept walking. "Are you Blaise Savage?" The man flashed a crooked smile and kept pace with him.

Blaise pasted on his it's-always-great-to-meet-fans face and stepped on the escalator. "Yes, I am." Sometimes he'd get lucky, and that's all they wanted to know. Maybe a bet with a buddy.

But the man stuck out his hand and wobbled on the forming escalator step. "Brent." He pumped Blaise's hand like a well handle. "Holy shit. It's real cool to meet you, man. I'm a huge fan."

Blaise pulled his hand away. "Thanks."

Brent shook his head. "My buddies won't believe this. We've seen in you in concert a bunch of times. When you touring again? I heard some place you busted up your hand pretty good."

Blaise saluted with the brace.

"That sucks," Brent said.

The escalator dumped them off. Passenger pickup was to the right. "Looks like we hit the road again in the fall. I don't mean to be rude, but I'm picking up someone." He tipped his hat. "Nice to meet you, Brent." He kept his head down and navigated an escape.

Most times he didn't mind meeting fans. They were the reason he got to play drums for a living, but on days like today when his nerves were tied up tight like old guitar strings, he wanted to blend in and not be noticed. It was the best thing about being the drummer, though. Only the true fans knew him to pick him out of a crowd. The guys up front—Colton, Troy, and Patrick—got stopped way more. But even that was happening less and less. Maybe he should've stopped and talked to old Brent for a minute. He wasn't in a position to be throwing fans away.

He waited in the corner for the passengers on the LA flight to retrieve their bags. When Cash appeared, he'd move out of the shadows, but until then he'd try to stay out of sight. His heart beat in sixteen notes. His hand sweated inside his brace. He checked his phone every few seconds, as if some message from his son that he wasn't coming would materialize. How was he going to get through the entire summer with a son he hadn't spent enough time with?

A crowd pushed their way to the baggage carousel. Mothers dragging children, fathers staking their space out to grab their bags first. Young couples checking messages.

There he was, and Blaise's breath caught in his throat. It didn't matter how much time went by or how many fights they had over the phone. Every time he saw his boy, it was like the first time he held him in his arms. He was afraid to be a father then, and he was afraid to be a father now, but his heart swelled with pride as his son sauntered through the crowd.

Cash's hair was shaved on the sides and bleached on top. He wore more black eyeliner than some women did. He dressed completely in black, his jeans with rips in them, and a bunch of black bracelets up his arm. The telltale white wires every teen dangled from their ears plugged up Cash's. Blaise hated those damn things.

Cash had filled out since Blaise saw him last. He wasn't all arms and legs as he had been. His graphic T-shirt stretched across broad shoulders. He'd grown taller too. Cash must be close to Blaise's six feet. Other than sharing looks, they didn't share much else. Cash didn't want to play music, even though he could. Blaise had tried to encourage him, but it never stuck.

Blaise pushed away from the wall. He took a deep breath and shook out his hands. The left one protested, but he ignored the pain. "Cash."

Cash turned in the direction of his voice. A smile crept across his face but stopped as if it had never been there. He nodded his salutation instead and grabbed his bag off the carousel.

Cash stood before him. The hint of mint and spice drifted in his direction. Was that cologne or gum? There was only one reason for a teenage boy to wear cologne. Blaise shook his head. He wasn't ready to believe Cash might be having sex.

"Hey." Cash stuck out his hand.

He grabbed it and pulled him into a hug, but Cash kept his arms down at his side. Blaise pushed away with heat in his cheeks. "How was your flight?" He tried to grab for Cash's bag.

"Fine. I got this." Cash nodded at his bum hand.

"It's not that bad. I can take your bag." He reached for it.

Cash switched hands. "I got it."

He wasn't going to make this easy. "Let's get out of here. You want to get some lunch?"

"Nah. I ate on the plane."

"If you change your mind, I've got some food back at the house. And your room is all set."

That was met with Cash staring into his phone as they crossed the parking lot. Blaise wanted to tell him to put the phone down. He hoped for a chance to talk to his son and try to mend some fences, but he didn't want to sound like a hard-ass two minutes in. Cash followed him out to the truck, never saying a word.

"How was school?" He tried another approach as Cash dumped his bag in the back.

"Sucked."

"High school usually does. But you graduated. Aren't you happy about that?" Melissa had told Blaise to stay home. Don't fly out for graduation. Cash didn't want him there. The words hurt, but he gave his son his wish. He had been wrong. He should've gone.

Cash stared out the window as they sped down the highway. The truth of his not being there for so many important things shoved its way between them. He had let too many chances to be a father slip by. Could he make up for it in one summer? Not by the scowl on Cash's face.

"What are you going to make me do while I'm staying with you?"

He didn't want to talk about that yet. He still needed time to decide. "For starters, we're having dinner at Aunt Savannah's tonight. The rest we'll figure out."

"Great. Can't wait." Cash shoved the earbuds in and turned to look out the window again.

It was a long ride back to the house.

Chapter Eight

"How long do we have to stay?" Cash hesitated but forced himself out of the front seat of the truck.

They'd arrived at Savannah's with not more than a grunt between them. Blaise tried to broach the topic of the fire, but every time he tried, the words died in his throat. He vowed to have better conversation during dinner. They could talk about the fire later. Savannah would be able to bridge some of the gap tonight. He needed all the help he could get.

The smell of beef on the grill came out to meet them in the driveway. Even though the sun wouldn't set for hours, she had left the front porch lights on. It was Savannah's way of letting you know you were welcome.

The wood planks of the front porch creaked under his boots. Wearing boots and jeans in this summer heat was a pretty stupid thing to do. He should've thought about that before he left. Instead, he had found himself thinking about his new neighbor. When would she be back to start fixing up her house? The house given to her as a gift. Who does that kind of thing?

Savannah's porch was an extension of her warmth. On either side of the double-glass front doors were two sets of wood-slat chairs complete with pillows to lean against if the planks were too hard on your back. And each set of chairs met an oriental rug to curl your toes in.

"We stay until I say it's time to go. And where did you get that?"

Cash had pulled out a gold lighter engraved with the letter *S* and flicked the top back and forth, making the flame dance.

"It was Grandpa's. What's the big deal?"

"You have to ask me that? Put it away."

Blaise poked the doorbell with his bad hand and balanced a peach cobbler he'd picked up from Maybelline's on the way over in his good one.

Cash shoved his hands in his pants pockets. "Is Jud going to be here?"

"Probably. He does live here."

"I know he lives here, Dad." Cash punctuated each word with a snarl. "I was hoping he had plans or something."

Before he could answer, Savannah swung open the door. "You're here." She yanked Cash and folded him in a big hug. "My goodness, you are all grown up." She released him, looking up, and grabbed his face. "As handsome as ever. Come in. Come in."

Cash snuck past her, but before Blaise could take a step, she planted a kiss on his cheek and slid the peach cobbler from his grip. "He looks great, but he needs a haircut and a little makeup remover," she whispered. She stepped back. "How are you doing?"

He ignored the comments about Cash's appearance. "It's only been one day. We haven't had a chance to kill each other yet. Give us time."

"Nonsense. You're going to be great together. Let's go out in the back. Adam has the steaks on the grill."

"You didn't have to go to so much trouble."

She had set the table for seven and surrounded it with white wicker chairs. Fresh flowers, probably from her garden, in purples and pinks decorated the center, and she matched the place mats and napkins in the same pinks and purples. Even the glasses were purple.

"How often do I get to see my favorite nephew?"

"I'm your only nephew, Aunt Savannah," Cash said with a smile. This had been their joke since he was five.

"Uncle Blaise." Caroline dropped her hula-hoop and came running.

"Do we still hug?" He didn't know the rules with twelve-year-old girls, and he suspected they always changed. Cash certainly had.

"You bet." She threw her arms out, and he reached down to hug her. She smelled like bubble gum.

Adam, wearing his Chefs Do It Better at the Grill apron, left his post. "Good to see you, Blaise." His shake was firm and strong. "Dinner's almost done. Cash, how was the trip out?"

"Fine."

"What's your plans for the summer?"

"Adam, let's talk about that later." Savannah swooped in with pasta salad in a glass bowl. She'd made deviled eggs, corn on the cob, brussel sprouts, and a salad.

"You're going to say no, but can I help you with anything?" Blaise stepped out of her way.

"No." She rearranged some of the food on the table to make room for her pasta.

"You made too much food." Blaise swiped a carrot from the salad and popped it in his mouth.

65

"For three teenaged boys, Adam, and you? I think not." She walked inside and shouted. "Grey, Jud, dinner. Now."

"Looks like Jud is here." Blaise handed a carrot to Cash, but Cash pushed it away.

"Whatever." Cash dropped into the chair on the end. "Sit here." He pointed to the chair next to him.

Cash might only want him to be a buffer from Jud, but he'd take what he could get. "Give him a chance." But he knew that would never happen.

"Hey, Uncle Blaise." Grey stepped outside through the kitchen doors and high-fived him. He wore the typical fourteen-year-old teenage uniform of athletic shorts and T-shirt. Complete with bare feet and cuts and scrapes up his legs. "I didn't know you were coming, Cash." Grey took a step toward Cash, but the permanent scowl on Cash's face probably stopped him. To Blaise's surprise, Grey dropped into the chair next to Cash. "Did you graduate? Cause I heard you weren't going to."

"Greyson Montgomery." Savannah glared at her middle child.

"Sorry." Grey tucked his head.

"Yeah, I graduated."

"Cool. So did Jud."

"Greyson, did you wash your hands?" Savannah slapped Grey's hand away from the deviled eggs. She pointed to the kitchen, and he retreated.

Blaise had been at Jud's graduation because it was in town, he had been back in Heritage River, and Savannah had insisted. She had told him to go to Cash's, even though Melissa told him to stay home. Savannah had been right. Blaise looked across the yard to the forgotten swing-set. His chest tightened knowing he'd missed his son's graduation. He had a lot of making up to do. His son torched a house because he sucked as a father.

Jud glided out onto the patio. Blaise could never get over how he saw Savannah in Jud's face. Genetics freaked him out. His hair was windblown in all the right places. He wore a buttoned-down shirt with the sleeves rolled to his elbows, fitted shorts, and those boat shoes that must've come back in style because Blaise had a pair when he was that age.

He knew how good Jud's grades were. He also knew about the awards, the community service his mother encouraged him to complete, the student council he ran, and the colleges that wanted him. Was it any wonder Cash was trying to disappear inside the collar of his shirt?

"Uncle Blaise." Jud fist-bumped him. "How's the hand?"

"Better. Thanks."

Jud walked past Cash without so much as a hello and joined his dad at the grill. Had Savannah told him what happened? Or was it still the argument from Christmas? That day had ended badly, and even when Blaise had tried to get Cash to stay through the first of January or to come for a visit after, he wanted no part of it. Christmas was probably the reason Melissa told him not to come to graduation.

He wanted to get up and drag Jud back. Make him say hello to Cash. Force these two boneheads to let the past be the past. But he sat, unsure of how to handle things. What was the right advice to give his son? At Cash's age, would he have stood up to Colton?

Probably not. He had a hard time standing up to Colton now.

He leaned in and whispered to Cash, "Don't let him bother you."

"He doesn't." Cash shoved his earbuds in.

Blaise placed a hand on Cash's arm. "Can you do that later? We're guests here."

Cash yanked them out again. A small victory Blaise didn't think would last.

The dinner went off without any trouble. Silverware clanked against the plates. Glasses were refilled, and laughter sang like a choir. Blaise's shoulders dropped just a little, and for the first time all night, he thought he might be able to make the summer with Cash work.

"So, Blaise"—Savannah pierced a piece of meat and hovered it near her mouth—"I wanted to ask you something."

"You're in trouble, Dad. Aunt Savannah's got that look in her eye."

Whatever Savannah wanted would be fine with him just to see that smile on Cash's face and hear the teasing in his voice. "What's up?"

"Now that you're going to be here for a while, I was wondering if you'd play at the library's fundraiser next month." She popped the steak in her mouth and stuck out her chin, daring him to say no.

He held up his bad hand. "Can't exactly play the drums right now."

"I know you can't play the drums. Play guitar instead." She held up a hand to stop the protests he was about to drop. "I know you're hurt, but I also know you've been playing. Just a few songs. It would really help us sell tickets, and if this fundraiser is a success, we can get those computers we desperately need. What do you say, Blaise? Help save the library you rode your bike to as a kid. The place where you kissed Maryellen Thorpe between the racks."

Laughter and a few *oohs* hit the air.

"She kissed me, and it was the third grade."

Savannah stared him down. She wasn't going to give up. If he said no tonight, she'd just call him tomorrow and ask again. His hand could manage to run up and down the neck of a guitar. Maybe he could play some of his new stuff, and if the crowd liked it, he could sell the idea of new music to Colton.

"Surprise." Shouted a voice from behind him. A voice that came through the kitchen. A voice that wouldn't have to knock.

"Colton." Savannah jumped from her seat and ran over to her older brother.

Cash was fast on her heels. Colton pulled Cash into a tight hug, and Cash grabbed him back and held on. Colton pushed away first but kept his hands on Cash's shoulders and looked him in the eye. "It's good to see you, kid. I got that video you sent me. That was some cool stuff."

What video?

But he didn't ask because Jud edged his way over and stood to the side. Colton patted Jud on the back, and then Caroline and Grey shoved their way in between to steal hugs from their uncle. Colton scooped Caroline up in the air and swung her around. She squealed.

"Uncle C, are you staying at the house with me and Dad?" Cash asked.

"Maybe for just one night if your old man will let me." Colton fixed his gaze on him.

"I can put up with you for one night."

Savannah plied Colton with food and got him up to speed on the conversation before his arrival. "It would be a sold-out show if both Savage brothers played at my event."

"No way," Colton said. "I'm not playing at some library fundraiser. What would that look like?"

"Like you gave a shit." Blaise realized what he just said. "Pardon me, Miss Caroline Montgomery, miss." He resurrected his old southern drawl and tipped his imaginary hat. Caroline giggled.

"Honestly, with that mouth," Savannah said.

But she wasn't too mad. He'd heard her say worse. Of course, not in front of her daughter.

"That means you'll do it, Blaise? You'll play?"

"I didn't say that. Let me think about it." He'd backed himself into a corner.

"I think you should do it, Dad. It's for a good cause."

"I'll do it if you'll play with me." His words sidelined Cash. The color drained from his face. "You said it yourself, it's a good cause."

Cash dropped his napkin on the table and stood. "No thanks. I don't play much."

"You going someplace?" Blaise pointed to the chair.

Savannah jumped in. "Cash, we could use some volunteers at the library this summer. I think that will cover your community service time."

"You want me to work with books?"

"How soon can he start?" Blaise said.

"Tomorrow." Savannah shoved a piece of lettuce in her mouth. Her knowing eyes said it all.

"No way, I'm not doing it. I hate books."

"You're doing it," Blaise said.

Savannah passed Blaise the brussel sprouts. "See you at the fundraiser."

Chapter Nine

What had she done? Grace turned in circles in the kitchen of the Disaster House. She'd handed the keys of her old house to Larry, deposited his check for his half of the house, put most of her things in storage, and driven down to Heritage River. Panic climbed up inside her skin while she stood in the kitchen.

The floor would need to be sanded. Beau had said the cabinets would need to be torn out. He'd take everything in here down to the studs.

"It will be beautiful, Miss Grace." He insisted on calling her Miss Grace. While the salutation was sweet, she felt like a preschool teacher.

And he was still looking for help with the job. His old crew had gone on to other work since he let them go. "Yours is my last job. I was about to go into retirement when Miss Dixie called and told me about you. Said you were a client of Hoke's. Now, I couldn't turn away someone like that. I'd never hear the end of it at poker on Friday nights."

He promised he'd have things done by September. "If we ain't done by the time your girl goes off to that school of hers, I'll hold the fort down while you see her off. Then you come right back here, and we'll finish the job. Have you out of Heritage River in no time."

And that's exactly what she wanted.

But in the meantime, she'd search for the person

who gave her this house. Dixie had the cable company come in and install the internet and update the wires for the televisions while she was back in Silverside.

Grace set up a makeshift office of a card table and chair in the living room where she could look out at the poplar tree and the activities of the street.

Beau wasn't due to start until tomorrow. That would give her plenty of time to try to get some information. She said a silent prayer for modern technology. Otherwise, this search would have her at the county hall of records, buried in oversized books and dust.

The search didn't reveal much. The public records site listed her as the current owner of the house. The owners prior to her were a Mr. and Mrs. John and Nancy Templeton. They bought the house in 1964 and sold it just a few short months ago to Grace. Well, to Grace's gift giver.

Grace searched for information on John and Nancy Templeton. She found an obituary for John dating back to 1987, which stated he was survived by his wife and his sister. No children. And no word on where Nancy Templeton was.

Did her neighbor know the Templetons? How long had Nancy been gone? How long had the Disaster House been sitting empty? If she could find Nancy Templeton, she might be able to figure out who bought the house, because a paper trail followed the sale of any home. She hated the idea of going next door. She convinced herself it was for informational purposes only. She wasn't interested in seeing him again. She hadn't forgotten what Jenn told her about the affair with the blonde bimbo.

The doorbell rang and startled her out of her thoughts. She ran to the door. Dixie held a casserole dish covered in plastic wrap. She had her pink lipstick on, and her floral-print suit struggled to stay closed. You weren't going to miss her coming.

"Howdy, Grace. I hope you don't mind my stopping by unannounced." She handed over the casserole. The dish was still warm. "I thought you might like some food on your first night in town. I know the oven here isn't much, but it works. I checked it myself. Just plop that in for a few minutes to heat it up."

"Thank you, but I wasn't planning on eating in this kitchen at all. It's so, so..." Any word she thought of sounded snotty.

"Gross, dear. It's gross. You're right, but the inside's clean. Heat kills everything." Dixie waved her hand.

Grace shook her head and crinkled her nose at the idea of sticking food in that oven. She tried to see past Dixie to Blaise's, but Dixie blocked the view. Was he home?

"No bother." Dixie waved her hand in the air again. "You can eat it cold right out of the dish too. It's a cheeseless lasagna. It's good either hot or cold." She handed over a bag Grace didn't realize she was holding. "Plastic forks and knives and some paper plates."

"It's very kind of you. I was about to run out, but would you like to come by later and join me?" The idea of eating alone didn't appeal to her, and she hadn't realized it until that moment.

"Thank you, but I can't. Book club night. Though that's part of the reason I'm here. Beau is going to bring by a kitchen table with some chairs tonight. You can use them until this place is fixed up and your new stuff gets here." She stuck her head inside the door and looked around. "You can't make do with just that card table."

"I'm not planning on furnishing the house. I'm just going to fix it and sell it."

Dixie waved her hand again and sent the smell of gardenia's in Grace's direction. "Don't be silly. You need a place to put your backside while you're here, and houses always sell better when they're furnished. Gives people the idea of what it will look like when they live there. Most don't have any imagination." She leaned in for that last part, as if telling a secret. Then she righted herself. "I'll help you shop for some bargains."

"I'm not sure the allowance I've been given covers furniture." She'd have to ask Hoke.

"There's a separate fund for furniture and curtains and things like that. It's smaller than the renovation budget, but we can stretch the dollars. I checked with Hoke myself."

Or Dixie could check with Hoke instead. Grace wanted to laugh. She liked Dixie.

"Did you know John and Nancy Templeton?" she blurted. She should wait to ask, but she had to know.

Dixie shoved the bag at Grace. "That poor man died such a long time ago. He had the "C" word. Pity. Nancy, well, I don't know what happened to Nancy."

"Do you know who bought the house for me?"

"Not me, darling. As far as I know, the only one with any information is Hoke, and his lips are tighter than a witch's tit in the cold."

"Dixie." Grace couldn't believe what she heard.

"But you didn't hear that from me." Dixie laughed and headed down the steps. "You can return my dish when you're done."

Grace put the dish in the kitchen and waited until Dixie's car was out of sight. Before she could talk herself out of it, she crossed the lawn to Blaise's house.

The house was built like hers, with a matching porch. Only Blaise's didn't sag. Two black rockers invited you to sit for a while and relax. He'd perched on the end of one that night she watched him play guitar. A swing with yellow and blue pillows hung where the porch turned right. An empty table sat beside the swing ready to hold a drink and a book. The decorations were simple, but inviting.

She marched up the steps, raised her hand to knock, but turned on her heel and made it down two steps before she stopped. "You are being ridiculous. He doesn't bite." Or maybe he did. Her cheeks flamed at the thought. Plus, how many women had he bitten to begin with? "Stay focused."

She opted instead to ring the bell she hadn't noticed.

A tall young man came to the door. His bleached crop of hair on the top of shaved sides was a little startling. He had five piercings in each of his ears, one ear plugged with an earbud, the other earbud dangling over the top of his ear, and one piercing defiantly in his nose like Chloe had. She would never understand why young people pierced their noses. How did you blow it? The black eyeliner was thick, but his eyes were bright. His lips were full, and when he raised them to smile, his teeth were white and perfectly straight. He had a dimple in his chin. He looked the way Blaise must've at that age. He held a soda can in one hand and his phone in the other.

"Can I help you?" His voice was rich and deep and absent of any southern accent.

"Hi. I'm Grace Starr. I live next door. I was wondering if Blaise was home."

The young man looked in the direction of her house, as if he could see it through the walls. "You live over there? The house that needs all the work? I didn't think anyone lived there ever."

So Nancy Templeton hadn't lived next door in some time. "I just moved in. Could you get Blaise? If he's home, that is."

"Sorry, my dad's not here right now. Can I give him a message or something? Or I could text him if it's important."

"No." Her hands flew up. "I mean, no, but thank you. It isn't that important that you have to bother him. I'll come back another time. Thanks."

She scurried off the porch with heat in her cheeks to match the heat of the day.

****

Grace drove into town for dinner because there was no way she was heating up Dixie's casserole in that stove. She'd spent two hours cleaning the refrigerator properly just to put the dish in there. She'd buy a small microwave tomorrow.

Heritage River had the kind of Main Street expected in a small town, with quaint shops flanking each side of the road and angled parking along the way. It was different from her hometown. Silverside lacked a Main Street with cute little stores. But she liked having the convenience of box stores that allowed for one-stop shopping. She didn't have the time to go from place to place. The idea was lovely, but not practical. Maybe if she were someone else, living a different life. She paused. Wasn't that what she wanted since the divorce? To be someone else.

She passed Maybelline's Bakery, a hardware store, and a café with Eat at Jake's lit up in the window. She found a spot and parked, but decided to walk a little first.

Reds and purples filled the evening sky. A slight breeze lifted her hair and pushed around clouds, keeping the air cool. She pulled her sweater closer.

Across the street was an ice cream place, Cream and Sugar, where a long line of families, older couples holding hands, and young couples maybe on dates waited to place their orders at the window facing the street. Another window had happy people greedily grab for their sugar cones and oversized cups.

The town was probably a nice place to raise children, but what were the schools like? Busy highways intersected Silverside, preventing anyone from gathering at the ice cream store. The store back home faced a four-lane road. When Chloe was young, Grace was always afraid she'd dart out into traffic.

Main Street met School Street in a four-way stop. Grace found a small library that looked more like an old-style train station.

A banner hanging in front advertised an upcoming event:

Library Fundraiser, July 17, 7 p.m.

And across the street on the other corner sat a Baptist church with a marquee that read

78

Come to Ch _ _ ch
What's missing?
UR!

The rest of the street past the library looked more spaced out and residential, so she turned around and went back. From the window, Eat at Jake's looked quiet. She felt for her book in her bag and yanked the door open.

The place was small and smelled like fried food and vinegar. Pocked and scarred wooden tables set for four crowded the area right inside the door. A table of three men sat huddled around their food. One wore a sheriff's uniform. The glass case filled with meats and cheeses also doubled as the place to order. A large chalkboard hung on the wall. Someone with a flowery hand had written the entire menu across it. She couldn't find any physical ones and had to get closer to the wall to make out the selections. Drinks were self-serve, but an older woman with red hair piled on top of her head in an old style fifties do brought out the food.

"What can I get ya, hon?" A thin man with salt-and-pepper hair and a white T-shirt covered in what looked like grease, ketchup, and sweat leaned over the counter. He pulled a pen from behind his ear. Maybe this was Jake.

She took a quick look around. If his shirt looked like that, was this place even clean? And if it wasn't, where was she going to go? She didn't want to search her GPS for a chain restaurant probably thirty minutes away. Jake's would do. And she'd be fine. She hoped.

"I'd like the Sophie salad, please. And could I substitute the bleu cheese for another cheese?"

"I don't have anything else. Well, I've got some

mozzarella—he pronounced it *motts-a-rel-la*—I could cut up. The misses makes me keep some in stock. Says I need culture."

"No, thank you. The salad without the cheese is fine, and could I have the dressing on the side, please?"

"Would you like a roll?"

"No, thank you. Just the salad." Grace grabbed a diet soda from the refrigerated case and found a seat. She pulled out her book.

The waitress slid the salad onto the table. "Thank you," Grace said.

"You're not from around here are you?" Her name tag read Donna.

"How did you know?"

"That accent and all your food requests. Locals order as is, or Jake makes a new version and names the dish after them. That's why there's no menus. Just the board." She pointed over her shoulder. "So where you from?"

"I'm from Jersey. I'm here for the summer."

"I said those same words some twenty years ago. This town got its claws in me, and I never left."

"I'm really only here on business." She pulled her salad closer and placed her napkin on her lap.

"I said that too. Enjoy your salad." Donna walked away.

Grace tried to ignore what Donna said about the town's claws and focus on her book, but the sci-fi romance wasn't capturing her attention at the moment. The Disaster House kept interrupting her.

"Are you having lettuce for dinner?"

Grace's head snapped up, and she bit her tongue.

Before she could respond, Blaise slid into the seat

opposite her and grabbed her book. "Reading something good?"

She tried to snatch it back, but he held it up high. "Looks a little steamy. You sure you should be reading this?"

"Give that back to me." She lunged for it again, but his long arms kept the book away by a foot.

She plopped back down in her seat and folded her hands in her lap. "Keep it."

He closed the book and placed it on the table. "Nah, it's a lady's book. I only read *Drummer* magazine anyway."

Of course he did. She was surprised he could read at all. "Is there something I can do for you?"

"I think it's you who would like me for something." He smirked at her, his gray eyes twinkling.

"I beg your pardon?" Heat filled her cheeks. Was he propositioning her?

The man wearing the sheriff's uniform walked up to their table. "Evening, Blaise." He offered Blaise a thin smile.

"Evening, Sheriff Jones." Blaise nodded.

"Heard your boy is in town for the summer."

"That's right."

"He having some trouble back home? Heard that's what brought him to you."

"My son is fine, thank you for asking. Now if you'll excuse us." Blaise raised his chin toward Grace.

It didn't take a detective to see the sheriff didn't like Blaise's son. What did the man know about the boy, or was his dislike rooted in the young man's strange style? How often had she made a judgment on someone's look? Wasn't the reason she hated Chloe's blue hair that she didn't want others to judge her daughter's appearance? The sheriff turned on his heel without so much as a word for Grace.

"Cash said you stopped by earlier today looking for me." The smile was back on Blaise's face.

Cash. That must be his son. She took in a deep breath and repositioned her napkin in her lap. He wasn't propositioning her. Was she disappointed? Impossible.

"I did," she said. Now that he was sitting opposite her and his smell of clean soap clogged her brain, the reason for racing to his door seemed stupid. "It was nothing." She could find out about Nancy Templeton another way.

"Can I get you something, Blaise?" Donna had returned.

"He isn't staying," she blurted out. She wanted to eat her salad in peace and not share a meal with a man who treated women like objects. At least that's what she assumed a man in his line of work would do.

He shot her a look. "Can I get three burgers to go? And some of that potato salad? The one with the red skin."

"You got it, sugar."

He drummed on the table with his fingers. "Why'd you stop by? You must've wanted something. Come on. You can tell me. I won't tell anyone. I promise."

"And you're not going to leave until I tell you? Is that it?"

He leaned back in the chair and stretched out his long legs. "Something like that."

"Do you always behave like a twelve-year-old?"

"Every chance I get." He crossed his arms over his chest, making room for his braced hand, and laughed.

His laugh was rich and full, and the lines on his face deepened around his smile. He was good at laughing.

She picked at her salad, but thinking about Blaise's laugh filled her belly. She pushed the plate away. "All right. I was wondering if you knew the people who used to own my house."

"The Templetons? Sure. Why?"

"I want to find out who gave me the house, and I thought if I could locate Nancy Templeton, I might get some answers." She folded her hands in her lap, then smoothed out her napkin. "Is it chilly in here?" Her fingers fumbled with the buttons on her sweater.

He leaned over the table, and she leaned back against the chair trying to put some distance between them. "It's really not that cold in here. Why does it matter who gave you the house? You have it now."

"It does matter. A lot. Who does something like that? Yes, it's generous and all, but it's crazy too. And I'm crazier for taking it, but that's another story. I need to know why they did it. Why pick me?"

"If it were me, I'd say thank you and move on. It's all legal, isn't it?"

"Of course it is. I would never be involved with something that wasn't legal." Her cheeks heated up at the thought.

"Don't get angry. I'm just asking. The house is yours. That settles it. Who cares about the rest?"

"Do you go through your life not wanting to know things? Not wanting to have all the details and information? Do people just randomly give you things and you say no big deal."

"Sure. On tour we get stuff all the time. Bras. Panties. I don't always know who they belong to, but we take them." He winked.

She crumpled up her napkin and threw it on the table. How many times had he figured out who those panties belonged to? She couldn't sit there any longer. The room was suddenly stuffy. She needed fresh air.

"If you'll excuse me." She tried to push her chair back to leave, but Donna returned and blocked her way.

"Here's your burgers." She handed over a plastic bag.

He pulled cash from his pocket. "Thanks. I'll pay for Grace's lettuce too."

"Oh no, you won't. I can pay for my own dinner."

"A guy can't buy you dinner, but it's okay somebody bought you a house?" He gave her that laugh again.

She wanted to be mad, but it was getting harder.

"When a man wants to buy you dinner, sugar, you should let him. Especially this man." Donna squeezed Blaise's arm and took his money.

Grace rummaged in her bag for her wallet. "Does every woman flirt with you?"

"Hazards of the job."

She shoved her money at him.

"Keep it. You can get the next one."

"Never."

Chapter Ten

Blaise threw the plastic bag onto the floor of the passenger's seat. His tires screeched as he pulled into traffic. Grace said *never* to him. She would never buy him dinner or never have dinner with him. What had he done that was so bad?

He wiped his hand over his face. He didn't mean to race down Main Street. Not with all the kids around, but that woman had gotten under his skin. Sitting there, she folded and unfolded her napkin, as if it were some shield to protect her from him. And the buttoning up of that sweater, pretending she was cold. What did she think he was going to do? Reach across the table and grab her breast?

Not that he hadn't thought about what her skin would feel like under his touch, but he wasn't some uncontrollable teenager with raging hormones. Though she thought he acted like a kid. *Do you always behave like a twelve-year-old?*

He pulled into his driveway, the front of his truck hitting the dip at the end. He let out a loud sigh. No one had ever made him so mad. No one except Colton and he was inside with Cash waiting for dinner. The inside of his house was lit up like a stadium. Those two boneheads had turned on every light. The whole street could see what they were doing. He shook his head. He was thinking like his father. Cash and Colton held guitars. Were they playing together? Was that video Cash sent to Colton of him playing?

More anger bubbled up in his belly. His son refused to play with him, but somehow Colton got him to strum? Why did Colton get the best of Cash? Did he really need to ask that? Colton charmed the best out of everyone. It was his gift. A gift Blaise did not possess.

Grace wasn't home yet but would be soon. It wasn't as if she had many places to go. Who'd she even know in this town? He didn't want to have to see her every time he walked out onto the front porch. Or every time he went into town. Hopefully, her house would be fixed up fast and she'd go back to wherever it was she came.

"Bro, you ever bringing those burgers in?" Colton yelled from the front door. "We're starving in here."

He grabbed the plastic bag as Grace pulled into her driveway. She turned off the car and sat there. If he hurried, she might not realize he was outside. But she hadn't moved. She rested her head on the steering wheel. Did something happen on the way home?

Should he go over and see if she was okay?

"Dad, the food."

Cash's words dragged him away from the car. Grace would be fine. She didn't need his help. She had said as much.

****

Grace pulled into her driveway. The house dark. She'd forgotten to turn on a lamp, and she didn't have her lights on a timer as she did back home. She didn't want to go inside. What was waiting for her? Nothing.

Why did she say "never" when he said she could

pay for the next dinner? She hadn't meant to say it. It slipped out, and she wanted to shove the words back as soon as they were loose.

She wasn't trying to be mean. They were just so different, and he wouldn't understand what she had been through. How could he know how it would feel to be dumped by a man you thought you loved for a younger, prettier version? It was as if her expiration date had hit and Larry was tossing her aside before she had a chance to start living.

Asking Blaise questions about the house's previous owners was stupid. She should have planned it out better before she raced across the lawn and pounded on his door earlier. She would stay in her yard from now on. He wouldn't want to talk to her, anyway, after she was so rude.

She dragged herself out of the car. Blaise's house was lit up like a Christmas tree. She pulled out the small flashlight she kept in her purse and made her way up the rickety steps. A wooden table and four chairs had been plopped on the porch, practically blocking the front door. A note was taped to the table.

Miss Grace,

You weren't home when I stopped by. Don't go dragging this heavy thing in by yourself. I'll be back in the morning at seven to start work. I'll take it in then. The weather will hold tonight. Hope you like the table. It's been refurbished.

Beau Carroll

The table was hard to make out in the dark, but she could smell the wood and the finish on it. He must've put down the brush and brought it right over. Dixie had been right. The table was a good idea. It might make the place feel like a home, and she could leave it behind for the new owners. She wasn't expecting something so nice.

A quick glance at the sky told her the weather might not hold. But what did she know? Lately, it didn't feel as if she knew much.

She wanted to wash her face, put on her pajamas, and flip through the home-renovation magazines she'd picked up. She would make a vision board, pulling out all the pictures that inspired her and taping them up for Beau to see and use as a guideline. There was an app for that, but she wanted to be able to hold the vision board in her hands, turn it in the light. Maybe she'd pull some pieces of fabric and materials and tape them on too.

Chloe would call her old for pushing aside the technology. Grace laughed. Chloe was right. She was old. And alone. And in a house ready for the junkyard. A tiny part of her, just a flicker, was excited about the new adventure. That, or it was dinner upsetting her stomach.

She carefully removed pages with pictures of white kitchens and wide-planked mahogany floors. She peeled out pages of fireplaces and front porches. Before she knew it, all three magazines were in shreds and covering the small folding table and much of the floor. She'd have to get poster boards, but that would have to wait until morning. She could leave the pictures where they were, but she didn't want them scattered around when Beau arrived. If he was beginning work, her vision would likely get trampled.

Rain pattered against her roof. Was it going to leak? She ran around from room to room checking, but the place seemed dry. The table. She ran for the front door.

She flipped on the overhead lights in the living room, but the ones on the porch didn't seem to work. No bother. She'd manage to get the table in. She could push it if it was too heavy to pull.

The chairs went in with no problem, but she'd built up a nice sweat. She lined the table up with the door. She didn't need a measuring tape, which she didn't have anyway, but the table looked as if it would fit. The rain was coming down harder and hitting the edge of the porch. If the wind shifted, she and the table would get wet.

Using the weight in her legs, she gave the table a good shove forward. It stuck in the door. She tried again to push it, but no go. She tried to pull the table back out. Maybe she could set it on its side and try that way. The table wouldn't move. She climbed over the table into the house and yanked with all she had. Nothing.

"Now what am I supposed to do?"

She grabbed onto the corners of the table and shimmied. The doorframe protested and started to splinter.

"Don't panic." What was she thinking? Why didn't she leave the table alone, as Beau had said?

She hoisted herself back onto the table. Maybe she could dislodge it from the other side.

"Do you need some help?" Cash stepped into the light spilling onto the porch from behind her.

Grace jumped and nearly fell off. "Oh, I didn't see you. No, no thank you. I'm fine."

"I was taking out the garbage." He pointed to the

cans on the street. "It looks like you're stuck."

"I'm fine. Really." Her neck and face burned. How could she accept help from Blaise's son after she was so rude earlier?

He threw his hands up, as if to say *whatever*, and turned away. She could see Chloe doing the same thing. Teens were very literal. An adult might push harder, sensing the hesitation, but teens took you at face value. Always best to say what you mean to them.

She wasn't getting anywhere with the stupid table on her own. She'd be at it all night, and the rain wasn't letting up.

"Um, Cash," she yelled into the darkness. "I think I might need that help, after all."

****

What was his son doing? Blaise watched Cash climb the porch steps of Grace's house. He didn't want to stand full on in the window and get caught staring, so he peered around the curtain. It was hard to tell from this angle, but it looked as if Grace was standing on something in the doorway. He had to find out what was going on.

"Where are you going?" Colton lounged on the couch, plucking his guitar.

"I'll be right back." He wasn't about to say more. If Colton heard about a woman in distress, he'd be on his feet faster than a sixteenth note. Blaise was sparing Colton from Grace's condescending pout.

Their voices drifted over to him, mixed with the song of the rain, as he crossed the lawn. Grace laughed at something Cash said. A large raindrop smacked into his head. His insides burned. Why did everyone get the best of Cash and not him?

"It was really stupid of me."

"It happens. Sorry about your door."

"No need to be sorry. You were right."

"Howdy, neighbor," Blaise yelled.

Grace pulled on her shirt collar. Cash unpeeled himself and stood at full height, staring at him.

"You guys okay?" he said.

"We're fine. Cash was just helping me." Grace fluttered around the porch like a moth.

"I think it will move now." Cash handed her a screwdriver and the molding from the doorframe.

The *it* was a table. That's what Grace had been standing on, and it was stuck in her door. He laughed, releasing the tension he'd carried over from next door.

"What's so funny?" Her chin was up.

"You got a table stuck? How'd you manage that?"

She waved a hand in the air. "It doesn't matter. Thank you, Cash. I really appreciate it, but I can drag the table inside from here."

"My dad and I can do it. I don't mind."

"You heard the lady. She can do it herself. Besides." He waved his braced hand in the air.

She didn't want his help, but she took his son's. How was that okay?

He took a good look at her in the lamplight. She stood there chewing on her bottom lip, wearing a T-shirt, cotton striped pants that dragged on the floor, and slippers. She'd pinned her hair up with a pencil, but small pieces fell around her face. Dirt had streaked her jawline. He was suddenly aware of his out-of-beat heart.

"Are we having a party and no one invited me?"

Blaise dropped his chin to his chest and frowned.

Here we go. "Grace, this is my brother, Colton."

Colton stepped onto the porch as if he were stepping on stage. He beamed at Grace and offered a hand. "Ma'am, it's my pleasure."

Blaise wanted to stick his good fingers down his throat.

Grace looked at her palm, then wiped it on her shirt. "It's nice to meet you."

How nice?

"Looks like you've got yourself in a predicament." Colton inspected the table. "Is my brother here helping you out?" He smiled at Blaise, but the dare gleamed in Colton's eyes. If Blaise wasn't interested in Grace, Colton would be.

Blaise's insides heated up again. "Actually, Cash solved the problem. I was about to drag the table in."

"Allow us." Colton motioned to Cash, and they hoisted the table and carried it inside.

Damn his bandaged hand and his stupidity for getting hurt. But why did he care? If Colton wanted her, he could melt the iceberg. Blaise was done with that kind of woman. Unless his wallet was wide open, Melissa was frozen enough for the entire female population.

"This place needs a lot of work, if you don't mind me saying." Colton glanced around the front porch and stuck his finger in the soft wood of the doorframe.

Grace laughed again. It was a nice laugh, like a slow melody. "Beau Carroll starts tomorrow to renovate."

"Old Beau. Haven't seen him in years. Does he have a crew big enough for this job?"

She shook her head. "But he assures me he can

handle it. I hope." She pulled on her shirt again.

"Is he hiring?" Cash stepped out of the corner he'd slid into.

She squinted at Cash. "I don't know."

"Why do you want to know if he's hiring?" Blaise looked back at Grace. What was she thinking?

Cash shoved his hands in his pockets. "This might sound stupid, but I kind of like working with my hands. Fixing things. Building things. Maybe I could work for him and help Grace."

That was the most Cash had said to him since he got there. "You can't work for Beau. You have to put your time in at the library."

"I'm not going to be at the library eight hours a day. If Beau will hire me, and Grace, I'll ask him, and I can split the days between here and the library. What am I going to do all summer anyway? I'm not going to help you with that garden."

"Why does everyone hate my garden so much?"

"Bro, have you seen it?" Colton snickered.

"Asshole, Dad planted one."

"Language, a lady is present. Forgive my Neanderthal brother." Colton turned back to Blaise. "You didn't inherit Dad's green thumb."

Grace found something interesting on the floor to look at. Was she trying to hold back a smile?

Colton grabbed Cash's shoulder. "Sounds like your son has a plan. You might want to think about it."

"I don't need any parenting advice from you."

She inched toward the door. "Um, if you'll excuse me, it's getting late. Thanks again for helping with the table. Really."

"What about the door?" Blaise said.

"The door?" Grace stared at him.

"It won't shut without the frame. What are you going to do about the door?" Because something told him Miss Wrinkle-Free from the North wasn't going to want to sleep alone without that door shut and bolted tight. Got to watch out for the neighbors.

"I'll fix it," Colton said.

"I can." From Cash.

"I'll take care of it," she said.

Blaise's head hurt. "I'm going home. You three figure it out."

He crossed the lawn as the rain lightened up, and turned one final time to glance at Grace's house. Cash was banging the molding in with what looked like his shoe. Colton made Grace laugh again. He shut the door from inside. Shutting Blaise out. Like always.

He rubbed the back of his neck. His bandaged hand ached, but he grabbed his guitar and dropped into the rocker on the porch. A moth banged its head against the light. "I know how you feel, buddy."

In the morning, he'd talk to Beau.

Chapter Eleven

The hot water overflowed from her mug. Grace had hit the water button on the machine one too many times, and when she yanked the mug away, not bothering to look, hot water scalded her hand.

"How stupid can I be?" She ran her hand under the cold water. Her skin turned pink.

She could be so stupid because she wasn't paying attention. She didn't want to admit it, but she was thinking about Blaise when she should have been thinking about her house lists. Picking cabinets, flooring, counters, paint colors, but instead her mind would sneak back to the way he looked at her when he climbed onto her porch last night. As if he were trying to undress her. It would probably be better if Cash didn't work for Beau. As sweet as Cash seemed, it wasn't a good idea for all of them to interact very much. Blaise would be climbing her porch steps constantly if he thought his son was over here working. She'd tell Beau. No Cash.

And then her mind would slide over the image of the way Blaise's hair curled against the collar of his ridiculous shirt covered in Xs and Os, the sleeves rolled up to his elbows to make room for his brace. Or the fullness of his bottom lip.

"Stop it. It doesn't matter how attractive he is." Or that she couldn't remember the last time she noticed a man at all. She dried her sore hand on the paper towel. It was final. Cash would have to find another job.

Plus that brother. Colton. Trouble. He was a charmer for sure. Trying to impress her with his musical success after Blaise had left, as if she cared about that, but then slipping in little bits of information about old homes as if he were an expert. It didn't work. She saw him coming a mile away. He expected every woman in his path to fan themselves at the great guitar player.

He did have the same gray eyes as Blaise, but they lacked that twinkle. She might even say Colton was better looking than Blaise. Colton had a full head of salt-and-pepper hair, a dimple in his right cheek, not that she'd noticed, and his smile lines showed when he laughed. He didn't look too bad in those jeans either, but something about Blaise was different. Maybe it was the way his face lit up when he smiled or how protective he was of his son or how he never mentioned his rock status, as if he wasn't impressed with himself.

The doorbell rang. Well, it was more like a sick chicken clucking. She yanked open the door to Beau, holding a coffee mug and his face as red as a cardinal.

"Why is that table inside? I told you I'd take care of it. And I see you had to rip the doorframe off to get it in. That might've been the only thing we wouldn't need to replace, and I can tell from the job you did to fix it, we'll have to just rip it all out and start over." He stepped forward, forcing Grace to take a step back.

"Good morning to you too."

"Did you scrape the table? And how did a waif like you drag that heavy table in?"

"First off, please don't plow into my house barking

at me. Second, the table is fine and the neighbors helped me bring it in."

"Which neighbors? Not Mo Bucknell. That man doesn't know the up side to a hammer."

She pointed next door to Blaise's.

"Better. At least those Savage boys know a socket wrench from a two-by-four." He marched into the kitchen as if he expected her to follow, which she did because she was afraid if she didn't, the smoke already coming out of his ears would turn to fire and take the whole place down with him.

"Afraid I've got some bad news." He put down his coffee.

"What kind of bad news?" She took a deep breath to brace herself. He was going to quit, she'd have to find a new contractor, and that would take a while and throw her plans off track.

"The permits haven't come in yet. I was just down at the town hall. We can't start your demolition until we get them. It's going to be a couple more days because that fool Miles is on some fishing trip and no one can get hold of him. His wife said he left his cell phone home on purpose."

"Does it really matter if we have the permits? Would anyone really care if we started fixing this place up?"

"I do everything by the book. No permit. No work. I'll be back day after tomorrow. Until then go over to Chester's and pick some paint samples." He rinsed out his coffee mug in the sink and then dried it.

She was so glad he felt at home. Not really. "Anything else you'd like to order me to do?"

He marched back over to the door. "Don't go

moving that table again without me. But at least you put it in the right spot." He mumbled the last words, but she caught them.

"Was that a compliment, Mr. Carroll?"

"Never mind." He swung open the door to Cash and Blaise, standing there with the same lopsided grin. "What are you two doing here?"

Beau was feisty if nothing else. She had forgotten to mention Cash to him, and now it was too late. She knew what they wanted. There would be no way to delicately mention her concerns. Why couldn't they have at least waited until Beau was out of the house? Were there no boundaries in this small town? Was everyone always going to be up in each other's business? At least the disregard of personal space would become someone else's problem when she returned home. She didn't want this much closeness with the people she lived near. It only meant trouble. It was too hard to trust people. Her mother and father had proved that to her in different ways, but it was still the same result. She had trust issues.

"Hey, Beau." Blaise stuck out his hand to shake, and Beau took it.

Cash did the same. "Good morning, Mr. Carroll."

"Could we talk with you a minute?" Blaise said.

"I'm in a bit of a hurry."

Cash looked Beau in the eye. "We won't take long. My dad told me you're working on Grace's house, and I was wondering if you needed any help. I'm going to be here for the summer, and I need a job."

Grace was impressed. Cash had stood tall and squared his shoulders. He never let his gaze waver. He was a sweet and mature kid. His appearance was a little startling, but once you got past that, he was just like any other kid his age.

"Beau, I was about to mention it to you before you started to storm out." Grace jumped in before Blaise could say another word. "I'd like to have Cash helping out on the job. I'll talk to Hoke about using money from the renovation fund to pay him, and you could use the extra pair of hands."

"You any good with a hammer?"

Cash shoved his hands in his pockets. "I got Grace's table unstuck and fixed the door."

"Never mind that." Beau blew past them. "We start day after tomorrow seven a.m. sharp. You show up late and you're fired." He halted and turned to look at Cash. "You follow my rules on the job, and no one gets hurt. Safety first. I don't want you to end up like your old man there. I know you young folk do things different than in my day, but on the job, none of that stuff on your face. You'll sweat it off anyway." He pointed a finger at Cash and turned to her. "Miss Grace, don't you go bothering Hoke about that fund. Keep your money for the big stuff. You're gonna need it. I'll pay the young man myself. Can't take my money with me anyhow." He muttered the last words into the wind.

****

He didn't see that coming. When Grace opened her mouth, he thought for sure she was going to throw them off the porch. He never figured she'd want Cash to work on her house. Not from the look on her face last night. Blaise figured when he spoke to Beau about Cash working for him, he'd have to convince Miss Ice Cube to go along with it. And he never thought she would because that would mean she'd have to talk to him and she definitely didn't want to do that. If she had said no, Colton was his backup plan. Women very rarely said no to Colton, and he already had Grace warming to him last night when Blaise left.

"Wow. Thanks, Grace." Cash stared after Beau's truck as it rode down the street. "I thought he was going to say no."

"Um, yeah. Thank you." He wanted to say how nice she was for helping his son, but the words stuck in his throat. She made him feel like that geeky music teacher's kid he used to be instead of Blaise Savage, the drummer. Except he would always be that kid. All the years on the road and all the album sales didn't change that. He'd stopped running from it a long time ago.

His hand inside the brace began to sweat and itch. He pulled on the Velcro and yanked it off.

"How did you hurt your hand?" Her words were soft like a pianissimo.

He locked gazes with her. "It was stupid."

"He fell off scaffolding back stage at a show."

Blaise glared at Cash. "Grace doesn't want to hear about it."

"No, go ahead. Why were you on scaffolding? Wait, before you tell me, do you want to come in? I could make some tea. I don't have much else yet except for Dixie's lasagna, but we can't heat it up yet."

"How about I tell you over breakfast at my house?" Did he actually just say that? She wrinkled her nose. Miss Fusspot was disgusted by him. Why offer the tea, then? He would never understand women.

"Excuse me one second." She held up a finger and pulled a phone from her pocket. "It's my daughter. I'm sorry. I have to take this. You'll have to tell me that story another time."

He wanted to say they would wait, but that seemed desperate. Grace stepped back inside and began to shut the door. She glanced over once more and offered a small wave.

"Hi, honey. How's it going?" she said into the phone. Her smile lit up her face.

Blaise watched until the door clicked shut and Grace's voice trailed away.

"Crash and burn, Dad."

"What are you talking about?" They headed across the lawn.

"You asked her out, and she denied you. Total crash and burn." Cash laughed.

Even if he was busting Blaise's backside, getting rejected by a woman in front of his son was worth the laughing. "I wasn't asking her out. I was being neighborly. That's all."

"Yeah. Okay. You making me breakfast?"

He pushed open the door, and the smell of cigarette smoke smacked him in the face. "Forget it. I only cook for pretty ladies."

"You mean the pretty lady next door with the long legs?" Colton stepped into the hallway with a cigarette dangling from his mouth. "Bro, leave her to me. You can't handle a woman like that."

And the competition was on.

Chapter Twelve

Grace had barely shut the door on Blaise before Chloe blurted out, "I can't stand living with them. Could you please talk to Dad?"

"Well, hello to you too." Grace returned to the kitchen to freshen up her tea. The morning sun was streaming in through the back door. Finishing the tea out in the backyard might make this conversation more pleasant, but there wasn't anywhere to sit. She'd have to navigate the cinder blocks posing as steps.

"Mom, this isn't the time for jokes. You don't know what it's like here. Can you please talk to him?"

"Talk to him about what?" Grace pinched the bridge of her nose. She hated that every conversation with Chloe had the knots in her neck twisting and turning until they were so tight she thought her neck would snap right off. When were the teenage years going to end? She loved her daughter more than anything in the world. She would lay her life down for Chloe, but her daughter was exhausting. Being a parent was exhausting.

"He fusses all over her all the time. He won't let her do anything, like she's sick or something instead of...you know."

"Yes, I know." How could she forget?

"So she sits there on the couch with her feet up, directing him to unpack boxes and put things away, all the time calling him some gross pet name. And he loves it. He laughs every time she says it, like it's the funniest thing in the world. And never mind me. I might as well be invisible for all the attention he pays me."

There it was. The real problem. "Chloe, there isn't anything I can say to your father about how he behaves with his new wife." Boy, was that going to be one she'd have to get used to. "Just ignore them."

"I can't ignore them. They are always around."

Grace plopped into the chair and pushed her tea away. "College is right around the corner. Does it really matter what they do? You'll be gone soon."

"I knew you wouldn't understand. You decide to go start a new life and leave me behind, and Dad has his new life. What about me? Doesn't anybody care about how I feel in all of this?"

"I didn't leave you behind. You wouldn't want to live here while the renovations are going on." The idea of leaving behind the fighting and the battles with her teenager had offered up some peace, if she were going to be truthful. The Disaster House was going to give Grace some of the space she had craved for a long time. When was the last time she didn't have to answer to anyone? Explain where she was going? She wanted to know what it was like to be on her own for once. "And you're forgetting you're leaving for college to start a new life there."

"I'm supposed to go off to college. You've been telling me that since I was four. You weren't supposed to relocate to the South, and dad wasn't supposed to marry some woman half his age and have another baby."

"Life has a way of messing up our plans."

"Thanks a lot, Mom. I call you and tell you how I feel, and all you can do is sit there and crack jokes. My feelings don't mean anything to you."

"I wasn't cracking jokes." But she couldn't help it. She laughed. The whole conversation was ridiculous, and she was being sucked in again. When was Chloe ever going to learn the whole world didn't revolve around her, and what had Grace done wrong that made her daughter think it did? She took two deep breaths. "Chloe, I've got to run. The contractor is here, and he's starting work today." She had to change the subject but felt guilty about lying. "I'll talk to you soon, and if you want to come stay with me, then you know my arrangement."

"Yeah. Bye."

She deposited the phone on the table and made another cup of tea. Maybe this one would release the weight on her shoulders. How could she turn Chloe away? Chloe was feeling the cold shoulder Larry so often offered. He wasn't a soft place to land. Grace didn't blame Chloe for feeling left out, neglected. Should she call her back and tell her to come and not worry about finding a job?

"No. If you want things to be different, you have to start acting differently, Grace Starr." But it was so easy to slip into old habits. She looked around the kitchen. Wouldn't it just be easier to leave all this behind and go home? She wasn't even sure if she cared that much about Nancy Templeton and who gifted the house. She could find a place to rent back in Jersey for a while, and she and Chloe could live there. Chloe would be happy, and Grace wouldn't have the stress of fixing up the Disaster House.

She yanked open the back door, needing to feel the air around her, and teased the cement block with her foot. It held enough. The yard was overgrown in most places, and the fence leaned like an old man. A hole in the fence gave her a clear shot into Blaise's backyard.

He was growing a garden. Well, it looked like one anyway. Small plants shot up out of the ground, and green mesh surrounded his small squared area. Not much. She couldn't picture him as a gardener.

He came outside but didn't see her. He dragged the hose to his patch of growth and sprayed the water, wetting himself in the process. He let loose a string of curses, and Grace couldn't help but laugh.

His breakfast offer had startled her. Why was he being so nice? Or was that invitation a rehearsed move he used to win over the ladies? That brother of his certainly had moves. Blaise was at least subtle about trying to pursue a woman. He didn't parade around like a peacock in heat.

The sun warmed her skin. The birds sang their morning songs, and honeysuckle scented the air. She could stick it out in Heritage River a little longer. Once the renovations got underway, she'd feel better. She'd have a purpose, and that's what she needed. She hadn't had one in a long time.

In the meantime, she'd go into town and poke around. Stop at the library, get a library card. She was craving a new book to read. Maybe ask about Nancy Templeton, after all. Who knew what she'd discover.

Chapter Thirteen

"You ready to give up on that garden yet?"

Blaise didn't turn at the sound of Colton's voice. He rolled up the hose and brushed the dirt from his brace.

Colton handed him a tall glass of iced tea. "Figured you be sweating your ass off out here playing in the dirt."

"I like the garden. It reminds me of Dad, but I don't know what the hell I'm doing. I think I drowned the tomatoes." Blaise held up his glass. "Thanks. The day is warming up fast. Are you headed down to the lake while you're here?"

The fishing was best at night this time of year. The water would be cool, and the wildflowers were in bloom. When they were kids, their mother would pack a picnic lunch and they'd spend the day there. He and his siblings would swim out to the center and hang on the dock, letting the sun cook their skin like bacon. Colton would hold diving contests to see which Savage kid could do the best dive. He'd play and play until he was certain he had won. And sometimes, when Savannah could be convinced, they'd sing rhythm-and-blues songs as loudly as they could. He would drum on the wood, and Colton would make guitar noises with his mouth.

"Nah. No time to drag out the poles. I'm going

back tonight. I've had enough of the old homestead for a while."

Colton never hung around long. It's why he never married. Marriage required too much commitment. Hell, a relationship lasting more than twenty-four hours was too much for Colton.

Looked like it would be now or never. "I want you to hear what I wrote before you go."

"Not this again. Christ, how many times do I have to say it?"

"Listen to what I have. You're going to like it." Blaise turned for the house and hoped Colton would follow. He didn't understand why his brother was being so stubborn about the whole music thing. What was he afraid of?

"Did you sell your car?"

That stopped him in his tracks. "What?"

"Have you sold your Porsche yet?" Colton flopped into the Adirondack chair and stared over the top of his glass.

"What does that have to do with what we're talking about?"

"Everything. You need the money."

Blaise wiped his face with his hand. He didn't want to talk about his money, or the lack of it. He'd trusted the wrong person, and now he was almost wiped out. He woke up one morning to find out his investments were gone. As if they'd never existed. He had some cash in a few checking accounts and his cars. He was trying to sell the Porsche. He hadn't told Colton about selling the place in Nashville.

"Don't worry about the car. I've got it under control."

"You'll make more money when we tour. If we sell out, we're set to make big bucks this time. We could all use it. Especially Patrick."

Patrick had been in and out of rehab more times than Blaise could remember. Patrick was like a brother to him, but he carried too much baggage and trouble. Blaise was getting too old for Patrick's bullshit. Finding someone to play behind Colton wouldn't be too hard.

"Cash got a job working with Beau on the house next door, and he has his community service at the library. Savannah pulled strings for that to happen. He's staying put, and so am I."

"He's going to be working for your pretty neighbor?" Colton tried to see over the fence. "That fence isn't ours, is it?"

"No, it's not mine." He emphasized *mine*. "The fence is hers. It should be torn down."

"You know, I could stick around and help her too. Maybe get another look at those legs."

"She's not your type. She's too uptight. Five minutes and you'll be gone."

"I don't know. I've been known to melt a few hearts. Besides, I had her laughing pretty loudly the other night." Colton wagged his eyebrows.

"Forget it." He never cared about the women Colton went after. His attitude was they were grown-ups and responsible for themselves, but there was something about Grace that didn't feel right with his brother. He loved his brother and knew he would never hurt a woman on purpose, but he did have the commitment thing. The only thing Colton was attached to was the band. Everything else came second. Grace didn't strike him as the kind of woman who would want to come second to anything.

"Are you saying I can't date her?"

"I'm saying she won't want to have anything to do with you."

"We'll see about that. More importantly, the band needs you, bro. I need you." Colton was never going to quit.

"So wait until after September when Cash goes back to California."

"Can't do it. The dates are being worked on as we speak. We can't cancel again. People will stop showing up."

"You shouldn't have agreed to any new dates without talking to me first. Before Cash even got here, there was still the problem with my hand."

Colton unfolded himself from the chair and set his iced tea down. "We can't wait for your hand to heal. This was supposed to be *the* summer tour for us. We can't reschedule all the meet and greets. We have to give that money back."

"So give it back."

"Are you nuts? I'm hoping we can give those people a signed photo or something like that, cancel the meets, and keep the money. I'm not returning that money because you're the ass that fell off the scaffolding."

"You dared me."

"What are you? Twelve? You don't have to listen to me."

The same words Grace used. They felt cold inside his head, like the iced tea in his good hand. When would he stop behaving like Colton's younger brother instead of a grown-up?

Colton kept talking, unaware of the look on Blaise's face. "We all shouldn't suffer. We hit the road when the dates are ready. That's it, man. Either with you or without you."

Blaise cleared the distance between them. They stood nose to nose. "Don't threaten me. I will kick the shit out of you with one hand. This is my band too. It's my name as much as yours, and it won't take much for me to convince Patrick and Troy to take my side."

Colton backed up. "I didn't come here to fight with you. I came to see my nephew, which I did, and I wanted you to know where I stand. And Patrick and Troy are with me. I told you Patrick needs the money, and Troy doesn't have the guts to stand up to me. He's just happy he has a gig. He's getting so old his voice is shot. No one wants him, and he knows it."

The anger seeped out of him. At one of the last shows, Troy couldn't hit the notes. Right on the mic, he'd asked the rest of the band to help him. "If we write some new music, the fans, they'll come back." Blaise turned back toward the house. "Come inside and listen to my stuff. If the whiskey didn't drown all your brain cells, you'll see it's good."

A horn honked from the street.

"Uncle Colton, your car is here." Cash came through the back door, holding Colton's bag.

"Send me a disc. I'll listen to it. But I'm not making any promises. And tell Grace I'll be seeing her soon."

Chapter Fourteen

When Grace was a child, she would escape the world of her chaotic house by riding her bicycle to the library. She often found her mother sitting at the kitchen table, staring off into space, the sink filled with dirty dishes, a trail of shoes and coats discarded on their way from the door to the closet. Corners of rooms were filled with objects her mother collected in hopes of using some day. Rebecca Somerall scavenged broken sewing machines, weave-back chairs minus the weave, and plenty of lost and forgotten items from garbage bins or curbsides.

Beds were never made, and sheets never changed unless Grace pulled and yanked her own and dragged them to the basement of their tiny bungalow to wash. By the age of ten, she had learned to operate the lawn mower because her mother was either too tired or too excited about a new adventure to be bothered.

The library was a place that made sense to Grace. The books arranged by classifications, arranged by numbers. Something she could always count on to be there. Something she could trust. She loved her mother up until the day she died, but trusting her was something altogether different. She hadn't seen her father since she was too little to remember him. She hadn't had a parent to lean on—ever. It was probably why Larry had been so attractive to her. He was older, stable, and reliable. Until the end.

She pushed open the door to the Heritage River library, and the familiar smell of old books and new paper greeted her. The tension eased from her neck as she stepped into the cool surroundings, leaving the heat at the door. She could take in most of the library in one swoop. It was much smaller than her library back home, but that wasn't surprising. The place was empty except for a mother and her child sitting on the floor in the children's section. They were hunched over a board book, pointing at pages. Her library had an entire room in the back for children to sit and read or participate in activities, many of which Grace had planned.

Like most libraries, the circulation desk was right in front, ready for someone to slip up to and ask for help or check out their books, and for a moment Grace longed for her volunteer job back in Silverside. She pushed the thought away. No time for self-pity. She took on this adventure. She would see it to the end.

A tall woman with long, wavy dark hair stared into a computer monitor. The woman furrowed her brows and leaned in to get a better look.

Grace wanted to offer this woman her glasses. "Excuse me," she said.

"Oh, I'm so sorry." The woman turned. The lines around her gray eyes crinkled when she smiled. She seemed familiar, but that was impossible. "I was so caught up in what I was doing." Her voice held a hint of a southern accent, but not as much as Grace would've expected. "How can I help you?"

"I'd like to apply for a library card, please."

"Of course. Are you new in town? Well, you must be. I've harassed everyone in town to have a library card by now. Let me find the papers." She shuffled things around on the desk, then squatted down to look beneath it. When she straightened, she yelled over her shoulder, "Has anyone seen the paperwork for library cards?"

The outburst startled Grace, but then the gesture seemed more like something done in a home when a mother wanted her child for dinner and didn't want to climb the steps to say so.

"I tell them to keep things in the same place so we can always find them, but no one listens to me. We don't have much of a staff, just Arlene and Robert and me and a few volunteers, mostly kids." She continued to push and shove things around the desk.

"Maybe now isn't a good time?" Her heart sank a little at not being able to take a book from the library. Her library was more organized, but she did have a bigger staff and probably more volunteers.

"No, no. We'll find what we need. I'll be right back. Don't go away."

"Is this what you're looking for, Aunt Savannah?" Cash rounded the corner, a pile of paper in his hand.

Aunt Savannah. Of course. She should have seen the resemblance.

"Hey, Grace." He punctuated his words with a nod.

Savannah's eyebrows squished together. She looked between her nephew and Grace. "You know her?"

"She moved in next to Dad." Cash handed over the papers. "I'm going to work with Mr. Carroll fixing up her house. Can I take a lunch break?"

"Which house? The dilapidated one?" Savannah pulled her shirt up over her nose, as if she smelled something rotting, and shook her head.

"That's the one." Grace straightened her shoulders. The house might be in bad shape, but it was hers and she was starting to take a liking to it. Well, a liking to the way it would look when she could sell it.

"I'm sorry. Where are my manners? Savannah Montgomery." She stuck out her hand. "Please forgive my obvious disdain for that house. It's been neglected for decades and become such an eyesore it's bringing the property values down. I'm glad someone finally saw fit to purchase it and fix it up. You're going to love living in Heritage River."

"Aunt Savannah, can I take that break now?" Cash glanced at his phone.

"You're only here for four hours. Can't it wait?"

"Not today. Today I'm here for eight. Remember?"

"Well, no, but I've had a lot on my mind with this fundraiser." She checked her empty wrist. "What's today's date?"

"You always have a lot on your mind. You're like Grandpa was."

"You were too little to remember Grandpa." Savannah reached up to ruffle his hair, but he ducked away. "Okay, go have lunch. Wait. Did you bring something healthy to eat, or is it those sponge cakes with the oozing cream filling?" she shouted after him.

"Aunt Savannah, no one my age eats that junk. Dad gave me some money to walk down to Jake's." He tossed his words back over his shoulder. "But I can bring you a sponge cake back if you'd like."

"Get out of my library." She shook her head but smiled again. "All Savage men are jokers. Lucky me."

Grace liked the banter between the two. She didn't

have this ease with Chloe at the moment and had no siblings, so she didn't know what it was like to have a nephew to joke around with.

Savannah handed her the forms for the library card. "I don't know why I bothered to ask if Cash brought lunch," she said in a conspiratorial tone. "I can't remember the last time my brother actually made a meal."

Grace thought of Blaise's offer for breakfast earlier. Her insides warmed, but she reminded herself not to take that offer seriously. It was just his way with women, and Grace wasn't anything special. Especially not to him.

She filled out the forms and handed them back. "What fundraiser are you planning?"

Savannah twisted her hair in a knot and secured it with a pencil. "This hair is driving me crazy. The library needs money. What library doesn't, right? I wanted to make this one a big deal, though. A big summer barbeque complete with entertainment."

"How are the plans coming?"

Savannah punched some things into the computer. "Like you'd expect. A million things need to be done, and I have to do most of it myself. My husband will tell you I don't know how to delegate, but I would if there was someone around I could trust." She handed Grace her new blue-and-gold library card. "I love Arlene and Robert, but sometimes it's just easier to do the task myself. But don't tell anyone I said that."

"Your secret is safe with me." Grace tried to shove the next thoughts right out her head. She didn't know this town. She wasn't going to stay in this town longer than she had to. The Disaster House would take up

115

most of her time. But somehow she couldn't keep her lips together. "I volunteer at a library back home."

Savannah held her gaze. "Please don't tell me you're joking."

Heat filled her cheeks. "I do. Or I did. But if you need the help—"

Before she could even finish, Savannah jumped from her seat and ran around the counter. She gripped Grace's hand in her own. "I need help."

Grace laughed. "Do you want to see a resume or get references or anything?"

"Nope. I like you. I know people. You'll be a great fit here. How soon can you start?"

She didn't have much on her agenda today, only a stop at the hardware store and maybe buying a few more home magazines. Beau wasn't due back for another day. And there was no point hanging around the house, staring at those walls. Helping at the library would distract her from thinking about the arguments with Chloe.

She looked at Savannah and decided to take a chance. "How about I grab us a couple of snack cakes with oozing cream and we have lunch first?"

Savannah's face crunched up in confusion. The heat burned in Grace's cheeks. She'd made a mistake. She should have just said what she always would have said, a simple *I can start now or whenever you want*. It wasn't like her to be so forward without a plan.

But then Savannah's eyes opened wide, and she threw her head back and laughed. "I knew I liked you. You've got yourself a deal."

And without realizing what she'd done, Grace made her first friend in Heritage River.

Chapter Fifteen

Where was he? Grace paced the front walk, searching the street for the faded red pickup. Every time she heard the rev of a motor, her head turned to find anyone but Beau Carroll coming down the street. He had said seven a.m. sharp, and now it was seven forty-five. She tried his cell again, but it went right to voice mail.

"Maybe something came up." Cash sat on the front porch step, his head bent to his phone.

What else could've come up? Hers was the only job he had. Was it the permits? But why not call? "Is this how people in this town do business?" Every day they delayed the start was another day she'd be stuck in Heritage River. How were they going to get all the work done in time anyway? Everyone knew house projects took longer than expected. The clock was ticking.

"People in this town do business with integrity," Blaise shouted from his spot on his porch. He raised his mug in salute. "Your voice carries."

She hadn't seen him come outside. He wore a slouchy green tee with cargo shorts. His hair was wet and slicked back.

Her phone vibrated in her pocket. "Finally." She yanked it free, and her heart sank. It wasn't Beau. "Chloe. Hi, hon." Regardless of all the fighting, she missed Chloe.

"Mom, I'm coming to Tennessee."

"Okay, that's great, but our agreement." She didn't want to start another fight. Not then.

"Yeah, I know. I'll find a job. Somehow. But you said yourself it's a small town with not much going on. How am I supposed to find a job and only for a few weeks?"

"Chloe, I don't know. Right now I've got a problem with my contractor. Can we discuss the job thing later?"

"No, Mom, we can't because I'm at the airport."

"What?" She nearly dropped the phone.

"I'm at Newark. Dad dropped me off like an hour ago. My plane lands in three hours. Can you pick me up, or should I rent a car?"

Pick her up or rent a car? Grace's head spun. What was happening? "You're too young to rent a car. Why didn't you tell me you were coming? I would've planned to be there and tried to get a space ready for you because the extra bedrooms aren't livable yet."

She wasn't mentally prepared for what it would mean having Chloe with her and nothing to run as a buffer. Chloe wouldn't be able to hide in her room when the tension got tight, and Grace didn't even have her usual places to escape to, like her deck. She glanced over at Cash, who still flipped through his phone. She couldn't even sit on that porch for a little alone time. It was about to fall in. Well, it would have to do— wouldn't it?—if Chloe was on her way.

"I couldn't stay another day with Dad and Annie. Her belly is huge, and she complains all the time about being fat and how her feet are swollen. And when Dad gets home from work, she whines to him to sit with her and rub her back. It's so gross."

Someday Chloe might understand how uncomfortable it actually was to carry another living person inside you. Grace remembered that time with a hint of nostalgia: feeling Chloe hiccup, or sticking headphones on her belly hoping to make a baby genius, or all the planning for her arrival. She had painted the nursery in soft greens, labored over the perfect mobile, and spent hours washing and folding onesies, tiny socks, and blankets.

"Okay, okay. I get it. Your dad and his wife are over the top. I'll figure out a way to get to the airport in time. I'm glad you're coming."

"Me too. See ya."

Grace wanted to say she loved her and have a safe trip, but Chloe ended the call before she could. She slapped a hand to her forehead. How was she going to pull off being ready for her daughter? There just wasn't enough time to get what she needed.

"Everything okay?" Blaise shouted from his perch.

Did that man watch everything she was doing? "I'm fine, thank you." Where was Beau?

Her prayers were answered as Beau's truck turned onto the street. She let out the breath she was holding. Once Beau and Cash got started, she'd leave for the airport and stop at a large housewares store to pick up sheets and towels and toiletries. She'd pass some bleach over the floors before Chloe stepped foot on them.

Beau shoved his way out of his truck. He stood for a moment, holding the door and his lower back. He turned back inside the truck, moving as if he were made of china, and pulled a binder from the seat. Blaise

119

barreled down his front steps, but Beau caught him and waved him off.

"Are you okay?" Blaise said.

"What makes you think there's something wrong with me, young man?" Beau pushed past him.

Blaise was right to ask. Beau's color looked like dirty dishwater. She gave him space. He wasn't going to talk to a stranger about his pain. She knew that much for sure.

"Good morning." She pushed her voice up to cheery. There was no point in staying angry about his tardiness, especially since he looked worn out. "Something's come up. I'm going to have to run out."

"Not today, you're not. We've got demo to do." Beau patted Cash on the shoulder. "Young man, take my truck over to Maybelline's and get me her coffee and anything coming straight out of the oven. Pick yourself up something too." He shoved money into Cash's hand.

"I've got coffee made. I can bring you over a cup," Blaise offered.

Beau put up a hand. "I only drink May's coffee. You probably have one of those fancy machines that makes one cup at a time. May puts something special in her coffee you can't buy for your expensive coffeemakers."

"I just found out my daughter is on a plane here without giving me any notice of her arrival, and she knows I need to plan for something like a visit, even if it is from her. I hate surprises. You will have to start demo day without me. Leave me a list of what you need me to do, and I'll do it by tomorrow."

Beau tossed his keys to Cash. "Go get my coffee

and hurry." He turned to Grace. "You can't do any of this work by yourself. Go pick up your girl. You can help out tomorrow. There will be plenty to do. And don't go crazy buying stuff now. The decorating part ain't for a while."

"Listen, Beau, I really wanted to get this project started. I'm anxious to begin so we can finish as soon as possible. We're already two or three days behind."

"We're going to end up a lot farther behind than that."

Blaise laughed.

She turned on her heel. "What is so funny?"

"Not a damn thing. I'll be heading back to my place. Good luck to you all." He raised his mug.

"Hang on a second, Blaise." Beau rubbed the back of his neck. "How's that hand of yours?"

Blaise shook his head. "Oh no. Don't even think about it. My hand hurts plenty. As soon as I'm ready, I'm back on tour. I can't risk making it worse to help out here. Besides, Grace wouldn't want me to. Right, Grace?"

Her world was slipping out of her fingers. What was she supposed to say to that? And why would Beau suggest such a stupid thing? "Beau, maybe it's not too late to get your old crew back. You look like—"

"Not a chance. They all have other jobs. Never mind, Blaise. Miss Grace, go do whatever it is you need to do today. Cash and I will be fine." He shot a stink eye at Blaise, who ducked his head and turned for his house.

She left Beau ordering Cash around. That old man didn't have the capabilities to restore the Disaster House. Should she walk away from it? Hoke did say she could change her mind at any time.

But what message would that send to Chloe? When things get tough, leave? Or when you realize you're in over your head, bail while you still can. And she wanted to know who gave her the house. She hadn't had a chance to track down Nancy Templeton. If she walked away now, she'd never know. She wanted to know, even if only to say thanks, because no one had ever given her a gift like that before. Maybe, just maybe, the donor was related to her. A long-lost cousin she didn't know about. A family member of her father's she never knew existed. She knew so little about him because her mother had refused to talk about him.

"He's gone, Gracie," her mother had said. "Best to forget him."

But Grace hadn't. What kind of a man walks out on his family never to return? Grace secretly hoped her father would show up one day and apologize. A simple I'm sorry. Only, he never did. And he never would.

She'd have to find that family another way. Her disaster house couldn't give her a family. Instead, it gave her a cranky old man and a handsome but incorrigible neighbor. Now it was giving Grace her daughter for the summer.

She listened to the GPS and turned into the parking lot of the housewares store. Everything would work out. Wouldn't it?

Chapter Sixteen

Who thought it would be so difficult to sell a Porsche 911 Turbo with twenty years on her? Blaise shoved his phone across the kitchen table after another prospective buyer said no, and rubbed his aching wrist. He never thought he'd have to sell that car. For him, that car defined the moment Savage made it. No more playing in dive bars and dragging his kit around in a beat-up van. Fast Lane Records had signed Savage with a big signing bonus, and they found themselves in a recording studio putting their first songs down on tracks. After the album climbed the charts and they sold out more shows than anyone expected, he dropped the money on that Porsche. Now he'd come full circle. He needed the money that car would provide, and they weren't selling out shows the way they used to.

He pushed himself out of the chair and headed to his garden. The sun spread its heat over him before he got to the bottom of the deck steps. Sounds of banging and cursing drifted over the fence from Grace's house.

"Throw it in the dumpster. Then come hold this ladder."

Blaise shook his head. Beau was a drill sergeant, but that would be good for Cash, because Cash certainly didn't listen to him. They were fine if the discussion stayed on things like what to eat for dinner or what time Cash would be back from the library, but if Blaise dug a little deeper, Cash shoved those damn earbuds in his ears and locked himself in his room. Melissa was no help. She said he should figure it out for himself. He would, if he had any idea where to start.

He thought of his dad. Jedidiah Savage was a man who said very little, but when he did, he commanded the room. His presence had made him an effective teacher, and when Blaise or Colton got out of line, their father only had to say a few words and Blaise immediately felt the ice form in his belly and the need for the floor to swallow him up.

He scratched the back of his neck. The plants weren't growing. His dad would know what to do with the garden too, and he wished he could ask him. He wished he could play music with him again, and he wished his dad were around to knock some sense into Colton about recording new music.

"Anybody home?"

Blaise turned to Savannah's voice coming from the house.

"Out back."

His sister stepped into the yard, wearing a dress covered in pink flowers. Her dark hair was pulled back into a knot. Jud followed on her heels. She was always the mother duck leading her ducklings. What would she do when they all moved away? Probably herd them back.

Jud looked like his grandfather, the man he was named after, with the dark, wavy Savage hair Jud wore slicked back. He stood six feet four like Blaise's dad. And now he sported an almost-full beard much like old Jedidiah's.

"I brought over a summer salad and a roasted

chicken for you and Cash. It's in the fridge." Savannah leaned in and kissed Blaise's cheek. Jud offered a firm shake.

"Thanks, but you didn't have to. No one is starving over here." He patted his stomach.

"I had extra, and since Cash runs down to Jake's every day to grab lunch, I worried you two were only eating takeout. How's the garden coming?"

"Don't ask. What else are you up to?" Because there had to be more than just the food. She was buttering him up for something.

"I was hoping to catch your neighbor for a minute, but it doesn't look like she's home."

"You brought her food too?" When had Grace met Savannah?

Savannah's eyes grew wide. "Does she need some? I didn't think of it. How foolish of me. I should've brought a plate of brownies as a housewarming gift. I'm slipping." She pulled out a small notebook and jotted down *brownies*.

"Mom, you really have to get into the twenty-first century. You could keep a list on your phone." Jud let his smile spread across his face and light up his eyes.

Savannah and Jud always had an ease with each other. Blaise envied that, but Savannah chalked it up to mother-son relationships. She was certain he and Cash would be at ease if they worked at it. Blaise thought she was wrong. Or just trying to be nice.

Laughing, she swatted Jud away. "I like pen and paper. Keeps me sharp. All that computer screen stuff is killing my brain cells. I'll come back later with those brownies. Hopefully, she'll be home then. Do you happen to know where she went?"

"Why would I know where she went?" He didn't mean for his words to sound so harsh. "She's not all that neighborly. She really doesn't like me."

"Really? Doesn't everyone like you? She seemed so sweet at the library, and she offered to help with the fundraiser. I just thought you might know where she was since Cash is over there working with Beau." Savannah held her hands up. "No problem. I'll catch up with her at some point."

Grace was helping with the fundraiser too? Savannah would hook anyone within reach of her claws. He shook his head. Grace did appear to be the kind of woman who could plan an event. She liked things her way and clearly wanted to be in control. Hopefully, he could avoid her. Living next door was enough.

"Cash, I need you to hold this ladder." Beau's voice carried across the yard. "You want to send me to my death?"

The dumpster filled with a clatter and bang. "I can't haul and hold, Mr. Carroll. Sorry. I'll come right over." Cash's voice sounded like a drumhead pulled tight.

"They need help," Jud said. "Maybe I should go see?"

Jud was like his mother, always wanting to fix a difficult situation, but Blaise knew Cash wouldn't want his cousin nearby. "They'll be fine."

"Jud, go ask Beau. It's only the two of them over there."

"No, really. Beau doesn't want anyone else on the job. He told Grace that."

"Hey, Miss Savannah, that your young man with

you? He's grown a foot since I saw him last." Beau stood on the ladder with a clear view over the fence. "Send him over. We need extra muscle power. I'm paying if he needs a job."

Blaise's heart sank. Jud shrugged and jogged into the front yard. Cash was going to be pissed and probably take it out on Blaise, as if he were the one sending Jud over.

"He doesn't have a job for the summer?" Blaise pulled on the leaves of the tomato plant.

"He looked but was having trouble finding something. We just want him to have a little spending money before he leaves for college. Hopefully, Beau needs him for more than one day, and by the looks of the house, he will." She turned and locked her gaze on Blaise's. "Why did you say Beau didn't need any other workers?"

He squirmed under his sister's glare. "He fired his crew. I just thought he was scaling back."

"There still isn't trouble between Cash and Jud is there?"

Nothing got past her. He didn't know if he could lie and get away with it. "I think they worked it out." Holding her stare was harder than he thought. Sweat trickled down the back of his neck. He broke his stare first and looked over her shoulder to the still trees lining his property.

"Well, that's good. They can't fight. They're cousins."

Being related didn't always equal harmony— nothing was that simple. You couldn't pick your family, and sometimes you got stuck with ones you didn't jive with. He loved his brother, but right now he didn't understand him at all. He understood Colton's drinking better than this decision to stop producing music. Continuing down the same worn-out path was suicide for their band. Why didn't he see that?

"Hey, big brother." Savannah waved a hand in his face. "You still there? I'm talking and you're zoning. I have to get to the library. If you can't give Jud a lift home, tell him to walk, okay? And heat that chicken in the oven, not the microwave. You'll dry it out."

She followed the path Jud took, but stopped and turned. "Have you decided yet how you're going to play at the fundraiser with your hand like that?"

He hadn't thought about her fundraiser at all. "I'll figure it out."

"Is it just going to be you?"

"You heard Colton. He's not on board. The other guys most likely won't play without him. They're afraid of him and never go against what he says. I'll do some type of acoustic version of our songs." He'd arranged most of their music that way already. It had given him something to do in between shows when they were on tour. The older he got, the more he stayed away from the partying and kept to himself in the hotel rooms and on the tour bus. He was tired of being the circus leader. Wasn't that how he hurt his wrist? Being stupid and childish? When had he gotten so old?

"How about Cash?"

"How about Cash what?"

"Will he play with you?"

"Don't count on it. He doesn't do anything I ask these days."

"Then I'll ask him."

Chapter Seventeen

Honking a horn in traffic never made it move faster. Why did people do that? Grace pulled her hair back into a ponytail. She was hot and sticky from filling her car with supplies she needed for Chloe's arrival. Now she was stopped on Route 1. The traffic to the airport was backed up. A lane was out, and everyone passing by had to slow down to look. "There's nothing to see, people."

Chloe sent several texts wondering where Grace was. Did her daughter think she was arriving late because it might be fun? Didn't she realize Grace would be there as soon as she could? She wasn't likely to leave Chloe at the airport indefinitely, though it was tempting after the last text.

How much longer are you going to make me wait?

She found a spot in short-term parking. The doors to the passenger waiting area slid open, and cold air blasted her. Chloe sat in the corner, flipping through her phone with her purple suitcases lined up around her like a fort. Probably texting a friend about the terrible life she had.

Her heart swelled as she watched her daughter. Chloe had dyed her hair back to its natural medium brown, and Grace bit her lip to keep from crying. Was it relief? Maybe a little. Knowing Chloe chose to spend the summer with her was a joy. Even if it was by default.

She folded Chloe in a hug, whether she liked it or not. She missed the vanilla-bean smell of her daughter and inhaled it in. Chloe might not let her get this close again for a while. The nose piercing still took up residence, but Grace could live with that. Chloe could do worse things than wear an earring in her nose.

"How was your flight?"

"There was a kid screaming the whole time and nothing good to eat. I'm starving. Can we get some food?"

Grace checked her watch. She really wanted to get back to the house. Beau was going to need as much help as possible. A sit-down lunch didn't fit in with her plan. "How about we grab something along the way? I'm hungry too."

Chloe searched for a sandwich place on her phone while Grace navigated them back onto the highway. They ate while she drove. Chloe filled Grace in on everything going on in town and what her friends were up to awaiting the arrival of that college moving-in day. Grace listened to her daughter prattle on about who was dating whom and who got a brand new car for their birthday.

"I'm so over Silverside," Chloe said.

"It's not so bad." Grace missed her morning walks with Jenn and running into people she knew at the grocery store. She missed her deck but reminded herself it was Larry's deck. She would have to build a deck on the Disaster House or sit on the porch and hang on for dear life.

"Dad didn't get me a car for my birthday." Chloe pulled on the ends of her hair.

"How were you going to put gas into a car if you continued to refuse to get a job?" They had been around this a dozen times. Larry wanted Chloe to work. Grace did too. It would teach her responsibility with money. But Chloe used theater camp, SAT class, tennis lessons, and summer homework as excuses. Maybe she should have forced Chloe the way she was forced to get a job at a young age.

She had her first job at fifteen. She couldn't count on her mother showing up for work. The fear of not being able to keep the lights on or food in the fridge scared her enough to keep her working. Even in college she worked as many hours and at as many jobs as she could, giving up sleep whenever necessary. She'd even fallen asleep in the shower several times, thinking she was killing two birds with one stone. She'd been working ever since.

"He bought Annie a new minivan." Chloe stared out the window.

Grace's insides burned. How many times was Larry going to show his daughter she came in second to this new wife? She'd call him the first chance she got. He'd have to learn to include Chloe, or he'd lose her forever. Unless that was what he wanted. The thought made the sandwich in Grace's stomach turn sour.

"Well, it isn't practical to cart a baby around in a sports car. I'm sure if you'd gone out and found a job, your dad would've considered buying a car for you." What else was she going to say? That Larry was a big fat jerk? Tempting.

"I can't have a car at school this year anyway."

It wasn't like Chloe to concede so quickly, but Grace wasn't going to argue. "You can get a job on campus too. Save a little money and show him you're serious. He'll come around." She only hoped he did and that he didn't get caught up in paying for baby music classes, high-end strollers, and a tummy tuck for his new wife after the baby was born.

She pulled into the driveway on Dogwood Drive. Debris covered the front lawn like confetti shot from a cannon. What was going on inside? This place was a disaster for sure.

A young man she didn't recognize came out the front door, dragging a cabinet, and hauled it over the porch onto the lawn.

"Who's he?" Chloe checked her lip gloss in the mirror.

Before Grace could get out of the car, Beau barreled out onto the porch and waved a finger at the young man. "Jud, how many times do I have to say throw it in the dumpster? You're making more work for us. Get this mess off the lawn, or you can't come back tomorrow, and that's final."

Cash came out next, hauling a large piece of Sheetrock. He snickered at the young man, then bounced down the steps and tossed the Sheetrock into the dumpster.

"Fag." The young man named Jud snarled at Cash, yanked the broken wood off the grass, and tossed it in the dumpster. "You won't be laughing for long."

She didn't like threats and name-calling. What kind of thing is that to say? Cash gave Jud a wide berth but didn't respond.

"Mom, you didn't tell me you had guys like my age working for you. I would've worn something different on the plane."

"You're fine." Grace peeled herself out of the car. "Beau, what's going on?"

Beau clamored down the steps. "Now, Miss Grace, don't go getting all upset. It's not as bad as it looks." He turned and shot the stink eye to Jud.

"Who is that person helping you?"

Beau leaned in. "That's Savannah Montgomery's son, Jud. He's a good kid, but he's more brawn than brain. Keep telling him to follow Cash's lead, but he won't listen. They're like two foxes fighting to get in the henhouse. But don't worry about them. I'll take care of the boys."

"Are you sure he can be trusted?" Call it motherly instincts, but Grace got a weird vibe from Jud.

"No need to worry, Miss Grace. I've known that boy his whole life." Beau turned to Chloe. A smile spread across his face. "This must be your daughter." He wiped his hands on his jeans. "It's a pleasure to meet you. I'm Beau Carroll."

Chloe shook Beau's hand, but he held on a little longer before letting her go.

"Beau, did you tear apart every room? How will I live here?"

He patted her shoulder. "Don't fret. We aren't touching the bedrooms or the bathrooms. I put your card table in your room with the air mattress. I did my best to keep those pictures in a neat pile, but I'm not sure I did such a good job with that. We sealed off the rooms with plastic to keep the dust out. And I've got all the windows open. Now the kitchen and the front room are something altogether different. Keep your shoes on when you walk around. I left your lasagna in the fridge, and that's still plugged in. I don't think we'll have a problem with the electrical, just yet."

"Just yet?" Her voice climbed a few octaves.

"This is an old house. We're bound to find some problems hidden behind these walls. But there's nothing I can't handle. Anyone in town will tell you that."

"Mom, why didn't you tell me this place was so bad?" Chloe took in the mess, then climbed the porch steps. "It's worse inside the house."

"I told you it needed work," Grace said.

"Dad was right. You bit off more than you could chew. Sorry to say." Chloe flipped her hair over her shoulder and pulled out her phone. "Is there a hotel around?"

The knots in Grace's neck twisted into a braid. *Bit off more than she could chew?* Well, she'd show him. How dare he speak that way about her to Chloe? Grace had been trying so hard not to say anything bad about Larry to Chloe, even though she wanted to, and he couldn't do the same? She hoped there were twins hiding in that bimbo's belly.

"The house isn't so bad." Cash came through the front door with more Sheetrock. He gave Chloe a quick glance but kept walking. "I'll help clean up, Grace. I sent Aunt Savannah a text and told her I can't make the library today. I'll make up the hours another day."

Jud followed Cash onto the porch. "I can't believe my mother actually thought you being at the library was a good idea. You should've gone to jail for your stupid prank, and the only reason you didn't is because of who your father is."

Red splotches bled over Cash's face and onto his neck. He stole a glance at Chloe, then back at Jud. Cash turned on his heel and marched back into the house.

She hadn't heard about any prank. She didn't even really know if Cash lived with Blaise permanently or only part-time. She should have asked more questions. But he seemed like such a nice kid, especially when he came over to help her get the table unstuck. All kids make mistakes. Maybe she shouldn't be so quick to judge without knowing all the facts.

Jud stopped and gave Chloe the obvious once-over. He soaked in her legs sticking out of shorts too short and dragged his gaze to her bare shoulder. His smile was wide. "Hey," he said.

Chloe checked him out too, and Grace could watch no longer. "Chloe, let's get your bags and the things I bought out of the car. We can store them in the garage until the men are done and we've cleaned up some."

Chloe leaned in to the trunk and grabbed her purple suitcase. "Mom, who is that kid's father? Is he someone important?" She made sure no one was listening.

"His father is Blaise Savage. He lives next door."

"Who?"

"Never mind." When Grace turned around, Jud was standing behind them. She jumped.

Jud took Chloe's bags from her. "I'm Jud."

"Chloe." She tugged on her necklace.

Oh brother.

"Jud, stop all that yacking and get back to work. I want everything cleared out before we leave here today," Beau yelled from inside the house.

Grace changed her clothes and began helping. Beau had her swinging a sledgehammer against the cabinets. He handed a broom to Chloe.

She threw her hands up. "I don't want to get dirty."

Beau shook his head and shoved the broom at her. "You plan on living here, don't you?"

Cash laughed. "Don't fight him. He always wins."

Chloe took the broom with two fingers.

"I didn't know what I was getting into either." Jud had dirt in his hair, and his T-shirt was torn at the shoulder. "This place is a mess."

Only Cash didn't seem to mind the work. That made the knotted braid of her muscles unwind a little. Beau shouted orders, and they followed, working mostly in silence. Several times he had to tell Jud to stop talking to Chloe, but as the sun set behind the poplar trees, the front rooms had been stripped of all signs of their earlier life. Grace had scrapes up and down her arms, and her muscles screamed from all the work she put them through. She'd hurt tomorrow, but her insides were warm with a sense of accomplishment. She had helped with her bare hands, and she was making something new with this house. Something completely hers.

Up until that point, nothing had been just hers. First, she shared everything with her mother—what her mother had, she usually hoarded—and then she shared everything with Larry. Before long Chloe arrived, and Grace was caught up in the tide of motherhood. She dove headfirst into having someone to love unconditionally, hoping to do a better job than her mother had, but somehow over the years, when she wasn't looking, her identity had slipped away from her.

That thought drew her gaze next door. If she found herself again, would this new person be more interested in Blaise? There had been no sign of him all day. His truck had been missing, so she assumed something had his attention. Was it a woman?

"Well, Miss Grace, looks like we're done for the evening. I'll be back bright and early." Beau limped down the porch steps. He rubbed his lower back. "Have a good night now, ya hear? Come on, Jud. I'll give you a ride. You earned that much."

Jud had circles under his eyes, and his hair was stuck to his head from sweating. He used the bottom of his shirt to wipe the sweat off his face before he gave a small wave to Grace. He ignored Cash, slid in Beau's truck, and leaned his head back against the rest. Had that young man ever worked that hard before today? Chloe certainly hadn't. They'd lost her help an hour ago. She had dragged a folding chair into the backyard and shoved her face into her phone.

Cash stood tall, a smile still on his face. "Good night," he said and crossed the yard, almost bouncing on his feet.

Grace admired the way he kept his cool around Jud. That couldn't be easy for anyone. What was the story between those two?

"Beau, before you go." She had tucked this idea away all day. She didn't want to think much about it, because the answer could void her ownership, but when she tried to force the thought away, it kept coming back. "Do you know whatever happened to Nancy Templeton?"

A darkness passed over Beau's blue eyes. He looked away, and when he looked back, his eyes were clear again. "How do you know who Nancy Templeton is?"

"I know she owned this house before me. I was wondering where she went. She clearly hasn't been living here."

Beau pulled his keys from his pocket and twirled them. "No idea whatever happened to her." He headed for his truck but said over his shoulder, "Best leave things alone, Miss Grace. Digging where you don't belong just brings up dead bones. Now get yourself some food and a good night's sleep." He slid into his truck, slammed the door, and kicked over the engine.

He pulled out without a look back, but Grace stood there until his taillights turned the corner. "Dead bones, my backside. You know, old man. You know."

Chapter Eighteen

The house felt hot and sticky. Although the AC was working hard, the heat had been too much all day and Blaise had forgotten to turn it up when he left. Now he didn't feel like heating up Savannah's chicken in the oven. The microwave would have to do. Chewy chicken never hurt anyone.

Cash had said he was starving before he jumped into the shower to wash off a hard day's work. He wouldn't care what he ate. He had been smiling when he returned from Grace's house. Blaise thought for sure it would've been a bad day with Jud there or Cash would've caved under the heat or the workload, but that didn't seem to be the case. He was glad. Maybe tonight could be the conversation he'd been putting off.

Was Cash relieved they hadn't talked about the fire? Or was he wondering why his father hadn't brought it up? It might be better if he didn't realize his father was too afraid to bring it up, fearing he'd screw up that conversation the way he'd screwed up so many other things. He wasn't just a lousy father, he trusted the wrong person with his finances, he married the wrong woman, and he didn't have the courage to leave his dying band and start a new one. The only thing he had done right was buy his parents' house.

"Dad, have you seen Grandpa's lighter?" Cash stood in the kitchen doorway with a smile on his face

Stacey Wilk

instead of the permanent scowl. His hair was still wet, and his face was scrubbed clean of that makeup, but he needed a shave. He had shoved one earbud in and left the other dangling over the top of his ear.

"No, and why do you need that old thing anyway?" Was he being overprotective, worrying that his son who set a foundation on fire kept a lighter as a keepsake?

"It's all I've got left from him."

"We'll try and find you something else."

Cash stood at the island. "Paper plates?" He held the plates up in each hand.

"I forgot to run the dishwasher." He wasn't used to all the house chores with a kid around. Cash was ten when Melissa packed up their stuff and moved out while Blaise was on tour. She left him a note and a few pieces of furniture. He'd been so angry she took his son he punched a hole in the wall and broke his hand hitting a beam. Acting before thinking. Like always.

"How was demo day?" He spooned chicken and orzo onto paper plates. He handed one to Cash, and they settled in around the table.

"What?"

"Could you take out that earbud, please?"

Cash rolled his eyes but did as he was told.

"I asked you how demo went today."

"Fine." Cash shoveled food into his mouth.

Blaise pushed his food around, watching orzo juice soak spots into the paper plates. He opened his mouth, but shut it again. Would it be so bad to have a decent dinner without the tension or arguing that would certainly come up once he said the word *fire*?

"You're drumming." Cash picked his head up, fork halfway to his mouth, and stared at Blaise.

"What?"

"You're drumming your fingers on the table. You do it when you're thinking about something."

Blaise stared at his hands, one still in a brace. "I didn't realize."

"You never do." Cash went back to his food.

He didn't realize Cash paid so much attention. He was right. Blaise did drum his fingers on any surface when he was thinking about something or nothing at all. It filled space in his brain. He was stalling. "Cash, we need to talk." He pushed his plate away.

Cash looked up at him and dropped his fork. He leaned back in the chair and crossed his arms over his chest. Blaise cleared his throat.

"You're sending me back, right?"

"What? No. Why would you think that?" Things weren't perfect, but they were managing. If Cash could notice the constant drumming, why didn't he notice when Blaise went to talk Beau into giving him a job? Or the food shopping Blaise did every few days because Cash was a human vacuum.

"Uncle Colton got the dates, didn't he? And now you want to get back on the road, so I have to go back home." Cash shoved back his chair and started to get up.

"Wait. Sit." Blaise pointed to the seat, and Cash dropped down. "I don't want you to go anywhere." He wasn't sure what the right thing to say was. He didn't want to say too much and scare Cash away, and he didn't want to say too little. "I like having you here with me. Do you like being here?"

He shouldn't have asked such a dangerous question. What was he going to do when Cash said he didn't like living with Blaise in the modest home in a small town? He probably didn't want to go home and do the community service where everyone would see him. And he probably missed the faster-paced life he normally lived with Melissa.

Cash pulled his dish over and stabbed at his food. He kept his eyes on the chicken. "Yeah, I like it here. It's better than Beverly Crest."

"It is? Why?" He wished Cash would look at him, but he leaned back and waited for his son to explain.

Cash took a few bites, shrugged. "Back home the other kids only liked me because I'm a Savage."

"That can't be true." It was true for him. He never really knew who liked him for himself and who only wanted to hang around a celebrity. As things for the band started to die out, there were fewer and fewer people around. Blaise couldn't offer them much any longer, and they were on to the newest piece of meat. Wasn't that part of the reason Melissa left him?

"Yeah, it's true." Cash finally looked up. "I don't have a lot of friends. Actually, I only had one friend, but that's changed now too."

A little pang hit Blaise's heart. His fingers drummed on his chest. "I'm sure you have more than one friend."

"No, Dad, I don't. I'm a loser with no friends. You want to know why?"

He was a little afraid to hear what was coming next. "Sure. Tell me."

Cash threw his plate in the garbage and leaned against the counter. "I hate fake people. Kids at school would always come up to me and ask me if you or Uncle Colton were my dad, and I'd say yes or he was my uncle or whatever. And then they'd be high-fiving me in the halls and wanting to text me or game with me. At first I thought it was cool I was making friends, but I didn't realize why."

"I'm sure a lot of those kids liked you for you."

"No, they liked me for you. They'd ask if I could get any of your tour stuff so they could sell it. They'd want to know if you knew other musicians they liked and wanted to meet. Or if you had an agent I could hook them up with because they had a band and wanted a record deal."

"Kids can be cruel." Blaise moved around the kitchen, cleaning up dinner, hoping Cash would continue.

"Mom never misses a chance to tell someone she was married to you or I'm your son. She likes to get reservations at restaurants no one else can get into. Or tickets to shows or whatever other stupid things she does. I told her to leave me out of it. If she wants to exploit being a Savage, that's on her."

Blaise wished Melissa had kept her name-dropping away from their son. "Your mom is a good parent."

Cash waved his hand in the air. "Yeah, sometimes. I mean, she loves me and all. I know that. She doesn't want me to screw up my life. She's always telling me to get good grades and be responsible, but she likes the spotlight a lot. She told me she'd never remarry because she wouldn't want to give up your last name."

That sounded like Melissa. When they were married, she was always pushing him to use his name to get them into the fancy clubs, and when he wouldn't, she would get mad and throw a fit if anyone didn't know who they were. And then she'd have the nerve to

143

complain he was never home and always on the road and not giving her enough attention. Cash was the only good thing that came out of that relationship.

"Have you had any girlfriends?" That should be information a father had about his son, and the guilt climbed into his chest for not knowing.

"Nah. I would've told you that."

Blaise let a smile tug at his lips. "You're a good-looking kid. There has to be someone."

"I was never interested in getting involved. I didn't trust that they liked me for me." Cash plopped back down in the chair and downed the rest of his soda. "That's why I like it here in Heritage River. No one cares who we are. They knew you before you were famous, and they knew Grandpa and Grandma. We're just regular people in this town, and that's what I want to be. I don't want to go back."

He let Cash's last words sink in. His son wanted to stay. He might want the anonymity Heritage River offered more than he wanted to spend time with him, but Blaise could live with that. At least Cash wasn't off and running from him. Maybe in time they could be close.

"Well, you still have to finish the community service hours, and now Beau is depending on you. Plus, school doesn't start until after Labor Day. You'll have plenty to keep you busy through your summer stay."

"No, I mean I don't want to go back ever. Mom doesn't know this, but I unenrolled myself from school."

Melissa was going to freak out. She wanted Cash in school, and honestly, so did Blaise. If Cash didn't want to follow in his footsteps, he'd need a backup plan. "How did you manage to cancel your registration?"

"I called and said I was you since I'm not eighteen until September. I could do it myself then, but I didn't want to wait. The rest was all through email."

"Was there a deposit given?"

Cash smirked. "Yeah, they're mailing the refund here. It's your money anyway."

That was true. Melissa did voice-over work, and that came in spurts. She'd been living off Blaise's money since the moment she said *I do*. "I don't mind that you said you were me, and I admire your creativity, but you can't go around lying to get out of something you don't want to do." Was that the right kind of fatherly thing to say?

"I was hoping I could go to the community college here and stay with you." Cash looked away again.

"Listen, Cash, I'm glad you want to stay, and you can go to school here, but you need to know I will have to go back on tour when the time comes." It was Blaise's turn to look away. "I need the money."

He explained to Cash about the bad investor and the loss of funds. He told how he was trying to sell his car and how he sold his house in Nashville. "I had to remortgage this house. If I don't hit the road, I'll have to see if Beau can hire me too."

"I understand. I won't burn the house down."

Cash handed him the opening to the much-needed conversation. Blaise sat in the chair opposite Cash and looked him in the eye. "Why'd you do it?"

Cash stared at his hands. "It was stupid. I knew it the minute I lit the match, but it was too late then. Tim had dared me. He kept calling me chicken when I wouldn't do it. He was the only friend I had. The only person who liked me for me. I was wrong. He said he'd read a story about you and Uncle Colton when you were young and touring in bars and how you'd set the bar on fire because you were so drunk. Tim laughed and said that it had to be cool to have a father like that."

"Cash, that story—"

"I know. That's not the true story. But I was mad because I thought you didn't factor into my friendship and you had all along. Tim liked me because he thought I'd be just like you, and when he thought I wasn't like that, he said things. I just wanted to be liked. I wanted to show him I could be cool. I don't know what I was thinking. I guess I wasn't thinking at all. So I did it." Cash swiped at his face with the heel of his hand.

Blaise didn't know what to say. He never thought about how it must feel to be his son. His mother had had some fame, but being in an orchestra wasn't the same as being in a country-rock band whose music played on radio stations everywhere. And he and Colton and Savannah had grown up in the safety of Heritage River, where everyone knew them and his father was the music teacher.

He patted Cash on the shoulder. "I'd be really glad if you'd stay with me." He wanted to hug Cash, but he wasn't sure if he should. Did Cash want the affection, or would he push it away?

Cash stood and tossed his soda can in the recycle basket under the sink. "Thanks. Can we ask Mom to send my stuff?"

He had no idea how he was going to tell Melissa that Cash wanted to live with him, but he'd figure something out. "I'll call her later."

"I think I'm going to hang in my room. I'm tired after all the work today." He headed out of the kitchen.

"Hey, Cash, I had an idea."

Cash turned and smiled. "You're not going to climb on any more scaffolding, are you?"

"Funny. Would you like to play in Aunt Savannah's fundraiser with me?"

Cash opened his mouth, then shut it. Blaise's heart sank. "It's okay, don't worry, bad idea." He grabbed the serving forks and shoved them in the dishwasher.

Cash placed a hand on his shoulder, and Blaise turned. "Can I think about it?"

At least it wasn't no.

Chapter Nineteen

Grace gave a final wipe to the toilet and sink in the master's attached bath. Her legs ached, and she had a stitch in her back. She certainly didn't hold up as well as she used to, and by tomorrow every muscle would ache, even the ones in her toes. But it would be a good ache from a hard day's work.

A hot shower might do the trick, and then she would crawl onto her air mattress and get some sleep. Chloe had taken the second bedroom and shut herself behind the door right after they ate pizza on the front porch. Grace was thankful for the quiet. Tomorrow would be a long day too. Not only would they be starting the process to put the rooms back together, but she was going in search of Nancy Templeton. Someone had to know what happened to that woman.

She wiped the steam from the mirror and dried her hair with a towel. She didn't think she had the energy to hold a blow dryer to it. Her hair would be a tangled mess in the morning if she went to bed with wet curls, but within five minutes she'd be covered in dust again. Did it really matter? She checked to make sure the front door and the sliding doors out to the backyard were locked. She almost sighed with the thought of pulling a blanket up around her shoulders and closing her eyes.

Someone banged on the front door. She jumped. At this hour? Did Beau forget something or have an order he needed to give? The lights in the front room had been torn out, and the one on the porch still didn't work. She went for her flashlight in her purse, but the banging continued. Almost insistent. Urgent.

The top of a head appeared in the door's window. That height and that much banging must be a male. She opened the door a crack, using it as a shield in case she had to slam it shut on the pounder.

"I'm sorry to bother you so late, but I need some help and I don't know who else to ask." Blaise stood in the darkness of her porch. He ran his hands through his hair. He wore a T-shirt and basketball shorts. He had nothing on his feet.

She came out from behind the door now that she could identify the person on her porch and be fairly certain it wasn't a serial killer. "What's the matter?" He honestly couldn't find another person in this town willing to help him? Was this some creative come-on?

"Cash is throwing up, and he won't stop. What do I do?" He turned back toward his house, as if he expected Cash to appear on the lawn.

"Take him to the emergency room? You do have one of those in this town, don't you?"

"I thought of that. He refuses to go. And I already called my sister, but she's not home and not answering her cell. She's probably turned her phone off. I also can't reach her husband. I really don't want to think about what they might be doing at this hour." He forced a half smile onto his face.

"How long has it been going on for?"

"Um, maybe an hour. He stops and starts."

"I guess he doesn't get sick often if you're not sure what to do with him. Chloe used to throw up all the

149

time. It might just be a bug or something he ate. If he's still at in the morning, call the doctor."

"He doesn't have a doctor in town."

"You mean the doctor in Heritage River doesn't make house calls?" She pulled her mouth in an *O* and fanned her fingers in front of her face.

"What do you think this place is? *Little House on the Prairie*?"

"You watched that show?"

"My sister liked it. Can you help us, or do I have to watch my kid get sick all night?"

"I can't make him stop, if that's what you're asking. But I can come over and try to make him more comfortable. If it's a virus, it has to run its course. You just don't want him to dehydrate."

He raked his hands through his hair again. "How do I do that?"

"Are you new to this parenting thing?" Grace chuckled to show she was kidding, but Blaise stared back with a straight face. "Really?"

"He lives with his mother in California. He's staying with me for the summer. I've never been with him when he got sick. My ex always took care of him. I don't know what to do."

She pressed her lips together. "Where is this mother of his?" Not that she didn't want to help.

"The last thing I wanted was to admit to her I didn't know what to do, but helping him is more important than my ego. I tried to reach her too, but no luck."

"Let me just tell Chloe I'm leaving." She returned as quickly as she could and followed him across the lawn.

The night air was thick. Sweat began to form on her neck before she got to Blaise's porch. Lightning bugs chased each other around trees. Cicadas sang their lullabies.

He let her into his home.

The place smelled like pine and lemon. Clean. His house was similar to hers. They walked into a living room. He had leather sofas facing the fireplace and a large television hanging above it. The dining area sat behind it, filled with a table for six. She guessed the kitchen was to the left, whereas in her house, the kitchen was to the right.

"He's this way." Blaise led her down a long hallway.

She stopped short of the closed door. "I doubt your son wants a perfect stranger in his room at a time like this. Why don't you check on him, and I'll wait here?"

He raked his hand through his hair again. "Good point." He slowly turned the knob and pushed the door open.

Grace leaned against the wall to wait. Pictures hung along the opposite wall, all black and whites framed in different sizes. Three children in various moments of their lives—running under a sprinkler, roasting marshmallows, and carving a pumpkin—smiled for the camera. Those same three were posed on the front porch of what looked like this very house. More pictures of a couple who looked at each other with love hung on the wall too. The man always seemed to have a violin in his hand. She took a step closer.

"Those are my parents." Blaise closed the door with a click.

She stepped back. "These are lovely pictures. Whoever took them had a good eye."

"Mostly, my father took them. I'm not completely sure who took the ones with him in them, though."

He stood beside her, taking in the pictures too. He smelled of soap. Also clean. She could feel his heat against her arm, and she stepped away. "How is Cash doing?"

"He was asleep, so I didn't want to bother him. Now what happens?"

The hallway felt tight with the two of them standing there. She turned toward the front of the house. "Maybe we should move so we don't wake him."

He followed. "Do you want to sit?" He pointed to the sofa with his bad hand. He never did tell her what happened to him.

"Uh, okay. The first thing I would do is make sure you have some ginger ale and crackers in the house. Besides keeping an eye on him to make sure he's done, you know."

"Yeah. I hope so." Blaise plopped down on the opposite end of the sofa and tapped on his legs with his fingers.

"What if he isn't done?"

"Really, Blaise, there isn't much you can do for him. But if it's still going on in the morning, I would call a doctor or take him to the ER. They can give him something to make it stop."

He popped up. "Would you like something to drink? I'm sorry I didn't offer before, but I could really use something."

His sudden need to move surprised her. "No, thank

you. I'm fine."

"Do you drink tea? You look like a tea drinker," he said over his shoulder on the way to the kitchen.

What was that supposed to mean? "What does a tea drinker look like?"

He returned with two glasses of iced tea and handed one to her. She searched for a coaster but didn't see one. "Can I put this down on your table?"

"That's what it's there for."

She held the glass, not wanting to leave a ring on his table. It looked as if it might've been made from a refurbished barn door. He had good taste. She figured she'd find an old brown couch held together with duct tape, a table standing on three legs, and the place reeking of smoke and beer. Not that she had ever seen him smoking.

He plopped back down. "No offense about the tea-drinker thing. It's just you don't strike me as someone who throws back a scotch at the end of the day. You're more of a 'pour your beer in a glass' gal."

She made a face. "I don't drink scotch."

He laughed. "I told you."

His laugh was full and filled the room. His eyes crinkled up, and the gray in them twinkled. He stretched out his long toned legs. His belly was flat behind that T-shirt, and his shoulders broad. His hands were muscular from all the years of playing the drums, though his fingers were calloused. She could see why women would fall for him. He was easy on the eyes, and the famous drummer thing was exciting.

"Okay, so if Cash keeps throwing up, I need to call the doctor or take him to the hospital?"

"Right."

"And if he stops? Is he out of the woods?"

"The worst is over, then. That's why I mentioned the ginger ale and crackers. That's about all he can eat tomorrow. If he insists he's hungry, then go to toast with jelly."

"Toast with jelly?"

"A baked potato with no butter would be okay, but not the first thing he eats. If you don't have ginger ale, I guess a Coke will do."

"Maybe I should write this down." He popped up again and ran back to the kitchen. She could hear him rummaging in drawers. He returned with a small piece of paper and a pencil and jotted down what she told him.

"I'm not sure if you thought of this, but you'll want to clean the bathroom so you don't catch whatever he has. If you have your own bathroom, it can wait until the morning, I guess." Though if it were her house, she'd be in there scrubbing as soon as she could. "I'd toss his toothbrush too."

"Toss his toothbrush?"

"Well, I like to be careful and don't want to give the germs any reason to spread." She looked into her drink. Larry always complained about her obsessive cleaning.

"If you say so, the toothbrush goes. You're the expert."

She looked back at him, and he was smiling at her. He wasn't wrinkling up his face as if she'd asked him for one too many favors or rolling his eyes as if she didn't know what she was talking about. He didn't say she worried too much about things that didn't matter, like throwing away a toothbrush.

154

Blaise tapped his fingers against his shin crossed over his thigh to a beat only he could hear. He glanced down the hallway and back at her, then back toward the hall again. His fingers never slowed.

"Do you always do that?"

"Do what?"

"That." She pointed to his hands, still playing a tune against his legs.

His eyes widened, as if seeing his hands for the first time, and he laughed. "Yes, ma'am, I always do." He exaggerated his southern accent, and she wondered if he worked hard to keep it quiet. "I drove my teachers crazy." He glanced down the hall again. "I never want to see my kid that sick again."

"You feel helpless when your child isn't well." She ran her finger around the rim of the glass. This man wasn't what she expected. He cared about his son in such an honest and open way. Larry always held his emotions for Chloe in check, as if it wasn't manly to express that kind of love. Or any kind of love, for that matter.

"You haven't touched your tea. Don't worry. It's low calorie. Not as low as that lettuce you like to eat, but close." He winked.

"Salad is good for you. You should try it sometime." She smiled at him. The conversation was easy, and she liked his innocent teasing.

He patted his stomach. "I like my meat and potatoes. Lettuce is rabbit food. Besides, I can't eat a salad and go on stage. I need real food, or I'll pass out. Low blood sugar, you know." But he winked again.

Laughter bubbled inside her. She liked the feeling of its effervescence on her lips. Every conversation with Larry had been serious, a constant list of things to do. Blaise reminded her what fun could be. She shook her head. She didn't want thoughts of Larry with her here. Here, at this late hour in a stranger's house, she could try to be the new Grace. Maybe it was too soon?

She hesitated to put the glass down and ruin the table. "I really should be getting back." She hitched her thumb over her shoulder. "He hasn't come back out. Maybe he's done."

"Could you stay a little longer just to be sure? I hate to ask, it's late and all, but if he starts up again…" He let his words drop off.

It was late, and her eyelids were growing heavy. The only thing she could do for Cash or Blaise was call an ambulance, but that didn't seem necessary. Cash was in his room probably getting the much-needed sleep that comes from retching repeatedly. Blaise stared at her, his fingers still drumming on his legs. He hadn't touched his tea either.

She leaned back against the cool leather sofa. "Okay, a little longer."

"Thank you." His voice was filled with a huskiness not there before.

He took his tea, and she decided to try it too. The sweet cold drink felt good against her now-dry throat.

"How are the renovations coming?" he asked.

"Dad." Cash stood in the entryway. Dark circles threw shadows under his eyes, and his face was the color of dirty dishwater. His chest was bare, and his shorts a wrinkled mess.

Blaise jumped from his spot and ran to Cash. He placed a hand on his shoulder. "You okay?"

"I think so. Can I have a drink?"

Blaise turned to Grace. His mouth formed an open circle. "I only have milk, iced tea, and water."

She picked up Blaise's glass. A tiny, wet ring left its mark on the pretty wood table. "Hang on a second." She went into the kitchen to deposit the glasses on the counter. Dishes were piled in the sink, but other than that, things seemed in order.

"Grace is here?" Cash's words were strangled.

"She's here to help."

She heard them talking and knew Cash was probably embarrassed by her presence. Chloe certainly would've been. She didn't want to make it worse for him. Hoping to keep things quick, she returned to the bedroom. "Why don't I run out to a supermarket or something that's open twenty-four hours and get you what you need. How far out of town do I have to go?"

"Thanks, but I'll do it. It's easier. I know where to go."

"You're going to leave me alone? What if I start throwing up again?"

She shook her head, and her smile widened. No matter what age teens were and no matter how much they fought to be treated like adults, on the inside they were still young and needed their parents.

"Grace, will you stay?" Blaise said.

Cash glared at him, but Blaise didn't notice. He didn't realize his son didn't want her around. Chloe would have barked like a rabid dog at the idea of Blaise hanging with her at a time like this.

"I'm happy to stay if Cash is okay with that, but it might be better if I run out. Really, Blaise. I don't mind."

Blaise turned to Cash. "What can I get for you?"

157

"Something to drink. Can I have water?"

Blaise turned to Grace and raised his eyebrows. "Do you have ice cubes? He can suck on those until I get back."

Cash threw up his hands. "What's the difference? They're both water." He stormed into his room and slammed the door.

"That's a good sign. He'll be fine. How far do I have to go?"

Blaise gave her directions to a twenty-four supermarket outside of town. She spent thirty minutes driving there because she took a wrong turn twice. Her knuckles were white by the time she pulled into the parking lot, but she'd made it. She wasn't tired any longer.

"What kind of town doesn't have a twenty-four-hour drugstore?" She pushed herself out of the car. "People get sick in the middle of the night."

She returned to Blaise's faster than it took to get to the store—this time she only made one wrong turn—and with everything he'd need for Cash for the next day. She pulled in a deep, satisfied breath.

Blaise stood at the sink loading the dishwasher. That might be the sexiest thing she'd ever seen. She quickly shook the thought away. She wouldn't entertain the idea of anything intimate with this man. He'd been with too many women. She'd never be able to get that idea out of her head.

She cleared her throat to let him know she was there and pulled crackers and soda from the bag. "I also bought waffles and syrup in case he gives you a huge fight about the toast and jelly. No butter." She pointed a finger at him, and he laughed.

Heat filled her cheeks. "I hope you don't mind, but I picked up some bleach cleaners and disinfectant wipes for the bathroom in case you didn't have any." She kept her gaze on the items as she pulled them from the bag. "Oh, and"—she held up a toothbrush—"you can never be too prepared."

He took the toothbrush, and their fingers grazed. Her heart fluttered; heat ran down her neck. This man was trouble. So much trouble.

"Thank you."

"You don't mind about the cleaning supplies?" It was a presumptuous thing to do. What made her think he didn't have things to clean his bathroom?

He smiled at her. "Why would I mind that?" He picked up the spray bottle of bleach cleaner, tossed it in the air, and caught it. "Thanks. It's the best gift ever. Better than the first drum set I ever got. I paid for that myself, so I guess that wasn't a gift, huh?"

"You're going to drop that, and there will be a big mess. You don't want to get bleach all over your wood floor."

"Do you ever take time off?" He placed the bleach on the counter, crossed his arms over his chest, and stared at her.

She held his gaze, though she wanted to look away. "Time off from what?"

"From all the rules."

"What rules?" She wasn't following. Heat climbed back into her cheeks, but this time she was certain he was making fun of her. People told her over and over she had too many rules. Too stuffy. Be more flexible. She had forgotten how to let loose, to let go. Letting go was dangerous, or at the very least chaotic.

"What do you do for fun?" His lip twitched as if he was holding back a chuckle.

Her chin went up, and she planted her hands on her hips. "I do lots of things for fun. I'm not sure what this has to do with anything." She reached for her purse. "Cash will be fine. I'm going home." That last word bit her tongue, and she sucked in a breath. *Home? The Disaster House?*

Blaise stepped closer. She could smell his clean scent, feel the warmth rolling off him. She tried to step back but collided with the kitchen chair. She grabbed it to steady herself.

He smiled down at her, the twinkle present in his dark eyes. "How much do I owe you for the groceries?"

The words dried out in her throat. Why was his presence unhinging her? She smoothed her shirt down. "It's fine. I just hope Cash feels better tomorrow."

"I can't let you pay for all that stuff. I dragged you out of your house, and you drove out of town for my son. How much?"

"Really, it's fine. I don't want your money." What kind of a person would she be if she took his money when all she bought was a couple of things? The poor boy was sick and without his mother. Grace corrected herself. It didn't matter that his mother wasn't there. Blaise was with Cash, and Blaise was enough. She knew better than anyone you could get by without a mother, even if your mother was present and accounted for.

"Thanks again for coming over. I think I overreacted." He kept her pinned against the chair. In order to slip away, she'd have to push him back, but she didn't trust her hands to handle the job.

"Common for the first time. The first time Chloe was… I really need to be going. It's late. Big day tomorrow." She had no reason to explain about the first time Chloe had a stomach bug. She didn't trust the words in her mouth anyway.

"You never answered my question."

"What question was that?" Her brain had stopped working. She couldn't remember what he asked. She focused on keeping her gaze off his full lips and glanced at the tiny water stain in the corner of the ceiling above his head.

He tucked a hair behind her ear, sending electric current down her spine. Why was her body responding this way? She hardly knew Blaise. Larry never roused a fiery desire in her. What she did know, aside from him being a caring father, she didn't really like. His charm or the clean scent or the way he loaded the dishwasher was throwing her off balance. It had to be.

"What do you like to do for fun?"

"Um, I don't know. Lots of things, I guess. I really need to be going." Her voice climbed a few octaves, and she willed her hand to push him back. He stepped away, and the scorched air between them disappeared, leaving a cool breeze on her skin.

"Would you like to have dinner with me tomorrow night? I know a place you might like." His words followed her out of the kitchen and into the dining area. "It'll be fun."

He had to say that. The one thing that got her thinking. When was the last time she had any fun? She couldn't remember, and Larry had always been accusing her of not being any fun. She hated him for that. She'd gotten so wrapped up in taking care of their home and their daughter she pushed aside all that she had wanted to be. And she thrived under a schedule. Order made sense to her. She could count on it unlike anything else in her life. Now she was staring at a very handsome man whose whole life screamed disorder, didn't it? A music man would suffocate under all her plans and calculated risks. Larry was an engineer, and she had strangled the life out of their relationship, hadn't she?

"You can't eat in that house," he said.

"I have Chloe. I can't leave her."

"She can eat here with Cash. Or they can come if they want."

"I'm not sure Cash will feel up to the company or the food."

"Let's worry about that tomorrow. It's only dinner. I know you said you'd never let me buy you dinner, but I'm hoping you'll make an exception. Think of it as reimbursement for the groceries."

Her face and neck sizzled. She pressed a hand to her cheek, hoping to keep the red blotches of embarrassment from growing full bloom. He remembered her dreadful comment.

He was right about the state of the house. How would they eat? She figured takeout or something. But dinner with Blaise? What would they have to talk about? They were so different. Of course, if she did go, she'd have something interesting to tell Jenn the next time they spoke. Jenn would definitely scream like a crazed fan. But that wasn't the right reason to go to dinner with a man.

"Are you going to make me wait all night for an answer?"

She looked in the direction of her house. Wasn't the reason she came down here so she could be different than she was before? Wasn't she looking for a second chance to create herself?

"Okay. Thank you. Chloe and I will accept the invitation." She wasn't ready to throw caution completely away. If Chloe didn't agree to come along, then Grace would cancel the date. Not a date. An invitation. She wanted to smack herself.

"It will be fun. I promise." He winked.

That's what she was afraid of.

Chapter Twenty

Did he really ask her to dinner? Blaise ran a hand through his hair and scratched the back of his neck. Maybe he shouldn't have brought up the joke about her not wanting him to buy her dinner. Sure, she was beautiful, and when she was only inches from him, it was all he could do not to pull her to him and devour those lips. *Devour?* Was he using words like *devour* now when it came to women? No, not women. This woman.

He went back to the sink, shoved his good hand under the scalding water, and without soaking his brace, tried to wash what dishes wouldn't fit in the dishwasher.

His phone vibrated on the counter next to him. Only one person would be calling at this hour.

He wiped his hands on a dishtowel. "What's up?" He didn't mean to bark at his brother. Grace had gotten under his skin, and he was worn out from Cash being sick and the stress of not knowing what to do. The muscles in his shoulders had turned to stone. What he really wanted to do was climb into bed and shut his dry eyes. He should've thought about that instead of burning his hand in hot water. Did it really matter if the damn dishes were clean? But he saw the way Grace took in his place, as if surveying him, and he didn't miss the way she took his glass into the kitchen.

"I was calling to see how your neighbor is doing."

Did the man have a sixth sense? Did he know Grace was here? Blaise looked around to make sure Colton hadn't walked in while he wasn't paying attention. "What do you really want?" He checked the driveway just to make sure.

"I can't sleep, and you're the only person I can call at this hour who won't hang up on me."

"I'm not reading your ass a bedtime story." He turned out the lights in the kitchen.

"I was hoping you'd sing to me."

"Bite me." His fingers found the lamp switch and turned it, throwing the living room into darkness. He flopped onto the couch and rubbed his eyes. He heard rustling on the other end of the line.

"Listen, we're still finalizing dates, and until we hit the road, I've got nothing going on out here. I thought I'd come back to Heritage River and hang with you and Cash for a while. Do some Savage-men bonding."

"You'll get bored in a day."

"Do I really have to ask my kid brother to stay in the house I grew up in?"

"You do now that I own it."

"I'll even listen to your stupid song."

The last thing Blaise wanted was for Colton to come out and stay. He and Cash were just starting to get along. Colton would worm his way in between that. "What was the video Cash sent you?"

"What?"

"You heard me. Cash sent you a video. Of what?"

"Blaise, it's no big deal, really."

"Tell me."

Colton let out a sigh. "He played in some open mic

thing. Just him, strumming a twenty-five-dollar ukulele. Pop-punk music. He's good."

Of course his son was a good musician. He had no doubt, but hearing Cash had shared something like that with Colton and not him made his insides feel like a broken drumstick. Colton was still getting the best of Cash.

"I'm sorry, man. I shouldn't have mentioned it at Savannah's that night. I slipped. I knew it would hurt you," Colton said.

"I'm fine." He didn't want to talk about it. "When were you thinking about coming out here?"

"Tomorrow night. I can get a plane out in the morning. Be there by afternoon. Maybe we can get some fishing going at the lake."

"You must be desperate for something to do. Okay, come. I'm telling you. You're going to be bored. Cash is working and volunteering at the library. I'm just hanging around."

"Yeah, I know. With your stupid garden."

"When Savannah finds out you're back, she's going to try and make you play her fundraiser."

"We'll be on the road by then."

Blaise hoped not. He didn't want to let his sister down, and he didn't want to leave Cash too soon. Not now that things were getting better between them. And could he really leave his kid for six months? Blaise scratched at his hand in the brace. He glanced in the direction of Grace's house. He couldn't see it, but he wondered if she had gone to sleep. He was grateful for her rushing over to help earlier. She wasn't so uptight after all, and she was clearly not impressed with his waning celebrity status. He wanted to get to know her better. The Grace hidden under that need for control.

"Did you sell that car yet?"

Colton's voice brought him back to his dark living room. He was too tired for a conversation about money. "I'm going to bed. See you tomorrow." He pushed off the couch. His knees popped and crackled.

"I'm guessing that's a no, then?"

"Goodnight, Colton."

He carefully turned the knob on Cash's door. When he looked in, Cash was sprawled out on his stomach. The sheets were tied up around his legs. The room smelled of sweat. Cash snored lightly but didn't move when Blaise stepped in.

How did the years go by so quickly? How had he missed the most important moments in this boy's life? Would Cash ever forgive him? Blaise thought about that video and hoped he could.

Would he make all the same choices if he had the chance? Probably. He never thought things through. He didn't plan. He certainly hadn't planned on being a father. But now with gray hairs sprinkled throughout his head and wrinkles around his eyes, he couldn't imagine not having Cash. He wanted a chance to enjoy this time with his son. Jam together. Give him advice on women. The road wasn't calling Blaise as it had in the past. He was ready to leave her behind.

He stepped back into the hall and closed the door behind him. He shuffled down to his room and pulled back the covers on the bed. The sheets cooled his warm skin, but he tossed and turned, trying to find a cozy spot.

He might be ready to leave the road, but she had her hooks in him. She was a drug you couldn't kick, the provider of his life. The life he wanted to give to his son. Without her how would he survive? He was too old to start over. Who would buy the songs of a worn-out southern rock star?

He thought of the woman next door. "Grace," he said. She had made something warm up inside his belly. He hadn't desired a woman that way in a long time. He liked the idea of her under him, wrapped around him. Messing up his sheets. Messing up his life.

Colton didn't want to come just to stay with him and Cash. No, Colton wanted to see Grace again. Blaise was sure of it. It was like that time in high school when Jeanine Paris, the lead in the high school musical, the girl with the gold hair, had Blaise turned around in circles. He sputtered and stuttered like an old car engine around her. They liked the same music. He had made her a tape of her favorite songs. But Colton saw her and moved in. He flashed his smile and spread his charm around her. Charm that Blaise, two years younger, didn't have. Jeanine Paris forgot all about Blaise Savage, the wild-haired, skinny, impulsive drummer who sang out of key.

Blaise wouldn't let a girl come between him and his brother. He had let Colton have Jeanine. This time it would be different. He wasn't planning on giving up without a fight.

And it would start tomorrow night when he took Grace to dinner. He finally stopped tossing around and settled in. He closed his eyes, and sleep hit him like a mallet.

Chapter Twenty-One

The early morning sun poked through the trees and spilled through the windows of the kitchen. Grace made tea in the microwave relocated to the spare bedroom. This room would make a nice office. She pictured cream walls and a wool area rug in the center over walnut floors. Burlap drapes on the windows and a tall plant in the corner. But the new owners would choose the decorations. She would leave them the bare bones.

She took her tea and went outside. She was starting to like the front porch. It was quickly becoming her favorite spot in the house. Probably because it wasn't stripped down to nothing or completely covered in Sheetrock dust. She passed the plastic chair, the only place to sit for now, and bounded down the steps, trying to ignore Blaise's house.

Debris peppered the front lawn. Paper had blown into the bushes. Jud hadn't done a very good job of making sure everything went into the dumpster. Was that deliberate defiance? With her tea in one hand, she moved around the lawn, throwing garbage away.

The idea of dinner with Blaise had kept her awake all night. She'd tried to tell herself it was only dinner. Not a proposition. He was just being neighborly. Isn't that what southern folk did? But there was nothing neighborly about the way he stood so close to her or the way he touched her hair. No, that was a skilled romancer, and the skilled romancer scared the pants off her. *Oh, Lord. Bad pun.* She groaned and kept her gaze on the lawn.

She should just tell him no. She and Chloe could grab dinner at Jake's. But if she went, she could redeem herself for that awful no-dinner comment. Every time she thought of it or the way his eyes twinkled last night when he reminded her made her cheeks burn again. If she didn't know better, she'd think she was having a hot flash. Did he want to see her getting hot? She covered her face with her hand. What had she gotten herself into?

Caught in the branches of the spirea, she found receipts faded from the years, a pink sales slip for a refrigerator, and a letter from an assisted living. She stopped. *Assisted living?* The hairs on her arms stood up.

The letter was addressed to Nancy Templeton, welcoming her to Shadow Lawn Assisted Living. It was a standard form letter, but at the bottom, someone had handwritten a message:

"Looking forward to your arrival on March 29."

Based on the date of the letter, that was ten years ago. The house sat empty for ten years? No wonder it looked the way it did. And who had looked forward to Nancy's arrival at a place most went into and never came out?

The growling of an engine rolled toward her. Beau's faded red truck turned into her driveway. Jud slouched in the passenger's seat, head tilted back as if he might be asleep. Grace shoved the letter in her back pocket and threw the rest of the papers in the dumpster.

"They're back." Chloe stood on the porch, a mug

in her hand and a smile on her face. She had twisted her hair into a knot on the top of her head. She wore a blue T-shirt and gray sweat shorts that barely covered parts better left clothed. Her feet were bare and toes polished lime green. The nose piercing twinkled in the morning sun. Grace swore that thing mocked her.

"Go put on different shorts." Grace tried to swat her away, but Chloe bounced down the steps.

"Why? I just got these." Chloe stood beside her and watched as the men peeled themselves from the truck. "I don't have to help today, do I?"

"What else were you planning on doing?" The tension began to weave its way into her shoulders.

"I don't know. Get some sun, maybe. Walk into town and see about some kind of a job." Chloe pulled her phone from the pocket of her shorty shorts. How could shorts that size even have a pocket?

"There's plenty to do right here. You can pitch in and help Beau. That will be job enough."

"Mom, I didn't come down here to do hard labor."

"Too bad. That's what you're doing." Grace glided forward. "Good morning, Beau, Jud."

Jud offered a head nod as he pulled tools and lumber from the back of Beau's truck. *A little acknowledgement might've been nice.*

"Morning, Miss Grace." Beau saluted her with his coffee. "We're going to get started putting those two rooms back together today. I hope everyone is ready to work hard." He looked around. "Where's Cash? That boy better not plan on being late."

"He was sick last night. Stomach bug. I'm not sure he'll be up for work today." No sooner had she said that than Cash dragged himself across the lawn. The circles were still under his eyes, but his coloring had gone from dishwater gray to parchment.

She met Cash halfway before Beau could say anything else to him. "How are you feeling?"

"Lousy, but I can work."

Beau was on them in a flash. "You're going to do no such thing. Look at ya, boy. You're in no shape to work, and I don't want you getting hurt. My word is final. March yourself back in the house. You come back to work tomorrow." He turned on his heel and stomped away.

"I agree with him." Grace patted Cash's shoulder. "Go inside. Take it easy today. There will still be plenty to do tomorrow." They were already behind schedule. At this point what difference did another day make? Just that she might be homeless, but hey.

"Miss Grace, let's get a move on." Beau waved her in from the porch.

"Go home." She shooed Cash back toward his house. She took a quick glance, but there was no sign of Blaise. She ran across her lawn and up the front steps. "Beau, you have to get started without me. I have an errand to run."

"Mom." Chloe's voice echoed in the barren room. "You can't leave me here."

Grace searched for her purse and car keys. "You'll be fine. Beau will tell you what to do. I'll be back as soon as I can."

"Where are you going?"

If Grace didn't know better, she'd swear Chloe sounded three again.

"Your momma said not to worry. First thing is go change into something more suitable for work. The whole neighborhood is going to get a show they didn't pay for with you dressed like that."

Chloe glared at Beau, and Grace bit her lip not to laugh. She wanted to kiss the man. Chloe spun on her heel and tramped down the hall. She accented her departure with the bang of her door. Beau shook his head and laughed.

"Do you have children?" She suddenly wanted to know because he handled Chloe better than she did.

"Wasn't in the plan. Now go and come back. We're already shorthanded."

She didn't waste another second, but she did glance back at Blaise's. Cash had gone inside, which she was glad for, yet a part of her hoped to see Blaise. The crazy part, she was sure, the part of her that was anticipating dinner later, but a part of her nonetheless.

She hit the brakes at the end of the road. She hadn't thought about what she was doing, and that realization stunned her. She didn't know where she was going and had no idea what she would do when she got there.

A car behind her beeped. She threw on the blinker and headed toward town. The library parking lot offered a spot to gather her thoughts and come up with a plan. She fished the letter from the assisted living place out of her back pocket and opened the windows to let in the morning warmth. It was going to be another hot one, but the heat relaxed her. She wished it were warm in Jersey year round. What was it like in Heritage River in the winter? Did it snow? Did the neighbors decorate their houses in white lights for Christmas?

Grace punched the address into the GPS. It would take her an hour to get where she was going. That wasn't terrible, and if the traffic was light, hopefully, not much longer than that. She could be there and back by lunchtime.

Whom had Nancy Templeton sold the house to? That's all she wanted to know. Simple. Easy. And that would be the end of it. Her curiosity satisfied. No one would have to know where she went, so there would be no violation of the sales agreement. She wanted to know who cared enough to gift her the house. Was it really so much to ask? She'd spent her life afraid to ask for help because it always came with a price tag, and now a total stranger had helped her in a way she could never have imagined. Why the anonymity? If Nancy Templeton refused to say or threatened to rat her out, that would be another story, one she would have to deal with when she got there.

Going to see Nancy was the most impulsive thing she'd done since agreeing to fix up the house. Two things in one summer. She was starting to feel like a new person.

She dropped the car into reverse. A car pulled in alongside her. The driver waved frantically. Grace squinted to get a better look through the glare against the glass.

"Grace." The woman jumped from her car. "I'm so glad you're here. I was just thinking about you and wanted some input on the fundraiser."

"Savannah." Grace let out a long sigh. If she didn't leave now, she'd never be back before lunch, and possibly the whole day would go by with just Beau and Jud working on the house. Chloe wouldn't be much help, no matter what Beau threatened her with. She plastered a smile on her face. "It's nice to see you."

Savannah dipped her head into the back seat of her

car and came out holding a folder. "What a morning. The sun's barely up, and I feel like I've put in a full day." She yanked her dark hair away from her face. "I need some input on the seating arrangements." She flipped through the pages in her folder. "We have to accommodate a stage and seating area, or we could make it standing room only and then I want to set up tables for people to eat at. This is what I was thinking." She handed Grace a diagram.

"Could I take this with me? I'm about to head to an appointment. Sorry."

Savannah looked up from her folder, and her eyes grew to the size of coffee mugs. "Oh, my. I didn't even realize. I'm so sorry. I've been running on all cylinders. I'm not thinking you might have somewhere to be. Please forgive me. Adam is always complaining about me doing that."

"It's not a problem. I will look this over and give you any ideas I have. Maybe tomorrow?" She hoped Savannah didn't ask her to meet later. She didn't want to explain about the dinner.

"Tomorrow's fine." Savannah looked back at the library, then at Grace. "You weren't coming to the library?" She checked her watch.

Heat filled Grace's cheeks. "Uh, no. I just pulled over to check directions."

"Where are you headed? I can probably give you some landmarks."

Her tongue tripped over the lie she was about to tell. She had to swallow hard to keep from spilling like an oil tanker on its side. "It wasn't really an appointment. Beau wants me to choose a countertop. I'm headed to the big stores to compare prices."

Savannah wrinkled up her nose. "Beau is letting you buy from a box store?"

"He doesn't know I'm going. It's just to check prices. Please don't tell him. I'm trying to cut corners wherever I can. I don't mean any disrespect to anyone local. I just don't know how far I can stretch the renovation budget." As far as Grace knew, Savannah didn't know the house was a gift or that money had been put aside for the renovations, and she wasn't going to pick now to explain it.

"I can certainly understand staying in the budget. My lips are sealed. Okay, then." Savannah turned and waved her hand. She glanced back over her shoulder. "I'll see you tomorrow. Good luck with the counters."

Grace let out the breath she was holding. She checked the time on the dashboard. If she hurried, she might still be back in Heritage River before the end of the day.

****

Grace gobbled up the last of the granola bar she kept in her purse. She'd left without eating breakfast, and her stomach growled louder than a rabid dog, and she didn't want to stop anywhere and waste time. Thankfully, she always had a snack with her.

Finding Shadow Lawn Assisted Living wasn't as bad as she thought it might be. The main building, a Victorian-style house with gabled roofs and a wraparound porch, sat at the end of a long tree-lined driveway looking down on the property surrounding it. Behind it were smaller buildings, some resembling cottages sitting semicircle to an open grassy area. The website boasted a pond and walking trails for their more mobile guests.

She closed the screen on her phone and took a deep breath. What was she going to say to Nancy Templeton, if she even found her here? Maybe it would've been better to call first instead of taking an hour-long drive and lying to Savannah of all people. Planning did have its advantages.

She was here now. No point in turning back. She pushed herself from the car and marched up to the front door. Potted plants adorned the porch; a wind chime played its soft, sweet music. Wicker chairs offered places to sit and take in the rolling property.

The door swung open against her touch, and she found herself in the grand foyer. A staircase swooped down into the center of the room. Victorian sofas in soft-colored damask created a sitting area in front of a fireplace. A large rectangular wool rug with matching muted colors added the perfect cozy touch. A flower arrangement of white lilies in a crystal-cut vase decorated a marble-topped table made of birch. A reception area was on her left. The place smelled of flowers and antiseptic.

She approached the opening. A young woman with thick black eyeliner and blonde hair pulled back in a tight ponytail greeted her with a wide smile. "Welcome. How can I help you today?"

Grace smoothed down her blouse to keep her hands from shaking. "I'm looking for someone."

The smile dropped off the blonde's face. "One of our residents?"

Grace forced a smile on hers. "Yes. Nancy Templeton. I was hoping to visit with her." She hadn't considered whether a place like this had visiting hours. Probably not for the healthier residents. Did *healthy resident* even apply to Nancy Templeton? Boy, she really hadn't thought this through.

"Oh, Nancy. Sure." The smile returned. The woman punched something into the computer in front of her. Her brow creased, and she leaned closer to the screen. "Looks like she's been moved."

Grace's heart filled with dread. "Is the new assisted living close by?" She'd have to take the chance and drive to wherever she needed to. She'd come this far.

"Excuse me? Oh no." The blonde woman laughed. Her top canine tooth was yellowed, and Grace tried not to stare. "Nancy's been moved to our Rolling Hills section. You can follow the hall to the end and make a left. Go through those doors. Someone there can direct you."

"Thank you." She smoothed her blouse again and followed the directions. She should turn right around and go back to Heritage River. This was crazy. She was invading some stranger's space. Did it really matter who Nancy Templeton sold that house to?

It did matter. To Grace anyway. No one had ever given her anything that didn't cost her in some way. If she could figure out who gave her the house, she could prepare for whatever that price tag would be. And there would be one. There was always one. No one gave anything away for free.

She pushed through the double doors. Rooms were lined up on either side of the doorway. Patient names were posted alongside each door. Some patients had cards and pictures drawn by young hands and reading "I love Grandma" and "Happy Birthday, Noni" taped to their doors. Grace found a nurse's station and approached a young man with thinning hair, who was scribbling notes into a binder.

"Excuse me." Her voice came out garbled and rough. She tried again. "Excuse me. I'm looking for Nancy Templeton."

"She's outside on the patio. Go through the dayroom." He pointed at the end of the hall.

Grace hurried through the dayroom. Patients sat in chairs, their chins pressed against their chests, some staring off into space. A woman with a shock of white hair sat alone at a table, speaking to someone only she could see. The Rolling Hills section appeared to be for the patient with more advanced needs.

She pushed through another door, and the warm sun and fresh air greeted her. She took a deep breath. She stood on a paver patio. Several tables and chairs were scattered around for patients to gather, but the only person out here was a woman, sitting in a chair with her face to the sun. Her long, white hair brushed her shoulders. Her arms stuck out of her shirtsleeves like curtain rods. Her bony knees poked against her blue pants.

Grace took a tentative step. "Nancy?"

The woman turned from the sun. Her face was lined with years of experience. She glanced at Grace with confusion etched in her blue eyes. Nancy turned to look at the door, then back at Grace. "Hi," she said, but the look remained. "Thanks for coming by."

"My name is Grace Starr." She stuck out a hand, but Nancy ignored it. "May I sit down?"

"Sure. We're having lunch soon. You came in time for lunch. I'll tell them to set another place for you." She rose, but Grace placed a hand on her arm.

"Thank you, but please don't go to the trouble. I

179

won't be staying that long. I was hoping I could ask you a question."

"I don't know where that book is. I put it down, but I can't remember where. You're going to have to find it yourself."

"Oh, that's okay. I'm not here about the book." Grace sank back in the chair and yanked her hair away from her face. This whole escapade had been foolish. But she was here, so she might as well try. "Nancy, do you remember your house on Dogwood Drive?"

Nancy's face lit up. Her eyes brightened, and the lines on her face smoothed. For a second Grace could see a glimpse of the woman Nancy was a long time ago. "I love that house. I carved my initials in the tree in the backyard. My mother was mad because I used her good knives."

Was she talking about the house on Dogwood or another house? "Do you remember who you sold the house to?"

A darkness passed across Nancy's blue eyes. "My mother sold the house? She didn't tell me." Tears filled her eyes. "I have to stop her. She can't sell the house. I'm going home tomorrow." She began to get up, but Grace stopped her. Nancy stared at her as if she'd just noticed Grace for the first time. "Do I know you?"

"No." Telling this woman she lived in her house would be a bad idea. "I didn't mean to upset you. Your mother won't sell the house without discussing it with you."

Nancy eased back in the chair and clutched her shirt in a fist. "Thank goodness. But I should call her." She looked around the outside area. "I don't remember the number. Do you know her number?"

Grace's heart broke for this woman, and she'd come here and made things worse. "I'll get someone to help you. I'm sorry to bother you."

Nancy smiled at her. "It was nice to see you again." She turned her face back toward the sun.

Grace returned to the nurse's station. "I'm sorry. I might've upset her. I didn't mean to. But could you check on her? She seemed determined to make a phone call." She wrapped her purse strap around her shaking hands.

The young man stood and offered a warm smile. "She wants to call her mother. She always does. I'll go out and check on her, but she's probably forgotten all about it by now."

Grace forced her legs forward and made her way back to her car. She rested her head on the steering wheel. "Well, that was a bust." Just when she thought she might have a lead. But it bothered her more that the sweet woman was ill and she'd upset her.

She pulled back onto the road and turned up the radio to clear her head and keep the tears from running down her face. She didn't want to think about Nancy Templeton again because she was afraid that was how she would end up. Alone. Forgetful. Who would visit her? She had no one. No siblings, no cousins, no parents. Chloe had one foot out the door already, and Grace was certain when the other foot followed, she'd see very little of her daughter. That was Grace's biggest fear. The more the real world drew Chloe in, the further she'd go from Grace. Children growing up and moving on was supposed to be the cycle of life, but losing her daughter to adulthood still tore her soul out. The fact they hardly got along didn't make Chloe's leaving any

181

easier.

She swiped at the tears rolling down her cheeks. The real reason Chloe left Larry's was she knew somewhere deep down she could never outrank Annie. Two women in the same house fought for the alpha spot. So she hopped on a plane to be with her mother. The one woman she could push around.

The car sputtered and jerked. She glanced at the dash. In all the rush and emotions, she hadn't noticed the low fuel light. How long had it been on? She hit the signal and pulled onto the shoulder. The car coasted to a stop. She turned off the engine, and when she tried to restart, the engine coughed and stopped. She tried again. More coughing and no going.

She growled. Never in her life had she run out of gas. Where was the nearest gas station? The GPS could probably tell her, but she didn't have one of those red cans to hold the gas. Can one be bought at a gas station? She shoved her way out of the car and kicked the wheel, hurting her toe in the process. *That's what I get for kicking in sandals.*

Cars flew by in a flurry. Her car shook, and her hair blew up around her ears. Standing on the side of a major highway while cars passed was probably not a good idea. She hopped back in and checked the GPS for the gas station. Eight miles away. How long would it take to walk eight miles and back? By the time she got home, she wouldn't be able to help with the house. She'd have to call Blaise and cancel dinner. He'd think she was making it up. *Who runs out of gas?*

It would be faster if someone could bring the gas to her, but how would she manage that? Who could she call? And she didn't have AAA because Larry made her cancel it once she got a new car. "Bastard." Cursing made her feel better for about two seconds.

No point in calling Chloe, so Grace searched her contacts for the one person she could call.

"What?" was the response when the call was answered.

"Hi, Beau. It's Grace."

"I know who it is. Where are you? You've been gone a long time. We've got a lot of work to do, and this crew isn't getting much done. If you want to make that deadline, you've got to pitch in."

She wanted to roll down the windows to get some air, but she'd never be able to hear with the cars going by. "I'm sorry. I'm having car trouble. Is there any way you can bring me some gas?"

"I don't have the time to bring you gasoline. I can't leave the job. Call a tow truck."

She had to pull the phone away from her ear to keep his response from busting an eardrum, and she could still hear him just fine. She sat up straighter in the seat. "I don't know who to call. And don't yell at me. It was an accident." She would never have called if she wasn't desperate. She couldn't stay at the side of the road. Should she call nine-one-one? It wasn't exactly an emergency. Better leave the police to the real problems. Her face was impossibly hot.

"Where are you?" Beau's voice softened.

She told him.

"For land's sake. I'll call over to Lewis's garage and have old Pete send his truck." He ended the call.

Grace leaned her head against the seat and closed her eyes. "Dumb ass." Her stomach growled. It would be hours before she could eat. Something knocked on the window, and she jumped. She bit her lip to keep from screaming.

A tall man with sunglasses leaned close to the window. "Do you need help?"

"I'm fine. Thanks," she said through the closed window. Thankfully, the doors were locked.

"Can I call someone for you?"

"No. I'm fine, really. Thanks, but you can go." She made a shooing motion with her hand.

"Lady, you can't stay on the side of the road. I'll call the police for you if you don't have a phone."

"Get out of here." She shouted, and the muscles in her neck tightened. "I'm fine. I don't need your help."

Her screams made the man jump. He muttered "crazy," which she could hear and really wasn't about to argue with, and turned away. His car was parked behind hers. He hopped in and pulled into traffic.

Her heart crashed against her ribs. She gripped the steering wheel to keep her hands from shaking. She was not about to take help from a total stranger. Finding women stuck on the side of the road was exactly how serial killers caught their prey. Even that time her tire blew out coming home from work when it had been dark and cold, she had opted to walk down the highway instead of taking help. Walking down a dark highway was dangerous too, but that choice was the lesser of two evils in her mind. When the off-duty police officer had offered to change her tire, she wouldn't get in his warm car even after he showed her his identification. You could never be too sure. Safer to freeze on the side of the road.

Now she was sweating and didn't see much choice except to get out and stand by the car for a while. She might catch a breeze, but she'd keep her phone in her pocket and her keys firmly between her fingers in case she needed a weapon.

The sun beat on her neck, and the fumes from the cars turned her empty stomach. Some people honked as they passed, but thankfully, no one else stopped. The minutes dragged by and no tow truck. She tried Beau another time, but he didn't pick up.

She debated sending Chloe a text to see how her day was going but decided against it. She had enough stress to deal with and didn't really want to know if things weren't as Chloe thought they should be. As long as Chloe was listening to Beau, she'd be fine, and she couldn't do anything for Grace anyway. She tried Jenn just to pass the time, but the call went to voice mail and the mailbox was full. Typical.

A pickup truck glided off the road and stopped behind her car. The sun's glare bounced off the windshield, making it impossible to see the driver. She shielded her eyes with one hand and gripped her keys with the other.

A tall male hopped out of the driver's side. "Do you northerners make it a habit of running out of gas?"

Grace loosened her grip on the keys, but she looked around for a way to escape. Maybe a tornado would appear and suck her up in its funnel. She'd hoped Blaise would never find out about her stupidity.

"Did Beau make you come?" Her voice wobbled.

Blaise swaggered up to her. "Nah. After he was done yelling about women and cars, I offered. Figured I'd save Pete the drive and Beau the call to bark at him."

"Beau was yelling?"

"Whole neighborhood could hear him. Where were you coming back from anyway?"

She turned and looked toward the woods. That might be a good place to run and hide. "I'm sorry I inconvenienced you. I'm not the kind of person who runs out of gas."

"Lighten up, Grace. Ain't no big deal." He pumped up his southern accent. "Pop open your gas tank. You know where that button is?" He laughed. "You weren't trying to get out of dinner, were you?"

He poured the gas into the car, and she held her nose. "It would've been easier to call and cancel, don't you think?" she said.

"Depends." He dumped the empty can in the bed of his truck. "You should have enough gas to get you to the next station. Get back in the car. The side of the road isn't exactly the safest place to hang out. I'll pick you up at six for dinner. Unless you can't remember the way back." He wagged his eyebrows above his glasses.

She couldn't help but smile. "I guess I deserve that. You don't have to knock on the door or anything like that, you know, later on. I'll just meet you on the lawn." She walked around the back of her car, the need to run and hide a little less pressing. "Thanks, Blaise, for coming all the way out here. You didn't have to do that. I appreciate it."

"It's the least I could do for what you did last night for Cash." He looked down at the ground and kicked the gravel, then looked back up at her. "Guess we're even now."

A car whizzed by, leaving a cloud of dirty exhaust behind. "We better get going." Though she didn't want to just yet and surprised herself at the thought. "Thanks again." She jumped into the driver's seat before another car came and watched in the mirror as Blaise hitched his leg into the truck and slid inside, all smooth and masculine.

"Knock it off before you give yourself a hot flash." What was she thinking going to dinner with this man? It would be safer to grab takeout and eat in the back rooms of the house, watching *House Hunters* on her tablet.

She checked the mirror again, and Blaise pointed for her to go first. She edged out into the lane, and he followed. He followed her until she pulled into the nearest gas station, and honked as he drove past.

At least Cash and Chloe would be at dinner. Having the kids with them would be enough cold water to keep Grace from thinking about that man's dimple. Jenn would squeal if she knew Grace thought Blaise was attractive. Problem was half the female population probably thought that too, and half of that population probably knew how attractive he was under the sheets. She turned up the air conditioner.

It's only dinner. She tried to convince herself. She could handle a simple dinner.

Chapter Twenty-Two

"Chloe, please come to dinner." Grace stood over Chloe, who was sprawled out on her air mattress. She wore the too-short sweat shorts and a tee. She had one earbud plugged into an ear, and the other dangled.

"Mom, I'm exhausted. Beau wouldn't let us take a break because you were gone all day wherever you went, and when he finally let us eat lunch, after ten minutes he was yelling at us to get back to work. My whole body hurts. I'm not even hungry. If you don't want to go to dinner, just cancel. But I'm staying here."

Grace threw her hands in the air and marched out of Chloe's room. She learned a long time ago that once Chloe dug her heels in, there wasn't any point in arguing.

Beau had worked them hard. When she finally returned to Heritage River, the sun suspended low in the sky, dirt and dust covered Chloe in a white film. Spackle stuck to Jud's hair like a good hair gel, and sweat stained his shirt. Beau had summoned Cash after Blaise left to rescue her, either forgetting or not caring the poor boy was sick. When Beau saw her, his face turned the color of an overripe strawberry. Grace worried he'd pass out. He yelled about responsibility and her pulling her weight. She'd refused to tell him where she was, and he'd kicked a hole in the new wall they'd already put in.

They had begun rebuilding her kitchen, and Grace stood there now, admiring their work. The new walls were up. Beau changed the window over the sink, and the oversized, clean glass let in more light than the old one. He assured her it was energy efficient. He drew chalk lines on the floor to show her the new layout for the cabinets. His plan made better use of her space and even added an island for her—well, for the new owners.

"You need to pick the things for your kitchen. Don't go running off tomorrow," he'd said as he left earlier.

A knock on the door drew her away from her thoughts. She checked before she opened it. "You didn't have to come to the door."

Blaise had changed into jeans and a button-down short-sleeved shirt that accented his toned frame. He wasn't muscular in some gym-head way. All that banging on the drums had probably made him muscular without being bulky.

"I was checking to see if you needed help finding the front yard." He winked.

"I didn't get lost today. Surprisingly. I ran out of gas. There's a huge difference." She grabbed her purse and followed him onto the porch.

"Is Chloe almost ready?" He swung his keys on his finger.

"Um, she's decided not to come. Beau worked her hard. She wants to collapse and stay home." Grace shrugged. "If I forced her, she'd just be a pill all night."

"Cash gave me a big fat no too. Said all he wanted to do was take a cold shower and sleep. Guess it's just us, then."

His smile made the muscles in her belly dance a

tango. Having dinner with him alone wasn't really her plan. She'd already thrown caution to the wind once today, and that didn't work out so well. Maybe this would be different. Or maybe it would be disastrous, much like meeting Nancy Templeton and running out of gas.

"Where are we going?" She waved to Mo Bucknell watering his hydrangeas. He gave her an enthusiastic wave back.

Blaise pulled the truck out of the driveway and headed through town and then passed the town's edge where fields spread out long and flat. There wasn't a car in sight, something Grace didn't see back in Jersey. She enjoyed the space and solitude laid out before them.

"It's a surprise."

"I don't like surprises."

"That's what I figured." He glanced over at her, showing off his dimple.

What if she'd worn the wrong thing? She'd changed three times as it was, trying to find the right combination of stylish, comfortable, forgiving, and subtle. She didn't want her clothes writing checks her body wouldn't pay, and she didn't want to look like a middle-aged woman trying to be twenty-five. What if she didn't like what they were eating? She was a picky eater and didn't want to embarrass herself with her strange food requests.

He pulled off the paved road onto a dirt one. The flat land gave way to tall grass flanking each side of the road. The truck bounced up and down over the uneven dirt. She turned in her seat to see if she could still find the road they left behind.

"Where are we headed?" She tried to keep the panic out of her voice. So much for enjoying the space and solitude. Well, solitude she could handle as long as she could see what was coming ahead.

"You'll see."

"Just tell me."

"Take your hand off the door and relax."

"What?" She looked down at her hand's death grip on the door, her knuckles white. "Oh." She pulled her hand to her chest.

He grabbed her other hand. "It's okay, Grace. I'm not going to take you to a secluded place where no one knows where you are, and drag you into the grass and then do unspeakable things they won't even want to report on the five o'clock news before tossing your body in the marsh. If I wanted to do that, I could've done it today on the side of the road." He threw his head back and gave a fake villainous laugh.

She yanked her hand away. "You're horrible." But she could still feel his calloused skin against hers, even though they weren't touching. She liked his roughness against her soft skin. It made her think of wood and lace.

He pulled the truck into a dirt lot. "We walk from here."

He hopped out before she could ask walk to where. She followed, hoping her sandals were sufficient for whatever trek they were about to take.

Blaise grabbed a basket and a blanket from the bed of the truck, along with his guitar. A picnic? She would have never guessed. She imagined a table at Jake's in town because Blaise knew everyone there and the kids were supposed to be with them, but never a picnic. She

Stacey Wilk

didn't take him for the picnic type, and she wouldn't have worn her white pants.

"Can I help you carry some of that stuff?" She held out her hands, and he gave her the blanket. "I can take something else." She reached toward him.

He turned away with a wink. "Hands off, lady. No one touches the guitar but me."

She found herself laughing.

He led her down a sandy road. "I picked up sandwiches and fried chicken from Jake's. There's potato salad and coleslaw. I think he threw in some pickles and a couple of bottles of iced tea. Oh, and big chocolate chip cookies for dessert." He puffed up his chest at his dinner announcement.

She had the Jake's part right anyway. Sand kicked up between her toes. She thought about taking her sandals off. "The food sounds very nice." And it did, except she didn't eat fried chicken and cookies would go straight to her thighs. But she could nibble on half to be polite. He seemed so proud of his plan. Was he a planner? She doubted it. Just good with women. That was all.

"I got extra in case the kids came. We'll have leftovers for sure."

And a thoughtful father. Her belly did that dance again.

The road ended in a dirt lot adjacent to a large, clear lake. Grass and sand ran down to the water's edge. A dock stuck out into the water, large enough to allow a small boat to pull up to it. A raft made of the same worn wood floated out in the middle. Picnic benches sat under trees, and houses flanked the far side of the lake. The sun rested its head on the roofs of those houses, casting rays of gold and orange onto the lake's surface. Bushes of honeysuckle swayed in the breeze and filled the air with their sweet scent.

Blaise spread the blanket out and indicated for her to sit. He pulled the food from the basket and held out a sandwich. "I hope you're hungry."

She wasn't. Her nerves were braided tightly, but she unwrapped the sandwich anyway. "The lake is lovely and peaceful." She closed her eyes and tilted her head back, feeling the sun against her skin. "I would love a house on a lake." Were her shoulders relaxing a little?

When she opened her eyes, Blaise was staring at her. She grabbed the sandwich to keep her hands busy and her gaze on something other than him.

"We used to come here as kids. We'd swim. My mom would make us a picnic, and she and my dad would sit and watch us while we horsed around. Colton would always want to see who could swim the fastest or dive the best or hold their breaths the longest." He looked off into the distance, as if he were seeing those old times. A small smile played on his lips. "This is my favorite place. I'm sorry I don't get to spend more time here. Maybe I can now."

"Now?"

"I don't normally live in Heritage River. I have a place in Nashville. Well, I had a place. I sold it recently." He swapped the sandwich for his guitar. "I haven't told anyone that yet except Cash."

"Two houses are a lot for one person." Not that she understood what owning two houses was like. She'd only ever owned the one she lived in with Larry and now the Disaster House, but she wouldn't own it for long if things worked out the way she hoped. "I'm sure you travel a lot with your line of work and don't need another house. Cash won't mind, will he?"

"He likes living in Heritage River. He wants to stay here with me. No one was more surprised by that than I was. He hasn't told his mother yet, and when he does, you'll probably hear her all the way from California." He began playing a soft tune.

"As a mother, I can understand, but he's old enough to decide where he wants to live. What about college? Is he going?"

"He didn't have any big plans. He's been floundering at school for a while and recently got himself in some trouble, making his college plans unclear for a while."

She didn't want to ask what kind of trouble. It really wasn't her business. But Cash was working at her house, and Chloe was there. She had to think about that. "What kind of trouble?" The words tumbled out before she could grab onto them.

He plucked on the guitar strings and turned the pegs. "I really can't tune by ear. That's Colton's expertise. There's iced tea in the basket. I hope you don't mind I didn't bring any wine. I don't drink."

He was full of confessions, but he didn't answer her question. He continued to play.

"That's a nice melody. It's...it's, I don't know, soulful, maybe," she said.

He looked up at her. His smile was wide. "You think so? Thanks. I wrote it. It would sound a lot better if I wasn't wearing the brace."

"It sounds lovely." She stroked her throat and imagined what it might be like to sway with Blaise to this sultry song. Her face flushed. Where had that thought come from?

Blaise turned his gaze back to the guitar and continued to play. "You want to know what Cash did? He burned down the foundation of a house." He smacked the guitar's body and stopped playing the sweet melody. "There wasn't anyone inside. No one was hurt. It's no excuse, but his friend egged him on. His punishment is community service because he's still a minor." He looked away and then back at her. "And because he's my kid. My ex thinks the judge might have been a fan."

How would she feel if Chloe did something like that? Would she fight for a lesser sentence? Probably. No parent wanted to see their child suffer or be punished. "Has he been in trouble like that before?" Was Cash used to getting away with things because of his name? Had he learned that from his father?

"Nothing like that. Just stupid things. Skipping class. Not doing homework. Not caring about his grades. Playing video games till his eyes bleed. I blame myself. I wasn't around. I didn't get involved enough. I left it all to his mother, and I think Cash was acting out. Honestly, at first I didn't know if I wanted him to come and stay with me, because I didn't know how to handle him or what to say, but I'm glad he did come. Even if there's times he barely utters two words to me unless he's sick." He let a smile play on his lips and went back to playing.

Blaise wasn't always the perfect father. Was she really surprised, considering his life choices? Was he really sorry for not being there? "It sounds like you're trying to make up for the past, and you must've done something right. Cash is a good kid." She liked the boy, and if he was a little broken because his parents weren't perfect, well, she could relate to that. She was broken too, thanks to her parents. Wasn't everyone?

"He isn't a good kid because of me. It's his mother."

How often did she hear a divorced couple give praise to one another? Not often enough. "Do you miss being married?" She wanted to know more about him. Sitting together beside the solitude and lulling of the lake felt safe. Her tension eased, and she could ask questions.

"Do you?" He raised his eyebrows.

But did she? Sometimes, but not in the way she thought she would. When Larry first left, she thought she'd miss his opinion on things or sleeping next to him or having someone in the house when she arrived at night. After her pride recovered from being battered, she realized Larry never offered much of those things to her anyway. What she missed was someone to change the lightbulbs in the ceiling or to twist off a lid on a glass jar when she couldn't. And she missed the idea of marriage, but she didn't miss Larry. They were lost to each other a very long time ago.

Blaise put down the guitar and finished his sandwich before he started on the fried chicken. He held a piece out to her, but she shook her head. "Now, Miss Grace, it is impolite to turn down the kindness of others. Here in Heritage River we say *please* and *thank you*. Then when I'm not looking, you can discreetly toss my food in the trash."

"I like when you turn up your southern accent." Heat filled her cheeks again, and she busied herself with cleaning up their dinner. She barely knew this man, and she was feeling things she didn't think she'd ever felt in her life.

He stilled her hands, and their gazes met. "I like your accent too." He was so close she could smell his clean scent.

Grace licked her lips because her mouth had gone dry. His gaze dipped to watch.

She pulled back, giving herself some space to breathe and think for a moment. Her heart clamored in her chest. She wanted to know what his lips felt like against hers—and she wanted to run for the hills. If she fell for a man like Blaise, how would she ever know if his feelings for her were true? He'd been with so many women. How many times can it be the real thing?

He took her cue and leaned back. "Would you like to take a walk?"

"That's a good idea." She might feel better if they were moving.

He led her around the lake on a dirt path made by years of others taking walks and riding bikes. "You never did tell me where you were coming from when you ran out of gas." He shoved his good hand in his pocket.

The sun dipped behind the houses. The sky bled orange and gold. Clouds rolled in, kicking up a breeze that cooled her warm skin. Did she tell him the truth and risk it all? Would he tell on her? "I went to visit Nancy Templeton in an assisted living today." There. It was out.

"Why did you do that?"

She could lie. "I want to know who she sold my house to. I want to know who my giver is."

"This again?" He stopped and turned to her. "Grace, who cares who gave you that house? They did. It's legit. Move forward."

"I can't." Not yet anyway. What if this gift giver was an uncle or a cousin she didn't know about? She wanted a family, and this might be a chance to find one. A relative for Chloe. Didn't her daughter deserve to be a part of a family larger than just her parents and a new sibling she wouldn't be able to relate to for years? "You don't understand. I have no one except my daughter. I don't have siblings like you. You probably grew up with both your parents who were supportive of your dreams. Maybe if I can find the person Nancy sold to, I can find a piece of my history I didn't know existed."

"My mother passed away when I was young. She didn't get a chance to be supportive of my dreams. As for my father, he tried to talk us out of a life filled with rock and roll. I guess it was a good thing we didn't listen. Well, Colton didn't listen. If it wasn't for Colton, I'd probably be an accountant or something."

"Oh, I'm so sorry. I didn't realize." She'd assumed he'd had parents rooting for him. In a way, they had something in common.

"It's okay. You wouldn't know. If finding this gift giver means so much to you, I'll help you figure it out."

She squinted at him. "You would? Why?"

He held up his bandaged hand. "The garden isn't working out too well. I need something to fill my time until we go back on tour."

He would be leaving. It wasn't safe to trust him. That little voice in her head screamed at her to stay away. This man would only break her heart if she let him anywhere near it.

"I'm not supposed to find out who bought the house for me. If I do or even try, I lose the house all together, and then I won't have anywhere to live. I'm hoping to sell this house and move back to Jersey and buy a new one."

"There's something in New Jersey waiting for you?"

"Well, my old life, I guess." Would her old life still fit her?

"Then why not fix up the house and live here in Heritage River?" He started walking again, and she fell into step with him.

Their feet kicked up dirt as they moved, but she didn't care about the dirt. At least for the moment. "I don't know anyone here. I couldn't even find the twenty-four-hour pharmacy last night."

"You know me and Cash. You know Beau and Dixie. You've met my sister, and you're helping out with the library fundraiser. I'd say you were starting to fit in just fine."

"You just said you would be leaving to go on tour. I'm sure your sister is very busy with her own life, and Beau isn't exactly warm and fuzzy. Staying isn't the plan."

Showing Larry she didn't need him—that was part of the plan. The plan included proving everyone wrong who told her renovating a house in a strange town by herself was a mistake. The library, Blaise, and all the rest didn't factor in. It couldn't.

They returned to the blanket. The sun had dipped farther, and the deep gray of nightfall spread across the top of the lake. Lights came on in some of the houses. Fireflies ducked and chased through the air.

"It's getting late." Grace rubbed at her arms.

Blaise settled down and dug out the cookies. He handed her one. "What's the rush? The kids aren't waiting for us. They're probably glad we aren't home. Besides, the night is young."

Even if she wasn't. She handed back the cookie. "No, thank you."

He stood to face her. He was inches away, and she could feel the heat rolling off him. She wanted to step back, but he took her hands in his, keeping her in place. "Am I making you nervous?" His voice was low and husky.

She bit at her lip and kept her gaze glued to the collar of his shirt. She could see the soft spot of skin between his collarbones. What did it taste like? The thought startled her, and she snapped her head up to meet his eyes. *Dear Lord, I'm worse than a teenager.* He smiled down at her, and her belly moved to its own beat. The beat he played out on her wrists.

"Yes, you're making me a little nervous. I...I...didn't realize...we were on a, uh, you know."

"Do you mean a date, Grace? You didn't realize I asked you out on a date? What did you think this was?" His gray eyes twinkled, and the dimple in his cheek was full. He was teasing her again. And she liked it. *Dear Lord, she liked it.*

"I don't know. Just a way of saying 'thank you' for helping out with Cash. I mean, the kids were supposed to come along. They wouldn't be if this was a date." She nearly choked on the last word. How could she, Grace Starr, be on a date with a rock star, albeit a fading star, but bright enough? A handsome man who must've seen the inside of a million bedrooms in his heyday. She swallowed hard. What did this man see in her? Boring, no fun, predictable Grace.

"If you'd like to end our date now, I'll take you home."

He let her hands go, and his absence chilled her immediately. She laced her fingers together to keep from reaching back out for him. She didn't want things to end. She kind of liked feeling on the edge of something—daring and alive. The precariousness of her emotions made her giggle inside. "It might be best."

Blaise packed up the picnic without another word. He opened the truck door for her to slide in, dumped the basket and guitar in the bed, and slid in from the other side. He turned on the radio to the classical station and let the music fill the space between them.

He pulled into his driveway and turned the truck off. Her house was dark. His front porch light was on. "I'll make some calls tomorrow and see if I can find anything out about who Nancy sold to," he said.

"No one can know what you're up to."

"I've got it covered." He pushed himself out of the truck and met her before she had the door all the way open. "Can I walk you to your door? It's pretty dark over there."

He followed behind her with his hand on the small of her back. The tiny gesture spread heat through her body. At the door she turned to face him. The darkness offered a shield. "Thank you for a very nice night. The lake was beautiful."

"So is the woman." He lifted her chin with his strong fingers. His intense stare sent shivers over her skin. When was the last time someone called her beautiful?

He closed the distance between them, and her first instinct was to run inside into the safety of the house. The smile on his face eased the dancing in her belly, allowing her to close her eyes and wait for the feel of his lips against hers. She hoped her knees wouldn't give out. Did she remember how to kiss someone? How would she compare to the other women?

A car horn blasted the night wide open. Blaise yanked back. Grace jumped. An engine revved, and the low bass thumping of music made its way into his driveway. A shiny pickup skidded to a halt behind his truck, and a man hopped out.

Blaise stepped back further from her. "Colton."

Chapter Twenty-Three

At best, families were challenging. At worst, they were dangerous. Having Colton Savage for an older brother was challenging on the best days. Still Blaise loved his brother. Which was why he had no problem setting up the guest room for his indefinite stay. He had been able to put up with the years of Colton running the band as if he were a dictator. From the very first backyard party they played, Colton decided where the band would be seen, which interviews they did, when the gigs would happen, and even how much they got paid. As the band's popularity took off, Colton decided they wouldn't play other bands' music. They would play the music Colton wrote.

Colton was a smart businessman and a genius on the guitar, and Blaise had benefited from his brother's dictatorship. He was tired of being bossed around, though. A man his age should certainly be able to make his own career decisions. He had his own creative needs to fill. He couldn't walk away from the band. He needed the tour, and even though Colton would never say it out loud, he needed Blaise too. There wasn't a drummer out there who could copy Blaise's beats—and no one dumb enough to sit behind Colton's gigantic ego.

Blaise did have a major problem with his big brother, one that could affect how long he stayed at

Blaise's. Colton's interest in Grace.

"You have to share the bathroom with Cash." Blaise tossed the extra pillows at him. "And next time don't drive down the street making all that noise. You'll scare the neighbors. I don't need the sheriff knocking on my door."

"I was trying to stop you from making a big mistake."

He'd seen. Blaise was worried about that. "Don't worry about my mistakes. Worry about your own." Colton had definitely made his share. A battlefield of scorned women was left around the world, thanks to Colton. He'd even broken the heart of his high school sweetheart, Harley. "I'm going to bed."

"I thought you were done getting involved with women? Too complicated, you said."

Blaise leaned against the doorframe. "She isn't staying. Once her house is done, she's moving back to New Jersey."

"So she's safe, then."

"I'm not looking to get involved with anyone. She helped me the other day. I was just taking her to dinner to thank her."

"Looked liked more than that from where I was sitting."

"Yeah, well, you were sitting on your brains, so what the hell do you know?"

"You were always in love with the idea of love."

Blaise pushed off the wall. "Who said anything about love? You're an ass. Good night." He marched into the hallway.

"So you won't care, then, if I ask her out?" Colton called after him.

****

Blaise woke to the sound of banging and someone yelling. The sun was already making its way into the sky and bringing with it a trunkful of heat. His wrist hurt from lying on it all night. He tore off the brace and rubbed the skin.

He dragged himself into the kitchen for a strong cup of coffee. He went to the window and pulled back the curtain. Beau stood on Grace's porch, barking orders. Cash and Jud balanced debris down the steps and tossed them into the almost-full dumpster. Colton came out of the house holding what looked like house plans. He wore a tool belt around his waist.

"That bastard." Blaise threw on a pair of shorts and a T-shirt he grabbed off the floor. He grabbed the coffee in case he needed something to hit Colton with and marched across the lawn to the construction.

Beau met him halfway. "'Morning, Blaise."

"Beau." He sipped the coffee just to have something to do. "Looks like you keep adding to your crew." Blaise hated to admit it, but Colton was good with his hands. That should be obvious with all the guitar playing, but he could build anything. Colton was like their dad that way. Blaise never took much of an interest. He was sorry now. And there was the little problem of his hand.

"The ladies are fine for demolishing things, but I need some experience to put it back together again. Cash is a quick learner. Not so sure about your nephew. He's too busy trying to flex his muscles for Miss Grace's daughter. I spent half the day yesterday swatting him away. I was about to call in some favors, but Colton showed up this morning. I put him right to work. The boy hasn't forgotten a thing."

When they were kids, Colton had spent summers working with Beau to make extra money to buy guitars and pedal boards. Blaise preferred cutting grass and planting bushes. He even spent a summer painting houses. But he never built anything except his drum kits.

"Are you going to retire after this?" Blaise tried to do the math quickly. Beau had to be near eighty by now.

"That's the plan. Jud, knock it off." Beau marched away, swinging his hand in the air.

There wasn't a place for him there, but he refused to leave. He'd be underfoot if he went inside, but he wanted to know what Grace was up to. More importantly, he wanted to know what his brother was up to.

A car swung in and parked at the curb. He headed over to the driver's door. "What are you doing here?" He held the door open for his sister.

Savannah pushed her way out of the car. "Well, rumor has it my big brother is in town. I wanted to see for myself, and I needed Grace's help with some fundraiser stuff. I know she's busy with the house, so I thought I'd stop by. What are you up to? How's the hand?" She yanked a large tote out of the back seat and slung it over her shoulder.

"Healing, I guess. Colton has strapped on his hammer. He's helping out with the renovation."

"Are you kidding me? I ask that man to play a few lousy songs at my fundraiser and he says no, but Beau asks him to break a sweat and he can't say yes fast enough? Colton Thomas." She shouted from her spot on the curb.

"Someone is shouting my name as if they're my mother, and I know my mother can't be here because she's been gone for many years." Colton laughed from an open window. "That leaves only one person. I'm still not playing at your fundraiser."

"He makes me so mad sometimes." Savannah banged her legs with her clenched fists.

"No kidding." Blaise took another sip of his coffee.

She shifted her bag on her shoulder and marched up the front walk. "I don't want you at my fundraiser, you egomaniacal oaf. I have the brother I really like already playing."

Colton met Savannah at the door, scooped her in his arms, and twirled her around. She yelled something about still being mad at him and pounded his shoulders, but by the time he put her down, they were hugging. She never could stay mad at him.

Where was Grace? Was Colton wielding his charms on her too? Blaise wished he had kissed her, but he'd tried to be a gentleman last night and not rush her. If the red blotches on her neck and cheeks were any indication, she was more than a little nervous with him, and he didn't want to seem like an overeager teenager. Since he usually jumped first and asked questions later, it took a lot of restraint to keep from tasting her lips. He could still feel the softness of her skin against his rough hands and smell her scent of vanilla and cinnamon. He wanted to drink that scent in, to taste it on her skin, but he hesitated, and now his brother was playing construction man on her house.

His coffee tasted bitter. He dumped the rest on the lawn. He waved to Cash who was dragging large pieces

of Sheetrock down the steps. His wave was met with a
slight nod and a scowl. Now what? Was Cash mad at
him? Or mad at Jud? Or Beau? Just when Blaise started
to get a grip on having a seventeen-almost-eighteen-
year-old son, the chords changed and no one warned
him. Colton bounded down the steps, helped Cash with
the plaster, and then showed him the plans. Blaise
couldn't hear what they were saying over the banging
that had begun again, but the smile grew on Cash's face
while Colton spoke. His insides heated up like the
summer day. When was he going to stop being jealous
of his brother?

He marched past them into the house. Grace had to
be somewhere. The house's layout was the flip of his.
Her front room was empty except for dust on the floors
and spackle on the walls. The kitchen sat to the right
and through the dining room. The kitchen walls were
new. Jud covered seams with spackle. He wore as much
as he scraped on the walls. Blaise could help with that.
He had one good hand. Beau was going to need more
help, or they'd be here until Christmas finishing this
house. Not that he'd mind having Grace around until
then.

"Morning, Jud."

"Hey, Uncle Blaise."

The hall bathroom was down to the studs. Beau sat
on the floor rerouting the plumbing. "Blaise, hand me
that wrench, would you?"

Blaise did as he was told. "You need any other
help?" He looked over his shoulder for Grace, hoping
for a reason to stay.

"I'll let you know if I do."

"If you want, I can handle a little spackle."

Beau unfolded himself from the floor. "It's about all I can give Jud to do for now. When we're lifting the heavy stuff, I'll have him do that and you can step in and be my goffer." Beau patted him on the shoulder and turned back to the bathroom. "Need to get this finished today, or Miss Grace and Chloe will be using the facilities at your place."

It looked like they might anyway. "Do you have enough help?"

"I called some of my old guys. They're coming next week. A final favor for me. We'll be done by the end of summer, just like Grace wants."

Blaise went down the hall toward the bedrooms. Hers had two on the left and one on the right, the master with a second bath. *She wants to be gone by the end of summer?* He'd be on tour by then. He liked the idea of Christmas. Then she'd be here when he got back.

The rooms were empty, so he headed back to the kitchen and out the slider onto the patio. Grace sat with her back to him at a glass table with Savannah and Chloe. He watched for a second without moving. Her blonde hair was pulled back in a ponytail, exposing her slender neck. He wanted to kiss that neck even with his sister watching, but probably not a good idea in front of Chloe. Not that Grace would let him. They hadn't gotten to the necking yet. He laughed at his own stupid joke.

Grace turned at the muffled sound of his guffaw. Her smile spilled across her face, and her blue eyes lit up. A tightness spread across his low belly. This woman was starting to wreak havoc on him.

Savannah looked from him to Grace before she

leaned back in her seat with a smirk. Chloe kept her face in her phone and didn't even notice him.

"What are you doing here?" Grace stood. "I mean, that didn't come out right." She laughed, and her cheeks turned red. She smoothed out the bottom of her shirt. "Hi. We're talking about the fundraiser. Did you come by to discuss something with Savannah?"

He opened his mouth to say something and realized he didn't know what to say. What was he doing stalking around the house? He couldn't help, or better yet Beau didn't want him to. Everyone had something to do except him, and his excuse for looking around for her died on his lips. "Um, that thing you asked me to do last night. I have an idea that might help. I'll come back later to discuss it with you."

Savannah stood and shoved folders into her bag. "I was just leaving. You stay. Grace, I'll call you. Blaise, tell Cash he needs to be at the library later today, in case I don't catch him on the way out." She offered Grace a quick hug and leaned up to give him a kiss on the cheek. "You have that look," she whispered against his face.

He squinted back at her. She smiled and patted his arm. "Bye, Chloe," Savannah yelled over her shoulder.

"Chloe," Beau pushed past as Savannah went inside. "I've got something for you to do, love." He pulled money from his pocket. "Run over to May's and get me one of those cruller things she makes and another cup of coffee. Ask the blockheads what they want too, but go alone. I don't want anyone taking a break unless I say so."

Blaise had never heard Beau use a term of endearment on anyone. Chloe must've warmed that old cold heart of his.

"Looks like it's just us. Do you want to sit? You can tell me what you know." Grace pulled out a chair for him. "Do you like the patio table? Sady Bucknell was getting rid of it and thought I could use it."

He sat beside her and stretched out his legs. He took the brace off and rubbed at his wrist. "Sady and Mo are good neighbors. Always helping out."

"I have neighbors right next door back in Silverside who I've never spoken to. Sad. How much longer do you have to wear the brace?"

"A few weeks. Maybe longer. I remembered something last night after I dropped you off." The thought came to him while he tossed and turned, coming up with ways to keep Colton away from Grace.

She pulled a notebook and pen into her hand and leaned forward with all her attention on him, as if he were a teacher or something. He laughed.

"What?" She wiped at her face. "Do I have something on my nose?"

He leaned closer too and could smell her sweet scent. "Yeah, right here." He dragged his thumb across her lips, unable to ignore the pull in his belly for much longer. He didn't think about what he was doing. He leaned in the rest of the way and placed a quick kiss on her lips. She didn't pull away, and he let the kiss linger. She tasted as sweet as her scent, but unlike anything he ever did, he stopped the kiss. He didn't want to embarrass her making out with him on the patio while his son and nephew were a few feet away on the other side of that window.

"Oh." She placed her fingers against her lips. Her cheeks and neck blossomed red. She looked into her lap. "Is that what you wanted to tell me?"

"No."

She looked back at him. He winked, hoping to ease her nerves. What was this woman like in bed, if a simple kiss got her flustered? She had never been loved the right way. He could tell. He wanted to show her what it was like to let go.

"I remembered Nancy Templeton has a niece, her sister's daughter. Her name is Claire Phillips. I wasn't in town when Nancy moved out, but I had heard her niece came and helped her. We could try and find Claire. She might know who Nancy sold to, or if Nancy was already sick, it might be Claire who sold."

"How do we find Claire Phillips? I don't want to ask around town."

"I hear there's this thing called the internet. We could try using that."

She gave him a full, rich laugh, like the crescendo of a song. Blaise liked that laugh and the ease that settled over her when she did it. He laughed along with her because it felt good, and being with her felt good. He thought of what Colton said last night about Blaise being in love with love. He was wrong about that. He wasn't sure if he was ever in love. Not really. He wasn't feeling that with Grace either. He wasn't dumb enough to fall in love with a woman who had one foot out of the state already.

If he did fall in love, it would have to be with someone who could stay in Heritage River. This was his only home now and where Cash wanted to live. And probably the only place he could get a job if Colton kicked him out of the band. Which might happen if Blaise continued to insist they play new music.

"Um, Chloe and I were going to get dinner at Jake's tonight. Would you and Cash like to come along? After dinner we could try and research Claire Phillips." She stood. "You don't have to answer now. You can think about it. I really need to get back to helping Beau."

"Grace, there you are." Colton appeared in the doorway right on cue. Was he listening? "Beau's been looking for you."

"Thanks." She had to sidestep to get by Colton. She offered him a half smile as she tried to keep from rubbing up against his brother blocking the doorway.

Blaise's blood cooked.

"Hey, Grace," Colton called her back. "You and Chloe can't really have dinner in this house. Why don't you both come over to our place tonight?"

Our place? Blaise wanted to deck him.

"Thanks, Colton, but Chloe and I have plans. Maybe some other time." She pressed her lips together and turned away.

Colton messed with the measuring tape on his tool belt. "I'll get her next time." He shrugged.

"Why are you so interested in her? She isn't really your type."

Colton gazed off in the direction Grace went. "I don't know. Maybe I like her because she isn't my type. Time for something different."

He saw the dare in Colton's eyes. He wanted Grace simply because he suspected Blaise did.

"What's with you helping out Beau?" Blaise said. Colton hadn't mentioned anything about wanting work while he was here. There had to be a reason.

"The man needs a crew. He can't expect to build a

house with Jud and Cash. The girls aren't much help. I think he might be losing his mind, taking on this job at his age without the regular guys who work for him. Figured I'd do the right thing. I'm just marking time here anyway."

It was odd that Beau had agreed to this job without sufficient help. "Don't take on this job and leave the man standing with his pants down because you're ready to move on to something else."

"I don't plan on spending six months on this job. When it's time, I have to go. I already told Beau that. He was okay with it." Colton squinted at him. "You trying to take care of everyone? That's not like you."

Savannah usually took care of everyone. She was always the mother hen even when she was little. She would write plays and assign parts and then make herself the director and boss everyone around. Colton would last about an hour before something more interesting caught his attention. Blaise stayed until Savannah said time was up. Even back then, he adored his little sister.

"I'm not taking care of everyone. I'm just trying to make sure the right thing happens with Beau." Blaise certainly had made enough mistakes in his life. He didn't want to make any more big ones. "When are we getting back on the road?"

"I don't know. Maybe Joe can hold those dates, after all. I think I'd like to stick around for a while. Give your hand time to heal. Get Grace to go on that date with me." Colton turned and went back in the house, leaving Blaise standing in the hot sun, his skin burning from the inside out. Colton didn't mean that. There was no way on earth he would postpone that tour for a woman. Never happen.

Grace stuck her head back out the door. "Oh, good. You're still here." She met him on the lawn. Plaster dust coated her cheeks. She looked like a teenager in her sweat shorts and loose T-shirt with her hair pulled back and no makeup on.

He was starting to notice too many things about this woman, and yet he didn't want to stop. "I was just about to walk around to the front. You guys are pretty busy today."

"Thanks for coming up with the Claire Phillips idea. That might be the big break I'm looking for. If you want, I can look her up myself. I still have Wi-Fi here, even if most of my rooms have turned to rubble." She looked down at her hands, then back up at him, the light in her blue eyes bright. "I'm sorry. I'm rambling."

"It's fine. I like it."

"My offer for dinner still stands." Grace glanced over her shoulder. "Your brother is welcome to come too, if he'd like."

Maybe Blaise could smack Colton over the head with a hammer first. "I'll ask him."

Chapter Twenty-Four

The house was finally quiet. The sun was getting ready to tuck in for the night, and so was Grace, but her stomach rumbled for food. Chloe was taking a shower and promised to hurry since they were down to one full bath now. Thankfully, the bedrooms needed little more than some paint and the floors refinished. They were habitable, and all Grace and Chloe had to move around in.

That didn't stop Grace from taking inventory of their work. She ran her hands across the new kitchen walls. Plumbing stuck up out of the floor where the sink and dishwasher would go. A large space sat empty, waiting for the new refrigerator. She'd go tomorrow to pick out the appliances and cabinets and counters. Her time would be better served doing that than working here. She didn't know the first thing about construction, and Beau never wasted a second reminding her. He definitely had some old opinions about what women should do as careers. But he took a real liking to Chloe, and she seemed to take to him too. Maybe because she never had a real grandfather. Larry's dad had died when she was four.

Grace was doing it. She really was, despite the naysayers. She was building a home in a town she didn't know. Heritage River was growing on her. Every time she ran into town, someone else waved hello. The lake Blaise took her to was beautiful. Just the kind of place she could spend her days.

She liked Savannah and the fact she had opened her arms to Grace and took her in, asking advice on the fundraiser and using her ideas. She wished she'd had a sister like Savannah. She wished she had any family at all besides Chloe, and in little over a month, Chloe would be off at school to begin a new life and Grace would be left behind, alone.

"Mom, I can't blow-dry my hair." Chloe stood in the kitchen doorway in shorts and shirt, her bare feet on the filthy floor. Her hair hung long and wet around her shoulders. She held the hair dryer in one hand, as if it were a weapon.

Grace had to bite her lip about saying anything, but dirt wasn't the only issue. What if she stepped on a nail or something? "Why not? I think we still have electricity." She flipped a light switch, and the overhead light popped on. "See?"

"There isn't a mirror in the bedroom and you said you wanted to get in to take a shower so I had to hurry out. Now my hair will look like crap."

She took a step toward her daughter and without thinking, brushed Chloe's hair behind her shoulder. Chloe flinched as if she had smacked her instead. Watching her beautiful daughter standing there, Grace had forgotten touching wasn't allowed. Hadn't been allowed since she was about twelve. Even though this was part of the process of exerting independence and nothing personal against Grace, the flinching still stung.

She covered her mistake by fussing with sandpaper left on the windowsill. She tried to smile and hoped her face showed disinterest and not something more. "You could let it dry natural."

"My hair looks gross like that."

Grace took a deep breath and forced her shoulders down. "I'll be quick in the bathroom. You can dry your hair then." She brushed past her.

"Why do we have to have dinner with them anyway?" Chloe called after her. "Don't you think it's weird?"

She turned. "Why is it weird? I thought you liked Cash."

"He's all right. I guess."

"Well, I think he's a good kid. I want to do something nice for his father since he treated me to dinner last night. Don't you want to have dinner with a rock star?"

"Mom, please. Blaise is like completely old. No one my age cares about his band anymore. His fans are all like your age. Like Jenn is. She gets all corny every time you even mention his name."

"Still, it's neat. I've never met anyone famous before."

"You would say that."

"What does that mean?" Her shoulders began to creep back up.

"You think it's neat"—Chloe dragged out *neat* as if she were dragging a body—"because Blaise is from your generation. Would you think it was *neat* to meet a singer I like?"

"Sure." Would she?

"No, you wouldn't. You'd think I was being all stupid and acting immature if I wanted to have dinner with someone famous. You'd say he only wanted to have dinner with me because he was up to no good. I couldn't trust him. You would never let me go, but because it's you and Blaise is old, it's okay."

"I would never call you stupid. How could you say such a thing? And Blaise is also our neighbor. We didn't just meet him in a diner someplace. This is absolutely not the same thing as a random meeting with a stranger. Then no, I wouldn't want you to go. It's my job to protect you."

Chloe glared at her. "You don't have to keep protecting me. I'm leaving for college soon."

"It's part of the job. I will always want to protect you." Though at the moment she was ready to resign from the job. Were they really arguing about Chloe having dinner with a stranger versus dinner with Blaise? Chloe could find any subject to argue about, and no matter what Grace did or said, she would always be wrong. All of a sudden, she didn't want to go to dinner. "I need to shower."

By the time she was dressed, the anger had washed away some. The idea of eating alone was still appealing. She could take a book and sit with her food and read. She wouldn't eat without Chloe no matter how mad Chloe made her, but maybe Grace could ease up on her no-phone rule at the table so she could read.

Would Blaise understand if she canceled at the last minute? Of course he would. He couldn't really care if they ate together. He had his son and his brother. She wouldn't be missed. Voices drifted down the hall. Before she could open the door, Chloe burst into the bedroom.

"Oh my God, they are all standing in the house, and I'm not done with my hair and makeup." Chloe pushed past Grace and slammed the bathroom door.

Grace hoped Colton had decided to stay home and one of those voices was not his. She only asked him to come along because she didn't want to seem rude. His slick moves and sultry looks might work on some women, but not her. He was all show. Blaise had heart. She saw it in the way he looked at Cash and in the way he played his music or talked about Heritage River.

The three Savage men stood tall in her exposed living room. The sun had dipped lower, covering the room in ribbons of gray. A lamp would be nice. By the time they returned, the room would be in complete darkness. She turned on her heel and ran back to the bedroom to unplug a lamp and returned to her guests. "For later," she said.

Blaise wore his hair slicked back—she liked it like that—and that silly *X*s and *O*s shirt, with the sleeves rolled up. His fingers tapped on the top of his thighs. Colton was dressed in black, showing off his muscular frame. His gray eyes danced as he smiled. Cash was also dressed in his signature black shirt, black ripped jeans, and black sneakers. The eyeliner had made its reappearance on his face.

"Are you ready to go to dinner?" Colton took center stage. Something he was probably used to. "We're starving."

After Chloe made her grand entrance, they headed to Jake's. They took two vehicles, and Cash slid into the back seat of hers. He and Chloe chatted on the way while Grace listened. She had learned a lot about her daughter just through the years of playing chauffer. It was as if the kids could forget she was there and be themselves, sharing stories and sometimes even secrets. This night was no different.

Chloe told Cash about her plans for school while he sat quietly. When she asked about his, he said he wasn't sure because he was moving to Heritage River permanently, though his mother didn't know yet. Grace also learned he loved music but didn't want to play with his dad. He clearly admired his uncle as well. Those two things left Grace wondering why.

Jake's was busy for a Wednesday night. Almost every table was taken, and many heads turned when Blaise and Colton walked in. Grace felt like part of an entourage and smiled, thinking how much Jenn would eat this up. She'd have to call her later and tell her. Other than a few waves, no one got up from their tables to bother them.

She wished she and Blaise were alone. She wanted to ask more about Claire Phillips. She hadn't had a chance to search the internet for this woman. Could Claire Phillips be the break she'd been looking for?

Blaise chose the seat next to hers. She could feel his heat against her skin. A sense of relief washed over her as Colton sat opposite his brother. Chloe and Cash huddled at the end of the table, their heads bent over her phone, sharing something. Hopefully, Chloe used her good sense. As much as Grace liked Cash, there wasn't room in Chloe's near future for a relationship. Would Chloe think it weird if Grace and Blaise got together, especially if the two teens liked each other? The whole situation was weird, and she couldn't help but giggle.

"What's so funny?" Blaise said.

Heat filled her cheeks. "Nothing. What's everyone having?" She craned her neck to read the board with the menu selections.

The conversation turned to food and house

221

renovations. "Grace, I think you'll make your deadline," Colton said.

Donna, the waitress, slid up alongside Colton, her pen poised over her notebook. "Hi, y'all. Grace, how's the car?"

Grace stared at her. "My car? What do you mean?"

"You know... The other day, you were stranded on the side of the road and Blaise had to come pick you up."

"I ran out of gas. Wait. You knew about that?"

"Honey, everyone knows." Donna winked at her. She took their orders and sashayed away.

"I hope we make the deadline. Everything is riding on that." Grace thought about Claire Phillips and the possibility of finding out who bought the house for her. A lot was riding on that too. Maybe more.

"Old Beau is making good time, and now that I'm on the job, things will go smoothly."

Blaise threw a balled-up napkin at Colton. "Shut up. Please."

The conversation turned to music. "Did you ever listen to the songs I sent you?" Blaise leaned back in his chair and stared at Colton.

His strong leg brushed against hers sending shivers across her skin. She averted her gaze to the salt and pepper shakers. Better not to get caught staring.

Donna brought out the food. Colton smirked. "Yeah. They're not bad, but we can't put them into rotation."

Blaise sat up straight, dropping his burger back on the platc. "Why not?"

The tension took a seat at their table. The kids ignored them.

"The songs aren't our sound. The fans don't want to hear stuff like that from us. We haven't practiced them. I want to change the chords around. What about Troy's lyrics? You really think he's going to sing a song he didn't write the words for? The songs need work. Not this tour, another one maybe."

"My songs are good. You don't need to change anything, and I can handle Troy."

"Not how I see it."

"You don't have the final say. I sent the songs to Troy and Patrick."

Colton clenched his jaw. He gripped his glass of water and took a swig. "You sent those songs without telling me?"

"I don't need your permission." Blaise gritted his teeth.

Colton slammed his hand down on the table. Grace gripped her chair. Cash and Chloe jumped.

"We stick together. Always."

"Not when you're being an ass."

"Hey, guys, maybe we should change the subject." Grace kept her voice low. Other people were looking now. Someone was bound to take a video of this.

"I'll change the subject," Colton said with a smirk. "I have the tour dates. Joe called a few hours ago. We leave July fifteenth."

"Isn't that a few days before the fundraiser?" Grace looked to Blaise for an answer.

"He's going to have to miss it." Colton popped a fry into his mouth.

She turned to Blaise. "But you can't. You promised Savannah, and she's begun selling tickets because you're going to be there." Would he really let his sister down like that? Would Colton do that to Savannah? From the look on his smug face, Grace thought he just might.

Blaise shot Colton a look. "I can always fly in for the fundraiser and fly back out if I have to, but I don't anticipate there being a problem."

Grace pushed her salad away.

"If we've got a show that night, you're not flying back." Colton leaned back in his seat and crossed his arms over his chest. The tension got out of its seat and climbed on top of the table, sizzling.

"I'll speak to Joe. It's covered." Blaise stood and threw money down on the table. "Cash, you want a ride back?"

Grace handed Blaise his money. "It's my treat."

He threw his hands in the air. "Keep it. Cash?"

Cash looked up at his father.

"I can take him back if he's still eating," Grace said. Did that mean she'd have to take Colton back too because it was clear Blaise wasn't giving him a ride.

"I'll stay," Cash said.

Blaise weaved his way through the tables. Someone stopped him and shook his hand. Hopefully, that guy didn't hear the argument.

"My brother is moody." Colton popped another fry in his mouth. "He'll get over it, though. He always does."

"You were mad about the songs, so you wanted to get back at him. You knew he wanted to be in town for the fundraiser, but you didn't care. Is that what just happened here?"

"He would never have been in Heritage River in the first place if he didn't go and bust up his hand anyway. No one told him to climb the damn scaffolding. Well, that's not entirely true, but since when does he listen?"

"It was you who dared him? Weren't you worried he could fall and break his neck?"

He laughed. "You don't know my brother. He's always the one jumping first and asking questions later. Did he tell you about the time we got kicked out of a hotel because he jumped off a balcony into the pool? He missed some lady and the concrete by inches. I didn't have to dare him to do that, believe me. I don't have to dare him to race cars or drive motorcycles or the other crazy things he does either. This time he got hurt. Shit happens."

He was right. She didn't know Blaise at all. A picnic at the lake and a kiss on her patio didn't make her an expert on Blaise Savage. Did she think she was in some kind of a romance novel? She was the jilted house renovator swept away by the good looks and dashing smile of the neighbor. Now she was acting like a fool thinking she had some kind of handle on the kind of man he was. What kind of a grown man jumps off a balcony? Not one for her, that was for sure.

But the way he cared about his son. And the softness in his eyes when he played his music for her. He had offered to help her find the prior owner of the house. Or the clear hurt he felt because his brother disregarded him. What about that side of Blaise Savage?

"If you'll excuse me. Kids, I'll be right back." Grace followed the path Blaise took and hoped he hadn't gone too far.

The warm night air met her as she pushed through

the door onto the empty sidewalk. The businesses were shut up for the night. Only the Cream and Sugar up the street was crowded with customers. The on-street parking was full, and she searched for Blaise's truck.

"Blaise," Grace yelled as he bent to pick up something he dropped. Thankfully, he hadn't pulled away. He turned at the sound of her voice.

She mustered up the courage she needed and crossed the street. Happy children squealed into the night, laughing and chasing each other with ice cream running down their hands.

"What's up, Grace?"

She met his stormy gaze. "What just happened in there?"

"Nothing you need to worry about." He clenched his jaw and shoved his hand in his pocket. "Is there anything else? I want to get back."

"Did you know he was going to schedule the tour dates over the fundraiser?" She wanted to understand him.

"There was always the possibility."

"What are you going to do?" It wasn't her place to try to fix things, but she couldn't seem to stop herself.

"I'll talk to our manager, but if the shows are scheduled, it's too late. We can't cancel again. I'll have to go."

"But what about the fundraiser?"

"Savannah will understand. She's used to us."

But Grace didn't understand. "How can you make a promise and then just go back on it like that when people are counting on you?" She'd spent her entire life being there for other people. She couldn't just walk away from a responsibility.

"It's the nature of the beast. I have to go on tour. Look, my hand is bothering me. I'd like to get home and take some of the pain meds." He didn't meet her eye when he spoke.

She wasn't so sure he was telling the truth. He never complained about his hand. "Why is this tour so important?" She should let it go. Let him get in his truck and drive away, but she couldn't. Why was his appearance at this fundraiser so important to her anyway? Did she really care that much about the library or Heritage River? Wasn't she ready to go back to Jersey? Until that moment she thought she had one foot out the door already.

He let out a long breath. "Making a living is important to everyone. Touring is just how I do it. I need the money, Grace. You understand needing money, don't you?"

"Of course I do." She smoothed down her shirt.

"Do you mind if we talk about Claire Phillips tomorrow? It's getting late and my hand." He raised his bandaged hand and offered a sweet smile. His gray eyes twinkled in the lamplight.

It was late, after all. She was ready to climb onto her air mattress and forget about the day. Especially this disastrous dinner.

"I'll stop by tomorrow." He leaned in and kissed her cheek. The sensation of his soft lips against her skin lingered as he straightened up. "Be careful with my kid." He winked at her, the casual expression back on his face. He slid into the truck. He either didn't hold a grudge or faked his feelings well. She hoped it wasn't the latter.

She turned before he pulled away. Colton pushed

through the doors and stepped outside. He lit a cigarette and waved to her. She hesitated before crossing back over Main Street, not knowing what to say to him.

When she reached him, he handed her a fistful of money. "This is Blaise's. He won't take it from me. Slip it to him when he isn't looking, okay? I took care of dinner." She folded the money and put it in her pocket.

"Dinner was supposed to be my treat."

"I crashed the party and pissed off my kid brother. Lets me save face in front of my nephew." He blew the smoke away from her.

"That's kind of you. Paying for dinner, I mean."

"I'm not a total asshole." He smiled. The lines around his eyes deepened. He had gray stubble on his chin and more gray in his hair than Blaise. He was definitely easy on the eyes.

"What's it like being, you know, you?" The words stuck and stumbled out of her mouth, but Colton laughed anyway.

"You mean being in a country-rock band or being the older brother in the small Savage family from a little town in the South?" He leaned against the glass window, all his usual bravado slipping away.

What was it like being from this small place? Was he trying to run away from something his siblings seemed at peace with?

The sounds from the ice cream shop had died down. When Grace looked over her shoulder, most of the cars had gone too.

"No one expected much from me." He stamped out his cigarette, and she was secretly glad. "I never did well in school because all I wanted to do was play music. Since our dad was the music teacher, my lack of interest in academics was a problem. Every teacher made the extra effort to encourage me. I fought them all the way. Blaise, he was wild, but he did well in school. My father hoped Blaise would do more with his life. Not that being a music teacher was bad, but our dad wanted to be a musician in an orchestra. Like our mother was until she died in a bus accident on the way to a show. We were young and my dad needed to stay home with us, so he became a teacher. Until then they took us on the road with them. That life got in my blood and I couldn't let it get away, but my dad, he didn't want rock and roll in our lives. That wasn't real music to him. But that's what paid. And we were great at it." Colton looked off into the distance at some memory. "That's what it's like being me. Are you sorry you asked?"

"No, not at all."

"I'm going to walk home. The fresh air will clear my head and give Blaise time to simmer down. My brother likes you."

Heat warmed her neck. She liked him too. "He's very nice."

Colton smirked. "Way nicer than I am. Give him a chance. See you tomorrow, Grace."

His comment stunned her. He allowed his feelings for his family to peek out like a slip showing under a skirt. Her phone buzzed in her pocket. She pulled it out and watched until the screen said the call went to voice mail. She'd call Jenn back later. Colton's back grew distant as the night swallowed him up.

He was still hoping to get his father's approval. Grace could understand that. Their father might be gone, and Grace never really knew hers, but that didn't mean somewhere deep down she didn't secretly wish her father thought about her. She often wondered on her birthday or Christmas if the man was even still alive, if he thought about her at all.

She never bothered to try to find him. If he didn't want her, then she didn't want him either. She didn't need him or anyone.

Chloe and Cash pushed through the door. "Jeez, Mom, were you like going to leave without us?" Chloe handed Grace her purse.

"Yes, that was my plan all night. Drag you out here, feed you, and then leave you for some child snatcher to come along and grab two adult teens and whisk them away when no one was looking." She fished her keys out of the bottom of her bag. "You two ready? Let's go home."

Chapter Twenty-Five

Blaise watered his pathetic garden. He made sure to get at the roots of the plants and not just the tops. The dirt had to be saturated, so he kept the spray light and he lingered. Watering the garden wasn't much different from the melody of a sweet song, light and lingering, but for some reason plants didn't respond to his touch the way notes and rhythms did. Or the way he suspected Grace would.

The construction had begun for the day. Yelling and banging drifted over from next door. Today some of the yelling came from Cash and Jud. Their differences were coming to a head. Hopefully, they'd figure it out, but Blaise wasn't so sure. They should get along, but just because you were related didn't mean you had to like each other.

He certainly wasn't liking his brother much at the moment. He was avoiding Colton and so far doing a pretty good job of it. Blaise rolled the hose up and brushed the dirt from his brace. He had lied to Grace about the pain meds. He hadn't touched anything stronger than ibuprofen since the accident. The need to get away from Jake's and Colton was too strong. He couldn't stay around and risk punching his brother in the face. Not in front of Cash anyway.

Time was up. He couldn't avoid going next door any longer. Grace wanted to find out about Claire

Phillips. He promised to help her, and whether she thought so or not, he kept his promises. Well, he tried anyway.

Blaise rounded the yard as Jud ran out of the house and jumped down the steps. Cash followed, his face scrunched and his fist clenched. He dove off the porch and landed on Jud, knocking him to the ground. Both boys rolled in the dirt. Cash landed on top and raised his hand. Jud kicked and squirmed under Cash's strong legs.

"Cash," Grace yelled from the porch. "Stop."

Chloe pushed past her mother. "Cash, don't."

Blaise forced his legs forward and lunged for his son. He gripped Cash's arm, but not before Cash swung. Jud shoved Cash with a final push and rolled away. Cash's hand collided with Jud's shoulder instead of his face, and Cash fell over, almost taking Blaise with him. Jud pushed up from the ground, ready to pounce on Cash.

Blaise threw up his bad hand. "Stop," he yelled, wanting his voice to startle Jud into reality.

Colton bolted down the steps and stood between the boys. Cash shoved Blaise away and stood on his own.

"You assholes need to knock it off," Colton said.

"What the hell is going on?" Blaise wiped his hair away from his face. His heart hammered out quarter notes in his chest.

Cash wiped the spit from his mouth. "Nothing."

"This wasn't nothing. Now tell me what happened." Blaise knew by Cash's set jaw the possibility of getting an answer was slim. He didn't know what to do. Did he push for an answer or wait until Cash was ready to talk? Should he take his phone away or something? What did his dad do when he and Colton fought?

Cash crossed his arms over his chest.

"How about you? You want to tell me?" Blaise turned to Jud. Maybe some of his sister's sense would leak out of her boy.

"You saw it. He knocked me down and started a fight."

Blaise gritted his teeth. "Colton, did you see anything?"

"I was in the back of the house when they started yelling. By the time I got down the ladder, they were out here beating each other up." Colton spit on the ground.

"I'll tell you what happened." Beau limped down the steps and deposited himself between Cash and Jud. His face was a flaming red. "These two knuckleheads got a beef, and I don't want no beef on my job sites. You're both fired."

"He started it." Cash's voice cracked.

"Look at him," Jud smirked. "The makeup, the hair. He's a loser that starts trouble everywhere he goes. And he's got shit for brains. He started the fight. Not me. "

Jud glared at Cash, his face stretched into a snarl. Blaise saw his nephew in a way he hadn't before, and the hairs on his arm stood up. Jud was the instigator. He always had been, but Blaise wanted to keep the peace and believed Cash could be the troublemaker. How stupid could he be? Did he allow his son to be hurt by Jud? This fight was his fault too.

"I don't care who started it. I won't have it. You

hear me? Now, both of you, get off this property before I throw your sorry asses off myself." Beau's face cycled through a few shades of red. He hoped Beau didn't have a heart attack on the front lawn.

Grace pounded down the steps. "Beau, let's not be hasty. The boys are sorry, I'm sure. Right, boys?" No one said anything. She let out a big sigh. "If you fire them, we won't have a crew and I won't make my deadline. Please rethink this."

"Grace is right," Blaise said. "Let's think this through."

"There's nothing to think about. Now git." Beau turned on his heel and with as much strength as he could muster, limped back into the house.

"I don't want to work here anyway," Cash yelled at his retreating back. "I'm out of here." He marched across the lawn.

"Cash, come back," Blaise yelled.

But Cash didn't answer. He kept moving down the street and turned toward town. Jud grabbed his stuff off the porch.

"Where are you going?" Blaise asked.

"I'm not staying either. He's the criminal, not me. Why should I get fired?"

"Jud, shut up." Colton's eyes gave Jud a warning, but he paid no attention.

"I didn't say anything that wasn't true. He set that fire. He hit me first because he can't handle the truth. He's a loser."

"Knock it off." Colton stepped into Jud's space. Jud backed up.

Blaise's vision blurred. "Be very glad right now that you are my sister's son." His bad hand hurt from the tight fist he made.

"It isn't fair that I got in trouble because of Cash. I didn't do anything wrong. I'm leaving. I'll get another job. A better one." Jud waved to Chloe, but she turned without so much as an acknowledgement and went inside.

Blaise didn't know what to do. Did he follow Cash? Should he make Jud stay and apologize? What was Savannah going to say when she found out? It was going to be the bad preamble to the admission he might not be at the fundraiser.

Grace dropped down on the steps and hung her head between her knees. Colton moved up the steps, patted her on the shoulder, and went back to work. Blaise took up the spot next to her. He could smell her scent of vanilla and cinnamon.

"I'm sorry." That was all he could think of saying. It wasn't enough.

Grace cupped her chin in her hands and propped her elbows on her knees. Her blonde hair spilled out of the rubber band. He wanted to let his fingers run through it, but the moment wasn't a good one. He had at least that much sense.

"I'm not going to make my deadline with only Beau and Colton. Beau said he'd called his old crew, but they haven't come." She turned to look at him. Her blue eyes darkened. "What's going to happen when the tour starts? Beau can't finish this project by himself." She sat up straight. "You have to convince Beau to hire the boys back. And to find out when his old crew is going to start. You owe me that much."

"Me? What did I do?" He tried not to laugh because she was mad, but he liked the way her eyebrows squished together when she yelled at him.

"It's your son and nephew. Your entire Savage family has wrapped its web around me, and now I'm at your mercy."

He leaned in. "I'd like to see what you would do at my mercy," he whispered.

She swatted at him. "Now? You're going to flirt with me now?"

He couldn't help but laugh this time. He threw his hands up in surrender. "Okay, okay. I'm sorry. I won't flirt with you right now. Unless you want me to."

She smiled that slow, beautiful, lyrical smile, and his heart played a different rhythm in his chest.

"What I want you to do is help me find Claire Phillips."

"I can do that." He could try at least. "We can use my computer."

A black sedan pulled up to the house. A short man with a head of white hair pushed his way out of the driver's side. Hoke Carter adjusted his tie and his belt before moving around the front of the car and standing on her lawn.

"Morning, Grace, Blaise." He tipped his hand as if he were wearing a hat. "It's going to be another hot one today." He looked at the blue sky, then back at them. "How are the renovations going?"

"Good." The lilt had returned to Grace's voice.

Blaise couldn't look at her for fear he'd make a face at the lie. He stood and shook Hoke's hand. Grace stood alongside him.

"What brings you by?" She smoothed her shirt as she spoke.

He wanted to reach for her hand and hold it in his,

let her know she didn't have to be nervous, but this wasn't the right place or time.

Hoke hooked his thumbs through his belt loops. "Wanted to see how the progress was coming along. That deadline is coming down the track."

"She'll make it."

Grace smiled up at him.

"Glad to hear it. I was over at May's the other day, just sitting with my paper and my coffee—she makes the best coffee. Have you been over there yet?"

She shook her head, and Blaise wondered if he should stay around. "I should be going," he said.

"No, stay." She grabbed his wrist. She didn't have to ask him twice.

"Like I was saying, I was over at May's and heard some talk. There's always talk in a small town like Heritage River. You can't believe half of it, but as it was coming from a reliable source, I thought I might look into it further."

"Did something happen?" Blaise didn't like where Hoke was taking the conversation. Grace had given up on smoothing her shirt and had begun working her bottom lip under her teeth. She sensed it too.

"Nothing happened as far as I can tell. Just some nosing around going on. People sticking their noses where they don't belong."

Blaise stepped in front of her. "Who was doing that?"

Hoke ignored Blaise and continued to speak directly to Grace. "You do remember your agreement to taking this house, don't you?"

"Certainly." She shoved her chin up.

That a girl. Don't let him scare you.

"Then you remember if you try and find out who bought this house for you, the deal is null and void and all the money spent on the renovations has to be repaid."

"Hoke, I don't know what you're getting at," she said.

"I'm just here to remind you, that's all. Can I take a look inside and see how things are coming? I'd like to say hello to my old friend too."

Grace stepped aside. "Be my guest."

Blaise waited until Hoke went inside. "He knows."

Grace yanked her hair out of the rubber band and retied it. "How does he know? Who told him?"

"The assisted living, maybe?"

She gnawed on her lip again. He wanted to do that too and then berated himself for thinking about fooling around with this woman while she was in trouble.

"Do you think Beau could've told him?"

"I'm sure the whole town knows you ran out of gas on Route 1. Anyone could've told him where you were that day."

"But who knew I went to the assisted living?" She shielded her eyes from the sun.

"Besides me? I don't know. Who did you tell?"

"I didn't tell anyone. I don't think. Oh, I can't remember." She closed her eyes and rubbed her temple. "No, no. I didn't. I didn't even tell Chloe where I was going."

"What are you going to do now?"

"I'm going to find Claire Phillips."

"Are you sure?"

"No, but I have to know who bought this house for me. Are you going to talk me out of it?" She held his gaze.

"I gave up on that a long time ago. If you need to know so badly, I'll help you. But don't say I didn't warn you. You're risking a lot for information that won't change anything."

"It will for me."

"How?"

She looked back at the house, then at him. "What if I have a family some place?"

"What if you don't? Or what if you have a family that doesn't want to be found? Then you risked this house for nothing."

She hesitated, then nodded. "It's worth taking the risk."

"If you want to take a risk, I can help you find one somewhere else."

She fisted her hands on her hips. "You know, you sound like everyone who told me not to come down here and take this house. No one thinks I'm capable of handling a risk, but I can. If you don't want to help me, don't. I'll find Claire Phillips myself."

She was feisty and he liked it. He tried not to laugh, but he couldn't help but smile. "Okay, Ms. Starr, ma'am. I aim to please."

"You shouldn't hide your accent. It suits you." She dropped her gaze for a moment. He didn't miss the red creeping up her neck.

"I'll work on it." He winked. She was so easily riled. It was fun to see how she'd react to him. He bet her ex couldn't get her to respond this way because if he did, Grace wouldn't be standing toe to toe with him. Blaise was suddenly grateful for this anonymous person giving her the house next door to his. Maybe he should thank whoever this person was by keeping them hidden.

His phone buzzed in his pocket. He pulled it out. "Savannah. She must've heard from Jud."

"What are you going to tell her?"

"I'm going to ignore her for now." He shoved the phone back in his pocket.

"Why do those two boys dislike each other so much?"

He took a deep breath. "I don't know. I'll see if I can't get Beau to hire the boys back." His heart picked up tempo. He'd help Grace get her crew back.

His phone buzzed again. This time he saw Melissa's name. He debated on ignoring her too, but knew she wouldn't go away so easily. "I have to take this."

"Sure. I'll see you later." Grace turned and headed inside. Not so much as a grumble about being interrupted. Not a pout or a glaring eye. He could get used to that.

He slid his finger across the screen. "What's up, Melis?"

"Hello to you too. I just called Cash. Honestly, I didn't expect him to pick up because he never does, but he did and I managed to get out of him he had another fight with Jud and he got fired from his job. Is that right?"

Blaise wiped a hand over his face. He hoped to talk to Cash first or even Beau before Melissa had to find out. "It wasn't a big deal. Just boys being boys. I can talk to Beau and get his job back."

"You're supposed to be keeping an eye on him. If he's going to get in trouble with you, then I want him to come back home."

"I am watching him, but he's practically an adult. I can't hold his hand all day. He and Jud got into it, no big deal, and I'll fix it." He gritted his teeth.

"You can't fix it. He needs to learn to fix it himself. You can't go throwing your name around and making things all right again. When is he going to learn?"

"You're going to lecture me about throwing my name around? You've been doing that for years. On airplanes, in restaurants, concerts. You name it."

"Don't start that again. This isn't about us. It's about Cash and how he has to learn to take responsibility for his actions."

"You don't give that kid enough credit. He got this job himself, and he's doing his community service every day." Blaise couldn't believe how easy Cash had been overall.

"I want him home."

Should he tell her what Cash said or leave that to his son? "He wants to finish out his community service here. And I was thinking. Why not let him go to school out here?" He wasn't going to tell her about the tour. She was sure to throw a fit if she knew he would be on the road and Cash would be alone.

"His home is with me."

"I'm his parent too. He can live with me."

"Since when do you want him to live with you?"

"I never said I didn't want him, Melissa." A fire began burning in his stomach. "It just made more sense for him to stay with you because of my schedule. What kind of life would it have been for a child on the road?"

"If you wanted him so badly, why weren't you around more?"

She could never stay away from that sore spot. The fire burned in his veins, and it took all the control he could find not to punch a hole in the fence. "It was my schedule. Being on the road made us money. Money you went through like water."

"I wasn't the only one who spent money. You didn't need those fancy cars, and you had to keep that stupid house in Heritage River. And the instruments you collected."

"Those were antiques. An investment."

"A waste. Being home for your family, a few less shows a year, wouldn't have made a difference, but you couldn't wait to be away from us. You never wanted a family."

He couldn't hold the burning lid on any longer. The fire boiled over, and now the whole street heard him. "I was on the road so much to get away from you, not Cash. I couldn't stand to be around you any longer than I had to. I'm sorry I ever married you."

Colton stood beside him. Blaise hadn't seen him approach because all he could see was red.

His brother grabbed the phone from his shaking hand. "Melissa, it's Colton. I don't know what you and my brother are talking about, but I'm going to give you some advice. Shut the fuck up." He ended the call and handed the phone back to Blaise.

"Thanks." Blaise's voice croaked.

Colton shrugged. "Hey, what are brothers for? You really shouldn't let her get you that upset. At your age, you're bound to have a heart attack."

"I'll remember that." The fire returned to a simmer. "Was I really that bad of a father?"

"What do I know about being a father?"

"But I didn't stay home like Dad did. Should I have stayed home?" Were Cash's troubles because of him? Did his son know he loved him?

"Dad didn't think he had a choice. Three little kids. No wife. He wanted some kind of stability. He knew all the people here. He could have help at home. It was different for you."

"I'm not so sure."

"Cash seems okay."

"I'm not so sure about that either."

"You wouldn't have been happy at home. Touring was in your blood. You wouldn't stop Cash from going after his dreams, would you?"

"Well, no, but I had a responsibility to take care of my son. My dreams needed to take a back seat."

"Really? I don't think so. I've got to get back to work. Beau's going to blow his top in there, and Hoke isn't helping any. I don't know what they're talking about, but it isn't good. I can tell you that. You think that hand of yours is well enough to help us out?"

"It might be." His hand wasn't hurting as much as it had. His doctor appointment wasn't for another few weeks. "What did you want me to do?"

"Just follow my lead."

As he had his whole life.

****

The sun had set an hour ago. Blaise stood at the kitchen sink, trying to reach Cash. The call went to voice mail again. "Cash, call me. Just let me know you're okay."

Savannah had called again sometime after his fight with Melissa. Cash hadn't shown up for his community service hours, and he hadn't called her to let her know.

243

She knew about the fight, and she didn't care. She'd said the boys had to work it out themselves.

Blaise couldn't sit still any longer. He yanked his keys off the entry table and swung open the door. Grace stood there, hand in midair.

"I was about to knock." She dropped her hand. "Now must be a bad time. I'll go. I'm sorry." She turned, but he grabbed her arm.

"Wait. I was going to look for Cash. He never showed up at the library today for community service, and he hasn't come home yet. He's not answering his phone either." The sight of her hair hanging loosely around her shoulders, shorts to her knees, and a baggy T-shirt, the collar hanging off one shoulder, eased his tightly strung nerves.

"Let me text Chloe and see if she's heard from him." She pulled her phone from her pocket. "Nope." She held the phone up for him to see Chloe's response. "I'm sorry. He was pretty upset today. He might be cooling off someplace."

How did Cash cool off, exactly? Blaise didn't know. Add that to the list of things he didn't know about his kid. Was Cash off somewhere setting a fire? Was he drinking the way Blaise might have done at that age? Did he have his uncle's penchant for something stronger than alcohol? Wasn't addiction genetic?

"Would you come with me?" Here he was again, asking her to help him be a father.

"Of course." She typed away at her phone again. "Just letting Chloe know I'll be out for a while."

"I'm sorry. I'm taking you away from time with your daughter. Never mind, I can ask Colton to come with me." He didn't want Colton with him, but an extra pair of eyes wouldn't hurt, and Cash was more likely to talk to Colton.

"You need help, and Chloe's watching a show on her computer. She isn't interested in hanging with me, I'm afraid." She pressed her lips together and tucked the hair behind her ear. "Teenagers can be tough, can't they?"

"I'm seeing that." He shut the front door and hit the button on the key fob to make the truck come to life. He opened the truck door for Grace, and she slid inside. Her shorts rode up, and he could see more of her thigh. She definitely had nice legs.

"Has there always been a problem between Cash and Jud?"

He stole a glance at her while he navigated the streets. He didn't know where he was going to find Cash, but at least driving around gave him something to do. "For a while now."

"Why don't they get along?" She had pulled her leg up onto the seat and tucked her foot under. She'd slid her sandals off. The casual way she sat beside him made his insides warm up.

"Honestly, I have no idea." He was embarrassed to admit that. Cash would never tell him what the issue was. He didn't know how much to push, and Melissa was never worried about it because the kids only saw each other on holidays. Until now.

"There must be a reason. Otherwise, they'd get along. Your whole family seems to get along with each other. You might make each other mad, but it's clear you care deeply for one another. I heard Colton on the phone with your ex-wife today." Grace turned and looked out the window. "I'm sorry. I didn't mean to

245

overhear."

"It's okay. We're a loud bunch." She was right about his family. No matter what, they had each other's backs. Their dad had taught them that. He had hoped it would seep down into the kids, but it hadn't. Maybe Savannah's kids felt that way about each other, but her kids didn't seem to feel that way about Cash. Cash had never made it easy for them. He should've insisted Cash spent more time with him.

Blaise turned the truck off the side roads and headed to the edge of town.

"I hope you don't mind me saying, but does Jud pick on Cash because of...well..." She turned away again.

"Just say it."

Her head snapped back around. "Does Jud pick on Cash because of the way he looks?"

"Why should that matter?" But Jud had said exactly that earlier. Had he really been picking on Cash because of his appearance?

"It doesn't matter to you, but it might matter to Jud. Look at him, clean-cut, excels at school. He's an athlete, student body president, the whole package."

He gripped the wheel tighter. "Are you saying my kid isn't the whole package?"

Her hand went to her mouth. "Oh God, no. I'm sorry. He is. I didn't mean it like that. He's different from Jud. Cash is certainly smart and handsome— talented, I'm sure, with a family so proficient in music—but his look says he's different. He's part of the group on the outside. Sometimes teenagers like Jud pick at the scabs of kids like Cash. Do you know what I mean?"

He did. But that wasn't Jud. Not one of Savannah's kids. No way. "It has to be more than that. Maybe Cash said something to Jud or accused him of doing something Jud didn't do. I don't know what it is, and maybe it doesn't matter. I just want to find my son and know he's all right. I'll deal with the rest later."

Grace folded her hands in her lap and didn't say another word. He wanted to pull her out of the shell she'd covered herself with, say he was being a big jerk because he was scared. He had asked her to come along, and now he was being short with her.

"I'm sorry," he said.

"Nothing to be sorry about. I would be upset too if I didn't know where Chloe was."

"How do you stay so calm dealing with her?"

Grace laughed. How he loved that laugh. "Calm? You don't know me very well. Calm is the last word I'd use to describe how I feel with her. I haven't been calm since the day she was born. That might be part of my problem."

"From over here it looks like you're doing just fine. You've given me plenty of advice."

She turned to him and gave him a wry smile. "You don't know much about parenting, do you?" She laughed again.

"Go ahead. Make me the brunt of your joke." He winked. He liked the banter between them. She could joke around and take it too.

Blaise turned the truck off the main road onto a dirt road. The only lights were those of his truck. Tall grass swayed on either side of them.

"You think he went to the lake?" she said.

"I can't think of anywhere else to look." He

stopped the truck and they got out. He pulled a flashlight from his tackle case in the back. They walked over the edge onto the sand. The fireflies danced around them, and the cicadas sang their nightly lullaby. The air was thick and smelled sweet. Some of the houses on the other side were still lit. The moon draped its rays over the lake's surface. No one was there except them.

"Where to now?" she said.

His phone buzzed in his pocket. He yanked it out. "Yeah?"

"He's home," Colton said. "He walked in five minutes ago and went straight to his room. I tried to get him to tell me where he was, but he wasn't talking. I can try again if you want, or I can call Savannah if you think it's better he talks to her."

Blaise let out a long breath. "No. No. Don't call her. Leave him alone until I get back. Just don't let him leave. Can you do that?"

"You want me to stand guard?"

"Yes, dammit."

"Easy. It's no problem. I'll stay up all night if I have to. Where are you anyway?"

"Driving around looking for Cash. I'll be back later."

"Take your time. Kiss her once for me."

Colton ended the call before Blaise could say another word. Sometimes he really hated his brother. He was pretty sure he heard laughing right before Colton hung up.

He shoved the phone back in his pocket. "Cash is home." His heart slowed to a normal rhythm.

"Thank God."

"I'm not sure how to handle him." He hated

admitting how inept he was at being a father.

"Just talk to him. Find out what's really going on between him and Jud. You can offer advice, but it's up to him to use it or not. He's an adult now. The choices are his."

"You make it sound so easy."

"It isn't." She looked around and then back at him. "Should we get back?"

He didn't want to go. He wasn't ready to have a heart-to-heart with Cash. He needed more time to get his footing. The moonlight cast Grace in a warm glow. He could look at her all night like that.

"My brother thinks I should kiss you."

"What? Why?" She stepped back and tripped before righting herself.

"I don't know. I thought he had a crush on you, actually, and wanted you for himself."

She turned away from him and looked out across the lake. "That's silly. I'm too old for someone to have a crush on."

"You're wrong about that." He leaned against the hood of the truck and watched her. She tucked her hair behind her ear and swatted at the mosquitos biting at her legs. How he wished that was him. Biting her, not being swatted at. Well, maybe. He chuckled, but she didn't hear him.

She turned back. "He isn't planning on asking me out, is he? Because I won't go." Her hand covered her mouth. "Oh, I'm sorry. I shouldn't have said it like that. It's just...I'm, oh, I don't know how to act around men. I'm out of practice, not that I was ever good at it."

The dark night made seeing difficult, but he was pretty sure her face turned red. "You can't iron your shirt with your hands." He walked over and rescued the bottom of her top from her constant smoothing. Her hands were small and cold in his. He rubbed the tops with his thumbs. "So you don't like Colton?"

She didn't release her grip. "Not like that."

"Should I kiss you, then?"

Before she could say anything, Blaise leaned in and pressed his lips against hers. Her lips were smooth and warm. He wouldn't push her—she might run scared into the water—so he lingered like a violin in C minor. She kissed him back and parted her lips, inviting him in. He pulled Grace closer so their bodies were touching, his hands on her shoulders. His tongue sought out hers, and she let out a slight moan. His blood heated up, but he wouldn't rush her, even though his brain was three steps ahead, already taking her clothes off and lying on the sand with her. Instead, his fingers tangled in her hair while he took the kiss deeper. Her mouth followed his lead, as she reached her arms up around his neck. Her sweet taste made his head spin. He wanted this woman in a way he hadn't wanted a woman before.

He broke the kiss. Grace stumbled a little at the abrupt ending, but he held her close. He leaned his forehead down against hers.

"Was that bad?" Her voice trembled.

"That was the opposite of bad, but if I didn't stop then, I'm afraid I wouldn't be able to stop at all. I didn't want to sully your reputation, ma'am. What would the neighbors say?"

"If you keep using your accent, it's going to make it harder to let go and I will stop caring what the neighbors say." She continued to hold onto him.

He could stay there all night with her wrapped around him, standing by the hood of the truck. The engine ticked as it cooled down.

He wasn't sure he would be able cool down at all. He leaned in and kissed her again. She opened her mouth wider and took control. His head spun for sure. Her hands slid down his chest, learning his angles, then rested at his waist. His blood heated up further.

He was afraid to touch her. Afraid he'd scare her. Afraid he'd do it wrong. Afraid he wouldn't be able to stop. He felt like a teenager again, and kind of liked it.

His phone buzzed in his pocket, but he was going to ignore it.

Grace pulled away this time. "You should get that."

"It can wait." He was breathless.

"Considering what went on today. Get it. It's okay." She released him and stepped back.

It was Cash. She had been right. "You okay?" Blaise said into the phone.

"I'm going back to California. Uncle Colton said he'd drive me tonight."

"What? Wait a second. You can't go back to California tonight. It's late." That was a stupid thing to say, but it was out of his mouth before he could stop it.

"I don't care how late it is. We can stay in a hotel if we have to. I'm not staying in Heritage River anymore." Cash said it the way he might say pass the milk. He wasn't angry or upset. He'd come to a decision, and that was it.

"I thought you wanted to live with me." Blaise didn't understand where any of this was coming from. "This can't be all because you and Jud got into it

251

today."

"I don't want to live in the same town as he does."

"Don't go anywhere until I get back. I'm at the lake. I'll be home in thirty minutes." Cash didn't say anything. "Cash, please tell me you'll wait."

"Yeah. Okay." Cash ended the call.

Blaise looked at Grace. She was so beautiful, staring back at him with her eyes wide and her mouth in a little circle. "We have to go," he said. "I may have lost my son."

Chapter Twenty-Six

Grace climbed the steps to the front porch of her disaster house. Things really were becoming a disaster. The renovations were going okay, but they weren't going to make the deadline. Not after Blaise told her Cash wanted to go back to California.

She couldn't tell in the dark interior of Blaise's truck on the race back from the lake, but maybe he had tears in his eyes. He didn't want to lose his son. She knew that much for sure.

Hoke Carter was onto her investigation into who bought the house for her. He'd said as much, but that wasn't going to stop her. She'd go to the library tomorrow and look up Claire Phillips. Blaise had enough on his plate. He didn't need to help her.

She shut the door and leaned against it. She'd left a small table lamp on so the house wouldn't be in total darkness when she returned. The lamp sat on the floor because the room still wasn't finished, and maybe never would be at this rate. The place smelled of dust and spackle.

What would she do if she lost this house? How would she return to Silverside and still hold her head up? Jenn had said she was crazy for taking this project on. Chloe thought it too. Larry would probably have a good laugh at her expense. Would she have to tell the people at the Silverside Library about her failure?

Silverside might be bigger than Heritage River, but gossip still flowed at a quick rate. There would be whispers about Grace making a fool of herself. Isn't that what she had been doing down here?

What she needed was a cup of tea.

With a soft knock, she carefully opened Chloe's door and checked. She didn't expect Chloe to be asleep yet. She listened to her daughter's slow breathing. Watching Chloe sleep never got old, and old habits don't die. She used to stand at Chloe's crib and watch in fascination as her little baby lay on her side, sucking on her fingers. Then Grace would watch as her preschooler with chubby cheeks tossed and turned in her sleep.

As Chloe got older, she didn't check in as much. Larry always said it wasn't necessary, and Chloe liked Grace stepping into her room less and less as the years went on. But she couldn't help herself. Who was she if she wasn't Chloe's mother? She watched for a moment longer and then left as quietly as she came.

Grace took the tea and went out to the back patio. She could sit out there at least. Otherwise, she'd be confined to her bedroom, and at the moment, that had lost its appeal.

The lights were on in Blaise's house. If she positioned herself right, she could see him over the fence as he paced back and forth in the kitchen. Cash stood at the counter, his hands in his pockets. Colton leaned against the fridge, a mug in his hand. Nothing good was going on over there. She sank into the patio chair. It wasn't comfortable with its plastic lines cutting into her, but at least she could sit and see the stars.

She wanted to help Blaise. Offer advice, but she

didn't have any. She wasn't in any position to tell him how to handle his son. She didn't want Cash to go either, but her reasons were partly selfish. What was going on between the cousins? And why doesn't anyone see it? Maybe Grace would ask Chloe what she thought. If the mood was right.

The chamomile soothed her nerves, which had been on fire since Blaise pressed his lips against hers. Just thinking about it made her legs jittery. It was a good thing she was sitting. She pressed her fingers to her lips and could still feel Blaise. He had smelled good too. Clean and masculine. She had wanted to run her fingers against his skin, but she didn't dare. She hardly knew this man, but he was affecting her in ways no man had before. Making her act like a schoolgirl when she was a middle-aged divorced woman who should have some sense.

Did she really want to have sense? On the one hand, yes. He had been with so many women. She could contract a disease, and how could he possibly feel anything for her other than lust? She didn't want to be another Blaise Savage conquest. Making love had to mean something, didn't it? What would it mean to a man who could never stay in one place very long with hundreds of women lining up to get into his bed?

And what if she did try to have sex with him—her face flushed just thinking about it—and things went badly? She was out of practice. She and Larry hardly set off any fireworks. They had their routine, with its memorized steps. Lovemaking with Larry didn't amount to much. As soon as it was over, he'd reach for his reading glasses and check emails. She'd roll over and turn out the light.

Just that kiss with Blaise felt hotter than any sex she had while married. Yes, he was skilled and it showed, but there was more. His quick wit and sense of humor. The subtleties and his consideration. The passion in his music. She needed to stop thinking about him, or she might find herself on his front porch. And how would that look?

Besides, he would go on tour and forget about her. Some younger, hotter woman would wave her bra in his face, and he'd forget about Grace. She couldn't bear that. And she was leaving for Jersey as soon as she could. They weren't in a position for a romance, and no amount of learning to be more of a free spirit was going to allow her to have a sexual affair with a man. She wasn't ready to take that leap.

The lights went out next door. The Savage men had retired for the night. She hadn't heard a car start or slamming doors, so maybe Blaise convinced Cash to stay at least until morning. She hoped Colton was on Blaise's side through this. Colton's obvious connection to Cash didn't help matters any.

Grace drained the last of the tea. The night was warm and quiet. It might be nice to sleep outside if she had a way to do it. She could put up a hammock under the big poplar tree and a conversation set in wicker with green cushions under an awning would round out the backyard. A fire pit would be nice on cooler nights. This place could be a little oasis with half a chance. She pushed up from the chair. Something to think about.

Maybe she should think about staying. The thought took her by surprise, and she stopped with her hand poised at the sliding door. Stay? In Heritage River? Why? She glanced over her shoulder at the darkened house next door.

"It was just a kiss," she said into the night. "Nothing more. Don't get ahead of yourself. You're too old for fantasies."

****

The morning light slid through the kitchen window, draping the room in white. The heat hadn't arrived yet. Grace stood by the opened window. The breeze rubbed against her warm skin. She hadn't slept much with her mind racing in all directions. She was ready to start the day.

A truck rumbled into her driveway. Beau was there. Alone.

"Chloe, hurry. Beau is here," she shouted through the house.

"Mom, you don't have to yell." Chloe turned the corner. She wore shorts and a tee.

"That looks like underwear." Grace pointed a finger at the tiny pieces of cotton. "Why don't you leave something to the imagination?"

"I'm an adult, and it's my body. I can do what I want with it."

"Said every hooker." Grace yanked open the door before Chloe could stamp her feet and accuse Grace of calling her a hooker. Which she wasn't, but Chloe wouldn't see it that way.

"Good morning, Beau."

He held up his coffee cup in salute. "Miss Grace. Miss Chloe. We have a lot of work to do today."

"I hate this job." Chloe threw her hands in the air. "I should've stayed in New Jersey."

"You two have a lot of work today." Grace pointed to Beau and Chloe's retreating backs. "I have some errands to run, remember? I'm picking out the quartz counters and the appliances. I'll be back later. Beau, you really should hire the boys back, and when is your crew coming?"

He gave her a grumble and marched into the kitchen. *Stubborn old man.* There was no time to debate with him. She wanted to get to the library when it opened and hopefully be in and out before Savannah arrived. Her internet service had been glitchy since she moved the router to the bedroom. If she locked herself in her bedroom, before long Chloe or Beau would come looking for her. She didn't trust herself to lie well. Beau couldn't find out what she was up to. He'd already warned her to stay away from any searching.

Before she could get out of the house, Colton walked through the front door, wearing his tool belt, work boots, and that same dimpled smile Blaise had. The smell of cigarettes followed him in.

"You're not smoking in the house, are you?" It was out before she could stop it.

His eyes grew wide, and he threw a hand to his chest. "Who? Me? Never." He pulled a pack of cigarettes out of his shirt pocket. "You want one?"

"Don't smoke in the house, please."

"I won't mess up your new house with my bad habit."

"Good." She pushed past him and headed outside.

Colton called from behind her. "You know you could say thank you."

She stopped dead and turned around. The muscles in her neck twisted together. "Thank you for what?"

"For working on your house. I don't have to do that, you know. It's not like I need the money."

"So why are you?" She hadn't given it much thought. She was grateful Colton decided to join the crew. He seemed to know what he was doing, and the boys listened to him better than they listened to Beau. He was right. She was being rude. "Sorry, Colton. Thank you."

He stared at her in surprise. "You're welcome." He turned on his heel.

"Hey, you didn't answer my question. Why are you helping out?"

He stopped. "I have my reasons. But now it's mostly because Beau needs my help."

She took a deep breath and retied her hair in a ponytail. "Does that mean Cash is really leaving?"

"I'm not sure, and if he stays, there's no saying if he'll get his job back." He hitched a thumb over his shoulder, pointing to the direction Beau went.

Colton was more of a softy than he let on, but she wouldn't point it out. Let him have his bravado and stage presence. He didn't seem to have a whole lot outside of his immediate family.

"Thanks again, Colton. I mean it."

Colton waved with his hammer and went in.

Grace hurried to the library, but not without a glance at Blaise's house before she pulled away. Hopefully, Cash would stay. Hopefully, Blaise stayed too. His tour would be a problem for all of them.

Grace didn't recognize the one car in the library parking lot. That meant Savannah wasn't in yet. If she hurried, maybe she'd get in and get out.

The air-conditioning hit her as she pushed through the door. The place smelled like old paper and overhandled books. She loved that smell.

Arlene sat at the circulation desk, her face buried in the computer screen. Her brown hair was piled on top of her head. Her lips were painted blood red. She left a lipstick ring on her white coffee mug that had seen one too many turns in the dishwasher, as the writing was all but worn off.

"Good morning." Grace hoped she sounded good humored.

Arlene's head popped up. "Oh, Grace. I wasn't expecting you today."

"I'm not here to work. I wanted to use the computer for a minute. I need to do some research." She forced her sweaty hands to grip her purse instead of trying to smooth down her shirt. Her voice sounded strangled even to her.

"You don't have internet access at your new place?" Arlene put more lipstick on that mug.

Grace waved a hand. "It's so dusty there right now. I had a few errands to run anyway. I'll just be a minute." She scooted off to the back corner where the computer center was located.

The Heritage River library had only three computers for use. They were old-style personal computers with a wide monitor, but they still worked. Savannah wanted to use some of the fundraising money to buy new computers. Some of the town's residents couldn't afford computers or internet hookup at home and relied on the library to look for jobs, write resumes, and even stay in touch with friends and family faraway. Unfortunately, most of the fundraising money was going to fix the roof and update the checkout system. New books would be nice, but Savannah didn't think the money would go that far. If Blaise didn't play, the money raised might not be enough for the new computers.

Grace poised her fingers over the keyboard. She didn't have much to go on. Where was Claire Phillips even from? She should have asked Blaise. She punched in the name, and a whole page of Claire Phillipses popped up. Some on Facebook, LinkedIn. One even had a Wikipedia page, but she didn't look like a good fit since she was born at the turn of the nineteenth century.

Facebook was a good a place to try as any. Maybe Claire would have pictures with Nancy. People were pretty savvy with their security settings, locking Grace out of many of the photos. She scrolled and clicked, but not knowing where Claire was from had her going in circles. The search was pointless without more information. She should have planned better.

She tapped her fingers on the table and thought of the way Blaise always did that but with rhythm, unlike the awkward noise she was making. There was one other person she wanted to look up, although the library was the worst possible place to do it. She could ask around and hide her intentions better than punching his name into the search engine. If she was smart, she'd leave now. Instead, she checked around to make sure no one was nearby and typed *Jud Montgomery, Heritage River* into the search box.

As she suspected, articles from the local paper popped up. A full page of results with titles like:

Riverhawks Score Again!
Montgomery Soars with Three Touchdowns!
Riverhawks Give Their Opponents a Bath!

She skimmed through the articles. Jud was always

mentioned as the team hero. The coaches and players loved him. She scrolled onto the next page and found the school's honor roll listed. Jud's name came up repeatedly. Another article talked about Jud and some classmates helping to build homes for the homeless. The picture that accompanied the piece was of Jud and four other boys, all smiling, their arms wrapped around each other.

Grace sat back in the chair. This kid had it all. Two loving parents, a good family including famous uncles, smarts, looks, and athletic prowess. And he hated Cash because Cash was none of those things. Often times kids like Jud found the weakest link and picked and picked until there was blood. How could he do that to his own cousin? To his uncle? But blood had nothing to do with it. It didn't matter how you were related. Your closest relative could slice you up in ways no one else could.

"Grace."

She jumped in her seat and fumbled with the mouse to shut the screen down before Savannah was on top of her. A quick glance at the clock said she'd been there longer than she'd planned.

Savannah dropped her big tote on the table and flopped down in the chair next to her. "You're here early. Needed some quiet time?"

"Exactly." The woman had a sixth sense. "I was just about to leave." Grace jumped up and gathered her purse and keys.

"Before you go, I wanted to show you the seating layout I did for the concert." Savannah rummaged through her bag and pulled out an overstuffed yellow folder. "I thought we'd use the parking lot and set the stage up at the south end. I know it means people will have to park on the streets and walk, but we don't have enough grassy space for everyone to sit."

"How are the ticket sales going?" Maybe no one was coming, and the loss of the main attraction wouldn't be felt as much.

"Great. I think we sold a hundred tickets already. I'm salivating over that technology room."

A hundred tickets. "That's more than you thought you'd sell."

"What can I say? My brother is still pretty popular in these parts. If I could convince Colton to join him even for one song, ticket sales would triple. This whole place would get a face-lift. So what do you think of the layout?"

Savannah dropped the folder on the keyboard, waking the monitor up. Grace fumbled across the table to shove it back to sleep, but not in time.

"Oh, were you searching for something?"

"Just trying to get into my Facebook account."

"You're on Facebook? Me too. You should friend me."

"Thanks, I will." If she were on Facebook, wouldn't it stand to reason the Facebook page would be up and not Google? "I was just taking a quick peek before I researched materials for the new counters." She felt like the kid caught drawing on the wall with crayons.

"Don't worry about it, Grace. We all need a little mindless entertainment. I love all the pictures of people's kids. I won't tell Beau what you were up to. I'm sure he wants you back on the job site after yesterday."

"Why do Jud and Cash fight so much?" It really wasn't any of her business, and she expected Savannah to say so. Grace was an outsider. She had no right sticking her nose where it didn't belong.

"You know boys. They say something, get mad, duke it out, and it's over. Colton and Blaise were like that all the time growing up. Drove my dad crazy." Savannah offered a thin smile.

Grace pushed her shoulders back and took a deep breath. She needed as much confidence as she could find to say what she was thinking. "I certainly don't know them well, and don't pretend to, but during our time together I've noticed the constant bickering. They aren't getting over anything."

Savannah shoved her folder back in her bag. "You're right. You really don't know them, and of course a mother knows her son better than anyone."

Why did women think just because they pasted a smile on their face no one else could detect the disdain simmering below the surface? Grace nodded, but she knew where this was headed.

"Jud and Cash are going through a stage. They're the same age, their bodies are changing, their minds are forming, and this will pass. I'm not worried," Savannah said.

Grace's throat dried up. She tried to swallow. "I've heard them. Is it possible, just a thought really, that there's some jealousy?"

Savannah pressed her lips together. "You noticed. Please don't say anything to Blaise. I don't want to upset him. It stands to reason Cash would be jealous of Jud. Cash never sees Blaise. His grades were never great, and he doesn't participate in any school activities.

He doesn't have a lot of friends, and he gave up playing music. And don't get me started about his look. He's a handsome kid, and I love him to death, believe me, but what does he expect people to think when they see him?"

There was no denying people made judgments based on appearances. It wasn't always right, and often times people got things wrong—look at Ted Bundy—but Cash was a good kid. He didn't want trouble. He kept to himself. Something more was going on, and Savannah was blinded by her "mother eyes." Grace could understand that too.

"Would there be any reason Jud would be jealous of Cash?" Grace took a step backward to give Savannah as much space as possible to lob at the question.

Savannah pulled her shoulders back, studying Grace. "Did Blaise ask you to quiz me?"

Grace waved her hands. "He would never ask me to do something like that. I was just making an observation, that's all. I'm sorry I said anything." Grace gripped her keys. "I should be going."

"Do you think you know my brother well?"

Heat filled Grace's cheeks at the thought of how well she was starting to know him. His muscular chest, his thin waist. His soft lips and strong tongue. "No, certainly not."

"That's good, because you don't and you don't know his son well either. Thank you for your concern, but we have it all under control."

"You do. Again, I'm sorry I mentioned anything." Grace took her purse and headed for the front of the library. She understood Savannah was filling the role of protector of her family. She was the matriarch and had been for a long time. Women always stepped in and did whatever was necessary to keep the gears grinding, and she wouldn't want Grace questioning the harmony in the family.

Grace didn't want Cash to get the short end of the stick either, and he might be. She'd talk to Beau herself to get Cash's job back if Cash wasn't already on a plane back to California by then. She hurried to her car and pulled out of the parking lot before she remembered. Her breath caught in her throat. It was too late to go back. How would she explain her return? No, she'd have to keep going and just pray she hadn't pushed Savannah too far or that Savannah wasn't one to hold a grudge.

She'd forgotten to clear the history on the computer.

Chapter Twenty-Seven

By the time she returned to Dogwood Drive from picking counters and appliances, her head spun. So many choices. Did she pick something she loved and wanted for herself or pick something practical and economical another owner could change if they wanted? How could she even consider staying? Well, she was starting to see what was so special about Heritage River.

Blaise's truck was nowhere to be seen. Did that mean he was taking Cash to the airport? Grace pushed open the front door. Chloe, Beau, and Colton were in the kitchen.

"Mom, look what we did." Chloe pointed around the room as if she were a game-show model.

The brand-new white top cabinets were in. On either side of the enlarged window were the glass front cabinets she'd drooled over and pasted pictures of on her vision board. She hadn't realized Beau was paying attention.

"How did you mange that?" She didn't think they'd get that far, just the three of them.

"Let's hope they stay on the wall." Colton swept the subfloor.

Her new hardwood was on its way, and then her island could go in.

"Hush now." Beau glared at Colton. "Don't go

scaring Miss Grace. You should know Chloe was a big part of today. She really helped." His face beamed as he looked at her daughter.

"Thank you. Thank you, all of you. How about dinner on me?"

"No, thank you. I've got to go rest these old bones. Big day tomorrow. We're fixing that bathroom, then tearing up yours. Plan on getting dirty tomorrow. No errands that run you out of town. No time for that." Beau scooped up his toolbox and a dirty coffee mug. He knew about her visit to Nancy Templeton. "Miss Grace, you mind following me out to my truck?"

He didn't wait for her answer, and she followed as told. He kicked the gravel in the driveway before looking at her.

"Is there something going on with the house?" She licked her dry lips.

"You like this house?"

She turned back and glanced. "Sure. It's cute. A lot of potential. Why?" She noticed he hadn't answered her question.

"This house suits you and Chloe. None of my business, but she could use a place like this to come home to when she's not at school."

No, it wasn't his business, so why was he sticking his nose in it? "I don't imagine Chloe will be coming home much at all. She's been dying to leave home for years." Grace was just trying to prepare herself for that moment.

"All I'm saying is, don't keep going on jaunts that risk losing it."

Her chin went up. "I'm not sure what you're getting at." She knew exactly what he meant.

"Don't go digging. Leave it be. It don't matter."

It mattered to her. She wanted a family, a big one. She was losing her daughter with every day. She lost her marriage, and her parents. There was no one left. She glanced at Blaise's house. He wasn't offering her what she needed. Not emotionally. She didn't expect him to. He wasn't asking for anything. Why would he?

"Did Hoke say something to you?"

"I'm warning you. You'll lose it all. I'm killing myself to finish on time for you. Don't go ruining what I'm doing because you've got to know. You don't need to know. Leave it."

"Why are you killing yourself? Why didn't you tell Hoke to find someone else?"

"That's my concern. Not yours. Now I'm going home and resting my old, tired body. See you in the morning."

"Beau, I was wondering if you'd hire Cash back."

He shook his head.

"You need the help, and I don't think Cash is the one who started it."

"How do you know that? You weren't there."

"No, I wasn't, but it's an instinct. A mother thing. I don't know." She looked over her shoulder to make sure Colton wasn't coming out. "Jud pushes Cash's buttons." She lowered her voice. "There's something going on between them, and no one seems to know what it is. Please give him another chance. I want him to know I believe in him."

Beau scrutinized her with his cold eyes. He was going to say no. "He means that much to you?"

"He does. He's a sweet boy. Maybe confused and misguided." She didn't want that to come off in a bad way for Blaise. "It must be hard for him with his parents living in separate states. He's had a hard time at school. Can't we give him another try? I don't mind, and it's my house."

"It's my crew, and I don't allow fighting on my crew. Never have."

"Please, Beau. Just this once."

"You want me to hire Cash and not Jud?"

She hadn't thought about it all the way through, but that was what she was saying. "Jud has opportunities Cash doesn't." She thought of Blaise's money troubles. Would they affect college or how they lived? He never shared the details.

"I've got to live in this town after you go, Miss Grace. I can't hire Cash back without Jud and look Savannah Montgomery in the eye when I pass her on the street. You take them both or not at all."

"But Jud started it and has something against Cash. No, just Cash. I'm the homeowner, aren't I? Isn't that what everyone wants me to remember? Well, as the homeowner, I have the right to hire who I see fit for the job. I want Cash Savage to help out." She crossed her arms over her chest for good measure.

"All right." He waved a hand in the air. "You women will be the death of me for sure. I'll do it." He slid into the driver's seat and rolled down his window. "You know your Chloe likes him too. Asked me the same thing this morning."

"She did?"

He nodded and pulled out of the driveway. She watched as he turned the corner. Chloe liked Cash. As friends or more?

****

"That was an oldie but goodie, folks. Rumor has it Savage is hitting the road again after Blaise Savage's accident put the brakes on earlier this year. If you ask me, I say why bother? Time to enjoy retirement, guys, if you aren't going to make any new music." The disc jockey coming through the speakers in Blaise's truck let himself have a hearty laugh at his own joke. "Now here's a band I hope never stops getting on the road."

Blaise jabbed at the radio, turning it off before the music began. He didn't want to hear what band was about to play. He didn't want to hear new music, and he hated hearing his own music on the radio. It was tired and old. The DJ, asshole that he was, was right.

Anger burned his insides. How had things gotten away from him? He had been cruising along fine for years, making money, making music. He had even fooled himself into thinking Cash was fine without him. Cash wasn't fine. The boy needed his father, and Blaise had tanked and burned on that one.

He stole a glance at Cash brooding in the seat next to him. Cash looked out the window, his head shoved low in his shoulders. He bounced his leg and picked at a scab on his finger. At least Blaise was able to convince Cash, with a little help from Colton, to stay in Heritage River.

"I'm not pulling this truck over until you tell me what started that fight."

They had been driving around for an hour. He thought maybe the truck would be the place Cash would open up. It was doing the opposite. He didn't know what else to do, so he headed for Main Street and pulled in at Cream and Sugar.

"Ice cream?" At least the boy was speaking.

271

"Hungry?"

"No."

"I am." Blaise jumped out before Cash could say anything. He stood in line and forced himself not to look back. This whole thing was stupid.

He wouldn't even have bothered to try to force Cash to tell him except for the call from Savannah. She hadn't liked Grace's questions. She wanted Blaise to tell Grace to mind her own business. Savannah hadn't wanted to say anything herself because of the fundraiser. There would be a lot of work to do that day. She'd asked him to help out too, but he'd managed to skirt the issue, not wanting to tell her he might be gone.

He wanted to talk to Grace. What had she seen in such a short time that he hadn't seen ever? What kind of father didn't understand his child's pain?

He got to the front of the line and ordered two mint ice creams with cookie crunches in cones, Cash's favorite flavor when he was around five. Blaise knew that much at least. He didn't know if the boy still liked it.

He waved Cash out of the truck. At first Cash shook his head, but maybe the ice cream dripping down Blaise's hand and onto his brace was enough guilt to get his son on the sidewalk.

"Do you still like this flavor?" The words were thick and heavy in his mouth, but nothing else would come to him.

Cash shrugged but licked what melted down the cone. They sat on the bench facing the library. The sun poked through the leaves, and there wasn't a breeze in sight. The smell of cut grass filled the air.

Blaise stretched out his legs and leaned back. "I'm

glad you stayed," he said between licks.

"How long before you leave for the tour?" Cash focused on his task of eating the ice cream.

"Do you think because I'm on tour means I don't want you to live with me?"

Cash ate his way down the cone, keeping his eyes straight ahead. "I guess I know you do, but why can't you stay home?"

"Why do you want me to stay so badly? You're almost an adult. I thought you'd be glad to have the house to yourself for a few months." Blaise tried to make light of his sentence by knocking into Cash's arm with his own, but the attempt fell flat. Cash kept looking straight ahead.

Cash turned toward Cream and Sugar, and Blaise followed his gaze. A family walked up to the window. The father held his young son with big blond curls on his shoulders while the mother ordered. The little boy had his fingers laced through the father's hair. A smile spread across the little boy's face, and he laughed a deep belly laugh. The father patted the boy's leg and laughed too.

"Hold him, James." The mother reached up toward her boy.

"Don't worry. I've got him."

I've got him. Blaise reached out to touch Cash but pulled back, afraid his gesture wasn't enough. "If I could undo my mistakes, I would."

"Huh?"

"I'm sorry, Cash. I'm sorry for my bad decisions as a dad." He swallowed the knot in his throat. The ice cream lost its flavor.

Cash kept his head down and kicked the sidewalk.

"I'm sorry I lit that frame on fire."

Blaise laid a hand on Cash's back. Somehow they would be okay. "I let someone handle my money who didn't know what they were doing. I'm almost broke, Cash." He stared at the ground between his feet. "Touring is the only way for us to make money now. No one really buys our music anymore, and only stations that play older country-rock stuff play our songs. It's not like it was a long time ago when our music could be heard on every station or when people had to buy full albums to hear us."

"You guys aren't that washed up."

"We're washed up enough." He hadn't said that out loud before. The words hurt to hear and hurt worse to swallow.

"Hey, Blaise." A male voice broke into their conversation. Blaise looked up at Keith Mulligan who grew up in Heritage River, worked at the high school as a maintenance director, and had married his high school sweetheart, Margery. Keith lifted a bag of groceries on his hip and offered Blaise a hearty shake. "Man, I heard you were back in town. I wanted to stop by and say hello, but I've been busy all summer with the kids and stuff. Heard you're playing at the library fundraiser. A bunch of families got tickets. We can't wait to see you. Me and my buddies saw you guys a few years back— well, more like ten now—but it was an amazing show. You're killer on the drums."

"Thanks. This is my son, Cash."

Keith shook Cash's hand. "Cash? Like Johnny Cash? He was your favorite, wasn't he?"

"Your old man and your uncle really made something of themselves," Keith said before Blaise could answer. "We all knew they would. They used to play every high school party. Kids came for miles just to hear them. It was something else."

"Keith exaggerates." Blaise laughed. How much should Cash hear about those parties?

"No way. They were the best. You should put out a new album, though." He heaved the groceries up on his hip again. "Anyway, I've got to go. Margery is waiting for these ingredients. She'll be calling any second if I don't hurry home. I just had to come by and say hi."

Keith headed off down the street. He was right. They needed a new album.

"That guy still thinks you're cool." Cash finished off the last of his cone and wiped his hands on his shirt.

"One fan thinking that isn't enough."

"So write a new album. You're writing songs all the time. I see you doing it. A new album would probably sell like crazy. That guy can't be your only fan." Cash turned away from Blaise. "If you write a new album, you can wait to go on tour."

Blaise's head was heavy. "Even if I do write a new album, which Uncle Colton doesn't want to do, I still need the rest of the tour. I don't think Cream and Sugar is hiring."

"I don't want to live here without you, and I don't want Aunt Savannah checking in on me."

"What happened between you and Jud? Tell me. Please. So I can help."

"You won't believe me."

"Why wouldn't I?"

"Because no one has ever believed me."

Blaise got up and tossed the rest of his cone. In so many ways, Cash was still a boy.

"If I tell you, will you stay?"

"Ah, Cash. Don't ask me that, please. I can't stay, but I promise to help you get set up at the community college before I go. I'll check in with you every day. We can do that FaceTime thing. I'll even take your calls while I'm on stage. I promise."

"I'll do the fundraiser with you if you stay."

Blaise wiped his hand over his face. "I would like nothing more than to play with you. It's something I've always wanted. I was bummed when I found out you gave Uncle Colton that video of you and not me."

"Sorry. I knew you'd say it was good because you're my dad. I wanted his opinion because he always says it like it is."

"Well, that's true enough. Hey, maybe you can meet us on the road when you don't have classes. You can come up on stage, and we can jam. How about that?"

"I don't want to go up on stage. I don't care about that. All I want is for you to stay in town so I don't have to worry about seeing Jud."

"You can't avoid him forever."

"Yes, I can." Cash stood. "Can we go home now?"

"Why won't you tell me?" His voice bellowed into the air. Cash stepped back, his eyes wide, and Blaise clenched his fists so hard his bad hand protested. "I'm sorry." He didn't know what he was doing except making a mess of things.

"Look at me, Dad. Do you see me? Jud hates the way I look, what I stand for. He knows no one will pay attention to what he does to me because I'm the one who has no friends, who gets bad grades, who gets in trouble. All he has to say is I started it, and everyone believes him." Cash turned away and swiped at his face. Was he crying?

Blaise stood frozen. He wanted to grab Cash and grip him in a hug, but would the boy allow it? Blaise never remembered his father hugging him like that.

"Jud isn't who everyone thinks he is," Cash said.

Blaise searched for his voice. "What does that mean?"

Cash turned to him. "He hates that I'm your son because he craves the spotlight. All he wants is people to pay attention to him." Cash opened his mouth but clamped it shut.

There was more, but he wouldn't push. He took a tentative step toward his son. "I'm sorry, Cash. I'm sorry for everything." The tears were what made Blaise believe even more. Cash had never cried in front of him. Not even as a little boy. "What was he saying to you yesterday?"

"Doesn't matter. I was just tired of hearing his big mouth and wanted to shut him up. I threw the first punch. It was my fault. I'll need another community service job too. Aunt Savannah won't want me back. I'm sorry I keep screwing up."

Blaise patted him on the shoulder. "Let's go home." He unlocked the truck with a push of his key fob. "I screwed up plenty too. Still doing it."

He pulled into the driveway and looked at Cash. "Will you stay with me?"

"Will you?"

"Cash—"

"I'm going inside."

Every muscle in his body ached. If he hadn't stopped drinking twenty years ago, he'd pour himself a cold beer. Instead, he walked across the lawn and up to Grace's porch. The hour was late, and she was probably wiped out from the day's work, but he had to see her. Just being with her might soothe whatever aches he had. There was one ache she could definitely soothe. He shook his head to get the thought loose. *When she was ready*, he reminded himself and knocked on the door.

Chapter Twenty-Eight

The banging pulled Grace off the air mattress and away from the book she was reading. Her hair was still damp from the shower, and her sweat shorts were loose around her legs and probably a hair too short to be seen in, but there wasn't time to change if that banging was going to keep up.

Hopefully, it wasn't Hoke Carter coming to pack her bags because Savannah saw what she was searching for on the library computer.

Chloe opened her bedroom door. "Who is that?"

"Not sure."

"It's probably your boyfriend."

"I don't have a boyfriend."

"Yeah, okay." Chloe gave her a knowing smile. "Don't stay up too late, and remember children are nearby." She shut the door behind her.

Grace navigated around the ladder Colton left in the hallway and made her way to the front door. She flipped on the lamp before opening the door.

"Blaise. What's up?" She crossed her arms over her chest, suddenly aware she wasn't wearing a bra. She wanted to run a hand through her hair, thinking it must look messy hanging in strands around her face, but was afraid to move her arms away from her chest.

He smiled that slow smile of his. The gray in his eyes twinkled in the dim light. He pushed his hair away from his face. "Sorry to come by so late. Did I wake you?"

"It's not that late. I was just reading. Do you want to come in?"

"How about we sit out on the porch?" He motioned for her to join him.

"Let me change first." She turned to run back to her room.

He grabbed her hand. "You look great. Come on outside."

The warm air wrapped itself around her bare legs. When was the last time she shaved? If this had been wintertime, that answer could be days. Since it was summer, she was pretty certain she was safe if Blaise happened to touch her legs. Why was she thinking like that? She wished she were wearing a bra.

They sat on the top step. His thigh brushed against hers and sent shivers across her skin. He smelled clean and sweet. She clamped her hands in her lap and looked up at him. Shadows circled his eyes. A day's growth covered his jaw. The dark scruff speckled with gray made him even sexier.

"How's Cash?" she said, hoping to derail her thoughts.

"He wants me to give up the tour and stay home."

"Is that a bad thing?" She wouldn't mind hearing Chloe say something like that to her.

"No, not really, but he wants me around to run interference with Jud mostly, and I need this tour. I was hoping it would start later, but if it doesn't, I have to go. I'll be out of money in a few months." He didn't look at her when he said the last words.

She reached over and grabbed his right hand. It

was warm and rough in hers. She didn't know what else to offer this man who was so open with his problems. He gave her a squeeze.

"How long will you be gone?" she said.

"Probably three months. I don't want to leave him alone for that long. Maybe it's better if he goes back to his mother's. Only, I was looking forward to finally spending time with my kid."

"You can't spend time with him if you aren't here. Could he go to his mother's for just those months and then come back?"

"What if he doesn't want to come back?" He drummed on his leg with his other hand.

She had no answer to that. "Could he go on tour with you?"

"I want him in school. He needs stability, and I can't give him that. I'll tell him in the morning he has to go to his mother's, and when the tour is over he can come live with me, if he wants." The lines around his mouth grew deeper. He scratched at the back of his neck.

"Are you sure there are no other options to make money?" He had told her about the songs he wrote, but for some reason he wasn't ready to change the dynamic between him and his brother. "I don't mean to judge, but your son wants you to stay. How much longer will that happen? Can't you make Colton understand?"

"My brother only understands playing his music. It's better if Cash leaves for a while, then comes back."

Grace released his hand and straightened her shoulders. "I spoke with Beau this morning, and he's willing to give Cash his job back. You can't send him to his mother's yet." Beau wouldn't need him forever, but it could keep Cash in town for the rest of the summer and maybe force Blaise to rethink the tour. If that was even possible. She understood needing money.

"Wait a second. Beau wants to hire Cash back? Why?" He didn't wait for her to answer. "It won't work. Cash will never work with Jud again."

"Not Jud. Just Cash. I asked because, well, he's a good kid, and I told Beau only to hire Cash. He didn't want to hire one back without the other, but I insisted. It may be none of my business, but I don't think Cash is the one causing trouble between the two. I'm sorry. I know he's your nephew, and your sister already gave me an earful about it, but I don't care. I have to call it as I see it." She finally took a breath.

He smiled at her. "You did that for my kid?"

She looked down at her lap. He tipped her head back up at him. He was inches from her.

"Yes, I did that for Cash. He didn't deserve to be fired for sticking up for himself." She wanted to lean in and press her lips against his.

"Thank you." His voice was thick.

She licked her dry lips and pulled back. The tug in her low belly said *do it, dummy*, and her brain wanted to write a pros-and-cons list on kissing Blaise Savage.

He took her cue and went back to holding her hand. "Cash said Jud always started things between them. I never saw it. What kind of father misses something like that?"

"Don't blame yourself. Jud is very good at hiding it. He knows no one suspects him. That gives him a lot leeway. I don't like bullies." Larry was a bully. "I'm sorry to put it so bluntly, especially about your family, but he is."

Blaise stared toward his house. The front room lights were on. "No wonder Cash didn't want to talk to me about it. I won't say anything to Cash about his leaving for California just yet. He needs this job, and he needs his community service hours. I don't want to mess that up for him if Savannah is still willing to have him. I'll have to figure something out about the tour and his staying here. Thank you for making me see. I want to kiss you right now."

"I'd like that." She hesitated.

"But?" He rubbed his thumb against her palm.

She straightened up again. "Can I ask you something? You can tell me to mind my own business, but I need to ask."

"Grace, spit it out."

She couldn't meet his eyes. Heat flushed her cheeks, and she was grateful for the night sky to hide her. "Have you slept with a lot of women? I don't need a number or anything, but do you, have you, I mean…" She couldn't finish. The words stuck in her mouth and wrapped around her tongue.

He laughed.

"Please don't laugh at me," she whispered. He didn't know how hard this was for her. Just sitting next to him, feeling the heat of his skin, wanting to kiss him and so much more was a big jump for her. She didn't trust herself and was still a little afraid to trust him. "My husband left me for a younger woman, and it was mortifying knowing I wasn't enough for him. It could be like that for you. I might not measure up to the, the, others."

"Please look at me." He lowered his voice. "I wasn't laughing at you. I'd never laugh at you. You don't know how cute you are when you get ruffled, and I like that I can do that to you. I want to see how ruffled and flushed I can make you lying underneath me, but only when you're ready. I know my lifestyle might be questionable for you, but I promise you, I believe in monogamy. I never cheated on my wife, never."

"My friend told me about a scandal with you."

"Lies. Every word."

"You know what I'm talking about?"

"I think there was only one scandal that made the tabloids. I was never A-list enough for those papers. Was there another one?"

She couldn't help but laugh. "I don't think so. I never follow that stuff. I only know what Jenn told me."

"Remind me to strangle her." He winked, but she knew he was joking. "I left Melissa because she only wanted to be married to my status and my name. She never loved me the way I thought she did."

She knew the feeling. "So you didn't have a lot of women?"

He kissed her knuckles. "Grace, you don't have to worry about my past. It's only this moment that counts. The one with you and me in it. Nothing else matters to me."

Her heart swelled. She held tighter to his hands. "I haven't been with many men, and my ex-husband accused me of being cold." She couldn't look at him.

"He was a jerk. And I don't care if that sounds like I'm a twelve-year-old."

Her cheeks flushed again. "I'm sorry I said that to you."

"I am like a twelve-year-old. It's only since I've met you that I wanted to grow up. When I'm around you, I feel settled. I've never felt that way before. You've helped me be a better father too. Thank you for that."

"That's kind of you to say, but I'm such a lousy mother. I'm hardly a good example."

"You just went to bat for my kid. That's the kind of person and mother you are." He leaned in and whispered in her ear. "It's a giant turn-on."

She was turned on too, and she couldn't believe it. This man who jumped off scaffolding on a dare had made her feel things she never thought possible. He made her feel alive. "Kiss me, please."

He wagged his eyebrows and leaned in. His lips found hers, and she opened her mouth for him. She didn't wait. Her tongue sought his. He tasted sweet, like sugar. Her hands reached up around his neck, and her fingers tangled in the back of his hair.

His hands cupped her face, bringing her closer. She loved the feel of his calloused, strong fingers against her jaw. She didn't mind the scratchiness of the brace. Grace wanted those hands to touch her everywhere, and she let out a little moan at the thought.

Blaise pulled her closer. His hands slid down her arms and held her waist. She reached under his T-shirt, and her fingers traced every inch of his chest. This time he moaned. His hands sought her under her shirt. His fingers traced her belly and then slid higher to her breasts.

He pulled back and looked at her, his eyes shining. "Look who gets a surprise."

Heat filled her cheeks. "I thought I was going to bed. If I'd known you were stopping by, I would've dressed more appropriately."

"Grace?"

"Yes?"

"I know you're not easy. Now kiss me." His lips found hers again, and he turned her so she faced him better and pulled her legs around his waist. She was practically sitting on his lap. She thought of her too-short shorts leaving everything open and exposed. She wished she were twenty years younger with tight skin and a body that hadn't pushed a baby out. His ex-wife was pretty and perfect. She'd seen pictures.

Grace broke the kiss.

Blaise's breath came in ragged. "What's the matter? Did I do something wrong?"

She untangled her legs and clamped her knees together. "No. It was wonderful. I...I..."

He kissed her neck and shoulder, leaving a trail of warmth in the wake of his lips. "It's okay. When you're ready. Besides, we might need a room at the B&B. I can't come to your house, and you can't come to mine. Too many eyes and I won't make love to you in my truck. I haven't done that since I was seventeen. I have some sense now."

"You had sex in a truck?"

"Forget I said anything."

He helped her up and wrapped his arms around her waist, holding her close. "I'm not done with you, Grace Starr."

She hoped he wasn't. But for how long? What would happen in a few weeks when he went on tour and she went back to Silverside? Could she throw caution to the wind for the first time in her life and just enjoy him? Or would she think this whole thing to death and ruin a chance for some happiness, even if it was temporary?

Would it be better to finish this before it started?

She untangled herself from his hold. "I should go in."

He kissed her lightly on the lips. "Can I persuade you to go to dinner with me tomorrow night? Just us. Out of town where we won't run into anyone I know."

"I'd like that." More than she wanted to admit.

"All righty, ma'am. I'm fixin' to pick you up at six."

His southern accent spread warmth over her skin. "What should I wear?"

"Don't care. Just leave the bra at home."

Chapter Twenty-Nine

Cash dragged himself into the kitchen, wearing basketball shorts and no shirt. His hair stuck up in the back. He rubbed his eyes with his fists and smeared his leftover eyeliner. Blaise couldn't believe that tall young man was his son. He'd missed too many years. Too many moments. He was going to miss more, and that nearly killed him.

But his beautiful, sexy neighbor helped him see he could have time with his son. He was becoming a better father because of Grace. What a surprise she turned out to be and what a handful he got last night. Probably not the best thing to think about while his son was standing inches away. Blaise glanced out the window toward Grace's house. Maybe he'd get lucky tonight. Only if she wanted to. Should he get flowers? Or a tomato from his garden? One popped up so far.

"You want some coffee?" He handed Cash a mug.

"No. Do we have eggs?" Cash opened the fridge.

"I can help you make them if you'd like."

Cash kept looking in the fridge and shrugged. "I can do it."

"Step aside. Let the master show you."

"The one-handed master?"

"I'm managing." And he was. His wrist hurt less and less. He had a follow-up appointment in a few weeks. The brace would be off before he hit the road.

And if it wasn't, he'd take it off. He still couldn't hold his sticks the way he wanted with this thing on, but he could still whip up some mean eggs. He pulled out mushrooms, cheese, and spinach. An omelet was in order.

"I smell breakfast." Colton sauntered into the kitchen.

"I'm doing enough for you by letting you stay here. Make your own breakfast." Blaise handed him the carton of eggs.

"There's one egg left."

"You know where the store is. I believe you broke their front window once."

"Uncle Colton broke a window? Cool."

"Not cool." Blaise slid the eggs onto Cash's plate.

"I was a kid. I did a lot of stupid things back then."

"You're still doing stupid things." Blaise took the egg carton back and dropped four slices of bread into the toaster. "I'll make you some toast because I feel bad you were such a dumb kid."

Colton punched him in the arm.

"Hey, watch the bad arm, will ya? I've got a tour to go on."

Cash dropped his fork on the plate. "So you're going." It wasn't a question.

Colton grabbed some coffee. "Time to build a house." He mouthed *good luck* over Cash's head and left.

Blaise pulled out the chair next to Cash. "I've got some good news."

Cash kept staring.

"Grace spoke to Beau. You have your job back."

"Really?"

"I don't think I'd joke about that. What do you think?" What if Cash didn't want the job back? He hadn't thought about that last night.

"That was nice of her." Cash pushed his eggs around the plate.

"Do you want to go back to work with Beau?"

"Not with Jud there." He met Blaise's eye. "If you're really going on the road, I'll go back to Mom's when you leave."

"First, Jud isn't going to be there. Grace fought only for you. She's waiting for you to show up this morning. Second, I want you to stay while I'm gone. We'll figure out the details. You shouldn't be here by yourself for months."

"You don't think you can trust me. Are you afraid I'd burn down the house?"

"What? Of course not. Listen, Cash, when I was your age I had no business being on my own either. You're smarter than I was back then, but anything can happen. A pipe could break, the roof could leak, and the toilet could overflow."

"A house could catch on fire." Cash's tone challenged him.

"I'm not blaming you for making a mistake. I'm not. Truth is, a house could catch on fire. What would you do?"

"Call the fire department."

"Get out first." He ruffled Cash's hair. "Then call. Let's take things one step at a time. Take back your job and stay here, go to school. We'll figure out the rest." He could work it out. Not every detail needed to be planned. Cash was an adult, for Christ's sake. Blaise was on tour by the time he was twenty-four. He hadn't known shit about being an adult back then. He would have to convince Melissa that Cash staying alone was a good idea. That wasn't going to be easy, but he'd figure that out too.

"Now what about that job? Are you going to take it?"

Cash dumped his leftover eggs into the garbage and put the dish in the dishwasher. "I guess. I can handle living alone. That's not the worst part. The worst part will be seeing Jud or when Aunt Savannah wants me to come over for dinner."

"Jud is going to be away at college. You won't see him much."

"It will only take once."

"What did he say to you?"

"Doesn't matter. I need a shower." Cash headed down the hall.

Blaise called after him. "Does that mean you're going to work?"

His answer was the closed door and the water running. Good enough. Grace believed in Cash and so did he. Maybe a conversation with his nephew was in order. Man to man.

Blaise knocked on the bathroom door. "Cash, I'm running out. Hurry up and get next door. Make sure to thank Beau and Grace." Especially Grace.

While he was out, he'd get those flowers. He had some thanking to do himself.

****

Blaise pulled up in front of Savannah's house. He didn't bother to call before he came over. He didn't want to tip off anyone he was on his way. Hopefully, he'd catch Jud still asleep. He just wanted to talk.

Maybe hear Jud's side of things and drop the hint whatever Jud's gripe with Cash was had to stop. They were family. They should stick together the way he, Colton, and Savannah always had. No matter what went on between him and Colton, his older brother always had his back and Savannah was always the mother hen looking out for them.

The grass looked a little shaggy, and the bushes could use a cut. Not like Adam to ignore his yard. Blaise's brother-in-law spent all his free time cutting, trimming, spraying weed killer. Sometimes Blaise wondered if yard work was just a hobby or Adam's way of getting some peace from their busy house and his wife's constant planning and directing. The front lights were out too.

He barely knocked when the door swung open.

"Uncle Blaise." Caroline, with her hair pulled back and white shirt and tiny black shorts, squealed when she saw him. She threw herself into his arms. "What are you doing here? I'm about to go to practice. You almost missed us."

"Hey, kiddo. What kind of practice do you need those shorts for?"

"Oh, Uncle Blaise. You sound like Daddy. They're cheer shorts. Everyone wears them." Posing, she turned to the side with hands on her hips.

His niece was going to give her father a heart attack. Blaise was glad he had a boy.

"Do you want to see my back hand spring?" she asked.

"Not in the house," Savannah shouted from the kitchen.

"Hey, sis." He walked into the kitchen, where his

sister was packing lunches. The counters were covered in mail, papers, cardboard boxes, and flower arrangements. "What's all this?" Her place never looked out of sorts.

She waved her hand. "Stuff for the fundraiser. Those are the start of centerpieces for the dinner tables. I haven't had a minute to look through the mail. This place is a mess. What brings you by?" She zipped up a flowered lunch bag and handed it to Caroline. The other bag she shoved into her large tote. "Caroline, could you make sure Grey is out of the shower? We need to leave in fifteen minutes." Caroline skipped out of the room.

"I was hoping to talk to Jud if he's around." Blaise leaned against the counter and crossed his arms.

Savannah rolled her eyes. "Are you kidding? He's never here. He slept at Alex's house last night, and I don't know when he'll be back since he doesn't have a job to go to." She pointed her gaze right on him. "Honestly, Blaise, sometimes I think Cash is more Colton's son than yours."

He pushed away from the counter. "What does that mean?"

"Cash. He's so much like Colton. Always getting into trouble or getting into fights. Do you remember the time Colton flipped the vice principal's desk over? And it was his fault bringing a bow and arrow to school in the first place." Savannah dumped breakfast dishes into an already-full sink.

He smiled at the memory. "It was the archery unit in gym class. The teacher never liked him and wouldn't give him any arrows, so he brought his own."

"Stop making excuses for Colton's behavior and stop making excuses for Cash's. I love your son—you know I do, just like I love my brother—but Cash has no sense of right and wrong."

"Wait a second. That isn't true. He made a mistake. That's it. Some of us make mistakes, you know. We can't always be perfect."

"What about school, Blaise? Did he care about his future? He didn't join any clubs or activities. Why not the band at least? Why not play in the school band?"

"For the same reasons Colton and I didn't play in the school band. He's too talented for that."

"Give me a break. You didn't play in the band because only the nerds would do that and because Dad was the music teacher."

"Does it really matter what activities he was in during school? He's got his whole life ahead of him. He can't be counted out because he wasn't in the damn winter concert."

"The kids that don't get involved are the ones who find trouble. The experts say."

Anger burned his blood. "Who are these experts? You?"

She let out a breath and dropped her shoulders. She straightened some mail on the counter. "All I'm saying is, if he had some goals, he might have made different choices."

"Like Jud."

She slapped her thighs. "Well, as a matter of fact, exactly like Jud. I'm not trying to compare our boys, but Jud was captain of the football team and class ambassador. He was in the school band. He got good grades, and every school he applied to accepted him. He's got a future."

"And Cash doesn't. That's what you're saying."

"He's only going to have a future if he starts shaping up, and picking fights with his cousin isn't the way to start. Jud would never have lost that job if it wasn't for Cash. You know I'm right."

"You're wrong and you're blind."

"Excuse me?"

"You heard me. Your son isn't perfect. It's been him picking on Cash. I don't know what he says to Cash because he won't tell me, but my son wouldn't start a fight with anyone for no reason." He raised his voice, and Savannah stepped back. He never raised his voice at her.

"How would you know whether or not your son would start a fight? You never spend any time with him."

The blow hit him like a jab to his jaw. He gritted his teeth. She was right about that, and if he had been more involved, maybe Cash would've made better choices. Maybe not, but he'd never know. As he told Grace, the only moment that mattered was this one.

"I know he wouldn't start a fight because I'm his father. That's how."

He stormed out.

Chapter Thirty

Grace pulled into the packed library parking lot. She had some work to do on the fundraiser, and she hoped to quiz Savannah about the computer and if she was lucky, get back on it and erase the history.

Arlene was at the circulation desk, talking to Dixie, when Grace pushed through the glass doors.

"Oh, Grace. How lovely to see you." Dixie pecked her on the cheek. She smelled like gardenias. "How are the renovations going, darling? I've been meaning to drop by with another casserole, but Hoke told me that kitchen of yours ain't quite ready yet. That true?"

"I'm afraid so. I think another few more days before everything is back in place. They're almost done with the bathrooms, and then it's resand the floors and paint. I'm looking forward to not living in so much dust."

"When you're ready to list, you give me a holler. You must be about ready to get on home. We'll get that place sold in no time. As a matter of fact, I heard Betty Sue tell Harlan at church her daughter was wanting to move back to Heritage River with her new husband and baby girl. That house would suit them perfect, and who better to have for a neighbor than Blaise Savage?"

Grace hoped her cheeks wouldn't flush at the sound of Blaise's name and give her away. Dixie had someone in mind for the house already? Grace didn't think it would happen before she was even done with the work. What if they weren't the right people? Blaise deserved to have good neighbors, especially when he was out of town. Maybe even someone who could look in on Cash.

"There's no rush," she found herself saying.

"We're growing on her, Arlene."

Arlene just smiled and checked out Dixie's book.

"Grace, just the person I wanted to see." Savannah had appeared like magic, taking Grace off guard. Her smile was on her face, but it didn't reach her gray eyes.

"I wanted to work on the ad journal layout. I hope now is a good time."

"I'm right in the middle of a hundred things, so I won't be able to help you, but I did want to talk to you about something." Savannah's tone suggested Grace might be a teenager caught doing something wrong.

"Sure."

Savannah stepped away from the desk and into the doorway of her office. They weren't completely out of earshot from Dixie and Arlene. The two women stopped their conversation, probably getting ready to listen. Who wouldn't after how Savannah sounded?

"I like to know everything that goes on in my library."

Grace noticed the use of the word *my* and the turn of Dixie's head. "Maybe we should discuss this someplace else."

"Here's fine. This will only take a second."

Maybe it had to do with the details for the fundraiser. They hadn't coordinated the chair rentals for the show. The church across the street was going to allow them to borrow their chairs and tables, but the rate at which the tickets to see Blaise were selling, a lot of people would be standing even with the rentals. Rentals Grace hoped would be donated, but she hadn't worked on that the way she should have—she'd been so preoccupied with trying to find out who sold the house to her gift giver.

"I'm sorry I haven't finalized the chair rental. I can do that today. There's just been a lot going on with the house."

Savannah put up a hand to stop her. "It's not about the rentals. I've taken care of that. I spent most of last night on the phone with David, and he agreed to give us a discount on the rental if I'd let him in to see the show. It was hard to argue. We're still ahead in my book."

One extra person wasn't going to make much of a difference, especially if the chairs cost less. "You could've waited for me to do it." Grace's back was up. She didn't like being micromanaged. "I've dealt with plenty of vendors. I'm sorry you felt you couldn't leave it to me."

"It's not you, really. It's just been my experience if I want something done, it's best to do it myself. One of my mother's lessons."

"I would've handled it. Please don't feel like you can't count on me for this event."

Savannah leaned against the doorjamb. Dixie and Arlene had their heads together, deep in conversation. Probably about what was happening only yards from them. Grace had tried to keep her voice down, but Savannah didn't feel the need to do the same.

"I hope you'll still show up on the day of. We're going to need all the help we can get, but as for the ad journal, I've got that covered too. I thought I would need extra help, but it looks like I don't."

The words felt like a knife in her back. Who fired a volunteer? That was unheard of. "I don't understand. Did I do something?" A web was forming around her. Had Dixie and Arlene heard the last part? She was too embarrassed to turn her head and find them looking, so she kept her head straight and hoped her cheeks weren't too flushed.

"Why were you looking up Claire Phillips on the computer?" Before Grace could answer, Savannah kept talking. "I wondered how you would even know Claire existed."

There was no easy way out of Savannah's interrogation. They were headed down a dangerous path. She had no explanation for the search of someone she couldn't possibly know, but was tied to her house. Sweat popped out on Grace's upper lip. She forced her hands to stay at her sides and not swipe at it.

"I found some papers when we tore out the cabinets. I was curious." She looked away and waved her hand in the air, as if she couldn't care less about Claire Phillips.

"That makes sense."

Grace let out the breath she was holding and risked a glance at the circulation desk. The ladies were still deep in conversation. When would Dixie leave? How long did it take to check out a book here?

Savannah crossed her arms over her chest. The look on her face shifted from smooth to stern. *Here it comes.* Grace braced herself.

"Why were you searching my son on the internet?"

Someone gasped from a few yards away. *Gee, who could that be?* That little tidbit would be all over

Heritage River before noon. She would look like some kind of stalker at best and some kind of child molester at worst. She might as well go back to Jersey now.

She cleared her throat. "I wanted to know why someone like Jud, with the whole world at his fingers, keeps picking on Cash."

"My son is doing no such thing." Savannah leaned in and lowered her voice.

Now she lowers her voice. "Have you ever asked him?"

Savannah stood to her full height. "What kind of a mother do you think I am? Of course, I asked him. I don't know why I'm explaining myself to you. My family is none of your business. Stay away from us. And I have the right mind to tell my brother to stay away from you too, but he'll do what he wants, like he always does."

"I'm sorry I was searching out information about Jud and I understand the need to protect your child, but I'm telling you, Savannah, he's antagonizing Cash. You need to stop it before something bad happens."

"Go home, Grace. Or go back where you came from. I have work to do."

There wasn't anything left to say. Savannah was convinced, and what mother in her position wouldn't be? Who wants to believe her child is making bad choices? Especially a child who seems to have the world on a string? What other kids had been on the receiving end of Jud's taunts? She didn't want to think about it.

Grace turned, keeping her head up and feeling the heat come off her skin in waves. She stopped short. Dixie and Arlene were gone. When had they left?

Arlene could be anywhere in the library, but Dixie?

Grace hurried to the parking lot. Only three cars remained in the lot. She recognized the one Savanah drove. The other must be Arlene's. Dixie's was gone. Could she hope Dixie would keep what she heard to herself? Why didn't she insist Savannah close the door?

Because Grace was guilty. Wrongdoers had to pay, didn't they?

She was out of time. Word would spread Savannah set her loose. Dixie had people who wanted the house. Grace needed to find Claire Phillips today. She needed to find out who cared enough about her to give her this gift. Because by the end of the week, she could be on her way back to Silverside.

She didn't have time to waste. Still parked in the library lot, she pulled out her cell and dialed Blaise's number. The sun beat down on the car. She turned the engine over and kicked on the air conditioner. She melted from both the heat of the day and the heat of embarrassment.

The phone rang and rang. She was afraid it would go to voice mail, but at the last second she heard his smooth, deep voice.

"Hey. I was just thinking about you."

How nice that sounded. She could curl up inside that voice of his, and maybe in another life they would've had the chance. "Hey. Are you free now?"

"I might be. Depends on what it is." The insinuation filled his voice.

"I need to find Claire Phillips today. I think Dixie overheard your sister and me arguing. I'm not sure she won't tell on me."

"You had a fight with my sister? That was brave."

She had to swallow. "Yes. I'm sorry. I'll explain later."

He laughed. "I had a fight with her today too. I went to her and said what you said about Jud. She doesn't believe it's possible. What did you fight about?"

"The same thing. Now I really understand why she doesn't want my help with the fundraiser anymore."

"That's crazy. I'll talk to her."

"No, don't. It's okay. There's no point. You have to live with her. I'll be gone soon, and she can forget about me."

"You're definitely leaving?"

Was that tension in his voice? "I have to, Blaise. I have to go back to Jersey, find a job, buy a house, start over." She thought she would be ready to go back after taking on the Disaster House and proving to everyone she could handle a risk, but she didn't feel ready to return. She'd done more than anyone thought possible, but she hadn't found the peace she was hoping for. Not yet.

"You have a house. Drop the search, Grace. Stay in Heritage River. You can find a job down here. I like knowing my neighbors." There was that insinuation again. Oh, how she wanted to know him better too, but he was leaving and soon. He would forget about her once a younger, more beautiful woman starting waving her underwear at him. Or could she be foolish enough to hope he was asking her to wait for him?

"Will you help me with Claire Phillips?"

He let out a long breath. "Okay."

"Great. Can you meet me some place and bring your laptop? Mine is back at the house, and I don't want to stop there. Oh, did Cash go over and talk to Beau?"

"I hope so. I'm not home. I'm heading there now. Where do you want me to meet you?"

She hadn't thought about it. Was there any place they could go that someone wouldn't see them with their heads bent together? "Does Jake's have Wi-Fi?"

"I doubt it, but my phone can act as the signal."

Her phone buzzed. "Hold on. I'm getting a call." She pulled the phone away to look. "It's Beau. Hang on." She swapped calls. "Hi, Beau."

"Where are you?" His voice was gruff. His face was probably bright red.

"Did something happen to the kids or the house?"

"You're not out looking in places you shouldn't be, are you? I warned you, Miss Grace. Don't go digging."

Her heart jumped into her throat. She had to swallow the lump back down. "I don't know what you're talking about. I'm leaving the library and running a few errands." Dixie had told him. What else could it be? She was in on the agreement. Hoke had arranged for the realtor and the contractor. Everyone who would keep the secret. Why was this person so determined to stay hidden?

"I have to go, Beau. I'll be back soon." She flipped back before he could say more. "Blaise, are you still there?"

"Yes, ma'am."

"He knows."

"Beau? How?"

"Dixie. I told you. She ratted me out. How fast can you meet me at Jake's?"

"I'm pulling into the driveway now. I'll be there in

ten."

She tapped the screen and leaned her head against the seat rest. She should let this go. Go back to the house and work with Beau and the kids. What would knowing change? It might change who she had in her life. No one would be left after Chloe went to college. Didn't she deserve some family?

She pulled out into traffic. It would only take her seconds to get to Jake's, but she didn't want to stay in the parking lot any longer for fear Savannah would come out and yell at her more.

Blaise was right. She could live in the house, maybe find a job. She liked the town and most of the people she'd met. Savannah's protection of her son was understandable. Grace didn't take that personally. They might even be able to become friends if things worked out between the boys. Dixie had been lovely until she tattled, but why shouldn't her loyalties lie with Hoke? And she even liked Hoke. He was only doing what he'd been hired to do. She was the one rocking the boat.

"It's about damn time," she said and parked the car.

Her phone buzzed. It was Beau again. She let it go to voice mail. Blaise pulled into the spot next to her. He waved and she hopped out. "Thanks for coming." He looked good in his blue T-shirt and cargo shorts. He skipped shaving, and she liked that too. How would that rough chin feel against her skin?

He leaned in and kissed her on the cheek. Scruffy. Yeah, she liked that.

"Have you had lunch? I'm starving. Let's get some food while we search." He stopped and raked his gaze over her. "You look great, by the way."

She ran a hand through her hair. "Thanks." Her phone buzzed again, and she yanked it out of her purse. She held it up for Blaise to see. "Hoke Carter is calling me."

"He knows too."

"He does." Her heart sank. "Let's get lunch." The call went to voice mail.

****

Over turkey sandwiches—Grace's without mayo— they searched for Claire Phillips.

"Did you ever meet her?" Grace covered her mouth while she spoke.

"A few times when I was a lot younger. She would visit Nancy and John. They were very close to her because they didn't have any children of their own." Mayonnaise stuck to Blaise's chin.

Grace resisted the urge to wipe it off, but she did signal with her finger.

"Oh." He grabbed a napkin. "Something for later."

Grace groaned.

"What? That wasn't funny?" He winked. "I suppose you never get mayonnaise on your face. You're probably the neatest eater on the planet, right?" He moved her plate. "Not even a crumb on the table." He moved his own plate to reveal a ring of crumbs and bits of lettuce in a circle. "Do you have your sponge in your purse?"

"You're incorrigible." She yanked her plate back with a smile on her face. "So which Claire Phillips is she?"

They had the Facebook search page up. Blaise clicked on the picture of the woman with long white hair flowing around her shoulders and a floral print scarf around her neck. She laughed with her head tilted back, as if she had heard a great joke. She was lovely.

Grace grabbed his hand hovering over the touch pad. "Are you sure?" Her heart picked up speed.

"That's her."

Claire's privacy settings were secure. Obviously, she wouldn't let just anyone look at her photos or her posts. Her timeline was void of all personal information too. Grace liked her instantly. She didn't understand why anyone posted their addresses, just as she didn't understand why people announced they were on vacation. They were giving a personal invitation to the burglars to come right in and rob them.

"If I send her a message, it's going to look like it's from you. She may not answer right away." Blaise finished the last of his sandwich and wiped his hands.

They had logged in to her account. Blaise didn't have any personal social media accounts. The band had some, but they couldn't send a message from Savage.

"I don't know how much time I have left." Beau had called again while they were ordering, but she ignored it. What could she say to him? She'd deal with him when she got back.

Blaise's phone buzzed. "It's Colton. I'll call him back." He turned the phone screen side down on the table. "You want to message her?"

She nodded.

He jotted a short message, explaining it was him and Grace was a friend. He wanted to speak to Claire and could he call her? "Now we wait."

She couldn't sit still any longer. "Let's get out of here." She reached for the check, but he swiped it up before she could grab it. "Oh no, let me pay. You did me a favor." She lunged for the paper, but he held it out of her reach.

"Nope. This one's on me."

"That's not necessary. Let me give you half."

"If I pay for this one, then you will feel obligated to eat with me again just so you can pay."

Heat filled her cheeks. "I'm that obvious?"

"Kind of, but I like it." Blaise pulled money from his wallet and dropped it on the table.

"Why?" They headed out into the hot day. She had to shield her eyes to look up at him.

"Why do I like you?"

"Well, not why do you like me, all of me. Why do you like that I'm so transparent?"

He took her hand in his. "Because I know where I stand with you. You mean what you say, and you say what you mean. You didn't like me at first."

"Sorry about that. I was wrong." She never liked surprises, and he had been quite the surprise.

"Doesn't matter. You like me now." He winked. "I could tell by the way you kissed me and by the way your neck is turning red because I mentioned it. That means I'm probably a good kisser, right?"

He wagged his eyebrows at her, and she laughed. He was indeed.

He looked up and down the street, then back at her. "This probably isn't the best place to tell you this, but—"

His phone interrupted them. "It's Cash."

"Get it." She pulled her hand away. Her phone rang too. She dragged it out of her purse. Chloe.

"Hey, bud," he said into his phone.

Grace tried swiping at her screen, but the button

wouldn't slide.

Blaise's face darkened as he listened to Cash. Her finger slipped, and the phone tumbled between her hands, nearly hitting the ground.

"Are you sure?" he said.

Chloe's call went to voice mail. Grace tried to call her back. Her call went to voice mail too.

"When? When?" He shouted that time. "Okay, we'll be right there." He ended the call. "Put your phone away. We have to go home. There's a problem."

Chapter Thirty-One

Grace tried to reach Chloe on the ride back to the house, but she wouldn't pick up. She followed Blaise as he sped around corners and made sharp turns. Something was wrong. Did someone get hurt? He wouldn't answer her frantic questions.

"We need to get home," he said.

Grace had thought of every possible terrible scenario on the five-minute drive back. One of the kids was hurt. Beau had a heart attack. But wouldn't they go to the hospital if that were the case?

Her heart hammered in her chest as she skid to a stop behind Blaise. He jumped out. In her haste to follow, she lost her balance and sprawled onto the road scraping her hands. Her head spun, but she forced herself up, no one the wiser, and wiped little pieces of tar out of the heel of her hands. She'd have to clean that.

Chloe, Colton, and Cash gathered on the front porch. Chloe slumped forward with her elbows on her knees and her hands on her face. Cash rubbed at his arms and then stared at his palms. Colton raised an eyebrow at Blaise.

"What happened?" Blaise said.

Colton came down the steps first. "Beau packed up."

"Packed up?" Grace turned in circles. Beau's truck

was gone. She ran past them and into the house. The ladders were gone, the tools too. The kitchen was only half done, the bathrooms even less. The floors were covered in dust. The place looked like the cliffhanger ending to a house-renovation show. "Beau?" she asked, knowing he wasn't there.

That's what all the calls were about. Dixie told on her. Beau and Hoke were either trying to get her to stop or at least giving her the courtesy of knowing the project was done. The house was no longer hers. She'd lost it. She'd lost the chance to prove to herself and everyone else she had what it took to take a risk. Grace Starr wasn't a new woman. She was a fool again. Larry did know her best.

She leaned against the wall and slid down to the floor. She pulled her knees into her chest. Tears threatened and her palms hurt. She swallowed hard. She didn't want to cry. She had no job, no home, no family. Blaise had been right too. Why was it so important to know who gave her this house? Knowing wasn't going to change the fact her mother had a mental illness and her father wanted nothing to do with her. Knowing wasn't going to give her a big family to sit down to at Thanksgiving dinner. Knowing wasn't going to fill the void in her chest that not belonging to anyone created. She bit her lip to stifle the groan pushing its way out.

Blaise poked his head around the front door, and she looked away. His footsteps echoed in the empty room. He plopped down next to her and pulled his legs up to match hers. "You okay?"

She shook her head.

"Beau stopped construction. Hoke told him to. It seems Dixie did overhear you and Savannah at the library. I'm sorry, Grace."

She was afraid to open her mouth because the tears would come and she didn't want Blaise to see her cry. "You were right."

"If you want, I could try to talk to him. Maybe he'll listen since he knew my parents. Colton said he'd come with me."

"No, thank you, though. You and your brother are very sweet to offer. It's my fault. I knew the parameters, and I ignored them. Now I have nothing."

He placed his bandaged hand over her knee. "You took a chance. That's all. Sometimes they pay off, and sometimes they don't."

"I don't take chances, Blaise. I've always been too afraid to lose, and the one time I do take a chance I screw myself up. I should have known better."

"It's okay to make a mistake, Grace."

"Okay for who? You? It's not okay for me. I can't afford to make mistakes. I don't have anyone looking out for me. No one has my back." She thought of the way Blaise was with his siblings. She'd give anything to have a brother or sister to call at that moment because no matter how good her friendship was with Jenn, Grace would never call now and ask for help. Any help.

"You know, sometimes we have to rely on the people in our lives at the time. I've made some big mistakes in my life. I don't beat myself up over it. There isn't any point. What's done is done. I move forward and worry about the present moment. You could try that."

She wiped her nose with the back of her hand. "Right now I don't feel like trying anything. I need to make a plan." She pushed herself up off the floor and wiped the dirt from her pants.

"Don't make any decisions right now. Give yourself some time. Come to my house for dinner later."

They stepped out into the hot sunshine. Colton and Cash were gone. Chloe sat glued to her phone on the front steps. The street was alive with activity. Two boys raced down the road on their bikes, shouting to each other. Across the street the Bucknells weeded their landscaping. A lawnmower growled in the distance. Two women dressed in bright exercise clothes braved the heat and walked down the sidewalk deep in conversation. The poplar trees were full and lush, lining Dogwood Drive and offering spots for shade. Her own poplar bathed the front porch in cool shade. She really did picture a porch swing with floral pillows to rest against, but that wouldn't happen now. Not for her anyway.

"Grace, what do you say? Dinner, my place? I'll use the one tomato I grew in the garden."

She dragged her gaze away from the neighborhood and back to Blaise. He smiled at her. His gray eyes twinkled.

"No, thank you. We have to pack."

He leaned in and kissed her cheek. "The invitation is open. Just come by. See you, Chloe."

She watched him cross the lawn and amble up his own porch. He turned with a wave and went inside. Her heart hitched.

"Mom, what are we going to do? We can't stay here like this, and we don't have anywhere to live in New Jersey. What's your plan, Mom, because I'm not going back to Dad's?"

Grace threw her hands up. "Chloe, not now. I can't handle your questions. I don't have a plan, okay?" She plopped down on the top step and rested her head on her knees. The tears threatened again, and she had to bite her lip to stop them. She wouldn't cry now. Couldn't cry because if she started, she might not stop.

Chloe placed a hand on her back. "Mom, are you okay?"

Grace lifted her head and dropped her chin into her hands. She looked out onto the street. "It's nice here, isn't it?"

"Mom, what's going on? You're scaring me."

She looked at Chloe. She wanted to brush the hair away from her daughter's face, but she held her hands in place. "You're beautiful, you know that?"

Chloe made a face. "You have to say that. You're my mother."

"It doesn't matter. It's true." Grace looked back out to the street. "I'm sorry I screwed this all up. I had to know who gave me this house. I was hoping it was someone I was related to. I've always wanted a big family, and this was going to be my one chance."

"We're a family."

"You're right, but you're going off to college and you'll be living your own life soon. There won't be space for me." She bit her lip again. The idea of being alone cracked open her heart. It wasn't what she wanted. It wasn't what she planned. Her worst fears were being realized.

"I won't be far, and I'll come home on weekends and stuff." Chloe looked back at the house. "If we have some place to live." Her tone suggested Chloe was attempting to lighten the mood.

Pride tried to mend Grace's heart, but it wasn't enough. Her daughter wasn't hers to keep. She always knew that, but today with the loss of everything, giving Chloe over to her own life was irrefutable—and stung like bleach in the eyes.

"Having you visit will be nice." *Don't forget about me.* Grace wanted to beg, but the words screamed only in her head.

"It's going to be okay, Mom."

Grace patted Chloe's knee. "It will." But she kept staring out into the street, as if the answers would appear in the form of a neighbor carrying a pecan pie or the mailman waving as he passed. Did it snow in Heritage River? She wouldn't be around to see if it did. That thought made the tears want to come all over again.

She'd fallen for this little town. It had snuck up on her when she wasn't looking and warmed her insides like hot apple cider. The Disaster House, which she was starting to refer to with something like love, was taking shape. Grace could see her beauty under all the dirt and dust. This house could be a home, just not hers. How long would they give her to move out? Would Hoke be standing at the door before day's end with the sheriff, ready to evict her? When would Dixie shove the for sale sign into the lawn?

She'd fallen for her neighbor. His southern charm and twinkling eyes. His ability to live in the moment and take chances. He lived life. He didn't watch it go by, as she had for so many years. He made her laugh. She was learning not to take herself so seriously. Who else could show her how to do that?

"Should we start packing?" Chloe's words dragged Grace away from her sorrowful thoughts.

"I don't know." She didn't have the strength even to throw her few items into boxes. If Hoke didn't bang on the door tonight, they could start tomorrow. What would one more day hurt?

"I'm sorry, Mom. I know you wanted this house to work out for a lot of different reasons. But things will work out. You'll see. Don't you always tell me when one door closes another one opens?"

"It helps if you don't shut your own foot in the door in the process."

"What?"

"Never mind. Thanks for the pep talk." Chloe was a smart girl. She would be fine in the great big world. Maybe Grace hadn't screwed up with her daughter completely.

"Are you hungry?"

The last thing Grace wanted to do was eat. "Not really, but I can take you into town if you want to get something."

Chloe held up her phone. "Cash asked if I wanted to walk into town with him. He's kind of disappointed he lost his job again. Would you be okay if I went to cheer him up? I don't have to go if you don't want me to. We can order takeout and watch movies."

Grace smiled. "We can do a girls' night some other time. Go enjoy dinner." It would be one of Chloe's last nights here. She might as well enjoy it. "Don't stay out late and make good choices." She didn't want her to enjoy herself too much.

"Oh, Mom. Like I'd do anything stupid with college just a few weeks away. I'm going to clean up a little. Thanks." Chloe kissed the top of her head and ran inside.

Grace stayed glued to her place on the porch. She waved after Chloe and Cash as they glided down the street toward town. Just as they were turning the corner, Cash slid his hand into Chloe's. Hopefully, it was nothing more than a summer crush. They both had their whole lives ahead of them. Mistakes could so easily be made. She knew better than anyone.

The sun began its descent and cast long shadows on the lawn. The mosquitos kicked up and made a meal out of Grace's skin, but she didn't move. Where was she going to go? Not inside. She couldn't bear it.

When Larry found out she'd failed, he'd have himself a knee-slapping laugh with a side of I told you so. She'd want to wipe that smug look off his face. She never needed him. She just wanted someone to say I love you and mean it. He was the biggest mistake of her life. She only had Chloe to show for that marriage. That was enough, but she wanted more now. So much more.

Lights popped on in Blaise's house. What was he doing? Was he wondering if she'd take him up on his offer for dinner? Was he setting the table for three? She didn't want to sit with Colton and make small talk. She might choke on small talk.

There was something she did want to do. It would be another risk and she wasn't sure she was ready to take a chance again, but it was now or never. The loss of the house, the start of Savannah's friendship and the fundraiser, the possibility of a family, even losing Cash his job, made her insides burn. She didn't want to care anymore. She was tired of being Grace Starr. She wanted to be someone else just for one night. Someone who hadn't lived her life in fear.

She pushed herself off the porch and marched across the lawn. She didn't care what she looked like or how desperate she would appear. This was what she wanted. Just for one night. One moment in time. The only moment that would count.

She rang Blaise's bell. She scrunched her eyes shut, trying to keep the rational Grace from invading her thoughts. "Shut up." This was her time.

She was about to knock when Colton yanked the door open. Her nerve wavered. What was she thinking? "Hi." The single word was all she could manage.

"Blaise said you were coming for dinner." Colton stepped aside to let her in.

Grace wrung her hands, took a deep breath. "Could you ask him to come out here?" If she stepped inside and let the comfort of his home surround her, her thoughts would jumble. She would forget what propelled her across the lawn. And she didn't want to forget. She wanted to feel it. All of it. The anger, the pain, the fluttery stomach as if she were about to jump off the high dive.

Colton raised his eyebrows.

He knew. Heat filled her cheeks, but she didn't look away. "Would you mind getting him?" If she had to ask again, she'd lose her nerve.

"I'll go get him." He walked away, leaving the door open. He didn't go far before he yelled, "Blaise, someone's at the door for you." He laughed and turned down the hall toward the bedrooms.

Grace imagined this very same scene with them as teenagers. Heat filled her cheeks again. How many girls came calling for the young and irresistible Blaise

Savage? She shook her head. No time to think like that. Those other women or girls don't matter. Only now mattered.

Blaise came from the kitchen. He smoothed his hair back when he saw her and smiled. That damn smile would be the end of her. Her knees wanted to buckle.

"Hey." He leaned against the doorjamb. "I'm glad you made it. You want to come in? Dinner's almost ready."

"No. Would you…" She had to swallow the knot tying up her vocal chords. "Would you take me to the lake?"

"The lake? Now? Why?"

She couldn't say it with so many lights on. "Can I tell you when we get there?"

"Okay. Let me grab my keys." He stepped away from the door and scooped up his keys from the hall table. "Colton, I'm running out."

Colton yelled something back that sounded like "condom." Grace nearly ran back to the house to hide. Instead, she stepped off the porch into the shadows of the night and waited.

Blaise opened the truck door for her, and she slid in. He ran around the front and hopped inside beside her. They didn't speak until he was off Dogwood Drive.

"Can you tell me why you wanted to go to the lake?"

She watched his profile as he navigated the streets. She wanted to commit it to memory so she'd have something to think about on the long nights back in Jersey while she tried to sew her life back together.

"Once we get there." She didn't trust herself to talk. When they were at the lake with nothing more than the moonlight to guide them, she could show him what she wanted. She didn't have to use any words.

"You've got my curiosity up." He winked. He was silent as he drove the truck farther from town. "Have you decided what you're going to do about the house?"

"I'm going back to Jersey. I hope Hoke will let me have a few days to gather my belongings."

"What are you going to do when you get there?"

"I have no idea. Find a job, I guess. All my volunteer work at the library has to count for something, doesn't it?"

"You could stay here and find a job."

"Everyone will know by morning that I lost the house. I can't live here with people whispering behind my back every time I walk down Main Street. Staying wasn't the plan anyway. Fixing, selling, going back. That was my plan."

"Sometimes plans change."

She stared at him. Those words echoed in her head with a new vibration.

He turned off the main road onto the dirt road leading to the lake. The tall grass swayed around them as he navigated the bumps and divots in the dark. He pulled into the open area to park. Another car sat dark and empty.

"Looks like we're not the only ones out tonight," he said.

She hadn't thought about having the company of others to deal with. They were alone the other times they'd come. Why didn't she think that a place like this would be a haven for teens to come to and make out? She leaned her head back against the rest and sighed. "It's just not my day."

"Were you planning something?" He turned the truck off and faced her.

She stared at the truck's roof. "I wasn't thinking it all the way through. I'm sorry to have dragged you out here. We can go back."

He hit the ignition button and pulled the truck out, but he didn't head back down the dirt road. He circled to the backside of the lake, closer to the houses. The spot was more secluded with tall trees acting as cover. He hopped out but left the lights on.

He waved her out. "Follow me."

"Where are we going?" She tried to see around the trees, but the crescent moon didn't offer enough light, and the headlights casted their narrow glow straight ahead.

"See? Sometimes plans change for the better, Grace." He led her down a narrow path that opened to a clearing by the lake. A small dock jutted out into the water, and a set of cement stairs led to the house behind them. The truck's lights still shone, and she could make out two Adirondack chairs facing the water. The space was private; the other house was too far away to see this part of the lake.

"That house up there?" Blaise pointed to the darkened house up the hill behind them. "That's old Billy Lewis's house. He's away visiting his grandkids in Tulsa. Goes every summer for a couple of months when they're off school. That old dock is his. No one comes here because they're afraid Billy might run out with his shot gun if he catches them trespassing."

"You're sure we should be here?"

"He liked my dad. Said we could come fishing any time we wanted. Colton comes out here when he wants to be alone. Billy pretty much ignores him when he isn't telling him what to do."

"Do you always bring the ladies out here?" She didn't see a good spot that offered coverage if someone should walk up on them. Heck, she didn't even think to bring a blanket. Her nerve was shrinking. This was a bad idea.

"Hey, I was twenty the last time I brought someone here. I didn't have anywhere else to go. She still lived at home, and I couldn't exactly bring a girl back to my house when my dad was home."

He brought a local girl here. "Does she still live in town?"

"Nope, she married her college sweetheart. He played baseball for a minor league team in Texas. They moved away when he got signed. Haven't seen her in nearly thirty years."

"She won't be jealous, then?"

"Probably forgot my name."

"But you slept with her?" Her nerves were making her lips loose. Did it matter what he did all those years ago?

He took her hands in his and looked down at her. "I didn't sleep with every woman who threw herself at me. I wanted to be with someone who liked me for me, not because I was in some band."

"You expect me to believe that as a young man you didn't hop into bed with every woman who wanted to when there were probably thousands willing? Come on."

"I wasn't an angel, no way. I won't lie to you. Those women never meant anything to me, and after a while I wanted more than waking up next to a woman I wasn't going to see ever again. That was why I married Melissa. I thought she really loved me for me. I was wrong about that."

"You know what? None of it matters. What matters is right now. I want to forget about today and all that I lost. I want to gain something. I want to know I'm not the same person who flew down here weeks ago. Can you help me with that?"

He pulled her close and tucked a strand of hair behind her ear. "Grace, I don't want to wake up next to a woman I won't see ever again."

"I don't want to worry about the morning. Let's just concentrate on right now. Just the two of us. Nothing else matters."

"What matters is you're going back to New Jersey in a few days."

"You're leaving on tour soon. How is that any different?" She snaked her arms around his neck. His lines and contours felt good against her curves.

"It's not different. You're right. I live my life on the road, and I promised myself I wouldn't get seriously involved again. It's not easy being with a music man. I miss special events, holidays. Someone like you would resent me in time. I can't have you staring up at me with those blue eyes full of hate."

"I would never hate you, and I would never resent you." But she would worry and wonder all the time. Who was he with? Was he thinking of her? Could someone else pull him away from her? "Blaise, we've got tonight. That's all I care about."

"It won't be. And it won't be for me. I want more, Grace."

"What are you saying?"

He held her shoulders and took a long look at her. "Woman, I'm saying I don't want a one-night stand."

"So you don't want me, then?"

"No, I never said that. I'd take you right now on the sand, but I won't take advantage of how you're feeling right now. I won't take advantage of our situation. I couldn't live with myself if I hurt you."

"I don't understand. How are you feeling these things about me? We just met, and I'm nothing special." She knew he was attracted to her, but there was more and she didn't know why. Why her?

"Hang on a second." He ran back to the truck. She couldn't see what he was doing behind the glare of the lights, but music filled the air. A slow melody of a guitar with the low rumblings of a man's voice.

He returned and took her in his strong arms, his head close to hers. He smelled clean and masculine, and she wanted to get lost in his scent. "One more thing." He yanked off the brace and entwined his fingers through hers.

"Your hand."

"It's fine."

He held her hand against his chest. They swayed to the song drifting toward them like a breeze. "This song reminds me of you. I've wanted to dance with you to it since I met you."

"Blaise?"

He interrupted her. "When I first met you, I thought you were a gigantic pain in the ass." He laughed, and she relaxed against him. "But I saw how you fought for what you wanted even when everyone else told you not to. I've never really been able to do that. Fight for what I want. It's always been easier to follow my big brother around and let him tell me what I wanted."

She thought of the music he had written. "You can still fight for what you want."

"After the tour, maybe." He inched away and looked down at her. "Grace, you showed me how to be a better father and gave me a chance to save my relationship with Cash. Then it was you who fought for my son. You believed in him when no one else had. I knew then."

He stopped, and her heart caught in her throat. "You knew what?"

He held her close again. The music kept playing, and he continued to sway with her in the glow of the headlights. "I knew how I felt about you."

Her heart was bursting. She hadn't planned to feel so much. She just wanted to come here and have sex with him. Prove to herself she could win at taking a risk, but her heart was invested so deeply. The real risk would be believing in her feelings for him, trusting him.

"Blaise, this is what I want. It's what I've wanted for a while now, but I was afraid. I don't want to be afraid anymore."

He leaned in and kissed her lips with a gentle ease. "It's not right. You deserve more than a man on the road all the time. You deserve a man who can wake up next to you every morning and take care of you."

She pushed away from him. "Who cares about right? And I don't need a man to take care of me. I let a man take care of me because I thought that was what a marriage was supposed to be, and look how that ended up. I do want to wake up beside someone again, and I should have a say as to who that is. You don't want to be with me because I'm leaving and you're leaving. Well, stay then. Don't go on that tour. Produce your music. It's good. It would sell. Your fans would trip over themselves to hear new music from you. Stop following your brother around."

She hadn't meant to say so much, but the words tumbled out and she couldn't put them back in. He stared at her, mouth open.

He clenched his good fist. "Stay in Heritage River. Fight for that house. Tell Hoke and Beau you still want it. Forget about Claire Phillips and whoever bought the house for you. Take a chance on me."

He didn't understand her at all. "This was a mistake." She turned and marched up the narrow path and past the truck. The music had stopped. She didn't know the way back to the house, but she'd manage somehow to find it.

"Grace, where are you going?"

She ignored his shouts and kept going.

The truck door slammed, and the engine growled. The headlights lit up the path in front of her. He eased the truck alongside her on the dirt road. "Get in the truck."

"No."

"Grace, get in the truck. You can't walk back."

"I can walk back, and I will. I don't need you—or anyone, for that matter. I've been on my own my whole life. Never had parents who really cared, and then I married an asshole. Get away from me, Blaise."

"Get in the fucking truck, Grace," he shouted.

She jumped but kept marching forward. He wasn't going to upset her with his language. He sped up, and her shoulders sagged a little. He was going to let her walk back, after all. Stupid idea of hers. She'd have to call Chloe or a cab once she hit the main road.

The truck veered left and blocked her path on the road. Blaise jumped out of the truck.

"Get in." He stood with his hands on hips and his feet squared.

The anger seeped out of her. It was a long walk back, and she wasn't the bravest at night alone. "I don't want to get in."

He ran a hand over his face. "Please let me take you home. After that you can be done with me if you want."

She wasn't sure what had happened. How did this night get so out of control? She wanted to run to him, tell him she'd stay, but her feet wouldn't move. They weren't right for each other. Never had been.

She marched around him, careful not to get within reach. "Fine. Take me home."

Home. That was a joke.

Chapter Thirty-Two

Blaise pulled into his driveway and cut the engine. He kept his hands on the steering wheel, afraid if he moved, he'd grab Grace, kiss her with all he had and never let her go. Except she wanted to leave, and he couldn't stay.

She had been right about all those things she shouted at him at the lake. He was following his brother around. Had been since he could walk. He wanted to produce his own music, play in smaller places, maybe even nurture some young musicians. He could squeak out a living if he tried. He had enough connections, but he was afraid to lose what little he had left.

He felt Grace's stare on him. He turned to see something dark in her eyes. "I'm sorry, Grace."

She shrugged and fiddled with the hem of her shirt. "When are you hitting the road?"

Did he hear a hitch in her voice? That vulnerable sound squeezed his gut. "I don't know yet, but sooner than later, I suppose. I still have to talk to Savannah about the fundraiser."

She swatted at her face with the back of her hand. "Make sure she knows I had nothing to do with your leaving before the event. She'll think I sabotaged her because I accused her son of bullying Cash."

He pressed his lips together. "She'll blame me. Don't worry. She's mad at me too right now."

She reached for the door handle. He wanted to stop her, but he watched as she pushed herself out the door. "Good night, Grace."

"Good-bye, Blaise." She went into the house without looking back.

He ran a hand through his hair and scratched the back of his neck. He was an asshole. The night was already ruined. He might as well call Savannah. He slid out of the truck, dragged himself up the steps, and unlocked the front door. He stared at his hands. "Asshole." He'd left his brace back at the lake. Oh well. Guess his hand was feeling better.

Colton lounged on the sofa, his feet up on the table. He strummed the guitar. A cigarette hung from his lips.

He knocked Colton's feet off the table. "And put that cigarette out. It stinks in here."

"Looks like you didn't get any." Colton rested the guitar against the arm of the sofa and put his cigarette out in his glass of soda.

Blaise dropped into the leather chair and covered his face with his hands. "Shut up."

"If your pretty neighbor didn't come over here to proposition you, then what did she want that she couldn't say in mixed company?"

He stared at the ceiling. "She was saying good-bye."

"And that's a problem? Oh, wait." Colton slapped his leg and laughed. "I get it. You dig her."

"Why is that funny?"

"Bro, you've got to stop falling like that. Women are trouble. When are you going to learn?"

"Colton, seriously, shut up before I beat your ass."

Colton held his hands up. "Okay, okay. I'll quit it.

Here's some good news for you."

Blaise sat straighter in the chair. "Yeah? What's that?"

"We're hitting the road day after tomorrow."

"What?" That wasn't good news. He needed more time. He had to get Cash signed up for school. He wanted to make sure his son was settled before he left. Savannah was so pissed at him. Would she even look in on Cash while Blaise was gone?

"It will help you get over your lady friend faster. That's why it's such good news."

"But Cash. I have to explain it all to him." Where was Cash? Had he come back?

"He's a grown-up. He'll be fine. And the best part is we're getting paid for the first ten shows up front. Joe worked a miracle. That should make you happy. You'll be able to pay the electric bill and not have to sell your car."

He was tired of that car. He was still going to sell it. The money would give him a nest egg again. Maybe enough to live on for a while.

"You don't have to come on tour. I can find a replacement for you without much effort. There's that Otis Michael guy from Lacerate looking for work."

Blaise's insides heated up. "That guy sucks. He can't play my beats."

Colton shrugged. "So you're coming, then."

Blaise didn't see the choice. "Yeah. I'll be packed. I've got to call Savannah."

He took his phone and went out back. The phone rang several times before his sister answered, out of breath.

"You okay?" he said.

"Blaise. What's up? I've got a lot going on here right now."

"Everything all right?"

"No, if you're going to ask. Not that you're going to do anything about it. That's not your style—or Colton's, for that matter. Jud and Adam had a fight. Jud stormed out. Adam isn't feeling well. He's going to the doctor tomorrow."

He let the jab go by. "I hope Adam feels better." He wasn't about to give advice where Jud was concerned, but he figured Jud was like most hotheaded boys his age. He'd go blow off some steam and be back a few hours later with the whole thing behind him.

"What can I do for you?" Savannah kept the edge in her voice.

"I have some bad news."

"Oh no. Don't you dare say it."

"Savannah."

"You bastard. How could you ditch me at the eleventh hour? I've sold tons of tickets because of you, and now I have to let everyone down. And the library. What about the library?"

"I don't have a choice. I have to go."

"You do have a choice, but you're letting Colton make it for you like you always do. Do you even have a mind of your own? No. You. Don't. You know what? Forget it. Who needs you? I'll handle this like I've handled every other disaster this family has endured since Mom died."

"Savannah, I'm sorry. When I get on my feet again, I'll donate money to the library. I can get those computers for you. Colton will chip in too. I'll make him."

"Go fuck yourself." She hung up.

He couldn't win. He'd let Grace and Savannah down when they needed him, but avoiding the tour meant financial struggles and standing up to his brother. He wanted a minute's peace to figure the whole messy situation out.

"Dad, you're leaving the day after tomorrow?" Cash said from the doorway behind him.

Blaise didn't turn around. "Uncle Colton told you?"

"Why didn't you tell me?"

"I just found out a few minutes ago. I didn't even know if you were home yet." He sagged into the Adirondack chair.

"Do you know that Grace is leaving too?"

"Yeah." And there was nothing he could do to make her stay.

"So I can't see Chloe again."

"Jesus, Cash, I've got bigger problems right now than whether you can see your new girlfriend. Can't you use that camera gadget thing to talk to her? Besides, you're about to go off to college. So is she. In a month you'll forget about her."

"Is that what you're hoping to do with Grace?"

"You don't know what you're talking about."

"Neither do you."

He was screwing up again. He had to make things right with his son. Explain to him. Help him. But Cash didn't wait for a response. He turned back in the house.

Colton appeared in the doorway. He lit a cigarette and blew the smoke outside. "Sucks to be you about now."

"Yeah, it does."

Chapter Thirty-Three

Blaise threw the last of his luggage into the back of the town car waiting to take him and Colton to the airport. Cash paced the sidewalk with his arms crossed over his chest. His hair hung in his eyes, and an impatient sneer across his face.

Blaise stepped in his path. "Okay, I'll call you when we land. You've got that job interview tomorrow at three. Don't forget."

Cash held up his phone. "I set a reminder."

"Good. Okay, if you need anything, call Aunt Savannah or Billy Lewis. I left his number on the fridge. He'll be back in two weeks."

"Grace will be here for a few more days."

He looked over at Grace's house. "Don't bother her." Then he changed his mind. "Unless it's an emergency." Grace would never let anything happen to Cash. Blaise had been secretly hoping Grace would be the one to keep an eye on his son. He had been foolish to think like that. Colton was right. He fell too hard too easily.

He gripped Cash and pulled him into a hug. "I'll be a better father. I promise. I love you."

Cash pushed him away and ducked into the car to say good-bye to Colton. "See ya." He waved and walked up to the porch and sat on the top step.

Blaise stuck his head into the car. "I'll be right

back."

Colton jumped out. "We're going to miss the plane."

"I'll only be a minute," Blaise yelled over his shoulder as he ran across the lawn to Grace's house. Colton yelled something back, but he couldn't make it out.

He banged on the door. Banged again. Harder. He drummed out a solo until Grace yanked the door open.

"Why are you banging like that?"

"I'm trying to get your attention."

She crossed her arms over her chest. "Okay, you've got it."

"I came to say good-bye." Even though they had said good-bye the other night. "I couldn't leave with the last good-bye between us."

She leaned against the doorjamb. "I'm sorry about the other night. I shouldn't have come over like that and demanded, well, you know what I was after."

He raised his eyebrows. "Yes, I do. And I'm sorry it didn't happen. I'm sorry I hurt you by what I said. It's your life. You have to do what's best for you."

"I guess you do too. Good luck on the road."

"Call me, okay?"

"I don't think so."

"Blaise, let's go," Colton shouted.

"I've got to go. Please, Grace. Say you'll call me. I want to know you're okay."

"I'm fine. Thanks."

"Blaise," Colton yelled again.

The car horn honked.

He leaned in and kissed her cheek. "Call me." And he ran off.

****

Grace stood in the doorway, watching the long black car drive away with Blaise inside. She stood there long after it turned the corner and was out of sight. Her fingers traced the spot where he kissed her good-bye.

No sense standing around feeling sorry for herself. She had plans to make. She had started by calling Hoke yesterday and asking to stay a couple of extra days.

"No harm, I guess," he had said.

The next call had been to Jenn to ask if she and Chloe could crash at her house until Grace could rent something. Larry gave her enough money each month. She should be able to rent a small condo with two bedrooms. She didn't want to touch what she had made from selling her half of their house to him. That was her nest egg. She'd need a job in order to buy something of her own, but one step at a time. No more risks.

"I don't see why we can't rent something in Heritage River." Chloe came out of the kitchen holding a cup of tea. They still had to get water from the bathrooms. Someone would have a lot of work on their hands when they bought this house.

"Do you really like it here? What about your friends?"

Chloe looked into her mug. "Andrea is really the only one I want to keep in touch with. All the other girls are fake. They pretend to be your friend because you have something they want. I'm sick of their drama."

"I don't know, Chloe. It's embarrassing losing the house. Everyone in town will know. I want to start over fresh."

"Silverside isn't fresh. And aren't you always

telling me not to care what other people think?"

Nothing like having your own words thrown at you. "I just don't know. Are you going to see Cash today?"

"He says he's got a bunch of things to take care of. Maybe later."

"Maybe we could all have dinner together."

"Maybe. I'm going to get dressed."

Grace spent the day packing up what little they had brought with them. Tomorrow she'd take the boxes to the post office and ship them to Jenn's. Their personal items would travel back in the car with them. She'd spend two days on the road. She didn't want to make the fourteen-hour drive back to Jersey in one day, even if Chloe could take part of the drive.

The sun sank into the sky. Grace took her book and sat on the porch. She could stare freely at Blaise's house knowing he wasn't there. Had he landed yet? She didn't even know where they were going.

Her motives for dinner with Cash might have been slightly selfish. She could find out if Blaise had arrived safely and where the tour was beginning. Maybe even learn what cities he would be in. That information might be on the internet too. Safer to check there than to start asking questions.

She would've liked to know who bought the house for her. She pulled her phone out of her pocket and swiped open the Facebook app. She had a direct message. Her heart fluttered. Maybe it was Blaise. It wasn't.

Blaise,

It's wonderful to hear from you. I'm so glad you found me on this silly social thing. It does come in handy. How is your family? Please tell everyone I said hello. How can I help you? Anything you need. I think you left a phone number, but the last numbers were cut off. And say thank you to your friend Grace for allowing you to use her account to find me. Thank you, Grace! I always adored the Savage family. So did my aunt and uncle. Ta-ta.

Claire

Grace stared at the message with her fingers hovering above the keyboard. How easy it would be to write this woman back and ask what she knew. She might know nothing. Or she might know who bought the house.

She started to type but stopped. She hit the back arrow key and deleted what she started. Then she deleted the message all together. Blaise was right. It didn't matter. She wasn't going to be able to change her past by finding someone she might be related to. She wasn't suddenly going to have Thanksgivings filled with family members around the table either. She'd have to learn to accept that.

Her book about some unreliable protagonist couldn't hold her interest. She slapped the cover shut and let the remainder of the day wash out around her until she was sitting on the dark porch watching the fireflies skitter around the yard. They made her think of Blaise. Everything was going to make her think of him for a while.

Her stomach announced it would like some food. She pushed herself up and sent Chloe a text. She would eat alone and see Chloe later. One last dinner at Jake's wouldn't hurt anything. And then a quick walk to Cream and Sugar for a cookies-and-cream double scoop on a waffle cone. Calories didn't count when you're licking wounds, right? She really was a walking cliché.

Grace had locked the front door when a beam of white light splashed across the house. She turned to see a truck pull into her driveway and block her car. Her heart sank. She recognized that old, beat-up truck and didn't want to see its owner. She just wanted to eat a salad at Jake's and read her stupid book, and not be interrupted by this guy.

She clasped her hands together and waited for Beau Carroll to lumber over to her porch. "Evening."

"Hello, Beau. Did you forget something?" An unexplainable feeling of betrayal settled into her stomach. She was the one who had done wrong, but she couldn't shake it. Did she foolishly want him to defend her to Hoke? He had said he liked Chloe very much. How was he comfortable letting Chloe lose her home, or perhaps Beau didn't view things that way?

"I came by to see how you were doing."

He was worried about that *now*? Why didn't he worry about how she would be doing when he packed up his tools? "I'm fine."

He eased down onto the step and patted the place next to him. She stood frozen in her spot. He patted the step again. "Please, Miss Grace. Oblige an old man one last time, yeh?"

She dropped her purse and keys and marched down the steps to face him, her arms across her chest. "I prefer to stand. Thank you."

He shook his head. Even in the yellow glow of the porch lights, she could tell the whites of his eyes had red lines running through them.

"I'm sorry about packing up without waiting for

you to come back. That's not how I do business, but Hoke had his orders." His voice carried the weight of exhaustion on its back.

"You did what you felt you had to." She wasn't going to make this easy, no matter how much she wanted to go eat dinner and be done with this conversation. She shifted the weight from one leg to the other.

He lifted the cap off his head, ran a hand over his almost smooth scalp, and shoved the hat back on. "You ever do something you regret with all your heart?"

Marrying Larry was a mistake, but she had Chloe, so she couldn't quite make that statement. Letting Blaise go without feeling him alongside her was climbing the ladder of regret, though. A woman like her, a planner, rarely did something of that magnitude. Fear was always sitting on her shoulder and talking her out of leaping without looking.

"No, I can't say I have," she said. "Why?"

"Well, you're lucky. I have." He looked away, looked back. "I swore I wouldn't come here, but I kept thinking about those kids and their faces when I packed up. I let everyone down, and that wasn't my intention in any way."

"What are you getting at?"

"I know who bought this house for you. I've known all along, and I fought with myself to tell you the truth, but I didn't. I let Hoke talk me into keeping it a secret. Said you wouldn't understand if I told everything. Said let sleeping dogs lie."

Her heart jumped into her throat. "You knew? All along? Hoke had you and Dixie in on it, right? He knew he could trust you to keep the secret, but why tell you at all?"

He lifted that filthy cap and rubbed his scalp again. "I remember when you were born."

Grace leaned closer. "What did you say?"

He ignored her. "It was a cold January that year. There was even some snow on the ground. I drove all night to get to the hospital. Couldn't believe it was happening and so fast."

Her knees buckled, and she dropped onto the step near Beau, careful to keep some distance between them. She had been born six weeks early. A preemie. It wasn't something she talked about. What was the point? She remained in the hospital until she weighed enough to come home. She had developed like a normal baby. Even Chloe didn't know her story. "How do you know this?"

Beau looked at her again, and the rims of his eyes were red now. He shook his head. "I'm sorry, is all. I can't keep the secret anymore. It's eating me up like a cancer. I don't care that I promised."

"How do you know about me?" Her voice rose and trembled. She had to clasp her hands to keep them from shaking, or choking him. She didn't know which.

"Your daddy, Grace. Your daddy was my brother."

"That's impossible. My mother told me he was an only child. And your last name is different than his was." Her mother had kept her married name so it would be the same as Grace's and save all the explaining. Before she was Grace Starr, she was Grace Somerall. Grace Rosalyn Somerall.

"Your momma lied, sweetheart. About his being an only child. Your dad and me have the same mother, different daddies."

His term of endearment almost stopped her heart. "I don't believe you." Because believing him meant her mother had lied and that might be too much for Grace to handle. She had tried to accept her mother for who she was, but to find out she had lied too. It was just too much.

Once more he removed the cap, but this time he twisted it in his hands. "There's no easy way to do this, so I'm just going to spill it all out. Don't stop me till I'm done, all right? At the end you can ask questions if you want."

She waved her hands to stop him, but stopped herself instead. Her whole life she'd wanted to know more about her father and why he left them, but her mother would never tell her. A piece of her was always missing. She thought knowledge would fill the hole, but now faced with the prospect of finding something out, she was too afraid to hear it. *Afraid. No more.* She took a deep breath. "Okay, tell me the whole story."

"My brother had pancreatic cancer. That devil had its hooks in him so bad by the time he found out there was no saving him. He decided against the treatment. There was no guarantee it would fix him, and he thought he didn't have much to live for anyhow. I tried to talk him into it, but he was stubborn."

Questions raced through her mind. Where had he been all this time? Was Beau close to him? What was he like? But she promised to keep quiet, so she chewed on the inside of her cheek instead and wished he'd get on with it.

"He was sorry for losing touch with you. That was his biggest regret. There were a lot of good qualities inside Dustin, but he was a coward too. After your

momma told him to stay away from you, he was afraid to show his face. Figured you deserved a better father than he was."

"What?" She put a hand on his arm. "Wait. My mother told him to stay away? No, he left and never came back." The words swam around in her head, and she tried to grasp them, but they slipped.

Beau stared at her. "Dusty did some stupid things in his life, and he went and got himself arrested when you were little. Too little to remember, I guess. When he got out and came home, your momma told him to git. He thought she was right about that one. He was wrong. You needed your daddy around. I tried to tell him, but he wouldn't listen. Too ashamed."

"Where was he all this time?" She couldn't help herself.

"He came back down here and lived a few towns over. He kept an eye on you, though. Hired a private investigator to keep tabs. He found out you were married and had a baby. He knew what your husband was up to, and that was when he decided to buy the house." Beau hooked his thumb over his shoulder.

"He wanted you to have a second chance, and he wanted to make up for all the years he wasn't around, but he knew you'd need to live down here and let Heritage River seep into your bones. He knew you'd love it because you were his girl and he loved it here. You'd realize this was the place to call home."

"But why the secret? Why not find me and tell me if he was dying anyway?"

"Who knows? People don't always do things that make sense. You live with your demons long enough they start to look like you. Right till the end he thought you'd turn him away. How could he face you after so many years of hiding? The mistakes kept piling up, and the years kept going by. He believed you were better off without him."

The heat of anger rose from her belly. "You're right, Beau. He was a coward. He let me believe all these years I didn't have a father who cared one bit about me while he was a plane ride away. I don't want his house. I'm sorry I ever came down here." She pushed herself up, but he grabbed her by the wrist.

"Don't go yet. I understand you're mad, and you have every right to be. Dusty made mistakes, but the one thing he did right was buy you this house. He didn't want you to find out it was him 'cause he knew you wouldn't want it then. Don't make that mistake, Grace. Keep the house."

"How can I do that if Hoke pulled the plug?" Anger heated up more. "And Hoke went along with it all. He held up my father's wishes, knowing that man had lied to me my whole life. What kind of a human being does that? How could you keep it up too?"

He twisted his hat again. "That's my regret. I've got to live with that, but I'm trying to make it right. That's why I'm spilling. You need to know the truth. I can't let you go back without knowing why."

"Okay, I know. Now you can go with a clear conscience." She waved toward the truck.

Beau hoisted himself up by holding onto the railing. "I'm sorry. If you want to stay, I'll go to Hoke, tell him to call the whole thing off and let you keep the house, or I'll buy the house myself and sign it straight away to you. You belong here in Heritage River. This should be your home and Chloe's home." He lumbered back to his truck, eased himself inside it, and drove away.

Grace swiped at the tears streaming down her face.

Chapter Thirty-Four

Grace sent Chloe a text. *I'll be out late.* Then turned off her phone. Problem was, she didn't know where to go. Main Street was closing up, and she didn't have the stomach for food any longer. Not with the truth choking her. There wasn't a soul she wanted to call—well, there was one, but she wouldn't call him. She needed to vent or to process or something, but she was at a dead end.

A numbness settled over her. She just drove, turning right and left without even thinking. The car steered over the streets of Heritage River. Her father had been alive and keeping an eye on her. Coward. Why not risk coming to her? What kind of a parent stays away from his child? Her father never loved her, and buying her a house and attaching crazy stipulations to it proved he didn't care at all. Who does that?

And her mother. That woman had lied to Grace. Allowed her to believe her father didn't want her, when she was the reason he went away. She pounded the steering wheel.

She didn't want the house anymore. How could her father think a house would make up for not having a dad growing up? He thought the house was her second chance. What did he know about second chances when he didn't try for one with her?

The open road stretched out before her. She

searched the dial for some soothing music and stopped when she heard the melody of the song she danced to with Blaise. She wanted to know what he thought about this whole mess. What would he tell her to do?

Stay. That's what he would say, but he hadn't stayed for her. He picked the tour and his brother's shadow. No matter what she felt for him, she couldn't compete with Colton. It wasn't even worth trying.

She drove in circles for a while before she recognized the turn off for the lake and took it. The car bumped and rocked as she navigated the dirt road. The grass grew tall before it gave way to the clearing. Her headlights drenched the water in front of her. She got out and sat on the sand, letting the warm breeze wash over her. The air smelled sweet, and the quiet diffused her racing thoughts. She let her shoulders drop. "If I had a choice, I'd build a house right on the lake so I could sit on the porch and watch the sun rise over the fog with a big cup of tea clasped between my chilled fingers." She pictured the chair she would sit in with her legs tucked under her. And she pictured Blaise sitting beside her, playing a song for her.

Grace hung her head. She never thought the right love at the wrong time was actually a thing. She should go back and start packing. She should call Chloe and tell her to come home and help. She needed as much space between her and this town as possible so she could begin to forget about everything. She curled up on her side and watched the water lap against the shore.

Five more minutes.

****

Blaise dropped his duffel on the hotel bed. The plane ride had been long and turbulent. He actually prayed a few times. The room smelled as if someone had used bleach to cover up something worse. He tried the windows, but they weren't meant to open. His stomach complained about being neglected. He hadn't eaten anything since they left. He'd slept through the meal on the plane.

His neck creaked and groaned. A shower might ease the knots and then a good meal. He had a few hours before the show. Colton had texted. The other guys were grabbing a bite down in the hotel restaurant, but he passed. He wanted to be alone.

He stripped off his clothes in a long line to the bathroom and waited while the water heated up and steam filled the room before he stepped in and let the hot water work on his neck. Too bad it wasn't Grace's slender fingers working out his knots. He shook his head. No more thoughts of Grace. She was wrecking his head, and then he'd likely wreck his playing.

But he couldn't stop thinking about the words she threw at him. Telling him he was Colton's follower. He wasn't brave enough to take a stand. She was right, but he didn't see how he had a choice. He couldn't turn the money down, especially not with Cash living with him now. He hadn't been able to sell his Porsche. Eventually, he wouldn't be able to keep the lights on. He wouldn't be able to make the mortgage payment soon, and he shouldn't even have one of those.

He hated leaving Cash behind in Heritage River, but the boy was practically a man, and Blaise had to start trusting him sometime. His son deserved a second chance.

He turned up the heat on the water and let it scald his skin. When he couldn't stand it a minute longer, he hopped out and wrapped a towel around his middle. His phone lay quiet, and he tried to ignore the disappointment taking up residence in his chest from the lack of communication from Grace. Had she left yet? He wanted to call her, but he couldn't give her what she needed. She deserved a man who could be with her all the time. That wasn't him at the moment.

He dressed and went downstairs. He'd stop at the steak house down the street and get a porterhouse and mashed potatoes smothered in gravy. He'd top it off with dessert. Too bad he didn't drink. He wanted to wash it all down with a beer.

One step at a time. Focus on this moment. He looked down at his hands. Everything he needed, he had. Bullshit.

****

"Let's make some noise for your favorite band and mine. Savage!"

The crowd's roar shook the walls, threatening to blow off the roof. Blaise stepped onto the stage with Colton, Patrick, and Troy. The lights were blinding, but he could make out the seats up at the back of the theater. The place was packed. A smaller place than they used to play, but the fans had showed.

His insides vibrated. There was no place like the stage. Nothing in the whole world compared to the crowd chanting his name. They waved to the audience, and Colton let a chord rip. Blaise climbed up behind his oversized drum kit and rolled his sticks between his fingers.

It was good to be back.

Stacey Wilk

Chapter Thirty-Five

Grace blinked her eyes open. The lake surface glimmered from the glow of the night sky filled with stars and a half moon. The ground was hard and cool beneath her. She pushed herself up and shook sand from her clothes. Her neck groaned when she turned it. She was too old to be doing stupid things like falling asleep on the hard earth.

It was time to go back and face the music. She slid into the car and turned her phone back on, secretly hoping Blaise had called.

Her screen lit up. Chloe had called three times but hadn't left a message. Grace turned the ignition key and eased the car back down the dirt road.

Her phone lit up again. "Chloe, what's up?"

"Mom, oh my God. The house. It's on fire. You've got to come home right now." Chloe yelled into the phone over the sounds of sirens and shouts.

She hit the brakes. "What? How is the house on fire?" There must be a mistake. Was this a joke? She slammed down the gas pedal, and the car lurched forward.

"Can you hear me? The house. It's on fire. Where are you? I've been trying you for like thirty minutes. When arc you coming home?"

"Are you all right? Were you in the house when it started?" Grace yanked on the wheel to turn left, and

348

the tires squealed in protest.

"I'm fine. When I got here, I saw the smoke and called nine-one-one. The sheriff and the fire department arrived at the same time."

"I'm so glad you're okay. I'm on my way. I'll be there soon."

****

Red and blue lights threw up their brightness all over Dogwood Drive. Sheriff vehicles and two firetrucks blocked the road. Grace swerved to the curb and jumped out of the car, leaving the door open, and ran. The smell of burnt wood permeated the air. Smoke drifted up through the branches of the poplars. Neighbors, wearing their pajamas, lined the sidewalk across the street from her house. *Her house.*

She pushed through some of the deputies and firefighters standing back.

"Hey," someone called after her.

"Chloe." She grabbed Chloe by the shoulders and turned her around. "My God. Are you all right?"

"I'm fine, Mom. Really. The house is another thing. All that work for nothing."

"What happened?"

"I don't know. Cash and I were having dinner at Jake's. We had a stupid fight. He left. When I realized he wasn't coming back, I came home. You know the rest."

"Excuse me, ma'am. I'm Captain Hanover. Are you the owner?" A tall man with black curly hair and the greenest eyes she had ever seen stood beside her. He wore his full firefighter gear, and his face was smudged with soot.

Was she technically still the owner? "I live here."

349

"She's the owner." Beau's voice traveled over the noise.

Grace turned to him. "What are you doing here?"

"Ma'am, we've contained the fire. There was only some damage to the kitchen and one bedroom. Could've been a lot worse."

"What started it?"

"We'll start looking once things cool down a bit. For tonight, you'll want to find another place to stay. We don't want you inside until we can search the place. We'll be back in the morning." He turned and walked to the group of firefighters now rolling up the hose and stripping pieces of their gear off.

"Hanover, over here," a male voice shouted from somewhere near the house.

Captain Hanover ran in the direction of the shouts. Grace scanned the crowd still standing and gaping at the house. Jud stood huddled with some friends, their heads bent together.

"You two can stay at my place." Beau's voice dragged her gaze away.

"Thanks, but I think we'll just get a hotel room." She wasn't ready for his kindness. His words still stung. She hadn't even had a chance to tell Chloe what she knew.

"Nonsense." He glanced at Chloe, then back at her. "We're practically family."

"Mom, I don't want to stay at a hotel."

Of course she doesn't. Grace's head hurt. She needed time to think and make a plan. "Someone should call Hoke and tell him about the house. He'll need to be involved." She hoped their things hadn't been completely ruined. Would they be able to get in the house tomorrow to grab them? She still wanted to get on the road. Now there was more reason than ever.

"I'll call Hoke in the morning. For now, come back to my house." Beau put a hand on Chloe's shoulder, ready to lead her away.

Cash came running down the street. "What happened?" His chest heaved in between words.

"The house caught fire," Chloe said.

"Who would set the house on fire?" He rubbed his side.

"That's what we want to know." Captain Hanover returned holding up a gold lighter smeared with soot. He eyed Cash dressed head to toe in black, his thick eyeliner smeared from sweating. "Found this by the kitchen. It's what started the fire. Whoever did this wasn't trying too hard to hide it."

"That's my grandfather's lighter." Cash reached out and wiped the soot away to reveal an engraved *S.*

"He likes to play with fire," Jud shouted from his spot on the sidewalk. His buddies bent over laughing and slapped him on the back. *Yeah, hilarious.*

"Ask the loser about it."

"Jud, shut up." Grace said.

The sheriff sauntered up to them and glued his stare on Cash. "Where you been tonight, boy?"

"He was with me." Chloe jumped in.

"I'd like to hear it from him, miss."

"I was with Chloe until an hour ago. Then I was just walking around. I sat at the park for a while."

"In the dark?" the sheriff said.

"I needed to think."

"Sheriff, he didn't do this," Grace said.

The sheriff hitched up his pants. "I'm not saying he

did. I just want to know where he was."

She stood between Cash and the sheriff. "You don't need to know any such thing. He isn't a suspect because he didn't do it."

"He's started fires before. Why not this one?"

"I didn't do this. Are you crazy?"

The neighbors had moved in for a closer view. Grace wanted to scream at them to go back in their homes. Mind their own business. Someone had taken a picture with their phone.

"You're the pyro, cousin. My money's on you." Jud had moved in closer.

"Jud, go home." Grace gritted her teeth. She yanked her phone out of her pocket and dialed Blaise. It rang and rang, finally landing in voice mail. *Damn.* She hung up.

"Jud, you think this boy started the fire?" The sheriff spoke to Jud as if he were an authority.

"I think he did. He started a fight with me the other day and got me fired. He's always causing trouble. He set that house on fire back where he lives, and he got sent here to do community service at the library. Who else would do it?"

Cash clenched his fists. "Why would I set Grace's house on fire? I like her, and my dad likes her."

Jud shrugged. "Maybe it was 'cause her daughter didn't like you."

Cash lunged. Beau grabbed him. Jud jumped back. "See? See? He's always starting something. Why not another fire?"

The sheriff grabbed Cash by the collar. "Let's go to the station and talk this out. Give you some time to cool down from whatever it is got you pissed off. You can tell me more about that lighter."

Cash yanked away. "You can't take me in. I didn't do anything."

"You can't talk to him without his father present. Cash is still a minor." Grace jumped in again.

"He can call his father from the station. We'll conference him in." The sheriff led Cash away.

"I'll go with him," Beau said. "Try Blaise again."

Grace called Blaise three more times. "Answer, please." But the call ended in the voice mail again. He must've been on stage by now. Or he just wasn't answering any calls from her.

The crowd had thinned out once the fire trucks had left. Jud and his friends stayed until the last person walked away.

Grace turned to Chloe. "What did you two fight about? Tell me because his life could depend on it." The idea that Cash could get in trouble for this was choking her. She had to prove to the sheriff it wasn't Cash. Never would be.

"He's still mad at his dad for leaving. I tried to make him understand, but he didn't want to hear me. I said he has to learn to accept his dad for who he is. Focus on the good stuff Blaise does and not the bad stuff. I mean, Blaise went back on the road for Cash, didn't he? That's what I'm trying to do with Dad. He's not perfect, but he's still my dad."

Grace's heart swelled. "You're one smart young lady. I'm so proud of you. Let's get down to the station and see if we can't help out. I'll keep trying Blaise."

Chapter Thirty-Six

Colton stood on stage under the hot lights, ripping the best guitar solo Blaise had heard him perform. His big brother just got better with age, and Blaise was proud of him. No one was as talented as Colton.

Blaise wiped his face with a towel and downed a full bottle of water. He had a few minutes before Colton was done and they had to go back on stage. He went to his dressing room to have some time alone. His phone hadn't stopped vibrating against his leg the whole time he was playing. Something was going on.

Four missed calls from Grace. Had she changed her mind about him? She knew he was working tonight. Would she really have called so much knowing he couldn't answer?

The final call and voice mail had his hand shaking. He hit the voice mail icon. "Dad, I need your help. Grace's house caught on fire. They think it was me. They dragged me down to the sheriff's station. I'm here with Beau and Grace. Please call."

What the fuck? What was he thinking leaving his kid again? And Grace's house? What was going on? He had to get back to Heritage River. Now.

He ran onto the stage and gripped Colton's shoulder. Colton almost lost his guitar. He swung around with a look ready to kill the person messing him up. He stopped short. The playing stopped.

Blaise whispered in his ear. "Cash is in trouble. I've got to go. I'm sorry." He ran off the stage.

****

The car dumped Blaise off outside the Heritage River sheriff's station. Beau's beat-up truck and Grace's car were in the parking lot. The sun poked its head above the trees. He'd taken the first flight he could. A car waited for him when he got off the plane, and a note from Colton. *Kick ass.*

Blaise barreled through the glass doors. "Where is my son?" He nearly threw himself on the front desk. Jason Thompson was manning it. He wasn't much older than Cash.

"Sherriff's got him in holding. No one's talked to him. Grace won't let the sheriff near him. She's a pit bull that one." He pointed the way.

Grace was watching out for Cash. The idea made Blaise's insides heat up. He'd been a stupid ass. He was going to change things.

His breath caught in his throat. Cash sat behind bars. His head hung low. Beau was asleep in a chair. Chloe curled up on the floor, also sleeping. Grace sat straight up in her chair, eyes wide, ready to pounce.

He wanted to cross the room in two strides and scoop her in his arms, but he stayed in place. "Hey." He must stink from the sweat dried on his skin. He hadn't had time to change or shower. He'd been up all night and was probably a mess. Grace would hate that.

She stood and smoothed her wrinkled shirt. Dark circles surrounded her eyes. Her hair stuck up on the side, but she never looked more beautiful. "Hey. I'm glad you're here. The sheriff found Cash's lighter at the scene. He thinks Cash did it. I made them wait to

355

question him until you got here. He didn't do it, Blaise. I know he didn't."

He pulled her to him. She relaxed against his chest. "Thank you for helping him. I'm sorry it wasn't me."

She looked up at him with understanding in her eyes, and his heart skipped a beat. "Go to him," she said. "We'll wait for you in the lobby."

She roused Beau and Chloe awake. Beau wiped his face with his hand and shook his head. He patted Blaise on the shoulder and limped out. Chloe pushed up off the floor. The lines of her purse had left marks on her face.

Blaise approached the cell. "Cash. Cash."

Cash slowly looked up. It took a second before he realized Blaise was standing before him. "Dad." He jumped up and grabbed onto the bars. "Dad, you came. I didn't do it. I swear."

"I know. I'm sorry, Cash. I never should've left you. I was stupid, but I'm here now and we'll make this right."

"No, it's okay. I understand you went for me. You want to give me a good life. But just being with you is enough."

"Yeah, well, it might have to be. I just lost us a whole lot of money I really needed. But that's not what's important now. Tell me what happened."

Cash filled him in with what he knew. The question was who had taken the lighter to start the fire. There was only one answer, and Blaise didn't like it.

"I'm sorry I never believed you about Jud. He always seemed like the perfect kid." Blaise had thought he could trust Jud, and he was wrong.

"That's what he wants you to think. But I know

he's not that great. He deals drugs. That's what the fight at Christmas was about. I caught him, and he didn't want me to tell on him."

"Why didn't you?"

"No one would've believed me."

Cash was right about that. Blaise certainly wouldn't have. "I would believe you now. I don't know how we're going to prove it was Jud."

"I don't care as long as they don't pin it on me."

"That was your lighter."

"It's been missing for a month. I lost it that night at Aunt Savannah's. Jud must've taken it."

"Your word against his."

"Grace knows I didn't do it."

"Yeah, but can she prove it?"

Blaise's phone buzzed. "It's Uncle Colton." He turned his attention the phone. "What's up?"

"I called Savannah. She's on her way with Jud."

"Why did you do that?"

"I wanted to know what happened that would have you ending a show. It had to be pretty bad. You know I would kill you otherwise. She told me about the fire. I made her put Jud on the phone."

"You did? Did you know?"

"I had a hunch. I knew it wasn't Cash. That's for sure. Anyway, when Savannah threatened to beat him with a rolling pin, he caved."

The big bad southern rocker, Colton Savage, could never admit he wanted to offer sound advice and guidance, just as their father did for them all those years. "Thank you." The words choked Blaise.

"Yeah, well, don't go ruining my image, okay? Give the kid a hug for me. I'll see you in a few days.

357

You can meet us in Texas."

Blaise took a deep breath. This wasn't the best time, but it couldn't wait. "Colton."

"Oh for fuck's sake. You're going to fuck up the whole tour, aren't you?"

"Yeah."

"You're making a mistake, brother. Don't do this. We'll work things out."

"I'm done, Colton."

Colton ended the call.

****

Savannah arrived at the sheriff's station with Jud. The sheriff let Cash out of the cell with a look of disdain and led his sister and his nephew into the interrogation room that doubled as the supply closet. Savannah could handle it, but did Blaise tell her about the drugs? Not today, but one day. Maybe.

When they stepped outside, the sun was wide awake and heating up the day. "Thanks, everyone." The words weren't enough, but they took some of the tension in Blaise's body with them.

"I'm going to get my weary bones home. The offer still stands, Miss Grace."

"What offer?" Blaise said.

"They need a place to stay until the house is fixed and they can move back in," Beau said.

"I'm not moving back in, Beau. I'm taking my things and going back to Jersey."

"Oh land's sake, woman. You are stubborn. You going to throw this family"—he pointed to everyone standing there—"away on principal? Let the past go. You've got a second chance here. Take it." He threw his hands in the air and hobbled away.

"Feisty old guy," Blaise said. "You're still going back?" He didn't want her to leave before he could tell her a few things.

She kicked at the dirt. "I don't know what I'm doing. I do know we all need some sleep, maybe a shower and some food. I can drop you and Cash home. Chloe and I need to see what's salvageable and find a hotel. Once I get some sleep, then I can decide what to do."

"Stay with us. There's plenty of room. Take your time deciding what to do."

"You don't need us under your feet. Besides, you should spend time with Cash before you have to hit the road again."

"I'm not going back on the road."

Cash smiled.

"You're not?" Grace said.

"No. But I'll tell you all about that later. Let's go home."

Chapter Thirty-Seven

Grace dropped into the wood rocker on Blaise's front porch. She pushed with her toe and then tucked her legs under her. The night had cooled down. The fireflies were slower. The cinnamon apple tea calmed her still-raw nerves.

They had returned to Blaise's after leaving the sheriff's station. He made everyone eggs and bacon. He burnt the bacon, and the eggs were runny, but she didn't care. He was back, and they were together, at least for the time being. They still had a lot to talk about, but it could wait for now.

After their meal she had taken a nap and a much-needed shower. She was glad to see he had showered too. He might be the sexiest man she'd ever laid eyes on, but all that drumming under hot lights even made him need a bath. She preferred his clean masculine scent.

Chloe and Cash decided to take in a movie in the next town. Blaise had fallen asleep on the couch, so she'd made some tea and sat outside. He needed his rest.

Her house sat dark. Her house. She could have it if she wanted. Beau would help her. Blaise was staying now. At least he said as much earlier.

She didn't want to leave Cash if she could help it. She had grown very fond of him. But that was selfish.

Cash didn't need her. He had a family looking out for him.

Who was her family? Who would care about what happened to her? He'd given her the house by way of apology. Could she really accept a gift from a man who had abandoned her? Could she let go of the past and live in this moment?

"Hey." Blaise eased into the rocker next to hers. Sleep still weighed on his eyes.

"You should go to bed. You've had a rough couple of days."

"So have you." He hooked his thumb over his shoulder.

She sipped her tea. "My own fault mostly. Why do you think Jud hates Cash so much?"

"Jealousy, I guess. Of what, I don't know."

"Of you."

"Me? Why me?"

"You're the famous uncle. Cash gets all this attention just for being your child, and he doesn't want it. He wants to be left alone, be accepted for who he is. Jud likes being in the spotlight, and he can't have the biggest spotlight of all and doesn't think Cash deserves it. Hopefully, things will get better now that he admitted what he did."

"My whole family needs to be in therapy."

"At least you have a family. I only have Chloe. Well, I just found out that isn't entirely true."

"What do you mean?"

Grace told Blaise about Beau and the house. She gripped the mug through the whole thing. If she focused on her grasp, maybe she wouldn't cry. She only had to stop a few times to catch her breath and keep the tears from falling.

Blaise stayed silent until she finished. "That's a lot to absorb."

"I don't know what to do with the thoughts flying around in my head or the ache in my heart. My father loved me, after all? It doesn't compute, because if he loved me, why didn't he try and find me? I've been alone for so long, and not once did he try to come to me. How could he think a house makes up for all I didn't have?"

He took the mug from her hand and placed it on the table. He stood and helped her up. He wrapped his arms around her and pulled her close. She inhaled his scent and burrowed deeper against him. This felt too good.

He stroked her hair. "Listen, babe, you don't have to have all the answers now. It's going to take time to come to terms with your father's choices. Try to focus on the positive. He bought you a house to give you a second chance at life. He knew what you were capable of and allowed you a chance to prove it to yourself. That house has given you a new perspective, and it gave you to me. And you gave me back my son."

She looked up at him. "I don't know what to do. I don't have a plan." She held her breath.

"Stay. Keep the house. Build a new life here in Heritage River. Let Cash and me be part of your family. Beau too. In time, you and Savannah might be able to become friends. There's also Colton, if you can put up with him."

Blaise had told her what Colton did for Cash. Colton might have some rough edges, but his heart was in the right place.

A family. A home. Right here in Heritage River.

"Are you really leaving the touring behind?"

He leaned in and kissed her. She opened her mouth to the fiery advances of his tongue. She pressed against him, fitting into his lines and angles. Her body burned from the center out, but even though she wanted more, they had to stop.

She pushed away. "Blaise, I can't do this." She chewed on her bottom lip, afraid if she spoke another sound, the tears would fall.

He tugged on her elbow. "I'm sorry. I should've been here when you needed me. I should've held your hand while the house was burning. I was afraid to take a chance. That's why I went on tour again. But when I left you, all I could do was want you with me. Then when Cash called, I knew. I knew with certainty that what I wanted was my family around me. I'd figure out the money part later. I want to be with my son. I'm becoming a better father and that's because of you. You make me a better man."

He held her face between his strong, calloused drummer's hands and placed soft kisses on her lips, her eyelids, the soft spot in front of her ear. "I'd like to take you inside." His lips nibbled on her earlobe.

She wasn't sure she could speak or that her legs would carry her even one step. She nodded, and he took her hand and led the way. She could trust Blaise. This she knew in her heart. The house was empty except for them. The lights were out. Only the small light above the stovetop was on.

He took her to his room. The king-size bed was ruffled, as if someone had been lying on it. He doused the light. "I wish I had some candles. Candles are romantic, right?" He wiped his hands on his pants.

"We don't need candles." Her hands were shaking. She hadn't been with another man besides Larry in more years than she wanted to think about. What if she forgot how to do it? Or what if she was bad at it? She needed to sit, except she wasn't ready to sit on the bed, and he didn't have any chairs in here. Well, if her legs decided to have a mind of their own, the floor might do.

"We do need this." Blaise moved to the side table. Soft music filled the space around them.

Grace recognized the rhythm-and-blues sound accompanied by the melodic voice of a female singer gone before her time.

He went to her and placed one hand on her waist, pulling her close, and with the other he grasped her hand in his. They swayed to the music. "Is this music okay?"

"It's lovely." And it was. The singer said something about being sad, but her man showed up and held her close. He was all she needed. Those could be her own words.

He moved her with ease in the small space between the bed and the dresser. He was a foot taller, but she fit with him. She inhaled his clean scent. She was aware of the heat coming off his body. He held her close, which was a good thing. If he loosened his hold, she'd be a puddle on the floor.

"Grace?"

She looked up at him. His gray eyes twinkled in the dim light.

"I'm going to kiss you again, and this time I won't be able to stop. I just want you to be prepared." He winked.

For once in her life, she was ready to be taken

away with no thought as to the end. This was the only moment she cared about. She couldn't have planned for it or planned it better. She was about to warn him she was out of practice, but when she opened her mouth, he kissed her deep and long.

His hands cupped her face, pulled her closer. She wrapped her arms around his neck and tangled her fingers in his hair. He moved away from her lips to leave soft kisses against her neck. His warm breath sent shivers across her skin.

She ran her hands across his chest and down his flat belly. His drummer body was toned and strong. She'd never wanted to touch a man as much as she wanted to touch him.

His mouth sought hers again, while his hands reached under her top. His rough hands scratched against her skin, making the sensitive spot between her legs ache with need. "Can we get rid of this?" He tugged on the hem of her shirt.

"Can we turn the light off first?"

"I want to see you. You're beautiful, but if it makes you feel better." He stepped away and turned off the light. The room was swallowed up in the dark. He kissed her lips. "Next time we'll do it with the lights on." The smile was in his deep, sexy voice.

So there would be a next time. She stepped back and yanked her shirt over her head. Her nerves mixed with desire. She crossed her arms over her chest. "I haven't been with anyone since my ex-husband." He had to know how inexperienced she was. What if he didn't like her body or the way she touched him? She didn't want Larry's ugly words about her creeping into this moment, but they were.

He took her hands in his and kissed her knuckles. "Grace, I want you so badly right now. There's nothing you could do that I wouldn't like."

She reached up and pulled him to her. She kissed him this time, parting his lips with her tongue.

His hands sought her again. He cupped her breast over the silky fabric of her bra. His touch sent fire through her veins. Next time she'd wear something with lace.

She wanted his skin against hers. Her hands ran over his back, appreciating the tautness of his muscles. He stepped away and removed his shirt. She should have left the lights on. She wanted to see his body.

He reached behind and unhooked her bra. "Skin against skin," he said.

She pressed against him. His heart beat in time with hers. He cupped her bottom and drew her in. She could feel his desire against her belly. He kissed her again. His tongue was slow and lingering and driving her mad. She didn't care about anything except being with him and touching him. She was losing control for the first time in her life, and she loved the feeling.

"Blaise, could we, um, you know." She tugged at the button of his jeans. She needed to feel all of him.

"Yes, ma'am." He stepped back, unhooked his pants, and dropped them to the floor.

She reached for his waist, wanting him next to her. Her skin was burning, and the only thing that would help was him. Her hands slid over his backside and around to his hips. She hesitated, but only for a second, and wrapped her hands around him, feeling his fullness against her palm. He let out a low groan.

She planted little kissed across his collarbone and

over his shoulders.

"Grace…" He scooped her up and lay her on the bed.

His tongue left a wet trail over her breasts and down her belly. The aching need grew stronger. She had never wanted anything more than she wanted this man to touch her. He stopped at the top of her pants. "Can I take these off?"

"Please." She lifted her hips to help him drag her capris over her legs.

"How about this?" He tucked a finger under the side of her panties.

She pushed off the thin piece of lace. His hand rubbed her thigh. She was going to burn from the inside out.

Her hands ran over his back and his chest. He kissed her again. This time his tongue went deeper, and she moaned.

His hand left her thigh and found the heat between her legs. She called out to him.

"Grace, even in the dark I can tell your eyes are closed. Please look at me."

She opened her eyes.

"You're amazing, strong, and beautiful. And I want you more than I've wanted any other woman in my whole life."

She held his face in her hands. "I want you too." Her voice was a whisper. She wanted his hands all over her, exploring and finding. Wondering what he would do next had all her senses on high alert. She liked this new sensation of losing control.

When he entered her, white heat spread through her. She wrapped her legs around his waist and raised her hips to match his thrusts. He waited for her, and together they reached the explosive release that cooled the fire inside her.

He held her close as her heart returned to a normal beat. "That was amazing."

"It definitely was."

Chapter Thirty-Eight

Blaise held her in his arms. They were under the covers of his king-size bed. His chin rested on the top of her head. She snuggled closer, relishing the feeling of his body entwined with hers. She could stay like that all night, except the kids would be back from the movies soon. They couldn't find their parents in such a compromising position. What message would it send?

"Are you hungry?" He rubbed her back.

"Starving."

He threw the covers off, letting all their warmth escape, and jumped from the bed. "Good. Me too. How about I make us a snack? Pancakes? Do you like pancakes because I'm all out of lettuce?" He yanked on his shorts and wrestled with his T-shirt.

She was a little disappointed to see him wearing clothes again. She smiled at the thought. The new Grace was being bold.

"You have a wicked grin, Ms. Starr. What are you thinking about?" He planted a kiss on her nose.

"You, us, this."

He wagged his eyebrows at her, and she laughed. She wrapped the covers around her and searched for her discarded clothing. "I don't eat just lettuce. Pancakes would be great."

He kissed her hard on the lips. "Hurry." And he was gone.

Well, he wasn't the cuddling type, but that was okay. She always wanted to move around after sex anyway, but she wouldn't have minded his body wrapped around hers for a little longer. She straightened the bed in case one of the kids peeked before she joined Blaise in the kitchen.

"Can I help?"

"Nope. Sit tight." He pointed to the breakfast bar.

He moved around the kitchen, yanking out ingredients, bowls, and a pan. "Babe, this might not be the best time for this conversation, but I want to take advantage of the house being empty."

What was he going to say? "Okay."

He put down the flour and took her hand. "I know I'm not perfect, far from it. But I want you to stay in Heritage River, and if you don't want your house, you can live with me."

She wasn't expecting that even after what just happened between them. "Oh, Blaise, that's...that's more than I could have asked for. I still don't know what to do about the house. As much as I love our time together, I'm not sure Heritage River is right for me. I've made some people dislike me, like your sister. How would she feel if I moved in with you? I need some time. Is that okay?"

A darkness spilled across his gray eyes. He pulled his hand away and went back to the pancakes. "Sure. No problem."

"Can I ask you something?"

"Anything." He kept his back to her.

"Are you going to perform at the fundraiser now?"

He turned to her and leaned against the counter. "I'll call Savannah in the morning." He went back to pouring ingredients into the bowl.

"Blaise—"

The front door swung open. Cash and Chloe barreled in, laughing and joking. They came up short when they saw Grace and Blaise in the kitchen.

"Pancakes. Cool." Cash stuck his finger in the mixing bowl. Blaise knocked him away.

"You just ate a whole bucket of popcorn." Chloe slid onto the stool next to Grace.

"I'm hungry," he said.

They shared their late night after-sex snack with the kids. They laughed when Blaise dropped batter on the floor, and Grace slipped in the mess trying to clean it up. Chloe and Cash told them about the movie and how Chloe screamed at all the scary parts. Grace wouldn't have had it any other way. When the dishes were cleaned and the kitchen closed up tight, Cash went to his room. Chloe took one of the guest rooms. Blaise walked Grace to the door of the other guest room.

"If you want to sneak back in after they fall asleep, I'll wait up for you." He kissed her nose.

"I'd like that, but I think we'd better wait." She pointed to the closed doors. "The walls might have ears."

"They're just going to have to get used to it. If you stay, that is." He turned and went into his own room.

Grace closed the door to the guest bedroom. Did she really want to be alone? What was she so afraid of? She had given herself completely to Blaise a few hours ago. Her face burned just thinking about his skilled drummer's hands. She wanted more of him lying naked next to her.

Why did she still feel the need to put space

between this town and her? Was it because she'd never planned to fall for the handsome neighbor? Or was it because she never planned on knowing her father loved her, after all?

Chapter Thirty-Nine

The next couple of days went by in a whirlwind. Grace and Blaise were more like cars passing on the freeway than lovers or even roommates. He had begun practicing for his performance at the fundraiser. Cash had agreed to play with him.

Grace and Chloe started packing up their belongings. Even if Grace decided to stay, they had to move out for the cleanup. The smell of smoke was everywhere. The whole place would need to be repainted and cleaned. That job was too big for Beau to do with just a few hands. The insurance company would pay for a larger crew, but Beau wanted to supervise.

He also kept pestering her to stay. She'd stayed longer than she thought. She was getting comfortable in Blaise's house. That scared her a little. Blaise had come to her almost every night, and she opened her arms to him. She craved him and feared what it meant at the same time. She didn't want to make any more mistakes.

The fundraiser was that evening. Blaise left early with Cash and Chloe; they wanted to rehearse and sound check. They'd be playing some songs from Savage, acoustic form because they didn't have a full band, and some of the new stuff Blaise wrote. He was going to be wonderful.

Grace would head over right when they were about

to go on. She'd stay to the back of the lot, away from the stage. She didn't want to get in Savannah's way or hear any of the whisperings going on about the fire.

She had stalled long enough. It was time to go to the library, but one stop first.

She wandered through her disaster house. The beauty was there if given a chance. The house had been neglected, as she had. With a little love, they both could be okay again. She ran her hand across the top of the table Beau made for her. It really was a lovely piece and thankfully, not damaged in the fire. Families were made around tables filled with good food and stories and time together. So much thought went into making this table. Grace would dare to even say *love*. Love. Of family.

She walked over to the show, knowing parking would be tough. The poplars hung heavy and low along the walk. The smell of honeysuckle filled the air. The Bucknells waved and said hello as she passed. Heritage River had calmed her nerves and offered her a place to find herself again. Thanks to this town, she found Blaise and a chance at happiness.

Her steps quickened. This town still had so much to teach her. She hadn't even been inside the bakery yet. She had heard wonderful things about May's homemade muffins, and Beau couldn't start his morning without her coffee. May's was the Saturday morning gathering place to get all the local news. Friends met there. Families gathered around May's small tables.

She hurried around the corner onto Main Street. Her breath came in short bursts. Voices from a large crowd gathering drifted in her direction.

The Disaster House was really her second-chance house. Her father knew what she needed even when she didn't. Couldn't she be grateful for that? Could she in time learn to forgive him? Maybe if she sat with Beau and learned a little more about her father she'd understand.

In a few weeks, Chloe was leaving for school. Grace didn't relish the idea of wandering the streets of Silverside. No one sat on their front porches at night. It was a backyard town, and she was tired of being alone.

She ran. It didn't matter how foolish she looked. She had no plan and knew in her heart this time she didn't need one. Everything would work out.

The music had already started. She hadn't arrived in time. Grace waited in the back of the crowd. This was Blaise's time to shine. What she had to say could wait.

"Hi." Savannah slipped in alongside her. Grace's back stiffened.

"Hello. Looks like you got a big crowd."

Savannah clasped her hands behind her back. "Blaise really pulled through. We're going to get those computers now." Savannah turned to her. "Grace, I'm sorry. For your house, for not listening to you."

Her shoulders relaxed. "It's okay. Really. You were just being a protective mother. I would've done the same thing."

"I don't understand what got into Jud. He says no one prompted him to set the fire, but he couldn't have acted alone. He would never do anything like that." Savannah placed a hand on Grace's shoulder. "Anyway, I just wanted to say I was sorry." She slipped back into the crowd.

Savannah didn't understand what got into Jud? Was she kidding?

"Okay, folks, we're going to take a short break. We'll be right back. Get yourself some refreshments. May donated her famous cookies and bread," Blaise said into the mic, and the crowd cheered.

Grace couldn't wait another minute. She pushed and shoved her way to the front of the people gathered at the stage. Chloe and Beau sat in the front row. Chloe turned to her and waved. Grace's heart swelled. Beau tipped his chin at her. This was her family. The daughter she gave birth to and the tetchy old man she found along the way.

Blaise and Cash tried to make their way off the stage but were met by fans wanting autographs.

Grace tried to catch Blaise's eye. She jumped up and down, then waved.

He looked up from signing and smiled at her. He handed the pen and paper to Cash. "He's the guy you want." Blaise patted the man wanting the autograph on the shoulder and walked toward her.

Butterflies flapped in her stomach as Blaise came closer, his hair slicked back, his shirt wet with sweat. He smiled long and hard. His eyes twinkled. "Hey, babe. You made it."

"I need to talk to you. For a minute."

The smile on his face dropped. "Are you okay?"

She grabbed his hand and dragged him to a quieter spot near the dumpster. "This isn't the ideal spot or the best time, but I couldn't wait." Her heart pounded in her ears. She looked up at him and saw the truth. "You are my home. Before I moved here, I couldn't imagine I'd fall in love and stay, and now I can't imagine living anywhere else."

"I want each and every moment filled with you. You're where I knew you belonged—with me."

He cupped her face in his strong hands and leaned in to kiss her. He tasted salty and sweet, and she wanted more. But there would be time. A lifetime.

A word about the author...

Stacey Wilk wrote her first novel in middle school to quiet the characters in her head. It was that or let them out to eat the cannoli, and she wasn't sharing her grandfather's Italian pastries.

Many years later, her life took an adventurous turn when she gave birth to two different kinds of characters. She often sits in awe of their abilities to make objects fly, make it snow on command, and remain dirty after contact with water. She does share the cannoli with them for fear of having her fingers bit off if she doesn't.

Because of the extraordinary characters now in her home instead of in her head, including a king who surfaces after dark and for coffee, she writes novels about family: those that we are born to and those that we pick up along the way. You can find her message in her middle-grade fantasy novels as well as her women's fiction novels. Family are those that love you when you need them.

When she's not creating stories in make-believe places, she can be found hanging with the cast members of her house, or teaching others how to make make-believe worlds of their own. Stop by for a visit, and make sure to bring some cannoli.

http://www.staceywilk.com

Made in the USA
Middletown, DE
02 July 2018